MIDNIGHT IN MALMÖ

WITHDRAWN

Torquil MacLeod

M^CNIDDER & GRACE CRIME

P9-ECS-225

3   447   01499   7908

To the BWs

Published by McNidder & Grace
21 Bridge Street
Carmarthen
SA31 3JS
www.mcnidderandgrace.co.uk

Original paperback first published in 2016
©Torquil MacLeod and Torquil MacLeod Books Ltd
www.torquilmacleodbooks.com

All rights reserved. No part of this work may be reproduced or transmitted in any form or by any means, electronic or mechanical, including photocopy, recording, or any information storage or retrieval system, without permission in writing from the publisher.

Torquil MacLeod has asserted his right to be identified as the author of this work in accordance with the Copyright, Designs and Patents Act 1988.

A catalogue record for this work is available from the British Library.

ISBN: 9780857161307

Designed by Obsidian Design

Printed and bound in the United Kingdom by
Short Run Press Ltd, Exeter, UK

ABOUT THE AUTHOR

Torquil MacLeod was born in Edinburgh. He now lives in Cumbria with his wife, Susan. He came up with the idea for the Malmö Mysteries after visiting his elder son in southern Sweden in 2000. He still goes to Malmö regularly to see his Swedish grandson.

Midnight in Malmö is the fourth book in the series of best-selling crime mysteries featuring Inspector Anita Sundström.

ACKNOWLEDGEMENTS

I owe thanks to the following people: Susan for her patient and sympathetic editing; Nick of The Roundhouse for the latest cover design and enjoyable lunches; Göran for running a Swedish eye over the manuscript and not getting me into trouble with a handball star; Doctors Bill & Justine Foster for medical advice; Alastair, Lesley, Charlotte and Isla for being generous hosts and giving me some useful insights into Switzerland; Fraser and Paula for putting up with me during research trips and taking me to the Kallbadhus; and, finally, to Karin for her usual input, even if I've played fast and loose with Swedish policing yet again.

And I would like to thank Calum, Sarah and other family and friends for their support, and all those kind readers who have been in contact over the last year – your correspondence is much appreciated.

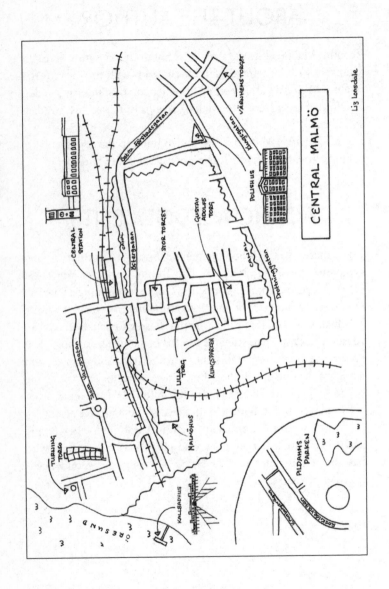

CENTRAL MALMÖ

Liz Lonsdale

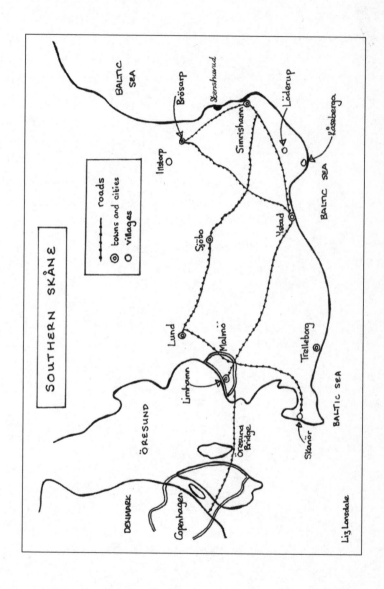

SOUTHERN SKÅNE

roads
towns and cities
villages

BALTIC SEA

Brösarp
Stenshuvud
Simrishamn
Löderup
Kåseberga
Iltstorp

Ystad

Sjöbo

Lund

Malmö

Trelleborg

BALTIC SEA

Limhamn

Öresund Bridge

ÖRESUND

Skanör

BALTIC SEA

DENMARK

Copenhagen

Liz Lonsdale

PROLOGUE

Were all Russians so greedy? I'd never seen anything like it. Certainly not in my time at the Savoy Hotel. It was as though they hadn't eaten for weeks. I had to admit that many of them didn't look well fed. They were certainly making short work of the beautifully prepared smorgasbord that we'd laid out on the long table a short while before their arrival. They called it zakuski. They were a motley collection of individuals – men, women, and a couple of young boys. Maybe it was the fault of the war. I'd read awful things in the newspapers. Germans fighting the English and French. Russians fighting Austrians and Germans. Terrible death and destruction, so the local newspapers had reported over the last three years. Not that we'd been immune to the effects of the war. Our trade had been seriously harmed, and national rationing was introduced later that year after a poor harvest. Yet the patrons of our hotel wouldn't have known that supplies were short when they sat down to dine. Money always has a way of overcoming such difficulties. By then, our guests were mainly Swedes, as foreign visitors had rarely appeared since the outbreak of the war.

Despite the ravenous wolves devouring all that was put in front of them, one of their number remained aloof. He didn't touch a morsel. He was in deep conversation with herr Fürstenberg, the Polish gentleman who'd organised the meal. The kitchen staff had been on high alert for three days. But during that time, there had been no sign of them. All we knew was that a special party of Russians was coming by ferryboat into Trelleborg. Augustsson, our head waiter, had told us that they were coming from Sassnitz. I couldn't believe this at the time, as we all knew that Russia and Germany were at each other's throats.

But this man who talked so earnestly with herr Fürstenberg was different from the others. Where herr Fürstenberg was elegantly dressed with a flower in his buttonhole, this fellow was unprepossessing at first glance, yet I found it difficult to keep my eyes off him as I served the other guests. Short, wiry and stooped, his clothes were baggy and crumpled. A thin strip of red hair encircled his bald crown. His beard was short and pointed, and he had penetratingly dark eyes. His features were almost Asiatic. I heard someone refer to him as herr Ulyanov. I'd no inkling who he was, or what he was doing in Malmö. We'd read that Russia was in turmoil and that the Tsar was no longer ruling. Such a thing seemed impossible, yet the world beyond our borders had gone mad. All I knew was that herr Ulyanov and his party were not staying at the hotel, but were leaving by the midnight train to Stockholm from the Central Station opposite, on the other side of the canal. I was pleased that they were going, as I didn't relish the prospect of serving these boorish people again over breakfast.

As I swiftly moved down the corridor outside, my hands full of dirty plates, I heard a loud thudding on the wooden floor behind me. I turned round. Herr Ulyanov was there. The source of the noise was his studded mountain boots, which seemed strange footwear for a train journey. He raised a hand to catch my attention and said something. I thought it was in French. He saw that I didn't understand. So, he spoke in English; a language I'd learned to use when dealing with our American and British guests before the war. 'I am trying to find a bathroom,' he said. His eyes engaged mine as he spoke. I remember how hypnotic they were as they narrowed in amusement.

I was about to direct him when another figure appeared at the end of the corridor and, after a moment's hesitation, made his way towards us. The man was short with a heavy coat, and he wore a wide-brimmed hat which virtually covered his eyes.

'Vladimir Ilyich Ulyanov?' he asked.

Herr Ulyanov nodded.

The man in the hat reached inside his coat. I suddenly realised that he was pulling out a pistol.

CHAPTER 1

Rivulets of sweat were now trickling down her face from the bunched blonde hair under her baseball cap. She was really pushing herself, pumping those legs. Those much-admired legs. It was important that she was in good physical shape; hence her pacey jogging. Yet she wasn't exactly sure why she was driving herself so hard round Pildammsparken this late on a summer's evening. Was it to expunge the last few hours? Was it self-loathing? That was silly.

She rounded the lake. The lights from the hospital buildings on the other side twinkled and danced in the half-dark. Though it still wasn't dusk, the heavy cloud cover was taking its toll on the available light. She strode on. There were few people about at this time. She virtually had the park to herself. She liked that. She liked being anonymous. That was the beauty of cities, yet she could never live in one now. Maybe it was her upbringing in a small, rural town. She remembered how her father used to bring her to Malmö as a youngster. It had seemed magical then, especially around Christmas when the shops were lit up and the electric holiday candles gleamed from every office and apartment window. He had brought her here to the park, taken her to the cinema, and usually rounded off their day with a meal at a nice restaurant in somewhere like Lilla Torg. Later, Malmö had lost its charm, but that wasn't the fault of the city. And her poor father? The thought spurred her on. That and the horrid shock she had had earlier in the day. She had seen *him*. It had upset her badly. It had brought back all the old fear, dread and revulsion.

She sprinted down the bank, over the road that cut through Pildammsparken, and across into the trees. She would finish with a circuit of the "Plate" before heading back to the apartment. Now she was alone in the tall trees, the moon flitting through the branches as it dodged one cloud before being swallowed up by another. It would soon disappear altogether, as the forecast had predicted heavy overnight rain. She would get back to the apartment before that started.

With the end of her run in sight, her practical mind took over, and she slowed her pace. She would make final arrangements after she had showered. There would be an early start in the morning for her next appointment. But at the weekend, she would have that well-deserved break she had promised herself. A bit of "me" time.

As she ran on, she became aware of someone close behind her. Another jogger. How annoying! She was enjoying the park's emptiness. Someone was invading her privacy. She upped her tempo so she could pull away from this unwanted presence. Yet the other jogger seemed to be gaining on her. She slowed down so that he or she could pass, and then she could return to her own pace.

She didn't turn round, but she could hear the controlled, rhythmic breathing of the runner, now almost next to her. It was an unpleasant feeling; her space being occupied. She had reduced her speed to a trot when she felt a sharp pain in her back, like a gigantic pinprick. Then she stumbled. Something had been stuck into her. The momentum propelled her forward, making it impossible to turn round to see her assailant. She tried to twist so that she could reach behind her with her hand, but she lost her balance and collapsed to her knees. Her jogging top felt sodden. She realised that it must be blood. Then the object was forcibly removed and, a second later, driven back in. And now the searing pain. Her attempted scream of terror came out as a grunt as myriad images swirled around her brain then sank into an abyss. Her last coherent thought was why was this happening?

CHAPTER 2

Anita Sundström hoped she wasn't making a ghastly mistake. A decision made in haste to be repented at leisure. Well, over the next two weeks. She stood nervously on the single platform of the small station in Simrishamn. The end of the line from Malmö. The day had turned out bright and warm after the previous night's heavy rain, though she found herself shivering slightly as she looked down the deserted track while she waited for his train. She knew he was on it as he had texted ahead. She glanced across to the red-brick police station. Windows were open to let in much-needed air. Police life would be going on as usual. It reminded her that it was good to be on holiday. Her month-long summer leave had begun three days ago. When the weather was like this, it was good to get out of the city and escape to the countryside and coast of her beloved Österlen.

She instinctively felt for her snus tin in her bag. Of course, it wasn't there. She had given up for nearly a month now. She knew it was a filthy habit, but it had kept her cravings for a cigarette at bay for a few years. Now, giving up the snus was the next step. She knew she had done it with him in mind; snus was a thing that the British couldn't get their heads around. She had also spent more time than usual getting herself ready before she set off for the station. This afternoon, she had stood in front of the mirror longer than she'd done in the whole of the last month. She decided she didn't look too hideous for someone coming up to forty-six. Mind you, she had increased her jogging over the last couple of months to try and lose the bit of extra weight that had crept up on her, particularly round the tummy. But her exercise regime had done the trick, and she could now wear clothes that hadn't fitted her at Christmas. Today, she had forsaken her usual jeans or trousers and decided to give her legs an unaccustomed airing. The floral dress she wore was short, and she began to worry that her legs weren't as brown as she would have liked. If this weather continued, then a few days on the beach would remedy that. Another concern was whether he'd like her hair. After having it short for many years, she had grown it out over the last few months, and now it reached her shoulders. She wasn't sure it suited her, though Wallen had been complimentary at work. So had Lasse and Jazmin. At least *they* were less of a worry now that they had moved into an apartment together. However, the Mirzas still didn't approve of their daughter living with her son, and Anita had been forced to play the role of peacemaker on a couple of occasions.

And now Jazmin's brother, Hakim, was back to help. It was great to have him at the polishus again. After a year and a half up in Gothenburg, he had returned last month, when an opening had become available in the Criminal Investigation Squad. Now he was a fully-fledged detective. Even the miserable Chief Inspector Moberg seemed vaguely pleased that he was around. In fact, Moberg's moods had been more equitable of late since his third wife's patience had snapped and she had walked out on him. The only change in his lifestyle, as far as the team could see, was that, now his domestic cook had downed utensils and left, he ate out even more than before.

It had been a strange year and a half while Hakim had been away. She had been given a long compassionate leave after the Westermark incident, in which her detective colleague had blown his brains out in front of her. The therapy sessions had been more useful than last time, though the image of Karl Westermark's final moments still plagued her, and often she screamed in the night. She wasn't sure if she did it any more. Since Lasse had moved out, there was no one to tell her. The disturbing dreams persisted, though. The team hadn't been the same again on her return to work. Too many scars that would never heal. The loss of her mentor, Henrik Nordlund – murdered by Westermark – had been particularly hard on her. As a group, they were still professional, but it often felt as though they were just going through the motions. Maybe Hakim's return would help.

Anita eyed the police station across the road again. Maybe she had had enough of Malmö, and she should spend the last years of her career in a quieter backwater like Simrishamn. She still had school friends living in the area. And she didn't see much of Lasse these days, so the ties with the city were loosening. It was something to ponder during her month off. She was pleased that she had managed to secure the same holiday home overlooking the sea that she had taken in the early months of last year when she was mentally sorting herself out after Westermark's bloody exit.

She became aware of the people around her stirring and staring up the line. She followed their gaze and could see the sun glinting off the outline of the train. Once again, she hoped that this wasn't going to be a disaster.

CHAPTER 3

The rain pitter-pattered on the roof of the crime-scene tent as Hakim Mirza zipped up his white plastic suit and pushed his way through the canvas opening. It had been raining all night, which wasn't going to help Eva Thulin and her forensics team. Eva looked up from the body she was examining and gave the tall, young detective a wan smile.

'Ah, Anita's prodigal son has returned. Welcome back. Where is she?'

'On holiday,' he replied as he cast an eye around the scene. Klara Wallen was already there, but there was no sign of Pontus Brodd.

'Where's Brodd?' he asked Wallen. The short, slightly muscular detective, with dark hair severely scraped back into a ponytail, replied with a resigned shrug. 'The chief inspector's on his way,' Hakim added as a warning. The prospect didn't improve her mood. With Anita away, Chief Inspector Moberg might ask her to front the investigation. She wasn't sure whether she was up to it.

'What have we got?' asked Hakim.

'Female jogger, probably in her mid-thirties,' Wallen answered. 'As she was out running, we don't have any identification. Only had a key on her. And a pendant in the shape of a cross.' With that, she left the tent.

Hakim could see the blonde hair behind Thulin's arched

body. A baseball cap lay on the ground close to the victim's head.

'How did she die?'

'Stabbed twice in the back. The second incision killed her. It looks as though her assailant came up behind her.'

'Was she running away from her attacker?'

'I can't be sure, but the cleanness of the first stab indicates that she may not have known that someone was about to harm her. The second one isn't as precise, as she was probably beginning to fall forward from the impact of the first blow. But the second thrust did the damage.'

'Which side did the attacker approach?'

'Judging by the angle of the initial wound, her assailant was coming up behind on the woman's left shoulder.'

'So was probably right-handed?'

'Yes.'

As Hakim tiptoed round Thulin, he could see that the woman lying lifeless on the ground had attractive, long legs. Thulin caught his glance. 'Beautiful girl.' Thulin lifted up the victim's right hand. 'Immaculate fingernails. She certainly looked after herself.'

'Was she sexually assaulted?'

'Doesn't appear so. We'll need to get her back to the lab to make sure. But her running shorts don't appear to have been disturbed. Pity, as that would have given us some DNA.'

'Time of death?'

'Last night between ten and midnight. Again, I'll know more later.'

'Is this the spot where she was killed?'

'Probably. There's no indication that she was moved.'

Hakim observed the interwoven mishmash of muddy footprints close to the body.

'Who found her?'

'Unfortunately, it was a group of elderly runners first

thing this morning.' She nodded at the footprints. 'Trampled everywhere. After the rain last night, you can see the mess they've made. We'll never find the perpetrator's footprints under that lot.'

'So, if they were the first to see the body, it's fairly safe to assume that this happened when no one else was around.'

'Possibly. But when did the rain start last night?'

'I'll check that out,' said Hakim, making a note.

'The rain may have kept people away until this morning.'

Just then, the vast figure of Chief Inspector Erik Moberg waddled into the tent. He was bursting out of his plastic suit. Wallen trailed in his wake. Hakim let Wallen update him, with Thulin throwing in the odd comment as she continued to examine the body.

When they had finished filling him in, Moberg sighed. 'I don't think the world will miss another fucking jogger. Bloody waste of time.'

Hakim realised that working for Moberg was going to be exactly as it had been in his trainee days. The man was all heart.

'Well, those geriatric runners may have buggered up the ground here, but I still want a thorough forensic search of the area.'

'Don't we always do that?' Thulin muttered from her squatting position.

Moberg chose to ignore her comment. 'If she's a jogger, I assume she hasn't come too far.'

Thulin passed Moberg two small, clear plastic evidence bags. 'A key. Only thing on her. Presumably it's for her apartment. The pendant was round her neck. Looks quite old to me.'

'So, we'll have to start going from apartment to apartment round the perimeter of the park.'

Did Moberg realise how many apartment blocks were round Pildammsparken? Wallen thought wearily.

'And that includes the medical staff over there,' Moberg airily waved a hand in the direction of Malmö's Skåne University Hospital. 'Wallen, you and Brodd can organise the apartment visits. Where is Brodd?'

'Haven't seen him this morning,' Wallen admitted.

Instead of being annoyed, Moberg grinned. 'The poor sod can't take his drink. We had a few last night on the way home. Better give him a call, though. Tell him to get his arse down here. And we'll also need to speak to regular joggers; Mirza, that's yours. They may know who she is, so we'll need an artist's impression done pronto. Can't show ghoulish photos to the public, or we'll get into trouble.'

'Do you want me to get in touch with Anita?' Hakim couldn't believe that Wallen had made such a suggestion. She would be furious being dragged in from her holiday. 'She lives just opposite the park and jogs round here, I believe.'

'No!' Moberg snapped. 'You think we're incapable of solving this without bloody Anita Sundström?' Wallen shook her head in submission. 'We can't have the woman thinking we can't operate without her.'

CHAPTER 4

He noticed her blonde hair and glasses as he peered out of the window of the train as it approached the platform. He gathered his luggage together. His heart missed a beat. He'd been waiting for this moment for so long. He couldn't believe his luck when Anita had phoned him several months after they had worked together on the heir hunter's case. He had hoped that she would, but, after time passed, he had despaired of any contact. He realised that their brief, fumbled lovemaking during her time in England had been because she had lost someone close to her – it was in a moment of vulnerability. He still didn't know who the person was and had not pried further. Her call out of the blue was followed by the occasional email. She gave little away. And then he had mentioned in one that they should meet up. To his amazement, she had agreed, and they had got together for a weekend in London. It hadn't been an outstanding success, but it hadn't been the debacle it could have been either. They had got on fairly well, even if it was a case of him doing most of the talking. Having booked separate rooms at the hotel, they had ended up in the same bed on the last night. Both had performed a lot better than on the previous occasion. Less tense, more relaxed.

The problem was that when the weekend ended, he still had no idea where he stood with her. Were they a potential couple? Or was it a fleeting friendship? The emails continued

– more regular on his side. The tone of his messages became increasingly flirty. The ones she returned were newsy but emotionally deadpan. She gave nothing away, which was increasingly frustrating, as he was becoming more preoccupied with thoughts of her. He found himself waking up with Anita's face being the first image that popped into his bleary head. He suspected that while she was always his first thought, he was but an afterthought to her. She grew more attractive in his mind as the months passed. And then, she had suddenly suggested that he visit Sweden. And not just for a weekend; a fortnight in the summer. That was back in February. He had booked his SAS flight from Newcastle to Copenhagen immediately, before she could change her mind. And then he had counted the weeks and days. His colleagues at the Cumbria Constabulary headquarters in Penrith were both intrigued and envious to hear of his trip. To the British, Sweden is a bit of an enigma. Though they think they know it, with its dark nights, bouncy pop music and fictional serial killers, it's not usually on their "to visit" list. Most of his fellow police workers tended to fly south to Spain and Portugal for the sun. When you live in one of the rainier parts of Britain, heading north is considered rather strange. But then, they were never quite sure what to make of Detective Sergeant Kevin Ash. He wasn't local; worse, he was a southerner from Essex. And he was far too chatty for a community that was friendly but naturally reserved. Now that he was heading off to Scandinavia for a fortnight, the office would be a lot quieter.

Anita had actually made the effort to clean her second-hand Peugeot before picking Kevin up. It still wasn't spotless, but it was passable. The greeting had been awkward. The half-embrace had turned into a formal handshake. But the smiles were genuine on both sides, and Anita found herself relaxing as they passed through the resplendent green countryside of a vibrant early-

June day. They had already dispensed with the details of Kevin's journey that day, which had involved both car and plane before coming to a juddering halt at Copenhagen's Kastrup Airport. The train service that usually whipped freshly arrived passengers across the Öresund Bridge into Malmö was subject to an all-out strike. Such an action had surprised the Danes and Swedes as much as it had Kevin. Though striking was once a traditional British pastime, he had assumed that such a thing was beyond the efficient Scandinavians. As both employer and union seemed incapable of sitting down together, Kevin joked that the British could teach them a thing or two about the games that surround negotiations. It was the one thing that Britain still led the world in. As a result of the strike, he had to wait for a coach in the middle of what seemed like a rugby scrum – 'You lot don't know how to queue either.' – until he and his fellow travellers were transported over the bridge by road.

After the previous night's downpour, it was welcomingly hot. The sea shimmered on their right, and the trees and fields on their left were burgeoning with the verdure of the beginning of summer. As the spring had come unseasonably early this year, Anita explained that what they called the "white period" of hawthorn and apple blossom had already been and gone. When the conversation lulled, Kevin seemed quite content to drink in the sights of this new land. He hadn't been sure what to expect, but this beautiful, tranquil countryside was a million miles away from the bleak landscapes of common British perception.

The car turned off the main road and along a gravelled track. It curled round to the left, and Anita manoeuvred onto the grass next to a Falun red wooden cabin. There was a decked porch to the side with outdoor furniture on it, which was invitingly bathed in sunlight. Kevin was childishly delighted that the house lived up to all his expectations of a typical Swedish dwelling. He noticed that there were two other houses along from Anita's rented home. The nearest was a solidly built, white-painted Dutch bungalow with a tall, ugly stone chimney breast abutting the gable end. It had a grey-tiled roof, in the centre of which, above the front door, was a wide dormer window. It had probably looked very smart when it was put up in the 1970s; now it looked faded and tired. Beyond that was a stone cottage, the oldest building of the three. As he got out of the car, he noticed that in the gaps between the surrounding trees, he could see the waters of the Baltic stretching away to the horizon.

'This is fantastic, Anita. Is there a beach near?'

'Just down there,' she said, pointing to a path at the side of the house.

'Glad I brought my cossie.'

'Pardon?'

'Swimming trunks.'

'Well, why don't you go for a swim while I sort out the meal for tonight?'

At that time in the afternoon, there were several people on the beach, which Kevin could see zigzagged its way along the coastline. Despite the heat, the water was cold, and it took him some minutes before he plunged fully in and headed out to sea. Anita had warned him not to go out too far, as there were strong currents. Once he got used to the temperature, he began to enjoy the freedom. He noticed that no one else was swimming. A few youngsters were playing at the water's edge, with a grandfather ankle-deep keeping an eye on them. As he paddled on the spot, he took in the view. He could see the three houses amongst the trees on the bluff above the beach. He had immediately taken to Anita's rented home. It was, he presumed, typically Scandinavian. Sparsely but tastefully furnished. No unwarranted fripperies. It was the casual, informal feel that was so different from anything he was used to in Britain. Anita had given him a brief tour. It had a functional but comfortable living room overlooking the sea, a neat kitchen-diner, a bathroom and two bedrooms. Unsure where he was to be housed, he was about to put his luggage in the second bedroom when Anita pointed to the room she was obviously using.

'Aren't you going to stay in here?' she had said matter-of-factly.

No messing around, no British-style prevarication. He hadn't needed a second invitation, and any embarrassment had been avoided. Now, as he headed back towards the beach, he couldn't remember when he had felt so happy. A quiet couple of weeks with a gorgeous woman like Anita would banish, albeit temporarily, the cheerless emptiness in his domestic life and the stresses and strains of a police career that was stagnating.

CHAPTER 5

Chief Inspector Moberg sat thoughtfully at the top of the table in the meeting room. Behind him was a blank whiteboard onto which photos of the victim would be attached, profiles of possible suspects would be added, and theories played out. He wondered if he should have had something to eat before the team meeting started. It had been a couple of hours since he'd demolished a burger brought in from McDonald's. He found it difficult to think on an empty stomach. And where was he going to dine tonight? His apartment wasn't an option. The third, unlamented fru Moberg may have departed and taken her bile and ill-will with her, but at least there had been someone at home waiting for him when he returned from work. They may not have spoken, or even slept in the same bed latterly, but, strangely, that was better than having nobody. After the initial month of euphoria following her walk out, when he'd felt free to come and go as he pleased – be answerable to nobody – there was a moment when he realised that that wasn't a satisfying situation any more. He even began to miss their marital spats and vitriolic jousting, which had shown they had cared enough about something, however inconsequential or stupid. Could he not survive on his own? Did he need to live with someone he could kick against, blame or annoy? Is that why he had dived from one marriage into the next? It certainly wasn't for the sex.

His thoughts were interrupted when the team started to

file in. First came Wallen, whom he knew to be competent but not pushy enough to get things moving; unlike the irritating Anita Sundström. Then Mirza. He liked his enthusiasm, while still being wary of someone of his background. He had never been keen on the influx of Arabs that seemed to have swamped Sweden in recent years. Not that they were any worse than any of the other immigrants. They just seemed to cause more trouble because many didn't integrate; a matter that had caused fierce disagreements with Sundström. Mirza had undeniably come from that same cultural milieu, and yet was quickly becoming an integral part of the polishus, so Moberg pushed his prejudice into the back of his mind. Then, in came Pontus Brodd. Brodd raised his hand in a tilted drinking gesture. Moberg nodded in reply. He glanced round the team as they took their seats. It was at times like this that he most missed Henrik Nordlund's unruffled presence and wise counsel.

'Is Eva Thulin coming?'

'She's on her way,' replied Wallen.

Moberg hoped that Thulin had something positive to report, as he had a horrible feeling this investigation was going to begin with the situation he always dreaded – having no clue as to the identity of the victim.

They were all looking at the whiteboard. Thulin had attached various photos of the victim. The neat stabbing ensured the images weren't as vivid and upsetting as those of many of the cases they had investigated. Thulin told them that the woman was in her mid-thirties, was healthy and in very good physical condition at the time of her death. The weapon was a knife.

'As you can see, the fatal wound is halfway down the thoracic spine, just inside the inner border of the scapula – the shoulder blade. The knife blade travelled through part of the left lung, causing a pneumothorax, and lacerated the descending aorta. The blade also pierced the left ventricle of the heart, causing blood to escape into the pericardial sac. Death would have been rapid. The fast drop in blood pressure was followed by cardiac arrest.'

'What you're saying is she was stabbed to death.'

'Yes, Chief Inspector, that's exactly what I'm saying,' Thulin sighed. 'You're looking for a right-handed person. Could be male or female. The perpetrator was strong enough to stab the victim with some force, and presumably fit enough to run up behind her. As the victim was very fit herself, she was likely to have been jogging at a reasonable pace.'

Moberg frowned. This wasn't exactly helpful.

'Anything else?'

'Hakim asked if she had been sexually assaulted. She hadn't, and her running clothes hadn't been disturbed. But,' and there was a long pause, 'she had been sexually active not long before.'

'What do you mean "sexually active"? She had sex,' snorted the chief inspector.

'She'd had sex at both ends, as it were. Probably what you'd call "normal" sex,' Thulin stared at Moberg with the hint of a twinkle in her eye, 'and anal.'

Moberg pulled a face. 'Poofs' sex.' Brodd smirked like a schoolboy.

'Woman can enjoy it as well. Anyway, we might be able to get DNA from at least one end with a bit of luck.'

Moberg didn't want to hear any more. Even after all his years on the force, he still felt uncomfortable when intimate sexual details were discussed as part of a case. 'So, she was with a man, or men, before she went out running.'

'Husband?' Wallen queried.

'No ring, anyway,' observed Hakim.

'And having looked closely at her hands, she certainly hasn't worn a ring in a long time, if ever,' added Thulin. 'But those fingers were beautifully manicured. Care like that doesn't come cheap.' She glanced at her own hands and frowned. 'And another thing, your victim wasn't a natural blonde. The hair was dyed. Dark brown is probably her natural colouring.'

'Are we looking at a lover?' Moberg threw out the question to the room. 'After a lover's tiff, he runs after her and stabs her?'

'After all that sex, he wouldn't have the energy!' laughed Brodd.

Brodd was tall and wiry, with a hint of a stoop, yet his slow and lugubrious movements were those of a much heavier man. He was usually unshaven, and had a mop of dark hair that seemed to have a life all of its own. He was often found to be sitting; any walking appeared to be an effort and was accompanied by a grimace. In short, he was lazy. Hakim had surmised it very quickly; Wallen confirmed the impression through her bitter experience. Why, Hakim wondered, did Moberg put up with a member of the team who offered so little and, more worryingly, was prone to incompetence? 'Since the Chief's wife left him,' Wallen explained, 'Brodd has become his drinking buddy. Brodd's his wife substitute.' Hakim shuddered to think what Anita made of their colleague.

'I wouldn't have thought that likely,' ventured Hakim, ignoring Brodd's facetious comment. 'She got changed to go out running. Not the easiest thing to do if you're in the middle of an argument. You might as well stab her where the argument took place. This seems like a calculated killing to me.'

'And that's your opinion after all your years in the police.' Brodd said mockingly. He hadn't liked the way Mirza had cut across his joke in front of the boss.

'I bow to your experience.'

'Don't get sarky with me.'

'Shut it, Pontus,' ordered Moberg. He gazed across to the whiteboard.

'One other thing,' said Thulin, breaking the silence that had followed the altercation. She pointed to a photo of the victim lying on her stomach. 'If you look carefully, there's a scar here.'

She indicated a spot just below the right shoulder blade. 'It's an old one and has healed over time, but I think it's a stab wound.'

It took a few moments for this to sink in.

'So, it's happened before,' Wallen remarked. 'The same person succeeding where they originally failed?'

'That long apart?' Moberg weighed in sceptically.

'Isn't it striking that it's also in the back?' countered Wallen.

'Right. We'll bear that in mind. But first, we need to know who the hell she is. Have we had any luck with the trawl through the apartments in the vicinity?'

'We haven't turned up anything,' admitted Wallen. 'No one of the victim's description appears to be missing.'

'What about the pendant?'

'Old but cheap.' Thulin held it up to the light in its clear plastic bag. 'It's strange for a woman who can afford expensive manicures to be wearing such an inexpensive item round her neck.'

'Maybe it was a family heirloom,' Wallen suggested.

'Could be. It wasn't made in Sweden,' continued Thulin as she twirled the bag slowly around in the light. 'I'm going to have it tested to see where it might come from. Could be up to a hundred years old.'

'In that case, she could be a religious type,' opined Moberg. 'Ask around in the local churches.' He pointed at the other plastic bag. 'So, we've got a key but no apartment to go with it. Joggers?'

'No luck there either,' said Hakim. 'I'm going back down to the park tonight to ask the ones who go out late. If she was a regular, then they're the most likely to have seen her or know who she is.'

'I've prepared her description for the papers and the TV stations if that's what you think we should do. That may turn up something.' Why did Moberg feel surprised that Wallen had actually taken the initiative for once? Maybe he should let

Sundström go on holiday more often.

'Go ahead with that. And the hospital?'

'Brodd was looking into that,' Wallen confirmed.

'Em... nothing, Boss. So far that is.' Wallen wondered how much questioning Brodd had actually done. And she found it irritating that he always called Moberg "boss".

'So, we've got fuck all.' He really should have eaten before the meeting.

CHAPTER 6

Kevin felt invigorated after his swim. As he towelled himself down, he noticed that the beach was now nearly deserted. He must have been in the water longer than he thought. A fair-haired couple were coming towards him on their way off the beach. Kevin put them in their thirties. She was as tall as her well-built partner, and carried an ethnic woollen bag; and he, iPod earphones clamped to the sides of his head, had a windbreak tucked under his arm.

'Lovely day,' Kevin said as they passed, and flashed them his best grin. He was in the mood to be friendly with the locals.

The man's hooded eyes didn't even flicker, and he offered no acknowledgement, but the woman smiled back in surprise.

'*Hej*.' Then she paused. 'Are you American?'

'No,' he laughed. 'I'm English.'

Her square-jawed, sour-faced partner seemed anxious to move off. She ignored him.

'Are you on holiday?'

'Yes. I'm staying with a Swedish friend at that house up there.' He pointed to Anita's rented cabin.

'We are staying here, too.' Her English was good, if somewhat stilted. 'We are in the house at the end.'

'It's so fantastic here,' Kevin said with genuine enthusiasm.

'It is. Are you walking up?'

He nodded.

Without saying a word, the woman's partner wandered on ahead, making absolutely no effort to join in the conversation.

'Sadly, we have only one day left of our holiday. We have rented the house, but we have to go back to Stockholm on Friday.'

They started to climb the bank.

'Benno and I will be back in our offices on Monday.'

Kevin now couldn't think of anything to say, so, to break the silence, he asked what they did for a living.

'My husband, Benno, does IT. I am in marketing.'

'Sounds exciting.'

'Not really.'

By this time they had reached the top of the bank.

'I am Fanny.' Kevin managed to cut off a silly smirk before it spread across his face. 'Nice to meet you.'

'I'm Kevin.'

She smiled once more and then hurried after her silent husband. Kevin wondered why a nice girl like Fanny was married to a miserable sod like Benno.

There was no sign of Anita when he returned from the beach, so Kevin showered and changed. As it was still warm, he made the bold decision to wear shorts. They never did his thin legs any favours, and he was conscious of how pallid he looked, particularly with his shaved head, compared to the Swedes on the beach. In fact, he found his body rather unappealing and envied many of his more muscular colleagues. At least at the age of fifty – a milestone he had reached in April – he hadn't run to fat like many of his contemporaries. Smoking helped, too.

Anita wasn't to be found in the kitchen or the living room. So, he wandered out onto the porch, which faced the side of the next house. He lit up a cigarette. It felt good, though he had a tinge of guilt smoking in such beautiful, natural surroundings. Another assumption he had made was that the Swedes were incredibly health-conscious. Yet he had been amazed watching people jumping off the trains arriving at Malmö Central Station and immediately lighting up on the platforms. That would not be allowed in Britain in this day and age.

'Over here!'

He turned his head and saw Anita waving to him from the back of the house next door. She had a glass in her hand. A second later, she had disappeared round the corner. Kevin stamped out his half-smoked cigarette and wandered over to the neighbour's house. More sensibly, it had been built with the whole of the back of the building facing the sea, not side-on like Anita's cabin. It had a verandah, with stylish, cedar outdoor furniture. Sitting on one of the chairs was Anita, who was sporting light-blue, short-cropped trousers and a striped blue-and-white sleeveless T-shirt. Her sunglasses were perched on the top of her head – it was strange to see her without spectacles on. But it was the neighbour who really caught Kevin's eye. A large man with a thinning mane of white hair sat upright in a wicker chair. He wore a light-beige summer suit with a white, collarless shirt. A neatly folded, faded red handkerchief protruded from the breast pocket of his jacket like a dried blood stain. He must have been even larger at one time, but the years – or illness – had taken their toll, and his figure had diminished. The wide blue eyes that shone out from his gaunt face were searching and alert. The long fingers of his right hand were wrapped round a tumbler, while the left clutched a wooden stick that was resting against his chair. If he was in pain, he didn't show it. Kevin estimated that he must be in his eighties. Yet, for all his physical frailty, it was impossible not to be aware of his compelling presence, even before he uttered a word.

'This is Albin Rylander,' said Anita, introducing him. 'And my friend from England, Kevin Ash.'

Rylander raised a sardonic eyebrow. It was the bloody shorts! Kevin knew he shouldn't have put them on.

'Welcome to Sweden. Please forgive me for not rising. It takes a lot of effort. Help yourself.' Rylander waved at the table.

On it was a tray with a bottle of gin, a very good malt whisky, a couple of small bottles of tonic, a glass dish with slices of lemon, and a plastic ice box. Kevin could have murdered a beer but was too polite to ask, so he fixed himself a gin and tonic.

'Cheers!' Kevin said, raising his glass and taking the seat next to Anita.

'And whereabouts in England do you come from, Kevin?' The English was perfect, with the vaguest hint of an American accent.

'From Cumbria. But originally from Essex. That's near London.'

'I know Essex, or parts of it,' Rylander said, with a gleam of recognition in his eye. 'I once visited Greensted Church. They say it's the oldest wooden building in Europe. I'm not a religious man myself, but even I found it a deeply spiritual place. I was based in London for a couple of stints.'

'Albin has been all over the world,' added Anita for Kevin's enlightenment. 'A diplomat.'

'Yes,' murmured Rylander reflectively. 'I liked London a lot. But I hope I don't upset you by saying that Washington was my favourite haunt. Of course, I spent more time there.'

'I'm not upset. It must be living up north for so long that these days I can't take more than a short visit to London without wanting to escape.'

Rylander looked nonplussed. 'I cannot understand that. I love the rhythm of the city; the constant clamour, the restlessness, the intrigue... the knowing that you're at the centre of things.'

'So, why are you here, away from all that buzz?'

Rylander smiled at Kevin pleasantly. 'To die.'

Two gins later, they were back in Anita's kitchen, and she was briefing Kevin on her neighbour as she prepared a salad. They had moved on to red wine.

25

'Cancer. Less than a year left. Perfectly open about it. Doesn't seem to worry him unduly. But he's come back to Skåne. This is where he was brought up.'

'Returning to his roots.'

'I suppose so.'

'Any family? Wife and kids?'

Anita shook her head with a wry grin. 'He's gay.'

'Ah.'

'He's not everybody's cup of tea, as you say, but I like him, even if I don't always agree with his political views.'

'I thought diplomats weren't meant to express their views.'

Anita started to mix up a salad dressing.

'After he retired, he was often on TV giving his opinions. And I'm sure that his views were well known behind closed embassy doors during his time in the diplomatic.'

'And what did he talk about on telly?'

'East-West relationships mainly. He'd been posted all over the place in his early days. Then he had a spell in East Germany before eventually getting the top prize: Washington. He was very pro-Reagan in the 1980s. Much of this became public after he retired and returned to Sweden. The Americans loved him, apparently. Always gets a warm welcome when he goes back; not that he's ever likely to make it there again now. You'll find lots about him on Google.'

'I read something the other day about how close the links were between Sweden and America during the Cold War. Stuff's come out recently. I thought you lot were meant to be neutral.' Kevin, who had a natural love of history, had been boning up on Sweden before his visit.

'We've always been scared of Russia. That's why we were neutral during the Second World War.'

'Not that neutral.'

Anita poured the dressing onto the salad and put the wooden bowl on the table.

'Sore point.'

Kevin finished his drink. He looked up at Anita. 'Help yourself,' she said, nodding in the direction of the bottle. He poured himself some wine and topped up her glass.

'I must ask Albin about his political views next time. That guy Edward Snowden, who leaked all those sensitive documents from the US: according to him, Sweden's been working with the Yanks since the Fifties. And apparently, your lot had an agreement with the American National Security Agency about ten years ago. He claims the Swedes have actually been spying on the Russians for the Americans.'

'I'm afraid I'm not into all this spying stuff.' When she saw that she had deflated Kevin's escalating enthusiasm, she felt bad. 'But I'm sure Albin will be more than happy to chat to you. Just don't get him started on Putin, if you want my advice.'

After a leisurely meal, Anita sent Kevin out onto the porch while she did the dishes. He had offered to help, but she said it was his first night, so he was excused. It was slightly cooler, and Kevin wanted to change out of his shorts and put on a jersey, but thought it might look a bit feeble. He put the second bottle of wine Anita had opened on the table, poured himself another drink and took a seat. He cradled his glass against his chest. He could hear the lapping of the sea below. It was a beautiful spot, and the evening promised even greater delights once they retired to Anita's bedroom. He was taken by surprise when she suddenly appeared in a tight-fitting tracksuit and baseball cap.

'Just a fifteen-minute run along the beach.'

'Oh, I met the other people holidaying in the house beyond Rylander's. On the beach, after my swim this afternoon. She seemed very nice. Fanny.'

'You'll find that funny. Isn't that what you British call—'

'I know. It's pathetic.'

'So, you're chatting up other Swedish women behind my back?'

'No chance of that. Her miserable husband was there. Didn't say a word. Very rude.'

'Stockholmers!' she snorted contemptuously. And then she was off.

Kevin took advantage of Anita's disappearance to slip into the bedroom and change into a pair of trousers and a jersey. When he returned, he lit up a cigarette and happily inhaled. Life was good. He just hoped that Anita's exercise wouldn't make her too tired for what he hoped would be an active night. The sun was fading fast, and dusk enveloped the landscape. There was a light coming from Rylander's house. He might have a chat with him in the next day or so.

Was that a movement in the trees where the bank began its slump to the sea? Maybe it was a bird, or some kind of animal. He took a sip of his wine. Was it instinct that made him stare hard into the gathering gloom? It was something, but any further inspection was swiftly dispatched as Anita came jogging up the bank and stood panting in front of him.

'That was quick.'

When she got her breath back, she said, 'I shouldn't have had all those drinks first.'

She took a few paces towards the door. 'I'm going to pop into the shower. Give me five minutes and then bring the bottle to the bedroom.'

CHAPTER 7

Hakim was tired when he dragged himself into the polishus. He had been at Pildammsparken until nearly midnight, long after the last jogger had gone off to bed. The numbers had dwindled as the light had faded, though there were one or two diehards who made it through the gloom. He had spoken to a number of people, most of whom were annoyed that they had to stop mid-run, and some even jogged on the spot while he tried to talk to them. He had gleaned one possibly useful piece of information. There was one particular blonde woman, who sometimes wore a baseball cap, who was known to run early to late evenings reasonably regularly. Could this be their victim?

His first port of call was to report to Moberg. The chief inspector wasn't in his most communicative mood. Hakim wondered if he'd had another night out on the town with Brodd. Moberg merely grunted when he gave him his update.

'I'm afraid there's no clear description of the regular jogger, but it could well be our victim.'

'Follow it up.'

Hakim got himself a coffee and returned to his office. Much as he liked working with Anita, he was grateful that, this time round, he wasn't squashed into a single room with her. Here he had space to work and think. He sat down at his desk and looked at the phone. Should he contact Anita and ask her if she knew who the blonde jogger might be? That was her running patch. Then he dismissed the idea. He knew her British "friend" was holidaying with her, so she wouldn't be too happy to have that interrupted. He had never met Kevin Ash, but he hoped that it would work out because Anita needed a man in her life. He had sensed that after Lasse had moved out to cohabit with his sister, Anita was lonely, restless. Though Lasse was still in Malmö, it wasn't the same.

Pontus Brodd wandered into the room unannounced and plonked himself in the spare chair. This wasn't the first time he had done this since Hakim had moved back to the polishus a month ago. It bugged him.

'Had a bit of a night of it. The boss can't half drink,' Brodd said, shaking his head. 'You should come out sometime.'

'I don't drink.'

Brodd gave him a sceptical glance. 'Never?'

'Never.'

'Ah, religious thing is it?'

'Look, Brodd, what do you want?'

Brodd blew out his cheeks. 'I'm just about to see the boss. Going around first to find out if anybody has any updates to tell him about.' Sucking up is what you mean, Hakim reckoned silently. 'Klara Wallen has nothing, but she did put out the description of the victim to the press et cetera.'

'I've already reported to the chief inspector about what I came up with.'

'Oh, have you?' Brodd's tone managed to combine surprise and annoyance.

He levered himself out of the chair with accompanying sighs. 'Anything then?'

'Ask the "boss" himself.'

Kevin couldn't keep the smile off his face as he supped his breakfast coffee. He hadn't enjoyed sex like that since... he couldn't remember when. Anita was a good lover. No, she was better than that. The day was warm and promised to get hotter.

They were sitting on the porch having strong coffee, with a choice of egg, ham or cheese to put on slices of bread. There was also a tube of caviar, which Kevin had tentatively tried. He'd spooled out a worm of pink gunge and spread it over his bread. It tasted salty. He wasn't sure if he could cope with Swedish breakfasts for the next fortnight.

'I thought I'd take you to Glimmingehus today. It's a castle. Not far.'

'That sounds good.'

They exchanged smiles. Then Anita glanced beyond him and waved. Kevin stretched round to see who she was gesturing to. The man with a satchel slung over his shoulder was squat and was wearing a black leather jacket and trousers. Above the biker's outfit, the grinning face sported a thick red beard. Kevin put him at about his own age, perhaps a little younger.

'*God morgon, Anita.*'

'*Hej Klas! Vilken härlig morgon!*' He walked over the grass towards them. 'Klas Lennartsson, this is Kevin Ash. From England.'

'Hi there. Nice to meet you.' He sounded American. They shook hands. 'Is this your first visit?'

'Yes, it is.'

'And do you like Sweden?' he asked, with a willingness in his voice that Kevin would say the positive thing.

'Very much so.' Kevin glanced at Anita. 'Very much so.'

'Are you visiting Albin?' Anita put in quickly.

'Yes. Another session.'

'Klas is writing Albin's biography.'

'Yeah. He has a wonderful story to tell. He's had such an amazing career.' Lennartsson couldn't stifle his excitement. 'It just fell into my lap. He actually asked *me* to write it.' He shook his head incredulously.

'Klas is our local historian.' Anita felt the need to clarify the situation for Kevin's benefit.

31

'Yeah, but I've never written anything like this before. Of this importance. He's such a well-known person in our country. He could have had his pick of biographers, but he said he wanted someone who was local and who he could trust.' He looked delighted at the compliment that Albin Rylander had paid him.

'Any juicy bits?' Kevin joked.

Lennartsson was taken aback for a moment. 'Not like that,' he answered severely. Then he leant forward in a conspiratorial way. 'But he has promised some shocks.'

'What sort of shocks?' asked Anita with a grin.

Just then, a middle-aged woman with neat, nut-brown hair swept up into a bun, and wearing a blue medical smock appeared from the back of Rylander's house. She waved to them.

'That's Moa. She comes in every morning to give Albin his medication. She's devoted to him. Of course, my sessions with Albin are restricted to about a couple of hours, as he gets very tired.' When he judged that the nurse was out of earshot, and even though they were alone and there was no sign of Rylander, Lennartsson lowered his voice. 'I don't know what shocks exactly, Anita. He's promised me these revelations when we've done the rest of the book. One thing I already know, but I can't say what it is yet. It's extraordinary.' For a moment, Anita thought he was going to spill the beans, but then he thought better of it. 'He's sworn me to secrecy. I'm not allowed to tell anybody anything until after he's dead. I fear that may only be months away. The manuscript mustn't be presented to any publisher until a month after his funeral. I've had to sign a legal document, you know.'

'Sounds as though he wants to get things off his chest,' said a now-intrigued Kevin. 'Guilty conscience?'

CHAPTER 8

Kevin loved Glimmingehus. The castle was unlike any other he had seen, albeit his knowledge was restricted to British versions and the more flamboyant châteaux he had dragged his bored wife Leanne round on a disastrous holiday in the Loire Valley. (He had wanted an alternative to her usual choice of vacation destination, which was invariably some Spanish beach. Needless to say, they went to Benidorm the following year.)

Glimmingehus, an imposing rectangular medieval fortress, was remarkably well preserved, with its cream stone walls and crow-stepped gables. There was a holiday atmosphere as the crowds – tourists and locals alike – soaked up the history, admired the views from the garret, marvelled at the jousting displays, then retired to the restaurant, satisfied that their cultural knowledge had been expanded in such a pleasant, entertaining way.

As Anita and Kevin stood in the courtyard, the conversation turned to Klas Lennartsson. Kevin had noticed the rapport that Anita and the local historian seemed to have. Ridiculously, it had awoken a pang of jealousy. Was Lennartsson a former lover? They hadn't really discussed her past sex life. He knew all about her ex-husband, Björn, but had never dared venture further. He had certainly never tackled the subject of the man whose death she was so upset about when she was over in England during the heir hunter's case. It was too private.

'I was at school with Klas. I've known him since we were teenagers. He was a couple years ahead of me. He's very nice. Very enthusiastic.' Kevin started to admire the crude wooden pillory. 'Not quite sure why Albin chose Klas. He's fine writing about local rituals and ancient stones and things like that, but a major biography is quite an undertaking. I'm sure there'll be a lot of publishers interested when it's finished. They'll probably bring someone else in to polish it up, I expect.'

'I know Klas is local, but he sounds like a Yank.'

'Picked up the accent when he had a couple of years over there at Penn State University. Went away Swedish, came back American!' There was real affection in her voice.

'He's not an old boyfriend, is he?'

Anita giggled. 'Klas? You're kidding.'

Kevin was infuriated with himself for asking, but relieved at the answer. In celebration, he stuck his head and arms in the old pillory and began to pull stupid faces. He made Anita laugh with his antics. She was starting to loosen up with him around. This could be a good holiday. She had to admit she had enjoyed last night's lovemaking. Kevin was an attentive lover, even if he wasn't particularly demanding. She liked that. She knew she had been spoiled by Björn. He had taught her so much. But the trade-off between good sex and a disintegrating marriage wasn't worth hanging around for. And Kevin was funny, and that was important to her. He would do nicely for the time being. The future would take care of itself.

Hakim stood at the murder site. The tent was still in place, and the police tape still cordoned off the killing ground. He knew that Thulin's team had been over the area again and that there was a constable on guard over night. He had had a word with him about asking anybody passing who might be able to identify the blonde jogger – and also to make a note of anyone hanging around the site. Killers were sometimes known to return to the scene of their crime. It was a long shot, but they had nothing else to go on.

The day was beginning to drift away as he wandered around the perimeter of the Plate. He took a seat and watched the sun disappear behind the trees and the area being thrown into shadow. A man in his sixties, with a large, fluffy labradoodle in tow, came along the path. Hakim wearily stood up.

'Excuse me, sir,' and he asked for the hundredth time about a late-night, blonde jogger. Hakim showed him the artist's impression of the victim. Again, there was the familiar shake of the head.

'Don't recognise her. But there's a regular lady jogger that does the circuit round the Plate a lot. This time of night sometimes. Bit older. I think she's a policewoman.'

'About mid-forties? Lives on Roskildevägen next to the park?'

'That's right. Do you know her?'

Hakim nodded. So, the regular jogger was Anita! Moberg wouldn't see the funny side of that.

It was another warm night. Kevin sat on the porch in the darkness, though the grass that ran across to Rylander's house was bathed in clear moonlight. He could count on the fingers of one hand the number of nights he had been able to sit outside at this time during his years living in Cumbria. He had left Anita's side to come out for a smoke. She had fallen asleep in his arms after they had made love. He had enjoyed the sensation of holding her until his arm had started to seize up, and he carefully manoeuvred himself out of bed.

He slowly exhaled the smoke from his lungs and watched it dissipate into the night air. This was a heavenly spot. It fulfilled all his romantic visions of Sweden – the wooden house, the gentle sound of the sea, and the clear, star-spangled sky. And a lovely blonde Swedish woman in his bed. Life couldn't get better.

He finished his cigarette and stubbed it out. He was about to get out of his seat when he thought he saw something in the trees facing Rylander's. It was like the previous evening. Then, he hadn't been sure what it was. This time it was different. He was almost certain that a man was hovering in the shadows. And a large man at that. In a glint of light, there was the shape of a head. Was he watching the diplomat's house? Kevin wondered if he should call out. Then the figure was gone. He waited for a few minutes to see if he would return, but no one appeared again. He would mention it to Anita tomorrow. There was probably a totally innocent explanation.

CHAPTER 9

They had made an early start. Anita whipped along the main drag north before cutting off onto some minor roads. She said that Stenshuvud National Park was best first thing in the morning to avoid the crowds. They could have it to themselves. So, after a strong cup of Anita's coffee, Kevin had emerged, still sleepy-eyed, into the sharp morning sunshine. It was about a twenty-minute drive on the main road up the coast. At a bend in the road, they turned right up a tree-lined bank. Kevin pointed out the gently swaying profusion of white cow parsley on the verges, which reminded him of the back lanes of Cumbria at this time of year. Anita laughed when she realised that he was referring to what the Swedes call "dog biscuits". Past the trees the landscape opened out onto fields of yellow oilseed rape, now gone over; newly planted apple orchards; and swaying, unripened corn. Through a farmyard with a jumble of horseboxes, past a couple of hamlets hardly worth the name, and the sea came back into view. Down a steep, forested bank, they reached a dusty, deserted car park at the bottom. Kevin had Anita's small backpack with their breakfast wrapped up inside and a bottle of water. Of course, there was also the obligatory thermos of coffee. It promised to be a hot day. They set off walking past the closed information centre, plunged into a thick blanket of beech and hornbeam trees, and onto a well-worn path which wound its way upwards. Anita led the way, which Kevin was happy with, as he could watch her sashaying bottom in her khaki shorts in front of him.

'You must be used to climbing hills living near the Lake District.'

'You're kidding.'

'But you've all those wonderful fells.'

'I come from Essex. It's as flat as a pancake. That's how land should be. That's why I like it round here.'

'And I thought you'd like this – it's the only hill we've got!'

'You call this a hill? The only time I've been up a real fell was with an ex-Army friend. Mark used to be in the SAS. Fitness freak. Got me drunk one night, and I stupidly agreed to go up High Pike with him. So, we went up just before Christmas. It started out OK until the wind picked up. Then it began to pour with rain. I wanted to turn back, but he was so far ahead, I couldn't make myself heard above the wind and rain. Then there was a fifteen-minute hail storm. There's nowhere to hide on those bloody fells. Then thunder and lightning! It was a nightmare. When I eventually staggered to the top, the weather actually cleared. But Mark had been waiting there so long for me to turn up, that I hardly had time to admire the view before he insisted we head back down. There was so much rain that the sheep trails had turned into bubbling torrents, and, to cap things off, I bloody slipped and fell into one. I've never felt so miserable in my life.'

He could hear Anita chortling at his story. 'Do you always moan so much?'

'Only when I'm dragged up hills.'

Anita turned round, still smiling. 'At least you're not moaning about this one.'

'This one's fine. Besides, you're far better looking than Mark.'

'I should hope so.'

*

When they emerged from the trees, they had reached the South Head. Broad heaths and dry meadows stretched across level sand flats which met the sea. Anita pointed out the beach he had swum off way down the coast. 'Our house is somewhere over there.' A further five-minute walk through more trees brought them out onto the North Head – a bald, rocky outcrop. Kevin found the scene astonishing. In the early morning sun, the sea was a wonderful ultramarine, the light playing on the calm water like a woman dancing in a blue lamé dress. Stenshuvud provided an uninterrupted view of the curving coastline of Österlen, with an infinite, thin line of pale sandy beaches. Inland, below them, was a valley, its contours totally obscured by a thick canopy of foliage. They were surrounded by the sounds of birdsong. They had the hilltop to themselves. Anita found some low-lying rocks, and she laid out their breakfast. To Kevin, the usual fare of eggs, cheese and caviar, washed down with strong coffee, seemed so much better up here in the warmth of their Baltic eyrie. They didn't even bother to chat, as the view took all their attention. They watched a couple of yachts come close to the Head and then sail out again.

'Probably from Simrishamn,' Anita remarked as she shaded her eyes against the sun.

After a second cup of coffee, Kevin raised the subject of the person in the trees. 'That's the second night I've been aware of someone opposite Rylander's house. Almost as though they were keeping watch.'

'Are you sure?'

'Pretty sure. I'm a policeman after all. We tend to notice these things.'

Anita retreated into her coffee mug.

'Maybe someone out for a late walk,' she said eventually. 'A dog walker. At this time of year, when the nights are short, people are often about at funny times. Especially if it's warm.'

'Probably something or nothing.'

'Don't worry. Nothing much happens round here. But you can ask Albin himself later. I know you're interested in having a chat with him. I've asked him over for a fika this afternoon.'

'Fika? What's that?'

'If you want to know more about Sweden, you can start with fika. It's a sort of coffee break with cakes or something sweet with it. We'd better pick something up in Kivik on the way back. Anyhow, it's a national institution because having coffee is an important part of our culture.'

'Blimey! More coffee.'

'This is Sweden.'

When Hakim entered Moberg's office, Brodd was just leaving. He was smirking. He had probably been telling the chief inspector one of his dubious, sexist jokes. Hakim waited for him to go before speaking.

'The jogger that has been seen regularly in that part of the park turns out to be Anita Sundström.'

'Oh, for fuck's sake! I can't escape that woman even when she's on holiday.'

'What woman?'

They looked round to see that Eva Thulin had slipped into the room.

'What brings you here?' Moberg asked rather ungraciously. A case going nowhere was not a situation that brought the best out of the chief inspector, especially when he had the commissioner on his back demanding the usual quick result.

'I have some news.'

'Well, then you *are* welcome.' Moberg managed a half-smile.

'The murder weapon,' Thulin announced.

'The knife?'

'Yes. Interesting. I've come to the conclusion that it's probably a balisong.'

'What's that when it's at home?'

'A butterfly knife.'

'Ah,' said Moberg in recognition.

'As you know, the butterfly knife can be very dangerous. They tend to be about twenty-two, twenty-three centimetres in length. Blade: ten centimetres or so.'

'Why are they called butterfly?' Hakim asked.

'It's basically a folding pocketknife. It has two handles with the blade hidden within their grooves. It's opened by the handles counter-rotating and revealing the blade.' Thulin demonstrated the motion with her hands. 'It's possible to open and close it with one hand. It's also very light and easy to conceal until the last moment, therefore making it an ideal weapon when you're running up behind your intended victim.'

'Sounds lethal.'

'Oh, they can be. It was traditionally made in the Philippines and used as a pocketknife, with the added benefit that it could be used in self-defence. Because of the way they open, they're also known as fan knives.'

'And they're illegal in Sweden,' pointed out Moberg, whose interest had been piqued.

'Exactly. They're banned in many parts of the world. One place where there was a boom in butterfly knives in the 1980s was in America. There have been legal clampdowns in certain states since, but they're still easy enough to get hold of. Ten dollars would probably be enough to buy one.'

'Can we check these things out?'

'Not really. If it came from Sweden, it's illegal, so you can't trace who sold it because there won't be any records. And as we haven't actually got the knife, we can't identify a manufacturer. If I were a betting person, I might put my money on it coming from America, though it could be from the Far East. Then again, to cause the damage it inflicted on that poor woman, it was a well-made blade, and the likelihood is that it was made in the States, where a lot of the better ones come from.'

Moberg looked thoughtful, and his fingers started drumming on his desk.

'So, have we got to factor the United States into this killing?'

'All I'm saying is that it could have come from there. Doesn't mean it's an American – possibly a Swede or someone else who got hold of it over there.' Moberg pursed his lips. 'Oh, by the way, the cross pendant is probably Eastern European. Polish possibly, so I'm told by someone who knows about these things. But it's not worth anything.'

'It meant something to that woman,' observed Moberg. 'God, this case isn't getting any bloody easier.'

It was about midday when Anita and Kevin got back to the house. They had left their breakfast spot when the gunfire started from the Ravlund army firing range further up the coast, which coincided with the arrival of a boisterous group of teenagers on an end-of-term school trip. They stopped off at the ICA supermarket in Kivik and bought some cinnamon buns, berry muffins and Danish pastry twists for the afternoon fika with Albin Rylander. Anita would be the first to admit that she had bought what she liked and not what she thought her guests might.

As they rounded onto the edge of the grass, they saw Klas Lennartsson's bike. Anita was surprised because he was usually gone by now. Maybe Albin was feeling stronger today. When they reached the porch, they found Lennartsson hunched up on one of their garden chairs. His face was drained and his eyes had a haunted look.

'Klas, is something wrong?' she asked in English.

He seemed unable to speak. Then, very quietly, it came out: '*Han är död. Han är död*,' he repeated.

'Albin's dead?'

He nodded dolefully.

CHAPTER 10

'So, what happened?' Anita asked, using English for Kevin's benefit.

They had taken the shaken Klas Lennartsson inside and rustled up some besk that Anita's friend Sandra had left after a boozy night when she first rented the house. Lennartsson downed the drink in one go.

'Albin killed himself.'

'What?' Anita was appalled.

'Suicide.'

'Did he leave a note?' It was the typical response of a cop.

'None has been found.'

Anita exchanged glances with Kevin. They both knew that suicides tended to leave some form of communication.

'Why now?' Lennartsson said while shaking his head in disbelief. 'The book was going so well.'

'Maybe he woke up this morning and the pain was too much for him,' Kevin suggested.

'It was last night, according to Moa. It was poor Moa who found him this morning shortly before I arrived. She called the doctor. The police have been here too. There was an inspector called Zetterberg.'

'Alice Zetterberg? Inspector Alice Zetterberg?' Kevin noticed how surprised Anita sounded.

'Yes,' replied Lennartsson, still in a daze.

'Know her?' Kevin asked.

The frowning nod Anita gave warned him not to probe any further.

'I know he didn't have long. But he was so positive about telling his story. I just don't understand it.'

'Do you know how he killed himself?' Anita asked.

'He... em... he seems to have taken some pills. Drank whisky to help him swallow them.'

'Not uncommon.'

'It's just... not right.'

Hakim was surprised to see Moberg in the meeting room that was doubling as their murder incident centre. Not that there was much to see other than the original crime-scene shots, various body photographs courtesy of Eva Thulin, and now a few pictures taken off the internet of examples of butterfly knives.

'Not much to go on,' Moberg said grumpily. 'I don't suppose you've got anything for me?'

'Sorry.'

'Have you seen Wallen?'

Just then, she came in. She wore a broad grin, which wasn't her usual facial expression.

'We've got something!'

'What?'

'A response from someone who saw the picture of the victim in *Sydsvenskan*. It's the owner of an apartment on Kronborgsvägen, which is close to the park. The woman rents, sorry rented, the apartment from him. She's called Akerman. Julia Akerman.'

The sparkle in Moberg's eye told them that this was the breakthrough they had been waiting for. At last, some concrete information.

'The owner is called Mankad. He said he'd meet us down at the apartment in half an hour and let us in.'

'Well done, Klara.' Wallen beamed with delight. 'Take young Mirza with you, and I'll get people here to track down any information we can find on Julia Akerman. What are you waiting for?'

Kronborgsvägen is a wide street that runs parallel to Pildammsparken and ends up at a major crossroads opposite the city's theatrical hub, the Malmö Opera. The block was about halfway down Kronborgsvägen, and was a good example of pragmatic sixties architecture. Jutting out from the flat face of the five-storey, red-brick, red-roofed building, above the front entrance, was a V-shaped, windowed column that ran the height of the structure to give it some perspective. It was hardly worth the effort. In front of the wooden doors hovered Mankad. He was a young man of no more than thirty, with thick black hair swept back, and casually dressed in a white shirt and cream trousers. On seeing Hakim, he flashed a smile which said "fellow immigrant".

'Herr Mankad,' Wallen greeted him formally.

'Please call me Vinoo.' His Swedish was almost immaculate.

'Inspector Klara Wallen. We spoke on the phone. This is my colleague, Inspector Hakim Mirza.'

Mankad insisted on shaking hands with them both.

'OK, you want to see the apartment?'

Wallen nodded. Mankad clicked in a combination on the keypad and pushed the front door open. There was no lift, so they had to take the stairs to reach the fourth floor.

'Did you know Julia Akerman well?' Hakim asked as he took up the rear of the procession.

'Mankad stopped at the first landing. 'I met her only once. When I handed over the keys. She wanted a furnished apartment, and this was the only one we had.'

'When was that?'

'Over four years ago.'

They carried on up.

'Is that usual? I mean to only meet a tenant once over such a long time?'

'We usually see them more regularly. They ring up with maintenance problems, or they have difficulty with the rent one month, or they want to move. My family owns a large number of properties in Malmö, Helsingborg and Landskrona. But Akerman was different. She paid her rent on time, and we never had any complaints.'

'No leaky taps or bunged up sinks?' Wallen said with some feeling. Her own kitchen sink had flooded twice recently, and it had taken ages to get hold of a plumber to fix it.

'No.'

'Don't you regularly inspect the properties?' asked Hakim. 'Make sure that the tenants are keeping them in a reasonable condition?'

'We do. But according to our records, Akerman was never around when we called. Busy lady.'

'A very dead lady,' said Wallen severely.

'Yes, it's horrible.'

They reached the fourth floor in silence. Mankad produced a key at the same time as Wallen took out the key they had found on the body.

'I'll try this one,' said Wallen. 'To make sure this is the right apartment.'

The key fitted and turned in the lock.

Mankad was about to follow them in when Wallen held up a warning hand.

'We need to do this on our own without anybody getting in the way. But wait for us, as we might have some questions.'

The chirpy Mankad shrugged his shoulders at her rebuff. 'I've got calls to make,' he replied, and whipped out his smartphone.

Wallen and Hakim took out plastic gloves and slipped them on.

*

The apartment was unspectacular. Two bedrooms, bathroom, kitchen and living room – just like thousands of other apartments all over Malmö. What made this one slightly different was the balcony beyond the living room; as the apartment was at the back of the building, it had a view. Two blocks on, Roskildevägen ran at right angles to it – and beyond was the park. At this time of year, the trees were proudly manifesting their fresh new apparel, and nothing else was visible until the eye rested on the conical roof of the water tower by the park's lake. This was exactly the sort of apartment in the right sort of area that Hakim would like to move into once he had saved enough to escape his parents' home.

What struck both Hakim and Wallen was that there was nothing personal about the apartment. No photos or pictures or ornaments or books or DVDs or CDs – just a place to lay one's head. The kitchen cupboards were virtually empty of foodstuffs. In the fridge was a half-drunk bottle of water, a carton of goat's milk and a pot of strawberry yoghurt. The main bedroom was the only place that contained anything of interest. The bed was made. A plain white T-shirt and a pair of Rag & Bone jeans had been thrown on top; presumably what Akerman had changed out of to go for her run. The chair in the corner had an Isabel Marant cream cardigan draped over it. On a table next to the wall mirror was a black cross-body bag.

'Jimmy Choo,' said Wallen admiringly. Hakim was none the wiser.

Inside the bag, they found her passport; a mobile phone; a make-up bag; a compact mirror; a pack of tissues; a purse with a Credit Suisse credit card, 214 kronor and 107 Swiss francs; and a set of keys which included a car key. Wallen unfolded an A4 piece of paper.

'It's a printed-out Easyjet boarding pass.'

'Where to?'

'Geneva. For Wednesday, the fourth. So, she was travelling out the morning after her stabbing. There's also one for her inward journey to Kastrup, dated Monday, the second.'

On the bedside table was a Kindle.

'She certainly believed in travelling light,' remarked Hakim as he surveyed the cabin case on the floor. It was already half-packed.

The built-in wardrobe was more revealing still. Though there were only three dresses, one was a very elegant blue evening gown. Again, Wallen seemed to appreciate the label. What was also hanging up was a nun's habit.

'Bloody hell!' Wallen exclaimed. 'I knew she had a cross, but this is ridiculous!'

'Doesn't sit with her other clothes,' Hakim said, pointing to the drawer he had just opened. It was full of exotic underwear – skimpy knickers and g-strings, low-cut bras, black stockings and suspender belts.

'Sexy games?' Wallen ventured. 'Maybe that was her lover's "thing".'

Hakim felt embarrassed at the thought.

'I'll have a look in the bathroom. You go and ask our friend outside how he was paid,' ordered Wallen. She was actually starting to enjoy being in charge. 'It might give us an idea where she was based. It's obviously not here.'

Mankad quickly finished off his conversation when he saw Hakim. He had been speaking in English to someone.

'You said Akerman always paid on time. Do you know where the money came through from?'

'Yes. A bank in Switzerland.'

'Are you sure?'

'I double-checked this morning. Thought you might ask. She's paid up until the end of this month.'

'OK. That fits in.'

Mankad offered an apologetic grin. 'Em... when will you be finished here?'

'Soon.'

'I mean for good. It's just that we don't want the property lying empty. It would be better for business to get a new tenant fixed up for July.'

Hakim stared hard at him. They had a dead woman lying on a cold slab in Lund, yet the wheels of commerce would grind on regardless. 'We'll let you know, herr Mankad.'

'Why don't we trace her route?' Hakim suggested as they stood outside the apartment block and watched Mankad depart in an open-topped Porsche.

At the west corner of the block, there was a flooring store. Between that and a florist, there was a tarmaced path leading towards the park. Hakim noted down its name – Tuborgsgången. Past an electricity station with vibrant graffiti, the path ran straight to Roskildevägen between two blocks of apartments. The gardens of the one on the left were well tended with copious bushes, small trees and freshly mown grass, while the block on the right was verged by a low hedge between the entrances to the building.

They made their way onto Roskildevägen. Akerman's most likely route was either down Margaretavägen, which was a road you could drive along to the centre of Pildammsparken and park near the lake, or she had gone further along Roskildevägen and headed straight towards the Plate, where her body was found.

'The trouble is that we don't know what stage she'd reached on her run.' Wallen's gaze was drawn down the tall avenue of trees to the murder site. 'Was she starting, or was she near the end? A circuit round the Plate before she finished?'

'Your guess...'

'Right; we'd better get back to headquarters and tell Moberg what we've got. At least we know where she was going to and where she probably lives. Or certainly where she has a bank account.'

'That's all we seem to know. The neighbours I talked to had no idea who she was. In fact, the one next door had never seen her, though he had heard her through the wall. He reckoned that she was hardly ever there, and he's lived in the block since before Akerman arrived.'

'She should be easy enough to trace now we have her passport.'

Given what he had seen and heard in the last couple of hours, Hakim wasn't so sure.

CHAPTER 11

They sat listening to the sea and watching the sun go down. They sipped their wine quietly. Anita was disappointed that such a wonderful day up at Stenshuvud should have been spoiled by Rylander's death. She knew it was an awful, selfish thing to think. But he was an old man, racked with cancer, who was going to die anyway. He had just brought the day of reckoning forward by a few months. In a similar position, she would probably do the same thing. And in Rylander's case, he didn't have any family to live for. Maybe he wanted to die with his dignity intact instead of physically wasting away further. Her limited experience of Albin Rylander led her to the conclusion that he was a proud man who always took great care of his appearance, whether being seen in public, or in the sanctuary of his own home. He was vain. And why not?

'I hope Klas will be OK,' she said at last.

'I feel sorry for him. This was his moment of glory. Can you imagine the fuss that would have been made over his book if Rylander did have some saucy secrets to reveal? Radio, telly, magazines; all doing interviews. He'd be the centre of attention. And that's not even taking into account the money he might make from such a book.'

'I hadn't thought of it like that,' Anita confessed. 'I was thinking more about his relationship with Albin. They got on so well. It was like he'd lost his best friend. But, as you say, he's had the golden goose snatched from his grasp.'

'Maybe you should go round and see him tomorrow,' Kevin suggested.

'Yes, I think I will. And you can come, too. I want to show you Simrishamn.'

They went quiet again. It was an awkward hush where they were searching frantically for something to say to break it. They didn't know each other well enough to relax in those silent moments. That's why Kevin found himself asking, 'Do you know the inspector Klas mentioned?'

'Huh! Alice Zetterberg. Oh, I know her.' Kevin immediately wished he hadn't asked. 'We were at the police academy together in Stockholm. We have, as you say in England, "history".'

'Want a top up?' Kevin asked to quickly change what was obviously a touchy subject.

Anita smiled. 'Yes, sorry. It's just I can't stand that woman. Or, to be more precise, she can't stand me. She thought I'd slept with the guy who ended up as her husband. He was at the academy, too. We were friendly, but never *that* friendly. But being a typically boastful man, he obviously intimated that we were. Suddenly, Alice was being a bitch to me, and I ended up being ostracised by some of my new so-called friends.'

'If she married him, then what's the problem?'

'The problem is that after a couple of years, he ran off with another female cop. I'm sure she blamed me for supposedly leading him astray in the first place.'

'She sounds the bitter sort.'

'Oh, yes; a very bitter woman. Or she certainly was the last time I came across her, which was at a police conference in Germany a few years ago. She was in Jönköping then. I'd heard through the police grapevine that she'd ended up in Ystad. They oversee the police station in Simrishamn, but I'm surprised she should turn up here. A local suicide would usually just involve the team on the spot.'

'But he was a famous person. Politically, I mean.'

'I suppose. Anyhow, not our problem.'

Kevin raised a glass. 'Let's hope we don't run into your Zetter-whatever woman then. I don't want to see any more fights. I've come to Sweden to get away from punch-ups in Penrith.'

Klas Lennartsson's house was in Stenbocksgatan, halfway between the train station and the harbour. It was large for a single person, but Anita had told Kevin that it had been left to him by his parents. It was a rendered building painted the colour of blue slate that towered over the single-story fishermen's cottages it was attached to. Like its neighbours, this was one of the town's original buildings. Lennartsson welcomed them through the stout wooden front door into a high-ceilinged living room. He wasn't house proud, Kevin noted. Everywhere was a mess. On a genuinely distressed oak table was a tray of his uneaten breakfast, surrounded by books and newspaper cuttings. He had to clear a stack of notebooks off the sofa so he could offer them a seat.

'If I'd known you were coming, I would have tidied up,' Lennartsson said in English. He didn't want to be rude to his visitor.

'It's my fault, Klas. I should have rung first.'

Lennartsson waved away Anita's apology. 'I'm glad you came. I wanted to talk to you. I'll fix some coffee first.'

With that, he hurried out with the tray.

'He's always been like this,' Anita said, raising an eyebrow. 'I remember it used to drive his mother mad. She died a couple of years ago.'

'It looks like he hasn't cleared up since,' Kevin observed. For a man who liked everything orderly, he was still trying to get his head round Sweden's shambolic electrics (unattached light roses hooked to wires festooned across ceilings and plugged into a wall socket: there was one in Lennartsson's living room, too), and the peculiar bathroom in Anita's rented home. (The stand-alone bath next to the wall doubled as a shower. The only problem was that the water ran down the gaps around the bath, flooded the floor and soaked the bathmat. The only escape for it was a hole in the floor underneath the bath. When he mentioned this to Anita, all he got in return was a dismissive 'That's what the mop and wiper are for'.) Even the doors opened outwards, which Kevin kept forgetting.

Lennartsson returned with the same tray, but with a thermos jug of coffee and three cups. He distractedly poured the black coffee out, spilling some onto the tray. He was in such a state that Kevin didn't have the heart to ask for some milk.

'Are you OK, Klas?' asked Anita with genuine concern.

'Not really. I had a couple of local newspapers calling me last night to do obituaries on Rylander. I knocked something up, but my heart wasn't in it.'

'It's understandable.'

Lennartsson stared out of the window over to the patch of green grass and trees on the other side of the road.

'I still find it difficult to believe that he would kill himself. I sat with him for hours and, though I knew he was in pain, he seemed real determined to finish telling his story.'

'Were you any closer to his "secret"?' Kevin asked.

Lennartsson slowly shook his head. 'No. All he did say was that he wasn't ashamed of what he had done, but he still felt guilty about the person it most affected.'

'Sounds like some romantic interlude. A lover he shunned?' Kevin suggested.

'Whatever it was, the answer lies in Berlin.'

CHAPTER 12

It might be a Saturday morning, but Moberg had made sure the whole team was in – Wallen, Hakim, Brodd and himself. He had even avoided his usual Friday night booze-up with Pontus Brodd so that all his faculties were sharp for this meeting. He sensed that there was a chink of light in the case, where twenty-fours ago there had been none.

All the items retrieved from the Kronborgsvägen apartment were laid out on the meeting-room table. The nun's habit was draped carefully over a chair. Moberg had had to cut Brodd off in mid-sentence when he realised he was going to come up with some inappropriately smutty joke.

Moberg started the meeting with: 'Before we go through all of these items, we've drawn a blank on Julia Anna Akerman so far. We've found ten women with that name, and none are the right age. And certainly not one with a Malmö connection. I've still got people on it, but it's not as straightforward as it should be.'

'She could have changed her name,' Brodd suggested.

'But we've got a Swedish passport in that name on the table here,' Moberg said, pointing out the obvious. 'Right, let's go through what we know we have. Klara?'

Wallen pointed to the bagged-up objects. 'According to her passport, she is called Julia Anna Akerman; born May 20th, 1979. Birthplace: Malmö. Passport issued on February 16th, 2008.'

'It looks like the genuine article,' said Moberg, 'but we can find no record of a Julia Anna Akerman being born on that date in Malmö, or any other time. We need it checked out to see if it's a fake.'

'The Easyjet boarding pass shows that she was flying back to Geneva the next day. We've checked, and she made six trips to Kastrup in the last seven months. Always for no more than a couple of nights here. So, she doesn't live in the Kronborgsvägen apartment, but uses it for flying visits. Which also explains why she wasn't seen by regular joggers in the park.'

'Could she be an air hostess?' Moberg wondered.

'We're checking that out.'

'We've been on to the Swiss authorities to see if they can find a Julia Akerman. We've got a credit card from a bank in Switzerland, and she also pays her rent through them, according to Mankad, so there's a good chance she lives there, or certainly spends a lot of her time there.'

'Of course, if she *is* in the travel business, she may be based somewhere else, but Switzerland is a useful place to have a bank account.' This was Wallen again, who was increasing in confidence. Maybe it was Anita who intimidated her more than Moberg, she wondered fleetingly before she moved on to the next object. 'This key is for a Mercedes car. There was no sign of one near the apartment, so we conclude that she has one at home, wherever that is. It might be at Geneva airport. We don't know. The others are house or apartment keys. Again, for where, we don't know yet.'

'And the mobile?'

'It's a basic Nokia pay-as-you-go phone, so we don't know where it was bought, and it's difficult to trace calls. I would have expected her to have a fancy phone. Strange thing is: she hadn't received any calls. Of course, she may have deleted them. We're going to get that checked out as well. She only had one number in her contacts section. It's one in Skåne.'

'And?'

'We rang it, and it turned out to be a nursing home outside Sjöbo. They have never heard of Julia Akerman. And no one in the home is called Akerman.'

There was quiet as they all pondered this surprising piece of information.

'I suppose we'd better deal with *this*,' Moberg sighed incredulously as he waved a large hand at the nun's habit.

'As far as we can see, it is a proper habit. The kind an actual nun would wear. It's not one of those sexy nun outfits that Brodd probably fantasises about.'

'What do you mean?' Brodd reacted angrily.

Moberg was amused. Good for Wallen.

'So, she's not necessarily into sex games.'

'But she had lots of revealing underwear,' put in Hakim as he wondered how horrified his mother would be if she had seen him rifling through a woman's knickers drawer.

'You don't think she could have been a real nun at some time?' Moberg threw the thought into the open.

'Well, she hasn't half reformed!' Brodd snorted.

Moberg ignored his comment. 'The other religious connection is the cross round her neck. We've been told it's Eastern European. Probably Polish. Does that give us any clues?'

'Maybe that's why we can't trace her,' suggested Hakim. 'What if she was born in Poland and either changed her name to a Swedish equivalent or simply changed her name to fit in?' He knew Poles got just as hard a time as Iraqis. Swedes always assumed they were going to pinch their cars and whisk them back over the Baltic.

'So, we might have a religious Pole who has a Swedish passport and lives in Switzerland. It sounds like the start of one of your fucking awful jokes, Pontus. Right, there's still a lot of checking to do. Unless we can nail down who she is exactly, we're never going to come up with any suspects.'

CHAPTER 13

Anita and Kevin spent the rest of the day wandering around Simrishamn. Kevin seemed to enjoy the harbour, with its rows of colourful cottages huddled along cobbled streets. They had spent a couple of hours at the local *loppis* – 'A bit like a British car boot sale,' Kevin remarked – near the Nils Holgersson School. Tables were laid out with everything from second-hand clothes to unwanted bric-a-brac. A large crowd had gathered and business was brisk. Anita bought a couple of thick woollen jumpers – 'Winter will be here soon enough.' Kevin guessed it must be an example of Scandinavian pessimism.

Anita acknowledged the few familiar faces who greeted her with smiles of recognition. As Kevin was debating whether to buy a small porcelain shepherdess as a present for one of his daughters, he noticed Anita chatting earnestly to a ruddy-faced man in his mid-sixties with cropped hair like himself but with a far more impressive stomach. They parted with a burst of laughter. By that time, Kevin had abandoned thoughts of a purchase; the figurine was a bit tacky anyway.

'That was Stefan. He's a cop based here in Simrishamn. I've known him since I was a teenager; he used to come to our school and give talks.'

'You looked to be in deep discussion.'

Anita smiled. 'I was just being a nosy bitch.'

'Your *bête noire*?'

'Oh, yes. I was just wondering what she was doing here in Simrishamn. So are Stefan and his colleagues. Zetterberg just appeared yesterday and commandeered an office. They thought it might be something to do with Albin's suicide, but now the rumour mill believes she's been sent by Ystad to keep an eye on them. There have been large hints that there are to be job losses. They're talking about centralising things from Lund, so smaller police stations are under threat. As you can imagine, they're all paranoid now. But Stefan's not too bothered; he's coming up for retirement and looking forward to concentrating on building his boats.'

Now they were sitting at the side of the Maritim Hotel on the raised decked area overlooking the harbour. Though the early evening was still warm, it was cool under the canvas canopy, and the waitress had thoughtfully brought out a couple of rugs to cover their knees. They had decided on beers, and Kevin was tucking into his Skånsk sisker from a local brewery in Tomelilla as he surveyed the fish he had ordered. When eating in a harbour town, fish was an obvious choice, though it certainly looked different from anything that was served up in his favourite Penrith chippy. Anita couldn't remember the name of the fish in English but, after tentative prodding, it turned out to be fried plaice. She had gone for the steamed lemon sole with lobster and elderflower pickled vegetables.

'Quite a boat that,' remarked Kevin, pointing with his fork over Anita's shoulder at a two-masted tall ship swaying gently at its berth.

'That's the Sarpen,' Anita replied, squinting round to see. 'It's old. Used as a training ship these days. When the masts had to be replaced, the new ones were made by a guy called Sven Geistrand. Lives not far from where we're staying.'

'That's what I call woodwork.'

After a pause for some more food, Anita looked across at Kevin. 'By the way, I'd better warn you that we've got visitors tomorrow.'

'Oh, yeah?' Kevin said warily.

'Lasse and Jazmin are coming over from Malmö for the day.' She grinned. 'I think he wants to give you the once-over. See the unfortunate sap that his mother has dragged into bed.'

'Is that the way he sees it?'

'No. The other way round actually. He's very protective of me, so you'd better be on your best behaviour.'

'I'll have an extra shower so I smell nice. And I'll try and do it without flooding your bloody bathroom!'

Wallen had been working closely with Hakim all day. Fruitless calls and dead ends. They hadn't been able to find any evidence that Julia Akerman was an air stewardess. The mobile phone hadn't yielded anything either. No deleted texts or calls, except one to the nursing home a month ago. Wallen had dispatched a grumpy Brodd off to Sjöbo to see if he could find out anything. She had to admit that it was only to get him out from under her feet. He couldn't do much damage out in the middle of Skåne. They could find no criminal records for Akerman – or health records either. Nothing on the electoral roll, no registration for a driving licence, nor enrolment on educational courses. And to add to their frustrations, they were also having difficulty at the Swiss end, as it seemed virtually impossible to get hold of anyone at the weekend.

Wallen had gone out of the meeting room to get some fresh coffee, and was thinking of calling it a day, when she returned to see a smiling Hakim. 'Found her!'

She still held on to the two mugs. The butterflies in her stomach were a good indication that this was a pivotal moment.

'That was the airline. They've got her booking details, and we've got an address. It's in a place called La Sarraz in Switzerland. I've Googled it, and it's not far from Lausanne.'

'Brilliant! Is Moberg still in?'

A few minutes later, they were standing in front of the chief inspector's desk.

'Right, we've got to follow this up. One of you needs to go out there and find out as much as we can about this woman. Actually, you can go, Mirza. I need you here, Klara.' Wallen was secretly quite relieved. She was enjoying the responsibility that Moberg was giving her, and she wanted to remain at the heart of the investigation. Akerman may have come from Switzerland, but the murder took place here, and she was sure that the real answers lay in Malmö. 'I'll get it sorted out at this end and try to establish contacts with the Swiss police.' He pointed a large, chubby finger at Hakim. 'I want you on a plane on Monday.'

CHAPTER 14

Anita let Kevin drive back from Simrishamn after their meal. He had wanted to try out driving on the right, and as the insurance covered the car and not the driver, there was no problem. Anyway, she was weary after the day out and wanted an early night.

As they approached the house, there was the outline of a figure on the porch.

'Who's that?' Anita called out.

'Klas,' came the reply.

Anita inwardly groaned. Much as she liked Lennartsson, she wasn't in the mood to listen to his stories. She had other plans.

'It's important,' he said in Swedish.

'You'd better come in.'

Once the lights were turned on and Kevin had offered to make them all a cup of tea, Lennartsson sat down on the sofa. Anita could see that he was tense and worried.

'What's the matter, Klas?' The sooner she got to the point, the sooner he would go.

'It's Rylander.' She knew it had to be. 'I don't think it was suicide. I want you to look into it.'

Anita tried to keep the sigh out of her voice, but failed. 'Honestly, Klas, it's obviously suicide. It's disappointing, particularly for you. I understand that. But he'll have had his reasons. And anyway, there's nothing I can do about it. It'll be officially dealt with.' She plonked herself down on the chair opposite. After a pleasant meal with a nice male companion, this was not something she wanted to get involved with. 'Besides, I'm on holiday.'

'I'm sorry. But it's not that simple. For starters, he didn't leave a note. Isn't that unusual?'

'Yes. Suicides do tend to. But who was Rylander going to leave one to? He had no family.'

'To me then.'

'Why to you?'

'I guess I was closest to him at the end.'

'Is that all you have to go on?'

'No.' This was said with more determination. The self-pity of a moment ago was gone. 'I spoke to Moa this afternoon. She was just as surprised as me.'

'For the same reasons as you, I expect.'

'No. She thinks that something's not right.'

'And why?' One amateur sleuth was bad enough, but two! She just wanted to go to bed.

'He was taking morphine sulphate for the pain. Once every twelve hours.'

'Was this what he took to kill himself?'

'In theory.'

'Well, it'll come out in the autopsy.'

'That's not the point, Anita,' Klas said vehemently. 'To kill himself, he must have taken ten to twenty tablets. With all the whisky he drank, that would do it. But Moa says that he didn't have enough tablets left to take that kind of overdose. Moa says she usually gave him enough tablets to last four weeks. They were nearly finished. She was taking his next lot to him when she found him dead. Where did all the other morphine sulphate come from?'

'Maybe he hadn't taken all the tablets at the prescribed

times. Maybe he was storing them up for the time when he felt he had had enough. Look, who's going to bother killing someone who's about to die anyway?'

Lennartsson looked unconvinced, but it seemed perfectly logical to Anita.

'Anyway, after I'd seen Moa, I went to the police station and saw Inspector Zetterberg. She wouldn't give me the time of day. She'd only say that it was a straightforward suicide. End of story.'

'Oh, Klas. I know you're upset, but going to the police! You just make yourself look daft. Especially in front of someone like Alice Zetterberg.'

They both sank into a sullen silence. Kevin entered with a tray with three mugs of tea. He passed the milk-free ones to the Swedes.

'Did I miss anything interesting?' Anita flashed him a filthy look. She didn't want to start Lennartsson off again.

Lennartsson took a sip of his tea and reverted to English. 'Albin Rylander made a remarkable claim. It's one that can't be proved.'

'What's that then?' asked Kevin trying to lift the subdued atmosphere he'd walked into.

'He reckons that his father saved Lenin's life. In Malmö.'

Anita's amazement was mirrored by Kevin's.

'I didn't realise Lenin had ever been to Malmö,' Kevin said in a tone of disbelief.

'I must admit, I took it with a pinch of salt when he first mentioned it. Until he produced the old red handkerchief. He was clutching that when Moa found him, by the way.' He took another gulp of tea.

'What was Lenin doing in Malmö?' asked Anita, whose lack of historical knowledge had already been exposed by Kevin's questions on their trips out.

Lennartsson grimaced. 'Long story.'

'Short version please.'

'When the Revolution broke out in 1917 and the Tsar was deposed and Imperial Russia collapsed, the provisional government that took over was still committed to fighting what was the First World War against Germany and the Austro-Hungarian Empire. This was important to their allies: France and Britain. It meant that the Germans were still fighting on two fronts – in the West against the French and the British, and eventually America – and Russia in the East. However, the hard-line revolutionaries such as Lenin, Sokolnikov, Zinoviev et cetera, who had been living in exile for many years, were stuck in neutral Switzerland, and obviously couldn't have much impact on events back in Mother Russia. Of course at the time, there were lots of revolutionary groups, each with its own agenda, but many still supported the war that was being carried on by the Kerensky-led government, which was largely made up of liberals and moderate socialists. The one group that was totally committed to withdrawing Russia from the war was the Bolsheviks. They were small, but had a dynamic leader in Vladimir Ilyich Ulyanov.'

'Lenin,' Kevin put in helpfully. The First World War was a subject that had always fascinated him. His great-uncle's name was engraved on the Thiepval Memorial for those who had died in the Somme but whose bodies had never been found.

'Exactly. Of course, the Germans were keen to take Russia out of the war so they could concentrate all their forces in the West. Through a German Social Democrat called Alexander Helphand, known to history by his pseudonym of Parvus, channels were opened up with Lenin and the Bolsheviks. Eventually, an agreement was made with the German Foreign Secretary, Arthur Zimmerman, in Berlin. The Germans would facilitate Lenin's journey across their country from Switzerland to the Baltic coast, where he and his followers could then travel on their own through neutral Sweden and on to Finland and then Petrograd.'

'Where's Petrograd?' asked Anita.

'Saint Petersburg. The name was changed in 1914 to get rid of the German "burg". Anyway, the Germans backed up the transport of these revolutionaries with huge amounts of money for the Bolshevik cause to allow them to make an impact on their return to Russia. It was ironic that an absolute monarch like the Kaiser was bankrolling a communist venture. Anyway, a train was arranged to take Lenin and about thirty companions.'

Kevin asked: 'Couldn't Lenin have gone through France and reached Russia via England to Scandinavia? Wouldn't it have been safer through the Allied countries?'

'Interesting question: and one that possibly relates to the events that took place in the Savoy Hotel in Malmö. Basically, the British were worried about the Bolsheviks because of their stated intent to end Russian involvement in the war. They needed the Russians to stay in and, therefore, would have undoubtedly stopped Lenin going through Britain.'

Lennartsson swirled his mug of tea around in his fingers. 'Lenin and company crossed Germany in a sealed train. Both sides were wary. Lenin didn't want to be accused of being a traitor by being seen to deal with the enemy, which, of course, is what he was doing. That's why the official front man was a Swiss revolutionary called Fritz Platten. The Germans didn't want political émigrés fermenting trouble while they crossed the country. With the British naval blockades, food was short. There were few men around to work the farms and the factories because they were all at the two fronts. And Germany had its own revolutionaries to worry about. Everything was kept low profile as the train made its way across the country through various different railway systems. On Thursday, April the twelfth, the train reached Sassnitz on the Baltic coast, and the passengers boarded the Swedish ferry *Queen Victoria*.'

Lennartsson drained his tea.

'Anything else to drink?' Anita asked.

'No,' Lennartsson waved away the offer. He was enjoying telling someone the story which he had been sworn to secrecy not to reveal until after Rylander's death. 'Lenin arrived in Trelleborg, where his party was met by Jacob Fürstenberg. He was an interesting guy. He was a Polish Social Democrat who was regarded as a sinister character even by Lenin's trusted allies, because he not only had dubious criminal contacts, but also had links with the German Imperial Foreign Office in Berlin's Wilhelmstrasse. Despite this, he was a close friend of Lenin's, and carried out various missions for him. Before Lenin's journey back to Russia, he had been employed by Parvus in an organisation that was basically war profiteering, which made him a strange bedfellow for Lenin. Anyway, he was given the task of guiding Lenin through Scandinavia. He met the ferry, and there was a warm welcome from Swedish socialists and the mayor of Trelleborg. Then Fürstenberg, Lenin and company took the train to Malmö, where they headed over to the Savoy Hotel.'

'It's opposite the central station,' Anita said to Kevin to put him in the picture.

'Rylander's father remembered the debonair Fürstenberg. As a young man, Oscar Rylander worked as a waiter at the hotel. It was here that Fürstenberg had arranged for Lenin's rag-tag group to eat before they took the midnight train to Stockholm.'

'And it was here that Rylander's father saved Lenin's life?' Kevin couldn't keep the enthusiasm out of his voice.

'If it's true. Albin Rylander obviously thought so. According to the tale Oscar told his son just before he died, he was walking along the corridor, hands full of used dishes, when Lenin asked him where the bathroom was. Just then, another man in a large coat and broad-brimmed hat appeared in the corridor and asked Lenin if he was Vladimir Ilyich Ulyanov. When Lenin said yes, the man pulled out a gun of some sort. He was only a few feet away and couldn't possibly miss from that range.

Oscar instinctively threw the plates at the man, who was so taken aback he didn't even fire and ran from the corridor and presumably into the night. Lenin thanked the young Oscar and said that the new Russia owed him a great debt of gratitude. It was then that he gave Oscar that red handkerchief. He told him that he had saved the revolution. And then Lenin was gone, and his party left for the station and on into history. The irony was that Oscar got an earful from the head waiter for dropping the plates and making a mess in the corridor!'

'The red handkerchief? Could it possibly have come from Lenin?' asked Anita, whose police instincts demanded proof.

'I've read everything I can around the whole Lenin journey to see if I can find any reference to a red handkerchief. Though the party set off from Zurich, a group of five started out at Geneva. When they were boarding the train to Zurich to meet up with the rest, they were seen off by an enthusiastic crowd of well-wishers. One of them thrust a red handkerchief through the train window into the hands of a young comrade called David Souliashvili. It was to serve as a revolutionary flag. It's perfectly conceivable that Souliashvili passed it on to Lenin when he reached Zurich.'

'OK, I can buy that,' said Anita thoughtfully. 'But who was the assassin? Or, more importantly, who was he working for?'

'Albin Rylander looked into this. Of course, his father had no idea. He didn't even know who Lenin was until he rose to power in Russia later on and the whole world got to know him. Albin said it might have been a former agent of the Okhrana; the Tsarist secret police. After the original February Revolution, they had disappeared real quick. It wasn't safe to be a secret policeman after that. Bizarrely, the Okhrana had actively promoted the Bolsheviks before the Revolution because they thought they were relatively harmless compared to the more violent revolutionary groups. The would-be assassin may have come from one of those rival groups. The Mensheviks perhaps.

Lenin arriving in Russia would be a threat to their ambitions for power. Of course, Lenin was to outmanoeuvre the lot. Or, it might have been someone sent by the Kerensky government. Again, Lenin's presence in Russia would inevitably destabilise an already shaky regime.'

'You mentioned the British before.' Kevin was on the edge of his seat. This was a journey into unknown history for him.

'Rylander's money was on the British. We know that Arthur Balfour, the British Foreign Secretary at the time, was in contact with the British ambassador in Berne to find out about the train negotiations, and then was constantly in touch with the ambassador in Petrograd, Sir George Buchanan. He enquired of him – what were the words? – "whether the Russian government intended to take any steps to counter this danger". They were already holding Trotsky in Halifax, Nova Scotia, having taken him off a Russia-bound ship from New York. They knew that Trotsky was a revolutionary leader being funded by the Germans. Before Lenin reached Sweden, the ambassadors of the Allied powers in Stockholm met to discuss whether to put pressure on the Swedish government to refuse the "arch-revolutionary" Lenin transit through the country. Officially, they decided that they'd not interfere as it might make matters worse. The British ambassador, Lord Esme Howard, explained to Balfour that the plan to stop Lenin "seemed impossible". But Albin Rylander thinks that the British, independently of the other Allies, decided to take matters into their own hands. Anyway, whoever was behind the assassination attempt; they didn't succeed.'

'Why didn't Lenin talk about the incident?'

'Difficult to know. I guess he had no idea who was behind it. If he suspected the British were involved, or even the Kerensky government, he might have been able to make some political capital out of it. Or maybe it wasn't his style. When there were later attempts on his life, they were played down by the Bolsheviks. They didn't want to give the impression that they were not in control. Of course, his detractors might have accused him of making the whole thing up. After all, there was only Lenin, an obscure Swedish waiter and an unknown assassin who were in that corridor at the time. I suspect he was more concerned about how he was going to get to Petrograd in one piece.'

'Quite a tale,' Kevin said, with an appreciative nod of the head. 'Without the quick-thinking Oscar, history would have taken a totally different course.'

'Klas, I don't understand.' Anita had looked increasingly thoughtful. 'If this was Rylander's big "secret", surely no one was going to kill him for it?'

Lennartsson stared hard at Anita. 'Oh, that wasn't his big secret. The Lenin story was somehow connected. I don't know how. But there was something far more important, far more damaging. He didn't live long enough to tell me.'

'Why did his father only tell him about Lenin on his deathbed?' Kevin almost demanded.

'It seems that Oscar was horrified at what he had done after the Russian Revolution developed into the communist state that followed. He realised that by acting the way he did, he had altered history. He believed that he had, inadvertently, played a part in helping what he saw as an evil regime come into power.'

'How extraordinary. So, do you think that an impressionable Albin inherited his father's attitude to the Soviet Union?'

'It certainly makes sense. It explains his subsequent career and views.'

'It's a pity that he didn't live long enough to tell you everything. Is this where it ends?'

'No, Kevin, it doesn't end here. I have clues. Rylander once said that it began and ended in Wilhelmstrasse. I've got an address of someone in Berlin who might be able to help. Albin said that after he had told me his story, I could verify it over there through this contact. So, I've booked a flight.' Then he looked defiantly at Anita. 'And I also intend to find out the truth behind Albin Rylander's death, even if the police, and you, Anita, won't help.'

CHAPTER 15

The beach was well populated. The hot summer Sunday had brought out families and groups of young people onto the warm sands. Anita had prepared a picnic lunch, which had been devoured quickly. She wondered if Lasse and Jazmin were eating properly at home. Kevin and the long-limbed Lasse were having an impromptu kick around. She was pleased that they seemed to have hit it off. Football had been the key that had opened the door.

'How are things with your parents?' Anita asked while she had Jazmin to herself. She had grown fond of this feisty, sometimes explosive, pretty girl who wore eccentric clothes, sported wacky hairstyles and had strong views on gender politics; all of which had led to the inevitable battles with her Iraqi father. Anita admired her determination to be her own woman, which she herself had never really had the courage to do. Anita knew she was too Swedish, too conventional, too ready to accept rules and the status quo.

'So, so.' Jazmin had made an effort with a neat blue top and denim skirt which she had picked up from the second-hand chain, Myrorna. In her mind's eye, Anita could see Lasse pleading with her not to be too outrageous when meeting his mamma's new boyfriend. 'It makes it easier now that the *wonderful* Hakim is back home. Gives my mother something to fuss over.'

'Are they warming to Lasse?'

Jazmin smirked. 'Mother likes him because he's so polite. Makes a nice change from me! My father still wishes that he was an Arab or a Muslim, or preferably both, but I know that he likes him. Not that he will admit it.'

'And are you both getting on OK?'

'Is this a police interview?'

'No, no,' Anita said quickly before she realised that Jazmin was mocking her.

'Yes, we're good. I think Lasse has lost some of his friends because of me. But that comes with the territory.'

'Then they're not real friends.'

'And the same applies to me. But my best friends think he's nice. It's the first time they've mixed socially with a white boy.'

'This is the last question! How's Lasse getting on at the uni? He's never very forthcoming; doesn't chat to me like he used to.'

'And that's my fault?' A certain prickliness was evident in her voice.

'Don't worry, Jazmin. It's nothing to do with you. He changed after he went off to Norrköping.'

'Rebecka?'

'Yes, the dreadful Rebecka.'

'So, I'm an improvement?' The amused look had returned.

'Oh, yes.'

'To answer your *last* question, he's doing fine. Or so he tells me. He works hard and he never skips lectures. Well, not many.'

Just then, Kevin came over to retrieve a miss-kicked ball. He smiled at Anita. 'I'll show Barcelona Boy what Colchester United can do.' With that, he belted the ball back at Lasse, who dived to save it between their improvised towel goalposts.

Jazmin lay back on the rug and put on her sunglasses. For a while, she seemed happy to enjoy the sun, which was now high in the sky. Anita tidied up the picnic things. Yet she could sense that not all was right with Jazmin. She hoped that there wasn't a problem between her and Lasse. He was settled. He was happier than he had been for a long time.

'I think someone's watching our apartment. Watching us.' Jazmin hadn't moved a muscle and was continuing to stare up at the sky.

'Are you sure?'

'I think so.'

'Have you seen anyone?'

'No. That's the daft thing. It's just a shadow... a feeling.'

'Lasse didn't mention it.'

'I don't think he believes me. Told me not to fuss. Maybe I'm just being stupid. Too much imagination.'

'Or female intuition?'

Jazmin gave a soft snort. 'Something like that. It's just a bit creepy. It hasn't happened in the last few days. Before. Maybe they've gone, or I really am just imagining things.'

Anita knew Jazmin well enough to know that she wouldn't be easily fazed by much.

'Have you told your brother?'

'Phew, Hakim! You're kidding!'

'If it continues, let *me* know, then.'

Anita wasn't happy that they lived in Rosengård, a notoriously rough area of the city. High numbers of immigrants, high numbers of unemployed and a high number of crimes committed didn't make it the most salubrious place. She knew how much the police hated going there, particularly since the riots of 2010. The Malmö Fire Department wouldn't attend fires without a police escort. But a few did escape the hopelessness; like Zlatan Ibrahimović and Rebstar. But a young couple like Lasse and Jazmin couldn't afford to rent anywhere else. She could imagine that someone like Lasse might be looked upon with suspicion. This might be where Jazmin's anxieties were stemming from.

Jazmin propped herself up on her elbow. 'That'll make me the first person in Rosengård to turn to the police for help.'

'I'm not the police. I'm family.'

'He liked you.'

'That's a relief. I liked him, even if he does support Barcelona.'

'That's an annoying habit he picked up when he was with Rebecka, his last girlfriend.' Anita was in the process of making a pre-bedtime cup of camomile and honey tea. 'When she disappeared off the scene, I thought he'd come back and support Malmö FF.'

'His local team.'

'Exactly. But they obviously seem a bit of a comedown after the Nou Camp.'

'He should live in my world. Colchester isn't the sexiest team on the planet.'

Anita handed Kevin a mug, and she joined him at the kitchen table. It had been a good day. Kevin had passed the Lasse test, and she had felt more at ease with Jazmin. She hoped that was reciprocated. The young woman still had various chips on her shoulder which would take time to brush off, but she was what Lasse needed at this moment. Yet she couldn't help feeling a tinge of jealousy that her place had been usurped. And she had been unsettled by Jazmin's story, but hoped that there was nothing in it. She pushed it to the back of her mind.

'What have you got planned for tomorrow?' Kevin asked as he let his tea cool.

'I'm quite happy to take it easy, if that's OK with you. But later in the week, we'll go to Bornholm.'

'Where's that?'

'It's a Danish island out there in the Baltic. We can get a catamaran from Simrishamn, and it takes about an hour. It's beautiful.'

'Sounds great. I'll look it up on your computer tomorrow, if you don't mind. I like to find out about a place before I visit.'

Just then, they heard a motorbike heading along the road towards the house. Anita pulled a face. 'Please let it not be Klas. I'm not in the mood for him and his conspiracy theories just now – or another history lesson.'

'I thought it was really interesting.'

'Well, you can talk to him. I'm off to bed before he comes in.'

She nimbly slipped out of her seat and, mug in hand and a pitying look on her face, was in the bedroom before there was a knock on the door.

Kevin opened the door; Klas was standing there in his full leather gear. Under his arm was a large box file.

'Is Anita in?'

Kevin managed an apologetic face. 'I'm sorry, Klas, but she's gone to bed. She's had a busy day with the family over,' he added as though he had to give a plausible excuse for her absence.

'It's OK. Can you look after this?' said Klas, handing over the file.

Even in the half-dark, Kevin sensed his agitation. He looked at him with some surprise. 'What's in here?'

'All the notes of my interviews and all my information on Rylander. Some CDs as well that I used to record our sessions.'

'But why bring them here?'

'I'm off to Berlin tomorrow, and I don't want to leave them in my house. They'll be safer with you.'

Kevin hesitated. 'Do you think they might get stolen?'

'Someone tried to break into my house last night. I frightened them off.'

'You think they're after all this stuff?'

'At the moment, I only trust Anita. She'll look after them until I get back. I'll only be gone for two days.'

With that, Lennartsson got on his motorbike. Kevin watched him until he'd roared out of sight.

When Kevin came back inside, Anita appeared at the kitchen door. 'I'm amazed you got rid of him so quickly.'

'He left this.' Kevin put the file on the kitchen table. 'It's all his research material on Rylander. He wants you to keep it safe while he's in Germany.'

She raised her eyebrows. 'Honestly!'

'He seems to think that someone tried to break into his place last night.'

'I doubt if local burglars would worry about that lot.'

'He seemed genuinely concerned.'

'All right. Bring it into the bedroom. The wardrobe is the only thing in the house with a lock on it. We'll put it in there. Oh, bloody Klas!' She knew she would worry about the file until he took it back. 'He's just being melodramatic.'

'I hope you're right.'

CHAPTER 16

Hakim glanced out of the window. Below him, beneath the scudding clouds the plane was descending through, was the choppy expanse of Lac Léman. He was slightly disorientated, and it took him a few seconds to work out which side of the lake the city of Geneva was on. Throughout the flight, his nervousness had increased as the realisation dawned on him that he had never been abroad by himself before. His only trips out of Sweden had been with the family to Denmark and Germany, and, when he was younger, a visit to his mother's brother on the outskirts of Paris. The brother had long since died, and they had lost contact with that branch of the family. Of course, his father had reminisced last night about his own visits to Switzerland in the 1960s, when he had been a successful art dealer in Baghdad, and it had been a centre of westernised culture. Switzerland had been a good place in which to buy and sell paintings. Uday had even come across the odd famous film star, like David Niven, who was a collector of art. Hakim had never heard of Niven. But Uday's globetrotting days had been ended by a Saddam Hussein regime that distrusted the intellectual elite, and his comfortable lifestyle was to be replaced by a very different one in Sweden. For his new country's hospitality, Uday Mirza had always been grateful, even though a climate of mistrust and hostility had seeped in over recent years. But he was proud that Hakim was an upright Swedish citizen, even if his natural distrust of the police – a result of years of harassment in Iraq – had prejudiced him against the path his son had chosen.

At passport control, Hakim was left standing while the official took an inordinately long time to scrutinise his document. It was when Hakim flashed his warrant card that his passport was reluctantly handed back and he was unsmilingly waved through. He headed through the airport, making his way past smart shop units and down an escalator to the subterranean train station. The train that was waiting was stiflingly hot despite the drizzly day and, to his surprise, left five minutes late. What had happened to the renowned Swiss efficiency?

Ten minutes later, the train stopped in Geneva, and many passengers disgorged to be replaced by businessmen, shoppers and students. The rest of the journey picturesquely followed the lakeshore. The rich, fertile belt of land between the lake and the foothills of the Jura Mountains was heavily influenced by man. Domestic dwellings, both grand and lowly, and industrial units squeezed themselves between neat fields with grazing cows and early-growing ranks of vines. The train stopped at small towns, many of which must have been developed in recent years, judging by the modern buildings. From what Uday had described of his visits, Hakim thought his father wouldn't recognise the countryside. In his day, it had been almost totally agricultural between Geneva and Lausanne. But the stunning view on the other side of Lac Léman would have been the same; the Alps rose dramatically from the water's edge and disappeared into the mists that camouflaged the peaks.

After Morges, it was only minutes to Lausanne. Hakim had his appointment at the Prefecture at four. That gave him an hour and a half. He would find his *pension* and drop his cabin bag, wash, and then make his way to see Inspector Boniface. The *pension* must be near the station, as the address was Avenue de la Gare. From his map, the Prefecture appeared to be fairly central, so it should be an easy walk. Once he came out of the grand, early 20th-century Gare de Voyagers, Hakim ruefully discovered that the Avenue de la Gare was on a very long upward slope, and his hotel was near the top. At first, he couldn't find it, before he realised that some of the side streets were also part of the Avenue. The *pension* was in a tall, French-looking building that had seen better days. Probably built around the time the station was constructed. His room was very basic, but it had a basin in which he doused his face, and he also changed his shirt. It was somewhere to lay his head, and it was the best that the Skäne County Police were willing to fork out for.

Forty-five minutes had seemed to be plenty of time to reach the Prefecture in the Place du Château, according to the more detailed town plan he had picked up from the tourist office at the station. What the map didn't tell him was that Lausanne is built on a hill; a very steep one. He set off in good spirits, but his progress became slower, the higher he went. He knew that he must make for the cathedral. He thought he was there when he reached the Eglise Saint-François. But it was onwards and upwards; past the Place de la Palud, and onto the atmospheric covered wooden staircases that eventually took him to the cathedral. He was out of breath when he arrived at the top, and he stood for a moment in the small square under the impressive medieval edifice. He leant against the low wall that skirted one side of the square and allowed himself time to take in the spectacular panorama across the town's rooftops below, and over Lac Léman to the mountains on the French side of the lake. The mist had cleared and the sun was glinting off the water. It was a view which he didn't have long to admire. He was almost running late. Fortunately, the terrain now levelled out, and the Place du Château was only a few minutes' walk. The castle, an unshakeable massive rectangle of stone and brick, sported a round turret at each corner. Opposite was the Prefecture, which looked rather like a château itself of the more elegant French variety. The yellow parking spaces outside with 'police' written on them gave Hakim the clue he was looking for. Yet the building wasn't his idea of a police headquarters, as it seemed to contain a number of other civic departments. The mystery was soon explained when he was ushered into a high-ceilinged office fifteen minutes later to meet Inspector Boniface.

Boniface was a dark-haired, dapper man, with a pencil-thin moustache which made him look like a 1930s matinee idol. His handshake was firm and his smile easy. He apologised for keeping Hakim waiting, but he was in the Prefecture for a meeting. Having quickly established that English was the language of communication, he explained that this was the gendarmerie and was responsible for security and traffic, while he was a member of the Sûreté. They dealt with criminal matters. Each of the twenty-six cantons in Switzerland have their own police departments – in the German-speaking ones they are divided into three. In Basel it is different again. He shrugged. 'I know it is most confusing. It is even more complicated than I have said; but this is Switzerland,' he added with an apologetic smile. 'And it was easier to meet in the centre of Lausanne, as the Sûreté is out beyond the motorway.' Glancing at his watch: 'And it is nearly five, and I have a home to go to.'

Hakim was slightly taken aback, and then he smiled as he remembered the recent story of the hijacked Ethiopian aeroplane that had landed in Geneva. The Swiss Air Force hadn't been able to guide it in because it was out of office hours, and the French had had to do it instead.

Boniface opened a slim file.

'As you can see, we do not have much on Julia Akerman.'

'Neither do we. She doesn't seem to exist in Sweden.'

Boniface glanced at a couple of sheets of paper. 'She arrived here in November, 2009. She bought an apartment in La Sarraz in July, 2010.' Hakim noticed that he didn't pronounce the "z" in Sarraz. 'She is not a Swiss citizen, so she is really your problem, not ours. And as she was killed in your country, we can only offer help.'

'I understand. But we are not totally sure that she is even Swedish, despite her passport. Do you know what she did?'

Boniface made a great play of scrutinising the file.

'Businesswoman. Or should that be business person?'

'In what?'

'We have no idea. It is not the Swiss way to probe too deeply. She has enough to buy an expensive apartment, she pays her taxes; and keeps her head away from the view, I think they say in English. We respect the privacy of those who live here, unless they are undesirable. People come here for many reasons. Work. Or to avoid high taxes in their own countries. Switzerland is full of the famous who want to protect their wealth,' he said with undisguised distaste. 'Or they come to escape their pasts.'

'Was she married or had a family?'

Inspector Boniface shrugged again. 'There is no sign of a husband in the records. It does not mean that she did not have a partner somewhere.'

'If we could discover what she did, we might find a reason for her murder. At the moment, we have nothing to go on.'

'I am afraid I cannot help other than her car was found at Geneva airport. That was bought from a Mercedes dealer in Lausanne last year.' He glanced at another piece of paper in the file. 'She made regular trips around Europe in the last few months. According to this, none to Sweden.'

'She would have flown to Copenhagen. Malmö is just the other side of the Öresund Bridge. Fifteen minutes by train.'

'Ah, that explains it. Yes. Copenhagen most months. You can have a copy of this, of course.'

'Thank you.'

'There was nothing in the car that puts a light on her and

her activities. But I believe you have a key for her home, so you should be able to uncover many things. Tomorrow, you can take the train to La Sarraz. It only takes about twenty minutes. There you will be met by one of the local gendarmerie. He will show you where the apartment is situated. I am told he has a little English.'

'Maybe he can talk to the neighbours for me. Find out more about Julia Akerman.'

Boniface gave Hakim a pitying grin.

'You may find that they will not have much to say. The villages of the Vaud are very close. They do not welcome strangers, and this lady of yours was from outside. To tell the truth, they often do not like the people from the next village. There are many feuds. You may not get much information. I think your eyes will be a better guide.'

Boniface looked up the train times and made a quick call to arrange for the policeman to meet Hakim at the station – 'He is called Lacaze.' That concluded the meeting. Boniface walked Hakim out of the building.

'Have a pleasant evening. Lausanne is a wonderful city. Oh, and if you do find anything tomorrow, you will tell me, will you not? I would not like you to remove things like computers. That sort of thing might be useful for us.' The smile returned. 'Can you find your way back to the Metro station?'

'You mean there is a station?'

Boniface's face creased into a wide grin. 'It would have saved you a steep climb, no? *Bonsoir.*'

Hakim retraced his steps to the cathedral. Now he had more time to appreciate the view. He concentrated on the Alpine ridges on the other side of the lake. He had never before been this close to such huge mountains. Skåne was basically flat, and he had never been beyond Stockholm, so he hadn't seen Sweden's own higher ranges in the north. On the train from Geneva, he had

had a slightly uncomfortable feeling of claustrophobia, being hemmed in by the mountains on both sides of Lac Léman. Up on the cathedral promontory, it wasn't so bad. He wondered how people could live in the shadow of such colossi, however magnificent they may be.

He made his way down the stairs until he saw a little restaurant nestling under a high wall supporting the road above. Inside it was cosy, and had an Italian menu. He ordered a tuna salad and a coffee. Nothing extravagant. He had noticed the steep prices, and he didn't want to run up huge expenses that he would have to justify when he got back to Malmö. The rain had started again. He stared out of the window, watching the office workers and tourists coming down the steps. The music in the restaurant was too loud, and he tried to shut it out by thinking about Julia Akerman. What had brought her to this land-locked country in the middle of Europe? Was it work? Was it to avoid punitive Swedish taxes? Or, as one of Boniface's suggestions had been, was she escaping from her past? There was so much to speculate about. From Boniface's sketchy facts, she didn't appear to have a husband or a family. A boyfriend in Switzerland? That was unlikely, as she had had sex the day she died. Or was he just being naïve? He hadn't had enough experience of women to know. He had concentrated so hard on carving out a career that girlfriends hadn't really featured in his life, a fact that Jazmin constantly reminded him of.

But what of Julia Akerman? Was she Julia Akerman? Maybe he would find out tomorrow.

CHAPTER 17

The weather had turned, and the sun greeted Hakim as he walked down the slope to the station. This time he was less hurried, and he could appreciate the imposing exterior and atrium. Hakim had always been a fan of Art Nouveau, and the refined ornamentation on the façade immediately took his eye. He hadn't really noticed the interior the previous day, but now, as he looked for his platform, he admired the long window bays bringing in abundant light. He quickened his step; his train was leaving in five minutes.

The train passed through dull suburbs of featureless apartment blocks and yet more industrial units. He was surprised at the amount of graffiti on show. It didn't fit with his image of an ordered country of green Alpine slopes, contented cows and beautiful wooden chalets. Mind you, Malmö probably didn't fit with people's ideas of Sweden. After Bussigny, lush forests dominated the landscape, to be replaced by open fields. La Sarraz station consisted of a small building on one side of the track. As Hakim alighted from the train, the noise of roadworks greeted him, and only one other passenger disembarked at nearly ten o'clock that morning. A stout, pot-bellied, uniformed police officer was hanging around in front of the automatic ticket machine. His expression of disbelief was plain.

'You cop? You Swedish cop?' The voice was incredulous. Instead of a tall, blond Swede, he would be chaperoning a tall, dark Arab. What was the world coming to?

'Yes, I am Detective Hakim Mirza.'

Another Gallic shrug.

'Follow me.'

Hakim walked behind Lacaze to a waiting car.

'We go long way. Roadworks,' he said pointing down a street that bordered onto fields and a distant sports ground.

The car went up a hill into the centre of the village. Not that Hakim thought that "village" was an accurate description. More like a small town. It had a large castle looming above the main street onto which, hugger-mugger, spilled shops and houses of every era and style. Within minutes they had reached the edge of La Sarraz, and now the buildings began to look exclusive. There was a curious mix of old French houses and modern Swiss chalets, but they all looked expensive. Lacaze turned the car off the side road through a gateless gateway and up a tree-lined drive. At the top, surrounded by a swathe of tamed, neat lawns and a polychrome of wild-flower meadows, stood a large, graceful building in the typical style of a French manor house. It had a hipped roof, stuccoed white walls with cream quoin stones, and each window was flanked by open shutters. They drove round to the back of the house and came to a halt next to a couple of top-of-the-range cars on the gravelled parking area. This definitely wasn't a cheap place to live. At the back, there were two access doors under a portico supporting a balcony.

'Four apartments. Two from here; two from front,' Lacaze explained. The left-hand door had a name plaque with J. Akerman on it. Hakim produced the set of keys that they had found at Akerman's Malmö apartment. The thickest fitted the lock. He felt a prickle of sweat run down his back. He hesitated for a moment. He was going into a dead person's house. That beautiful woman who had been stabbed in Pildammsparken lived her life here. She'd done all those ordinary, inconsequential things that people do at home. When she'd left here, she had little idea that it would be for the last time. He was aware of Lacaze standing impatiently behind him. He pushed open the door.

There was a large hallway. It was painted a clinical white, but one entire wall was covered with an exotic Indian tapestry of an elephant. Against the opposite wall was a long, mahogany bench, on which was casually draped a blue, all-weather jacket; it must have been raining before she left. Immediately to the left of the front door was the kitchen. Hakim thought he would get his bearings first before he investigated each room individually. Straight ahead was a wall with glass panes from floor to ceiling. In the centre of it was a double door. He opened the door and stepped into the elegant living room. A piano stood in one alcove at the side of the plain wooden fire surround. Logs were piled neatly in a wicker basket next to the hearth. Above the fireplace was a huge gilt mirror, which made an already large room appear even more expansive. In the other alcove stood a heavy piece of furniture that looked like a wardrobe but Hakim assumed must be a cupboard. Two matching sofas in cream faced the fire, while beyond them was a dining table; bare except for a simple candelabra. There were eight chairs. To the left of the dining area was a door which led directly into the kitchen. At the far end of the room was a French window. Through this there was an uninterrupted view over to the Alps. Tasteful paintings, many of them of local Swiss scenes, adorned the walls. They gave the room the personality that the bland furniture failed to. Nothing about the room suggested any connection to Sweden – even the sheet music on the piano was Chopin.

Along the corridor from the living room were two bedrooms, both en suite; a luxury bathroom; and a storeroom for domestic appliances. All had the high ceilings of an early 19th-century house, and the renovation, though totally modern, had been carried out in sympathy with the original building. From his cursory glances around the apartment,

Hakim surmised that Julia Akerman was not used to having visitors; there was a slightly musty smell and an unmade-up bed in the second bedroom. Nowhere gave a clue as to what nationality Akerman really was – Hakim was beginning to think that she wasn't Swedish at all. However, the final room in the apartment set his pulse racing. It was an office. This was where Akerman must have conducted her business, whatever that was. The solid, plain, modern desk had a computer on it. But it was what was on the wall above that immediately caught Hakim's eye. Two small watercolours. He recognised the scenes and knew the artist; he was a Malmö-based painter named Hopp. One picture was of Sankt Petri Kyrka, Malmö's biggest and oldest church; the other was the distinctive Ribersborgs cold-water bathhouse that straddles the end of a pier jutting out from the city's main beach. This could be significant, though both pictures could have been picked up on one of her visits – they certainly didn't prove she was Swedish. Hakim knew that, as well as renting the Kronborgsvägen apartment, Akerman had made trips most months to Copenhagen from Geneva since the middle of last year.

The office had very little else in it other than a small wooden chest of drawers, a shelf containing a few travel books, and a CD player/radio on a table in the corner. There was a large diary on the desk. It was open at the first week of June. As they had discovered from her flight tickets, she had arrived in Malmö on the Monday. She had written "Malmö" in the diary on the Monday and Tuesday. In the space for each day, there was also written a couple of capital letters – initials? AI on Monday and MA on Tuesday. On Friday was written "Madrid" and another pair of letters – GT. The following week: Paris and Barcelona. Flicking through the rest of the month: London, Lisbon, Naples and Rome. Again with letters or initials. He went back to previous months, and there was much the same pattern – and the same letters. Maybe she was in the travel business, thought Hakim, though he would have expected to see more evidence of that.

Lacaze had followed him round like a faithful dog. Hakim wanted time alone in the office.

'Lacaze, why don't you look round the rest of the house again?'

'What I look for?'

'We need to find out what Julia Akerman did for a living. Her job,' as Lacaze looked puzzled. 'Anything about her that makes it easier to understand who she was. You could start with her bedroom.'

Lacaze shot him a suspicious glance.

'I'll try and get into her computer.'

As Lacaze left, Hakim turned on the computer. To break in was going to test all of those advanced IT courses he had been sent on during his time in Gothenburg. It was the very fact that they had tried to push him into cyber crime, at which he was actually very adept, that had made him look for a transfer back to Malmö and join a more conventional unit with a wider remit.

Ten minutes later he was still struggling with the computer, when Lacaze appeared at the door. He beckoned Hakim to follow him. They walked along the corridor to the master bedroom. Like the rest of the house, it had white walls. Fine when the sun was streaming in through the large window, Hakim thought, but when it was dull, it would be very stark. Above the large double bed, there was a small, simple wooden cross, and there were two bedside tables, both with lamps. Their uncomplicated design could have been Scandinavian. What intrigued Hakim was a framed photograph on one of the tables. It was of a middle-aged couple smiling at the camera – hers was natural while his was forced. They were on a beach somewhere, and a picnic was laid out before them.

'Here,' Lacaze commanded.

Beyond the bed, next to the en suite, there was another door, now open. It was a substantial walk-in closet. Straight in front of them was a rack of designer shoes. On either side of the rack were wardrobes with sliding doors. All were open except the one at the end on the right. In the open ones, there was an array of dresses in a range of colours and designs. None of them looked as though they came from Lindex! Akerman liked to dress well.

Lacaze slid open the final door with a flourish. '*Voilà!*'

It took Hakim by surprise. He was the first to admit he had lived a pretty sheltered life in a Muslim household, though he'd learned a thing or two up in Gothenburg. But this was like stepping into one of the sex shops that Copenhagen was famed for. There was a huge array of what he mentally described as "sexy outfits". Many of them would fight to cover the part of the body they were designed for. A range of scanty uniforms seemed to represent most occupations from soldier to French maid, air hostess to nurse. He couldn't work out which force the short-skirted policewoman's kit belonged to. The handcuffs looked real enough. And there were plenty of other titillating toys dangling from the back wall of the wardrobe. Hakim found himself blushing.

'*Putain!*' he heard Lacaze muttering behind him.

'What?'

'Whore.'

'Maybe she just liked dressing up for her lovers.'

Lacaze gave him a scathing look. He waved his hand at the garish costumes, voluptuous corsetry, languorous lingerie and associated ironmongery. 'This is work.'

'A prostitute?' Hakim wasn't totally convinced. Lots of people had fetishes, though maybe not on this scale.

Lacaze nodded. 'I go ask neighbours about her. Any visitors?'

Hakim agreed, and Lacaze left the closet. Hakim went back into the bedroom, picked up the framed photograph and took it with him back to Akerman's office. What struck him was that this was the only photograph to be found in the whole house. He put it down on the desk and stared at it. The woman was still pretty, though she was quite chubby. She was a brunette and wore a denim dress. Hakim put her at about forty. The man standing next to her looked slightly older. His hair was very black, and he was more formally dressed in a shirt and neat trousers, even though they were at the seaside. Hakim found it difficult to gauge the age of the photo. Parents? Might make sense of Akerman's natural colouring, which wasn't blonde. Relatives? Whoever they were, they must have meant something to Julia Akerman. Did they know about the sort of things she had in her closet?

Hakim glanced around to make sure Lacaze wasn't about. He turned the frame over, extracted the photo and slipped it into his pocket. He shoved the frame into the desk drawer.

The visit to the *Systembolag* was necessary, as the house was now very short of booze. Part of their relaxation had been over early beers – the hot summer was still continuing – followed by a bottle or two of wine over a meal in the evening. Kevin was intrigued by the fact that you could only purchase ordinary alcoholic drinks from a government-run operation. Though initially taken aback, he could see the benefits for somewhere like Britain, where he had to deal on a regular basis with youngsters out of their minds on cheap supermarket drink. He was also intrigued that the wine was laid out by price – rising from the cheapest to the most expensive – and not by the area of origin. Good idea, he thought.

Coming out into the sunshine, Kevin decided he wanted to nip into the church, which backed onto the *Systembolag*. Anita was quite happy for him to mooch around. When she was younger, she had been dragged into St. Nicolai too often by her mother to want to revisit it now, though she was quite willing to concede that it was a wonderful building. She parked herself on a bench outside, closed her eyes and let the warmth caress her. She had nearly fallen asleep when she realised someone was speaking to her.

'Well, well; if it isn't Anita Ullman!'

At first, she was startled by the voice and the fact that the speaker had used her maiden name. The sun was obscuring the face of the woman who stood before her. She assumed it must be some local who knew her from her school days in Simrishamn. As her eyes got used to the light, there was no mistaking the features: the deep-brown, chin-length hair; the square jaw; the wide mouth; and the round, dark eyes. Anita had once thought her attractive, albeit in a slightly manly way, before they grew to loathe each other. She was larger than Anita and could carry any extra weight without it showing too much. She had changed. To Anita, she looked harder. Maybe that was the nature of their unforgiving jobs. Hers certainly hadn't mellowed Alice Zetterberg.

'Still sitting on your fancy arse doing nothing. Of course, that's what attracted Arne. Not doing nothing... your arse.'

Anita didn't rise to the bait.

'Hello, Alice. I heard you'd suddenly appeared.'

'Things to sort out here.'

'So I believe.' Anita caught Zetterberg's momentary look of surprise. 'The station. They think you're here to appraise them.'

'Oh, that. Yes. Downsizing. That's modern policing for you.'

'I was surprised to hear you were out at Albin Rylander's.'

'The call came in and I went out. He was an important figure. We needed to make sure there was nothing suspicious. You know what the press are like.'

'And it *was* suicide?'

'Of course. All very sad, but I believe he was dying anyway. Just brought the inevitable forward.'

'I liked him.'

'Oh, that's right. You rent the house next to him, don't you?'

'How do you know?'

Before Alice could answer, Anita saw Kevin coming out of the church and waving behind Zetterberg's back. Zetterberg glanced round.

'Who did you pinch him from?'

Anita was about to say something nasty in return, but Zetterberg was already moving off. Kevin noticed the scowl on Anita's face.

'Did I miss something?'

'You didn't miss anything,' she said bitterly.

'Ah, your *bête noire*.'

They headed down towards the harbour, where they had parked the car. The cafés on Storgatan were full of mid-morning customers enjoying their alfresco coffees and pastries. Kevin wanted to take Anita's mind off her encounter with the Zetterberg woman by prattling on about the church.

'Did you know it was built up by the Premonstratensian brothers eight hundred years ago? There's one of their abbeys near Penrith at Shap. Lovely spot, well hidden.'

Anita nodded in response, but she wasn't really listening.

'Look, do you want a coffee?'

'No, it's OK.' Then she smiled ruefully. 'I mustn't let that bitch get me down. We're on holiday, and I'm taking you off to Ystad. While she's based over here, we won't run into her over there!'

Kevin was relieved. They were getting on well, and he didn't want anything to spoil the time they were having together. As they reached the car, Anita's mobile bleated. With difficulty, she eventually located it in her bag; a black hole that Kevin suspected would still be spilling its hidden secrets into the next millennium.

'Probably Lasse.' Anita flicked up the message. 'No, it's from Klas,' she said in mild surprise. 'Didn't even know I'd given him my number.'

'Is it something interesting?' Kevin asked expectantly.

'Phew. Yes. Em... it translates as "Very successful trip. All is revealed. Will make sensational book. Flying back tomorrow. See you soon".'

'Well, does that mean he's discovered Albin Rylander's big secret?'

'I'm sure we'll find out as soon as he gets back.'

CHAPTER 18

It had taken time, but at last Akerman's computer yielded up its secrets. And knowing his way round computers, Hakim had little difficulty locating the files that would be most pertinent to the investigation. Lacaze had been right. Hakim couldn't help being shocked. He thought he had got beyond that in his first few years in the police, as he had seen many horrific sights and been in life-threatening situations. And this was almost innocuous in comparison. Everywhere had prostitution. Maybe it was something to do with his Muslim faith. He wasn't a committed believer, nor did he attend the mosque regularly, and yet he couldn't shake off many of the tenets of Islam. Though he hadn't consciously thought about it, abhorrence of prostitution must be one of them.

On the computer there was no attempt to hide what Akerman did for a living. Hakim wasn't sure what the official position on prostitution was in Switzerland. But from what he could see, she didn't work locally. She was very business-like, with a database for her euphemistically titled company, *The Swedish International Friendship Service*. There were financial spreadsheets which showed that she was earning a huge amount of money from a limited number of clients. They had to be rich to afford her. Each one was listed; and the cost of each session. The only anomalies were the two Malmö clients. One paid very little, while the other paid nothing at all. Despite her huge income, the details of her travel arrangements showed she

95

didn't go first or business class as Hakim had expected. He had heard that Geneva was an Easyjet hub. Either she was frugal, or it was her way of keeping a low profile. With London, Paris, Barcelona, Naples, Rome, Lisbon and Malmö (Copenhagen) as her regular destinations, Switzerland was the ideal base. Being an hour from Geneva airport meant that Akerman could fly to her clients with the minimum of fuss. A quick check on the Easyjet website showed him that all her destinations could be reached by the low-cost air company through Geneva.

Most importantly, the letters in the diary *were* initials – they corresponded to the names of her clients. She appeared to have twelve regulars who were serviced every two months, or in three cases, every month; though she seemed to go to Barcelona twice a month to visit a specific client there. But it was the names of the two Malmö men who really interested Hakim. One he recognised – a well-known local politician. That was a real surprise. The other was the one who got his kicks for free. She had even made a list of each one's sexual preferences and foibles. The man from Barcelona was the most demanding, one of the ones in Paris was the most imaginative, and her two London clients had the shortest lists. Did that sum up their national characteristics? wondered Hakim as his horror grew at the calculated, yet graphic, nature of the descriptions. She had also made notes about the men and their families. Names of their wives and children, their birthdays, what they liked doing in their spare time, where they went on holiday. She was meticulous.

Hakim did a quick internet search of prostitution in the countries that Akerman regularly visited to check their legal approaches to the world's oldest profession. He was the first to admit that he was no expert on the subject, except in regard to Sweden. They varied from legal to tolerated to prosecuted. But none had the same attitude as his home country, where prostitution wasn't illegal, but what was against the law was paying for sex, so it was the clients who were the criminals and not the prostitutes. That might put the two Swedish men in a difficult position if it emerged they were using the services of an international call girl. That could give them both a motive for murder. This could be the breakthrough they were looking for.

Lacaze returned. 'You get in?' he remarked, pointing at the computer.

'Yes,' said Hakim. 'You were right. Any information from the neighbours?'

'*Non*. They see her little. She go away a lot. Keep by herself.' Then he laughed. 'So do everybody here!'

'What did they think she did when she was away?'

'Business. They do not know what business. One say she like to run.'

'Jog?'

'*Oui*. And on the bicycle. She go many kilometres. Very fit. Bicycle in hut in *jardin*.'

Hakim returned to the computer. He had made notes, but he wanted to download the relevant files he'd found. But Lacaze continued to hover.

'Shall we have a coffee?' Hakim suggested.

'*Bonne idée*. I smoke as well.'

'Can you go to the kitchen and see if there is some?' Lacaze nodded. 'I will come along in a minute.'

As soon as he heard Lacaze clomp along the wooden-floored corridor, Hakim whipped out a computer USB memory stick he always carried with him and furtively downloaded the relevant files. He had been warned by Boniface not to take the computer back with him, and he wasn't sure if the Swiss detective would be too happy about him taking vital files out of the country. He thought it was better not to enquire.

When Hakim reached the kitchen, Lacaze was sitting on a stool at the breakfast bar smoking a pungent Gauloise. He had found some coffee and that was percolating, its aroma unable to prevail over that of the cigarette.

Lacaze smiled. 'Finish the download?'

Hakim flinched. How did he know?

'*Pas de problème!* I not tell. Sûreté are shits. They are...' and Lacaze made a gesture by flicking his finger a couple of times against the end of his nose, accompanied by a soft snort.

Hakim couldn't think of the word in English either. 'Look down on you?'

'*Précisément!* And the photo also OK,' he added with a wink. He might appear a bumbling local policeman, but he didn't miss a thing, thought Hakim ruefully.

In a halo of smoke, Lacaze poured out two cups of black coffee. It was much needed. Hakim had been surprisingly shaken by what he had found out since entering Julia Akerman's home. He still needed to do a thorough search of the apartment. Now that he knew what she did and what she was doing in Malmö, he still wasn't sure who she really was. They already knew she wasn't Julia Akerman. Everything was false about her, including the colour of her hair. He wanted to discover more. The neighbours didn't seem to know anything useful other than to confirm her movements, which he'd already established. But what was she like? There was one thing that had struck him as odd. For a woman who had made her living out of prostitution – albeit high-class – why had she worn a cross and have one above her bed?

'Did you see the cross in the bedroom?'

'Yes. I not think that Swedish are religious people.' Lacaze gave Hakim a look. 'I mean Christian, not Muslim.'

'There are still Christians who worship. But I believe the numbers are falling.'

Lacaze suddenly smacked his head. 'I remember. Upstairs,' he said pointing to the ceiling, 'she say she think Akerman go to church. Church in village.'

'Roman Catholic?'

'*Non*. We speak French, but this is region, what you say...
Protestant.'

'Same word in English. In Sweden the church is Lutheran.
Similar, I assume.'

'You speak to *pasteur*?'

Hakim nodded his head thoughtfully. 'That's a good idea.
Bonne idée.' He was beginning to like Lacaze.

Hakim spent another hour searching through all the rooms in
the apartment. There was nothing to indicate who Akerman may
have been in her former life. Besides the two Malmö paintings,
the photo was the only connection with her past. It was also
difficult to assess her character. Her home was fashionable,
neat and cold. Add her computer files to the mix, and she was
obviously an efficient, well-ordered woman. She was wealthy,
yet nothing about her surroundings was overtly ostentatious.
She didn't mix with her neighbours. Did she have any friends out
here? Her emails were virtually non-existent; mainly practical
ones to do with travel, insurances and bills. She had no social
media contacts. Julia Akerman kept the lowest of profiles.

The apartment had few books. Most were romantic fiction
in English, probably picked up at airports to fill in time on her
regular journeys. They were similar to the types of book she
had on the Kindle they'd found at the Malmö apartment. They
seemed a world away from the life she lived. There seemed no
romance here that he could detect. There were no books about
Switzerland or guidebooks on the Vaud, so she hadn't taken
much interest in her chosen country, despite being here for five
years. Was it purely a place to hide away from the world?

Finally, he sat down on her bed. He had already been
through the drawer of the bedside table on which he'd found
the photo. Nothing unusual there. Now he looked through the
other drawer. It had one item in it. A Bible. It was well-thumbed.
He flicked to the front. There was an inscription – *Till Ebba,*

med kärlek från mamma. Juli 1990.

So, the murder victim in the park was called Ebba. That was a start.

Lacaze and Hakim walked into the centre of the village. Near the far end of the main street stood the church, perched above the road below. Steps ran up from the pavement to the concourse in front of the building. Four pollarded plane trees with tufts of leaves guarded the entrance. The 19th-century church had a bell tower moulded to the main structure of the building in the neo-Grecian style. Below the belfry was a clock, and below that, a pedimented doorway. The faded yellow sandstone softened any potential air of austerity. When the bells suddenly tolled three, they gave Hakim a fright. They were thunderous. He couldn't imagine living close to a sound that loud springing into life every quarter of the hour. After the third strike, and with the noise fading away into the now warm afternoon, a figure appeared at the entrance. Hakim had expected the pastor to be in a full black cassock. This fair-haired man of about forty was wearing tracksuit bottoms and a T-shirt.

'*Pasteur,*' said Lacaze to Hakim. 'His English, better than my English.'

'Hello,' said the pastor, and he held out his hand for Hakim to shake.

'Hello.'

'Come in,' the pastor said, waving his hand towards the door.

Hakim found himself hesitating. He had never entered a church before. There had been no reason to. The occasional visits to mosques with his father were his only experience of religious buildings. No case had ever required him to step inside a church or a synagogue. The pastor noticed his reticence.

'It is OK. All faiths are welcome in our church.'

Hakim felt obliged to follow him inside. He could justify

it to himself as it was important to the case in hand, yet, irrationally, it was a strange, uncomfortable moment. Once inside, he relaxed. It wasn't what he expected. Two blocks of modern beechwood pews were slightly unaligned, causing the aisle to taper to a central cross at the end where the chancel would normally be. Plain round pillars, painted a strident peach, supported a gallery on three sides, and an enormous organ filled the side above the door with its impressive array of pipes. It was more like a concert venue than a church. Hakim and the pastor sat down in one of the pews while Lacaze wandered around.

'It is about Julia Akerman.'

'The gendarme explained. It is so shocking. We will say prayers for her. This world can be so wicked.'

Hakim felt he had to nod in agreement. 'I know. And we intend to catch the person who killed her. But we know so little about her. This has been her home for the last few years?'

'Yes. I have been here three years, and she came here on a number of occasions. Not regular. She was away on business a lot.'

Hakim didn't think it was appropriate to elaborate. 'What kind of person was Julia? I am trying to build a picture of her.'

'Beautiful, of course. Swedish people often are.' Then he looked rather embarrassed as he realised he was addressing a Swede who had none of the physical characteristics associated with the country. 'Julia was always friendly,' said the pastor, hurrying on. 'She even came to one or two of our social evenings. They can be fun,' he added in response to Hakim's sceptical expression.

'Have you ever been to her home?'

The pastor shot back a puzzled expression. 'No, now I think about it. I am not sure if any of the other members of the congregation have either.'

'Did she seem worried about anything lately?'

'I do not think so. She was here two Sundays ago. She was as she always is. Very polite. Her French was improving. She was pleased about that.'

'You don't know if she had a boyfriend... or girlfriend?'

'Not that we knew. It did seem strange that someone so pretty did not have a husband or partner. Maybe she was too busy with her career.'

'Maybe.'

'But I think Julia liked to come here. She liked the peace. And the company of the congregation. Her escape from her busy life.'

Hakim called Chief Inspector Moberg. After his meeting with the pastor, he had bid farewell to Lacaze. The station was just round the corner and down the slope from the church, and the hourly train back to Lausanne would be departing in forty minutes. Hakim had gone up the bank at the back of the church and was standing in front of the castle. The twin towers of the medieval fortress soared skywards, their red pyramidal roofs resembling rocket heads. It was now a museum.

'A whore!' was Moberg's exclamation on hearing Hakim's discoveries.

'Clients throughout Europe. She flew in and out once or twice a month in most cases. Certainly to Malmö.'

'And have you got names for these clients?'

'Yes. She had two in Malmö. One is called Markus Asplund.'

'The name means nothing.'

'The other one will. Axel Isaksson.'

'Axel Isaksson!' Moberg was incredulous. 'The politician?'

'Yes, it's him; Akerman's got a wealth of information on all her clients.'

'Brilliant! He's the bastard that's always giving the police a hard time if we get the slightest thing wrong. He had a field day with the Westermark business. Axel Isaksson,' he repeated.

Then Hakim heard a bark of laughter. 'And the wanker is always banging on about family values and how people give up on marriage too easily. He didn't have to live with my wives! I'll enjoy hauling him in.' Moberg chuckled again. 'That's good work, Hakim.'

Hakim felt ridiculously pleased. The chief inspector had never used his first name before.

'Have the Swiss police been cooperative?'

'Reasonably. But Inspector Boniface in Lausanne doesn't want me to take any computer material out of the country. They like to keep tabs on their residents. Everything's a bit secretive here. You know they don't have freedom of information in Switzerland?' Hakim couldn't keep the disbelief out of his voice.

'We could do with that here. Too bloody open for our own good. Anyhow, I'll ring this Boni-thingy fellow.'

'It's OK. I've downloaded all we need.'

'You're learning,' Moberg said approvingly. 'When are you coming back?'

'Tomorrow. I've got to report to Boniface first thing.'

'Right. We'll get onto these two "clients". If they've got something to lose – and Isaksson has his reputation for starters – then they've got a motive.'

'One more thing. I think Julia Akerman's real name was Ebba. But Ebba what, I don't know.'

CHAPTER 19

Next morning, Hakim had a meeting with Inspector Boniface. For convenience, as Hakim had a plane to catch later in the day, they met at the Prefecture again. This time, he took the Metro up the hill. He explained what he had found out about Julia Akerman.

When Hakim had finished, Boniface said, 'So, she had no clients here in Switzerland.'

'Not that I could find.'

'Good. Nothing for us to investigate. Anyway, her activities would be legal here. But, as a precaution, I had Lacaze bring in her computer to the Sûreté last night. We might find things that we need to keep our eye on.'

As they shook hands outside the Prefecture, the rain began to fall again.

'At least you return with two possible suspects. Why you have such a ridiculous law on prostitution is beyond me – you prosecute the client, don't you?' Boniface gave a Gallic shrug. Hakim wasn't in the mood to argue with him. Despite his misgivings about the trade, he was proud that Sweden was liberal enough to see the prostitutes as the exploited partners in the exchange and that they should be protected.

The train journey back was miserable. The rain continued, and the lake and the mountains beyond were lost in the mist. He wanted to get back home to Sweden. The case was developing, and he wanted to be at the centre of it.

While he waited in a virtually deserted airport upper departure lounge away from the shops and the eateries, he noticed a sign in the corner: *Espace de recueillement*. He went into the small meditation room and found a curved wall, seats and a bench. On a table were carefully laid a Koran, a Bible and a Jewish book, which he thought might be the Torah. Appropriate religious clothing was also available for the traveller's use. The solitude was slightly marred by the piped music impinging from the departure lounge outside. Nevertheless, he spent fifteen undisturbed minutes in the room and found himself praying. He wasn't sure why. Maybe this case had disturbed him more than he realised. Maybe it raised issues about his own life that he hadn't faced before. Maybe he was beginning to feel that his relationship with Allah shouldn't be the only meaningful one in his life.

The plane back to Kastrup was on time. At the last moment, he made an impulse purchase at an airport shop. It was a silly little cowbell with the Swiss flag painted on it. His mother would like it. As he queued up for the security check, he felt the computer memory stick in his pocket. He was leaving Switzerland with a lot more than a tacky souvenir. What did play on his mind was how Julia/Ebba had found her clients.

The crossing had been fine, and Anita hadn't felt squeamish or seasick. She wasn't a good sailor, and had had second thoughts about taking the catamaran from Simrishamn to Allinge on Bornholm. But it was a favourite trip of southern-based Swedes, who enjoyed the charm, beauty and less-expensive beer of the Danish island an hour away in the Baltic. It was somewhere that she felt she must take Kevin, and, if the weather stayed pleasant, it made for a good day out. Kevin was already clicking away with his camera as the catamaran eased into Allinge with its brightly painted buildings and distinctive smokehouse chimneys artistically positioned above its picturesque harbour. As they disembarked, they could see that it was bursting with sailing boats of all sizes, from ocean-going yachts to small craft. A market was in full swing on the quayside, and, with the promise of bargains, Anita automatically gravitated towards it. With the Swedish krona relatively strong against the Danish krone, this was a good time to buy. Kevin soon lost interest in the stalls and wandered off to take some more photographs. They met up for a coffee and Danish pastry at a café above the harbour, where Anita showed off her two purchases – a summery blue dress and a new pair of sandals, which she was wearing.

'The others were pretty worn,' she explained as she tucked into a large cream-filled bun.

'Well, I've been to the tourist information,' Kevin said, producing a batch of leaflets. 'This is a very interesting island.'

'And I've a horrid feeling you're going to tell me what you've found out,' she joshed.

Totally unabashed, he went on to tell her about the history of Bornholm and how it had changed hands between Denmark and Sweden over the centuries. 'Then the Germans took it over in 1940. They used it as a listening station, as it was part of the Eastern Front. At the end of the war, the Russians bombed it because the German commander had been given orders only to surrender to the Western Allies. Then the Soviets landed and held the island for a year before handing it back to the Danish on condition that no NATO troops, particularly the Americans, were stationed here.'

'And that's it?'

'There's plenty more.' Kevin couldn't help noticing Anita's lack of interest. In fact, she was feeling slightly embarrassed that she knew virtually nothing about a place she had visited many times. 'But it'll keep.'

'Try again after I've had a couple of beers,' she joked. 'I might be more receptive.'

He laughed. 'I do go on. But when you've got no one in your life to natter to, I have to make the most of a captive audience.

And, sadly for you, that's what you are for the next week.'

'How do you want to play this?'

Wallen was sitting opposite Moberg in his office. The chief inspector drummed his thick fingers on the desk top. He had been wondering himself ever since Hakim had given him the names of Axel Isaksson and Markus Asplund.

'What do we know about Asplund?'

Wallen glanced down at her notebook, on which she had scribbled down the results of a few phone calls. 'He's a businessman.'

'What in?'

'Travel. He runs Malasp Travel. I think I've booked through them before. Tenerife. It's a made-up name; an amalgam of Malmö and Asplund.'

'I gathered that. They've got a few places.'

'Ten offices. Mainly in southern Sweden. He's fifty-one. Married with two grown-up kids and lives up in Växjö.'

'That's a bit of a trek.'

'But he's got an apartment here in Malmö. On Östra Rönneholmsvägen.'

Moberg gave a leer. 'So, while his wife is safely tucked away in Växjö, he can play away from home here in Malmö. Perfect arrangement,' he said almost wistfully. 'But why doesn't Akerman, or whatever she's really called, charge him? I suppose we'll have to ask. Do you know if he's in town at the moment?'

'No, he's not.' Wallen consulted her notebook again. 'But he's due back at the main office tomorrow morning.'

'That's your first appointment.'

'I'll sort that out. But what about Isaksson?'

Moberg blew out his cheeks. 'That's going to be trickier.'

'Because of what he is?'

'I know exactly what he is! He's a shyster politician who'll jump on any bandwagon that suits his cause. I don't have to tell you what a hard time he gives us in the police. Any wrong moves and he's on us like a shot. And each time, it increases his popularity. If we charge in – and I know I can be a bit like that...' Wallen suppressed a smirk. Everybody who had ever worked with Moberg knew he was exactly like that, but she was surprised by his self-awareness; not a quality she had associated with the chief inspector. 'We have to be damned sure of our facts before we tackle him. Our beloved commissioner and that harpy of a prosecutor will put every obstacle in our way before we're allowed near the sod. What background have we got on him?'

Again, Wallen turned to her notebook.

'Aged fifty-five, married with four children. Brought up in Sjöbo and started his political life there.'

'God, I might have known he'd come from Sjöbo.' Sjöbo was a Scanian town known throughout Sweden for being associated with strong opposition to immigration. It had made headlines when the municipality refused to accept refugees in 1987, and the result was the adoption of a combined immigration and integration system in the "Aliens Act" a couple of years later.

'He may be right wing, but he's not as far right as the Sweden Democrats. They had a lot of votes from there in the election.'

'Anyone who shits on the force is a prick in my eyes. What else?'

'He's been on the city council for ten years. There have been rumours that he may stand for parliament in the general election later this year. During his time on the council, he has been involved in education. And, more recently, the Real Estate Office.'

'That opens him up for dodgy dealing.'

'Not a whisper. He seems whiter than white. Regular churchgoer. And he makes a big thing of the family and how it seems to be breaking down in modern society.'

After splitting from three wives, Moberg wasn't in a position to cast any stones in Isaksson's direction. But he did. 'Can't stand sanctimonious people like that.' Then he brightened. 'But we know he's been a wicked boy. I wonder what his wife, church and council colleagues will think of him consorting with a prostitute. That'll wipe the smug look off his face.'

CHAPTER 20

Hakim made his way straight back to the polishus. He wanted to make sure that Moberg was up to date with everything, and find out if they had made any progress with the two names he had supplied from Julia Akerman's list. The sun in Malmö was hot, and its brightness was in pleasant contrast to the gloom of the Switzerland he had just left. He dumped his cabin case in his room and knocked on Moberg's door. He found the chief inspector in his shirt sleeves and with beads of sweat on his brow and upper lip; the small fan on his desk wasn't having the desired effect.

'Heat's all right in bloody Spain but has no place in Sweden.' He waved for Hakim to sit down.

Hakim produced his computer stick and placed it on Moberg's desk.

'From Akerman's computer?' Hakim nodded confirmation. 'Well done.' He wasn't sure if the chief inspector was praising him for his mission in Switzerland or for taking evidence out of the country without Swiss authorisation.

'Are we any closer to finding out who Julia Akerman really was?'

'No. We're going through all the Ebbas of about the same age we can find. But if she wasn't born in Malmö, as it says on her passport, then she might come from anywhere in the country. Or somewhere else entirely.'

Hakim now took out the photo he'd taken from Akerman's bedside table.

'This might help. There's a good chance that these are her parents, or some relatives. If we have it blown up, we might be able to find the beach, if it's in Skåne.'

Moberg picked up the photograph and examined it.

'Then there's the church connection. She went to the local church in La Sarraz. There was a Bible by her bed and a cross above it. She may have been a... anyway, she appears to have been religious.'

Moberg laughed. 'A frustrated nun!'

'Maybe she'd considered entering the church and somehow got sidetracked.'

'You can bloody say that again! But I'm not so sure. I think the nun outfit may have just been one of her kinky getups for some pious punter. Eva Thulin was on the phone half an hour ago and she says they've found semen on the habit.' Moberg went silent for a moment, and then he clicked his fingers in triumph. 'Now that would be nice! Axel Isaksson's dead religious. Maybe Akerman was playing out his fantasies.'

'Any DNA?'

'They're working on it. If it comes up as Isaksson's, then not even the commissioner, the prosecutor or the frigging mayor can stop us talking to him.'

They had a final drink on the quayside while they waited for the catamaran to return. The heat of the day had receded, but the early evening was soothingly warm, and the cold beers were most welcome. As far as Kevin was concerned, they had had a wonderful day mooching around Allinge. They had wandered along the coast and found a fish restaurant for their lunch. Afterwards, they had returned to the harbour area and, at a cluttered shop packed with arty metalwork, Kevin had bought Anita a chunky modern candelabra made of Danish iron, with square, clean-cut lines, which she had taken a shine to. She had been suitably grateful, and he'd been pleased because he'd got a better exchange rate using his British bank card than he would have had using Swedish kronor.

He observed Anita supping her beer as she watched an elegant ocean-going yacht glide into the harbour and its crew jumping off to secure its moorings. She was such a handsome woman. He felt lifted every time she smiled at him – the playful grey-green eyes alight, and the high cheek bones creasing up above the open mouth. She made him feel good. He was wondering if he could spend the rest of his life with her. Yet, deep down, he knew it would never happen. It wasn't practical. They lived in different worlds. To her, it seemed to him, this was a casual relationship with no strings attached. And he knew that she had been hurt in the past and that there would always be barriers that he would never be allowed to break through. He must count his blessings and take the relationship for what it was.

Anita turned to him and smiled. Even with her sunglasses on, her face lit up. 'Happy?'

He stared at her for a few seconds before answering. 'Very.'

'Well, you'd better drink up. That's our boat coming in.'

The journey back was as smooth as the one out. When they got back to the house, they opened up one of the bottles they had bought at the supermarket in Allinge – Anita wasn't going to pass over the opportunity to buy cheaper red wine. They took their drinks out onto the porch and watched the sun retreating into the shadows of the night, the sky aglow with vermilion and gold.

'Forecast is fine for tomorrow,' Anita commented.

'Is the weather in Sweden always this good?'

Anita's snort was an eloquent reply.

'What do you want to do tomorrow?'

'Stay in bed with you.'

Anita gave a coy giggle. 'I mean after that.'

'Why don't we chill out? Flake out on the beach. I still haven't really started that Scandi crime book I picked up at the airport. Turns out it's about Iceland, not Sweden, and by a British writer. Got a female detective in it.'

'You've got your own Scandinavian female detective already,' she said mischievously.

'Is that a come-on?'

'Might be.' Anita took a sip of her wine. 'Anyway, it's best if we stay here tomorrow because I expect Klas will turn up. He's obviously dying to tell us what he's found out.'

'Actually, I've been wondering about that. I can't think of any huge diplomatic thing happening in Germany in the late seventies or early eighties. Apart from all the Cold War rhetoric coming from Reagan and Thatcher that is. But something turned Rylander into a hawk.'

Anita could feel another history lesson coming on. 'Why don't we take the rest of the bottle to bed?'

The boyish beam on Kevin's face stopped any further Cold War speculations, and he happily followed Anita back into the house, bottle in hand.

They must have drifted off after their lovemaking, as Kevin woke up with a start when he heard a mobile phone. It wasn't his own boring ring tone but Anita's burst of jazz music.

'Anita,' he said as he gently shook her shoulder. 'It's your phone.'

In a daze, Anita rolled out of bed, totally naked. Kevin watched her as she walked slowly out of the bedroom and into the living room to find her mobile in her bag, which was slung over the back of a chair. Kevin glanced at his watch on the bedside table. It was just after midnight. Who on earth was calling at this time of night? It was bloody antisocial.

Suddenly, he noticed the tension in Anita's voice. She was

asking quick-fire questions. He didn't understand the language, but he could interpret the tone. Any detective the world over would recognise it. Something had happened. But what? He got out of bed and slipped on his boxer shorts. He found Anita's dressing gown on the back of the door and took it into the living room. As she continued to listen and talk, he helped her slip the dressing gown on. She gave him a grateful nod.

Kevin went off and put the kettle on. He could see that, whatever the news was, they were unlikely to go straight back to bed. A cup of tea was always the answer. He could hear the call ending. A moment later, she stepped into the kitchen.

'That was Stefan.'

'From the police station?'

'Yes.'

Anita was distracted.

'Tea?'

She nodded.

As he fished out a couple of teabags, she spoke.

'There's been a terrible accident. It's Klas.'

Kevin swung round to face her. 'Is he OK?'

'No. He's dead.'

CHAPTER 21

Wallen was relieved that she had Hakim with her and not that lazy sod, Brodd. Moberg had got Brodd chasing up the National Forensic Lab in Linköping, where Sweden's DNA national database is kept. The chief inspector was hoping that the semen stain on the nun's habit would lead them to Axel Isaksson. Wallen wasn't so sure that her boss's wishes would be granted. The man that they were about to talk to, Markus Asplund, might well be the sexual culprit. But even if he was, it wouldn't necessarily mean that he was their murderer.

The travel agency's main Malmö bureau was on Stora Varvsgatan in one of the plush new office blocks that had sprung up in the Västra Hamnen area north of the city centre. Gone was the huge industrial zone that had powered Malmö's economy for so long, revolving around the famous Kockums shipyards. In its place, the "City of Tomorrow" was rising; the first district in Europe to claim to be carbon neutral using aquifer thermal energy storage systems to heat the buildings in the winter and keep them cool in the summer. As Wallen parked their police pool car in front of the high-rise building, she thought it might be interesting to see if the new technology really worked.

It *was* pleasantly cool and calm as they stepped through the glass doors. A number of desks were neatly laid out, and already a couple of customers were in earnest conversation with a member of staff, who was pointing out figures on a computer screen while glossy brochures lay open on the workstation. Another agent was busy on the phone. Hakim noticed the posters on the back wall. Everything from the Swedes' favourite destinations like Spain and Thailand, where they could rely on the sun, to more intriguing and exotic holidays or short breaks in Europe's most sophisticated cities.

An enthusiastic young man with short, gelled hair and a ready smile looked up from his desk.

'And where do you fancy going? At Malasp Travel we can make your dreams come true. Let me help you plan that great holiday.'

Hakim couldn't help but give a little chuckle. He and Wallen didn't exactly look like a "couple". Klara was old enough to be his mother. Maybe he was her Arab toy boy!

'We're here to see Markus Asplund.' Wallen flashed her warrant card. 'Police.'

The smile of greeting vanished immediately.

'Is he expecting you?'

'No.'

The young man sat dithering, not quite sure what he should do.

'I don't think he'll want to keep us waiting,' added Hakim, realising that that the employee was worried about disturbing his boss.

'Of course not. Sorry, I only started last week. I'll... I'll go and fetch him. Would you just take a seat?'

He hurried off to the back of the office and knocked on a door. A few moments later, he reappeared. 'Please go in.'

Markus Asplund was a handsome man with the confident expression of someone who has made a success of his life. He was dressed in a pale-blue shirt and faded jeans. The look was casually downbeat, but the clothes must have come with a healthy price tag. His smile was broad and revealed a set of shining white teeth. Now Hakim recognised him. He had fronted some TV commercials for his company last year. It was the smile he remembered. He couldn't help his first thought – would a man like this need to go to a prostitute? His second thought was that Asplund was trim and fit enough to have run up behind Julia Akerman and stab her in the back.

'Please come in. Just bear with me for a second,' he said apologetically as he quickly signed a piece of paper which he added to a small pile. Wallen noticed that he was right-handed. 'Now, how can I help the police?' He emphasised the word "police" as though there was obviously nothing for him to worry about – he would just be a good citizen and be as helpful as possible.

'I'm Klara Wallen and this is Hakim Mirza.' They both waved their warrant cards at him. His response was to indicate that they should both sit down opposite his glass-topped desk, which had three computer screens on it. He wheeled his swivel chair round the desk and positioned himself in front of them.

'Can I offer you coffee?' he said, pointing at a large coffee maker sitting on a table by the window.

'No.'

'OK, then. Fire away.' It was as though he was opening a meeting that he had convened. He was in control.

'It's about the death of Julia Akerman,' Wallen started.

Asplund looked at them blankly.

'The young woman who was murdered in Pildammsparken,' she prompted.

'Ah, that girl. Awful. Not good from a travel-business point of view. As well as sending Swedes on holiday, we're also very conscious of how we appear to tourists coming to Sweden. I know a lot come now because they're into our crime fiction. But that's what it is – fiction. They don't want real murders.'

'Precisely. And this "real" murder is the reason we're here.'

Asplund wore a puzzled expression.

'You see, your name has come up in connection with this woman.'

'What did you say she was called?'

'Julia Akerman. Actually, that's probably not her real name. It could be Ebba something.'

Now he produced an apologetic smile. 'I'm afraid I don't know of anyone of that name... or an Ebba something.'

'That's strange,' Hakim put in. 'I found your name on her computer.'

'I'm a travel agent. I expect my name appears on a lot of people's computers.'

'This computer was in Switzerland. That's where she lived.'

'Well, there you are then.'

'It was more in connection with her business transactions.'

'We specialise in business travel. This office in particular. We're surrounded by companies here. Half of Malmö's business community uses Malasp Travel.'

'Her business was prostitution.'

This time, Asplund didn't know what expression to call upon.

'We certainly don't go in for that sort of thing, I can assure you. What clients get up to in their own time is their own business, not mine.'

Hakim pulled out a copy of Akerman's client spreadsheet showing their names, details, and the amounts paid by them.

'As you can see, your name is on here with another one that you'll probably recognise. It's a list of Julia Akerman's clients. I think the figures are self-explanatory.'

Asplund took the proffered spreadsheet and studied it. An eyebrow was raised; Hakim assumed he had reached Isaksson's entry.

'Do you know Axel Isaksson?' Wallen asked.

'Of course I know of him. Who doesn't in Malmö?'

'Have you ever met him?'

'Not that I'm aware of.'

'OK, apart from Axel Isaksson, do any of those names mean anything to you?'

Asplund's eyes flitted up and down the list. He shook his head. Then he handed it back.

'I can't explain it. I have no idea who this woman is. And as you can see, according to this, I haven't even paid her anything. So, I can hardly be a client.'

'True,' said Wallen. 'But she made regular visits to Malmö. At least once a month and—'

'You can see from that,' Asplund interrupted, pointing at the spreadsheet now back in Hakim's hand, 'that the woman travelled a lot. She might have used our services. I can check.'

'On her final visit last week,' Wallen continued, ignoring Asplund's comment, 'Julia Akerman had two appointments in her diary. On Monday there was one with AI. We can surmise from the spreadsheet that that is Axel Isaksson. On Tuesday, there's an appointment with MA. Again, that looks suspiciously like Markus Asplund.'

He threw up his hands. 'I don't know what to say. I repeat: I don't know a Julia Akerman. I'm not a client. And even if I was, from those figures it looks like I didn't pay for any sex, so I'm not guilty of anything illegal.'

'But you do like anal sex?' It wasn't the sort of question that Hakim was used to asking.

'I beg your pardon?'

'That's what she's got down for your sexual preferences on this spreadsheet. And she'd had anal sex a few hours before she was killed.'

'I'm not fucking answering that.' It was the first time that Asplund had appeared rattled.

'Where were you last week on Tuesday, the third?' Wallen asked, keeping up the pressure.

Without a word, Asplund reached over to his desk and

picked up his smartphone. He clicked away for a few moments.

'I was in Gothenburg Monday night. I'd been at our bureau there. I got the train down in the morning and reached Malmö after lunch. Went straight to the Södra Förstadsgatan outlet and was there for the rest of the day. We'd had a problem with a couple of hotels for a group we'd sent to China and Hong Kong. Needed to change them at short notice. Took a while to fix, but it got sorted. We're that kind of organisation. We believe in giving satisfaction.'

'And the evening?'

'I had a drink with a couple of my managers. Just an informal chat to touch base on various issues. And then went back to my apartment.'

'At what time?'

'When did she die?'

'At what time?' Wallen repeated, ignoring his question.

'Oh, I suppose about eight.'

'So, you have no alibi for the time of the murder.'

'I can assure you I didn't kill her or anybody. I'm not capable.' This was said with some vehemence. Then he became more matter-of-fact. 'I was in my apartment, and I skyped the family at Växjö. You can ask my wife. My youngest, Erik, has Down's syndrome. Sometimes Ella finds him difficult to cope with when I'm away. I wanted to check how everything was.'

'Do you jog?' Wallen continued to probe.

Asplund screwed up his eyes. 'That's how she was killed, wasn't it? I remember now. She was jogging. Well, I do run occasionally, but I prefer to do my exercise at the gym. When I'm in town here, I tend to go to the one near Triangeln station. The entrance by Sankt Johannes.'

'If you could supply us with your home number, we'll check the time of your skype.'

'There's no need for that,' he said hurriedly. 'It was about half eight. We talked for about twenty minutes.'

'So, you still don't have an alibi.'

He didn't answer.

'Thank you for your time,' said Wallen, rising from her seat. 'We'll be talking again very soon.'

As they were leaving the room, Hakim turned back to a shaken-looking Asplund.

'Do you ever go to America?'

'America?'

'Yes. Do you ever travel there?'

'Of course. It's a big destination for Swedes. Why do ask?'

Hakim's reply was an enigmatic smile.

They drove back towards the centre of town. They were held up by a procession of cars with honking horns, and young people hanging out of the windows and heads popping through sunroofs. At the front of the queue was a truck, on the back of which was a pack of excited teenagers shouting and cheering. They were all wearing their distinctive student caps resembling sailor hats with a white crown and black peak separated by a dark band with an insignia. This was the day when the school leavers of Malmö publicly let their hair down and celebrated leaving their place of education. It was always a joyous event, with the boys looking smart in suits and the girls putting on their best dresses, and all taking to the streets. Hakim's mind slipped back to his own graduation. It was a good day. Sunny like this one. They had paraded through the streets behind a drumming band of students and teachers. The only embarrassing element was that a number of parents – including his mother – had made placards with photos of the graduates when they were very young. His photo had not been flattering. Not all graduation traditions were good ones.

'So, what do you think of Asplund?' Wallen ventured.

Hakim was staring at the car in front. Two happy girls were waving at them. He waved back self-consciously. 'He's lying about not knowing Julia Akerman.' One of the girls blew him a kiss. 'I'm sure he knew her; after all, she had all his details. And he probably saw her the day she died.'

'We need to check out his movements that day. What train did he get? He could have caught an earlier one than he said and been back in Malmö to have time to meet up with Akerman for a quick session. His apartment's between the station and the Södra Förstadsgatan office.'

'I'll go to his apartment building and see if anyone recognises her. And check the neighbours at Akerman's place and see if someone recognises him. The streets run into each other, so they're only about five minutes' walk apart.'

The student procession turned off, and they made quicker progress.

'He wasn't keen on us contacting his wife.'

'Not at all,' agreed Hakim.

'We'll leave her until later. We need to trace his movements first. What was with that question about America?'

'The butterfly knife.'

'Ah. Yes, he could easily have picked one up. And he jogs; he's certainly fit enough to run up behind Akerman.'

'But why?' This was the question that still puzzled Hakim. 'What's his motive?'

'A falling out? Could she have been extorting money from him?'

'But she didn't appear to charge him in the first place. And she could hardly threaten him, as he pointed out. If money didn't change hands, he's not committed any crime. Unless, of course, they had some other arrangement which got round the law.'

'She might have threatened to expose him to his wife.'

'That's possible. But even if that's the case, why didn't he kill her earlier when they met for sex?'

'Maybe he couldn't do it then. If they'd met in his apartment, he could hardly get rid of her body easily. It's too central. Too many people about. Her apartment's the same. He must have cold-bloodedly planned it so there would be no connection between the two of them.'

'Maybe you're right.' Hakim lapsed into thoughtful silence. The fact that Asplund hadn't appeared to pay for sex gnawed at him. Why the freebees when Akerman was charging the others – except Isaksson – eye-watering amounts of money for her services? Why was he a special case? What was their real connection? Maybe they had to go back further; dig deeper. One thing he was sure of was that, despite his protestations, Markus Asplund knew Julia Akerman. More than that, he probably knew who she really was.

CHAPTER 22

Anita had been fretting all morning. Kevin had tried to persuade her to come down to the beach after breakfast. He wanted a swim. She wasn't in the mood to join him. She had hardly slept during the night. As she made herself yet another coffee, she couldn't get Klas out of her mind. It had been a real shock when she had spoken to Stefan. Klas had swerved off the road, and his motorbike had crashed straight into a tree by the roadside. What made it worse was that it wasn't far from her cabin. Klas must have been on his way to see her with his news from Berlin. If only he had waited until the morning!

He was such a lovely man. She felt guilty that sometimes she had switched off when he started to prattle on about his latest project or obsession. He was harmless. He was intelligent. He could be fun when he hadn't got his "serious" head on. Suddenly, both he and Albin Rylander had gone. They had been an essential part of her summer – other than Kevin, of course.

Stefan's details had been sketchy. There didn't seem to be another vehicle involved. No other driver had reported anything and, as there were no houses on that stretch of road, no one had heard the accident. Perhaps he was tired and wasn't concentrating, Stefan suggested. Anita thought it was more likely that his head was full of his Rylander discoveries, and that he had taken his eye off the road. He was often miles away, lost in thought. What a waste of a good human being.

Ten minutes later, she found herself jumping into her car and driving to the crash site. A ribbon of police tape round the tree marked the spot. In the Simrishamn direction there was a rise in the road; traffic came zooming over the top and into a slight bend. Maybe he came over the brow too quickly, had to adjust to the bend and lost control. But he had travelled this road nearly every day for weeks. As the traffic whipped past on this sunny morning, she could make out the faint impression of the motorbike's tyre tracks that led straight over the grass verge and into the tree. She found herself placing a few wild flowers that she had picked from the verge, next to the taped perimeter. It was a pathetically inadequate gesture.

She wiped away a tear that had sprung from nowhere. As she did so, she focused again on the tyre track. That was quite a sharp turn. If he had dozed off or had lost concentration, she would have expected more of an arc. This looked like a quick readjustment. More of a swerve. Had something been coming in the other direction on his side of the road? The thought made Anita uneasy. She got back into her car and drove home.

Hakim stood next to the small sculpture of a naked woman on bended knee holding a sheaf of corn above her head. What it stood for, he had no idea. Possibly something to do with fertility. Behind him was a grassy area where a number of young people were lolling about in the sunshine. To his left, Malmö's main theatre. Beyond that, Pildammsparken. A very central position to have a crash pad. As he sipped his takeaway coffee, it was the building opposite that most interested him. It was Markus Asplund's city centre apartment on Östra Rönneholmsvägen. Obviously, the travel industry was booming. Asplund lived in an elegant building with a Dutch-style façade. His apartment was set back off the street, secluded by the curvature of the design. The principal windows were tall and graceful and, at the top of the building, under the eaves, oval apertures were wreathed by sculptured laurel leaves.

The balconies looked large and substantial and were supported by voluted corbels. Not like ours, Hakim thought ruefully as his mind strayed to the flimsy metal protuberance on his parents' home. He had already been to Julia Akerman's apartment and asked the few neighbours who were in if they recognised Asplund from a photo taken from his advertising campaign, but he had drawn a blank. If Asplund had had a sexual assignation with Akerman, it was unlikely to have been at her place. Now they knew about Asplund and Isaksson, Moberg wanted forensics to go back into Akerman's apartment and search for any evidence that they had been there, but Hakim doubted that they would find any connection to the travel agent; he was too careful. But the close proximity of the two apartments was suggestive. They were also both close to Pildammsparken. Asplund might have known Akerman's Malmö routine – they had already met that day if her diary entry was correct. He could have caught up with her, killed her, and been back home within minutes.

There was a lot of circumstantial evidence building up against Markus Asplund. What Hakim needed now was to find someone who had seen Julia Akerman entering his apartment. Or, at the very least, seen her in the building. He finished his coffee, chucked the container into a bin and headed across the road.

'But I was having a great time on the beach,' Kevin protested as Anita dragged him up the bank towards the house.

'There's something I want you to see,' said Anita firmly, quashing any further dissent.

'Can I at least have a shower first? Get the sand out of my... crevices.' It didn't sound right, but it was the only word that immediately came to mind.

'Just change out of your swimming trunks. We won't be long.'

'Is it that important?'

Anita didn't answer as she strode on ahead. He hadn't seen her like this before. He decided it was best not to argue.

A quarter of an hour later, they were at the crash site. The route was particularly busy at that time in the morning. Though it was a single-lane road, it was fairly straight as it ran in line with the coast, and vehicles were hurtling along it. Once they had managed to park on the grass verge near the accident spot, Anita pointed out the swerve the bike had taken.

'Is there much traffic in the evening?'

'Not much. It was after ten.'

'I can see what you mean, but it doesn't necessarily indicate it's suspicious.' Kevin wanted to say enough to keep his new girlfriend happy, but not be too encouraging in case it developed into an annoying distraction from the holiday which he was really enjoying. 'He could have swerved for all sorts of reasons.'

'Such as?'

'Well, an animal for instance. There are lots round here, I assume. A deer? We get a lot of them in Cumbria around dusk, and they sometimes run into vehicles. Can cause quite nasty accidents.'

'True,' Anita had to reluctantly agree.

He laid a comforting hand on her shoulder.

'I know it's sad. You were fond of him. But there doesn't seem to be anything wrong. I'm sure your police will have done everything thoroughly. Checked the scene. All the usual stuff.'

He could see that Anita wasn't totally convinced, but he managed to shepherd her back into the car.

'Normally, I wouldn't even question this. But Klas was so sure that there was something wrong with Rylander's suicide. And then this.'

'Horrid coincidence.'

'It was you who raised doubts in my mind about Rylander's death in the first place. You seeing someone watching his house before he died.'

'Don't blame this on me.'

Anita turned on the ignition. The car sparked wearily into life. 'I think I'll have another word with Stefan. And the nurse. Klas said he'd talked to her.'

'I hope to God you're not turning this into a bloody case, Anita. I'd like to remind you, this is my holiday!'

'Well, this will make it a more interesting one.'

'I don't want an "interesting" one. I want boring. I'll take uneventful any day.'

All he got in return was a withering look.

'I always thought the English had plenty of get up and go.'

'I have, but it gets up and goes for a fortnight every summer.'

She relented. He was right. This was unfair on him.

'OK. I'll have a little chat with Stefan. He'll probably clear things up. And maybe a word with Moa, the nurse. And if there's nothing, we just get on with the holiday.'

Kevin sighed. He had a nasty feeling it wasn't going to end there.

Hakim glanced back at the elegant apartment block. He had knocked on fifteen doors. Seven had produced an answer. Some of the inhabitants had seemed wary of a detective with an olive skin. Apart from the suspicious looks and the shaking of heads, there had been absolutely no reaction. No one had seen a woman of Julia Akerman's description in or around the building, let alone slipping in and out through Markus Asplund's door; and there was no CCTV. Hakim sighed. He couldn't give up yet. He would have to return this evening and try and rustle up the absent neighbours. His feelings about Asplund were hardening. He had the means – the possible access to a butterfly knife. He had opportunity – he hadn't an alibi for the time and he lived in the vicinity of the murder. And motive? That wasn't entirely clear as yet. But as a prostitute, Akerman might well have known his guilty secrets. Or was *she* the secret?

CHAPTER 23

Lasse was supposed to be doing his course work when Jazmin was out. His attention had wandered, and he was playing Football Manager on the computer when she came back. Barcelona was his team and they never lost, certainly not while he was their manager. But he had made sure that Malmö had reached the Champions League semi-finals before succumbing to Lionel Messi's magic. Jazmin's return gave him a fright, and he quickly managed to replace the page on the screen with some notes he had been typing before he'd been lured away by his managerial duties.

'Sorry, I didn't hear you come in,' he lied as he turned round to see his girlfriend, who was clutching a bag of shopping from the ethnic Allfrukt supermarket. It was where her parents shopped, and it was cheaper than the nearest ICA. Once they'd paid the rent, there wasn't a lot of money to go round. She hoped that she was teaching Lasse to be more frugal than he was used to. Living at home with his mother had meant that he had got out of touch with prices of basic things like food.

Lasse followed her into the tiny kitchen of their one-bedroomed apartment in Rosengård. It was only twenty minutes' walk from her parents' home, but it felt like a million miles away. She was enjoying that freedom. Her movements weren't constantly being monitored – or commented on – by her strict father. Lasse put his arms round her as she unpacked the shopping. He kissed her tenderly on the back of her neck. She liked that. Then he slyly reached round her, and he tried to open a packet of biscuits. She slapped his hand in admonishment. 'They're a treat for later.'

Jazmin came back into the living room while Lasse made her a cup of coffee. She heard the rustle of the biscuits being surreptitiously opened. She smiled to herself, too tired to reprimand him again. She didn't mind spoiling him occasionally. Their one, real indulgence rubbed his neck round her lower shin. Messi the cat. The name wasn't her idea, but Lasse had called him after some boring footballer. And the cat was messy. He caused chaos in their small living space, and his ginger and white fur was everywhere. But he was an integral part of their little family. He jumped onto her lap and curled up for a snooze.

Lasse came in, bearing two mugs of coffee. There were still telltale biscuit crumbs at the side of his mouth, which he hadn't wiped away. Jazmin took her coffee.

'What time are you working till tonight?'

'Half eleven.'

Lasse worked in a café-cum-restaurant off Kungsgatan three nights a week. This was to supplement their student grants. She did a few hours in a corner shop run by a friend of her mother's. Between them, they managed to make ends meet.

'I saw someone last night. I thought whoever it was must have gone away, but they're back.'

Lasse sighed. Not this again. He had got in late last night after his shift, and she had been out early to get to her gender studies class, so she hadn't had a chance to mention it.

'I definitely saw a figure this time. About eleven.'

'What did this "figure" look like?'

'I couldn't tell; it was dark by then. He had a hoodie on.'

'Honestly, Jazmin, there could be a thousand reasons why someone was out at that time of night. Granted, he might have been up to no good. This isn't exactly a crime-free neighbourhood. You're getting upset over nothing.'

'Your mother didn't think so,' she said vehemently.

'Bloody hell! I can't believe you mentioned it to her. She's turned worrying into an art form. We'll never hear the end of it now.' He couldn't take the incredulity out of his voice.

'Forget it!' She was annoyed that he kept sweeping away her concerns.

They drank their coffees in moody silence. Messi sensed the unease and jumped off Jazmin's lap and wandered into the bedroom.

'Look,' Lasse relented, 'if you think you see anything when I'm out tonight, give me a call.' Then he smirked. 'You have got a mobile, haven't you?' he teased.

She managed to turn her sulky pout into a suppressed grin. A month ago Lasse had bought her a brand new mobile phone with all the bells and whistles. She suspected that he had borrowed some money from Anita to cover the cost.

'I'll call.'

'Let's review the evidence.' Moberg sounded more upbeat than usual. Wallen's visit to Markus Asplund was the most positive development they had so far encountered. 'Two suspects. Marcus Asplund?'

Wallen, Hakim and Brodd all sat round the table in the meeting room. It was late. Brodd was the least happy to be there and had muttered that he had better things to do.

'What we seem to have is a successful travel agent who has his family conveniently tucked away up near Växjö in Småland while he spends a lot of time down here in an apartment in the centre of town. And that apartment is an easy walk from the victim's. And he keeps fit, though he doesn't jog much – allegedly. We know that his initials are in the Akerman diary.' They had decided that they would refer to the murdered woman as Julia Akerman until they were a hundred per cent sure of her real name; "Ebba" would just confuse things at this point. 'We've got his name on her spreadsheet, even though he doesn't appear to pay for her services. Yet intercourse must have taken place at some stage, as she had noted his... em... sexual idiosyncrasy.'

Brodd's smirk elicited an angry glare from Wallen.

'And we know that that was the method of sex she had with her last client on the day she died. So, the probability is that she was with Markus Asplund on the day of her murder.'

Moberg turned to the whiteboard and tapped the photo of Asplund.

'We also know that he's a frequent visitor to America, so could easily have picked up the butterfly knife. He has opportunity and the possible means, which is all well and good – but where's the motive? Any thoughts?'

'It must be sexual.' Brodd could always be relied upon to come up with the obvious. 'She's a whore. So it's bound to be.'

'I think there's more to it,' suggested Hakim.

'You would,' Brodd muttered.

'If he saw her that day, why wait until later to kill her? I mean, the murder was very premeditated. I know Klara said that he couldn't do it at the apartment because it would be very difficult to dispose of the body in such a central location, and she's right. But what had got so bad between them both in a matter of hours that he turned to murder later in the day?'

'Are you suggesting he didn't do it?' Moberg asked.

'Not at all. I think there's a strong possibility that he did. But the reason must run deeper. How did he get to know her? Was it before she moved to Switzerland? He travels a lot, so did he make any trips to Switzerland in the last year? Did he meet her there as well as here? Shouldn't we be looking into his background more? We might find the missing connection there.'

Moberg nodded as he took in what Hakim had just said. He

couldn't help but be impressed by the boy from Rosengård. 'OK. There's stuff we can follow up there. I want to know everything about him, from his bank accounts to his eating habits. Talking of habits, have we had any luck on the semen stain, Pontus?'

'Sorry, Boss, we've drawn a blank there. Neither Asplund nor Isaksson are on the DNA database. No reason why they should be, as neither has a criminal record.'

'So, we'll have to get samples from them. That might be difficult in Isaksson's case. He's bound to kick up a stink. I had a meeting with the commissioner and Prosecutor Blom this morning, and they don't want us to approach the tosser until we have some definite proof of his connection with Akerman.'

'What about the spreadsheet?' Hakim pointed out.

'Yes, but the way you got hold of it wasn't exactly kosher.' Moberg suddenly felt awkward using the expression in front of a Muslim. Fucking political correctness! 'For it to stand up in court, we'd need to get the information officially through the Swiss police. I suspect that would take forever. Despite what our superiors think, I'm going to pay Axel Isaksson a visit tomorrow. Friendly, of course.'

Laughter tinkled round the room.

'Right, tomorrow I want everyone to concentrate on Asplund. Do we know if there's any connection between him and Isaksson other than that they both appear to be Akerman's clients?'

'Asplund denies ever meeting Isaksson, though he's heard of him,' Wallen answered.

'Haven't we all? OK, another visit to Asplund might be a good idea. Keep the pressure on. Asking him for a DNA swab should put the wind up him.'

Wallen and Hakim gathered up their notes.

'Beer?' Moberg suggested to Brodd.

'Sorry, not tonight, Boss.' Moberg's face fell. 'Having a drink with a rather attractive young lady.'

Moberg couldn't help betraying his scepticism.

'On a promise?'

'You never know!' Despite his cheeriness, his answer didn't carry great conviction.

'Oh, by the way, did anything emerge from your visit to Sjöbo?'

'Nothing of interest. The nursing home was a waste of time. I've got a list of staff and patients, but there's no Akerman connection. And I asked around about Isaksson. He's popular there, even if he's left them for the big city.'

'We'll see how popular he is when all this comes out.'

CHAPTER 24

Kevin was sitting by the harbour at Simrishamn. There was now a gentle breeze, which took the edge off the heat of the day. The crowds had dispersed now that the ice cream and fast food outlets had closed. He sat on one of the benches that faced the sea. Three old men along from him were busy discussing some important topic, or maybe what was on the telly tonight. He couldn't tell. Would he be in a relationship with Anita long enough to attempt to learn some Swedish? Or was it worth it? People seemed to speak excellent English here. And as long as they understood him when he ordered a beer, he would be fine. He was gasping. He wished Anita would hurry up. She had called into the police station to see Stefan. She was to do it casually in case Alice Zetterberg was about. That was half an hour ago. It was all right admiring the harbour in the bright evening sunlight, but there was a limit. It would look better with a glass in his hand.

'Beer?'

Anita was standing behind him.

'Bloody right!'

They went to a bar on Storgatan. In the summer it's a pedestrianised area and they sat outside.

'Well?'

'Well nothing.'

'Oh, that means that we can concentrate on the holiday.' Kevin was relieved.

'But I'm not happy with "nothing". It's as though no one at the station is involved. Except for Zetterberg. And she's not telling them anything.'

'Maybe everything is straightforward, and there's nothing to it. A suicide and an accident.'

Anita lowered her voice as though they might be overheard, though the nearest drinkers were a couple of tables away.

'Stefan says he doesn't know where the motorbike is. And they haven't had an autopsy report back on Rylander's suicide. That's nearly a week!'

Kevin looked at an animated Anita over the top of his glass.

'Maybe they've been busy.'

She shook her head. 'This isn't any ordinary body we're talking about. He was a well-known figure. He'll probably have a memorial service in somewhere grand like Lund Cathedral.'

'I'd like to visit that sometime. Sounds really interesting. Lund Cathedral.'

'Don't change the subject. I might give Eva Thulin a ring. She'd know. The point is: I'm beginning to think Klas was right about Rylander's suicide.'

'Stop it, Anita. This is fanciful.'

'Is it?' she came straight back at him. 'A man, albeit suffering from cancer, takes his own life in the middle of telling his story to the world. He actually chooses Klas to write it. We know from Klas that there was some big secret he wanted to reveal. It doesn't come out. Klas goes off to Berlin to see somebody who seems to have the answer. I get that excited text. Next thing, he's dead – and so is Rylander's secret.'

'You're turning this into a conspiracy theory.' There was too much talk. He wanted a second beer.

'No note either. And you saw somebody watching the house – twice.'

'I could have been mistaken.'

'You're a cop, for God's sake! You don't make these things

up. Have you seen this person since the suicide?'

'Well, no.'

'What about the couple next door? Your girlfriend on the beach?'

'They were just some young Stockholmers on holiday. Surely you can't suspect them. They were going on Friday, anyhow.'

Anita tapped her half-empty glass thoughtfully.

'No, I don't for a minute think they were involved. But they might have heard or seen something that night. What were they called?'

'She was Fanny. I think he was Benno.'

'Surname?'

'It wasn't a police interview. A few words exchanged staggering up your bank.'

'I can find out from the letting agent.'

'I'll tell you what,' said Kevin getting up.

'What?'

'I'm getting another beer. Top up?'

Anita shook her head. She watched Kevin make his way inside, and she could see him ordering another drink from the girl behind the bar. She knew that she might be reading too much into the situation. She had thought that Klas was just being ridiculous when Rylander died, but his own death had put everything into a different perspective. Though nothing in itself was out of the ordinary – and cock-ups did happen; people didn't do jobs quickly enough – there were little alarm bells going off. Yet why was she doing this? She was enjoying Kevin's visit. She had started to genuinely relax. Was she spoiling his holiday? Carry on like this, and their whole fledgling relationship might come to an abrupt end. Maybe she should just let it lie.

Kevin returned, sipping his beer. He sat down. 'Why don't we have a bite to eat here? There's some nice-looking grub inside. Then we can head home and maybe – I don't know – maybe have afters.'

Anita grinned back. 'OK. But between the meal and the "afters", I just want to make a small detour.'

'Where?' he said despairingly.

'To see Moa Hellquist.'

'Why?'

'Because she happens to live on the way back.'

Moa Hellquist lived off Kristianstadsvägen on Backgatan. Her home was a small cream house behind a neat hedge. It was as unassuming as the nurse herself turned out to be. Anita had left Kevin in the car because she didn't want to have to keep translating for him.

Hellquist lived alone with her West Highland terrier dog. If she had been married and had had a family, there was no obvious evidence. After Anita had refused a coffee, Hellquist fussed the dog as she waited for the inspector's questions.

'Moa, you must understand that I'm not here in any official capacity. I'm here because I know that Klas spoke to you after Albin Rylander's suicide.'

'I know. Klas thought it was odd.'

'Did you?'

Hellquist gave the dog another rub.

'Yes, I suppose I did. I know it's a strange thing to say about a man who was dying of cancer, but he was full of life. Does that sound stupid?'

'Not at all. What was he like the day before he died? Did he seem depressed?'

'No. Just as normal. Always had time for a chat. I think that's what he liked. He wanted to talk about things, anything really, while he still had breath to do so. That's why he always looked forward to his sessions with Klas.'

Anita could sense that Moa was uneasy talking about the subject. Rylander had been in her care. She wondered if there had been any official investigation by the medical authorities into the number of pills that Rylander had got hold of. The dog was acting as her comfort blanket.

'Klas said you couldn't understand where all the pills that must have killed him came from.'

Hellquist pulled a pained expression. 'I have no idea.'

'Could he have stored them up? Just pretended to take them?'

'I don't think so,' she replied slowly. 'He was on morphine sulphate. They're slow-release tablets so he could manage the pain. And though he didn't show it, he was suffering a lot. I saw him take them regularly. He took two one hundred milligram tablets a day. I gave him four weeks' worth at a go. But he had nearly run out, and I was due to give him his next batch when he... died.'

'So how many would he have needed with the alcohol to kill himself?'

'Between ten and twenty tablets, plus half a bottle of whisky. That seems to the amount he drank, apparently. That would depress his breathing and render him unconscious. Coma and respiratory arrest would lead to death.'

Anita took time to process the information before proceeding.

'What did you do you when you found him?'

'Well, I could see he was dead. I phoned for an ambulance and called the police.' Hellquist adopted a quizzical expression. 'That's odd. I hadn't thought about it before. Though I called for the ambulance first, the police arrived before the medics.'

'And this was Inspector Zetterberg?'

'I hope I'm not speaking out of turn, but I didn't like her.' Anita offered a sympathetic smile. 'She didn't want me to hang around.'

'Did she ask you about the tablets? Where he might have got that many?'

'Didn't seem interested.'

'And no follow-up questions?'

'No. I thought there might be some comeback, but no.'

'One last thing. The couple who were staying next door. From Stockholm. Were they still around when you arrived?'

'I saw them most mornings. Seemed nice. Well, she did. He looked moody. I can't remember seeing their car. I know she said that they were due to leave that Friday morning. Probably made an early start. It's a long drive.'

Anita got up. She leant over and made an effort to stroke the dog. The terrier immediately ducked out of the way.

'Thank you for talking to me.'

Hellquist stood up. Anita realised that she was glad to get rid of her uninvited guest. They walked to the door together.

'So sad about Klas, too. A lovely man.'

'He was, wasn't he?'

Hellquist held the door open.

'Just one more thing, Moa. Was Zetterberg by herself?'

'No, there was another detective with her. Well, I assume he was a detective as he wasn't wearing a uniform.'

'Local?'

'Might be, but I've never seen him before. I know most of the people at the station by sight through my work at the hospital. This man was a large fellow in his fifties. He was entirely bald. Didn't speak in my presence.'

As Hellquist closed the door behind her, Anita stood thoughtfully at the top of the small flight of steps. Now, who was this other detective?

CHAPTER 25

Axel Isaksson's detached house was modest. It wasn't too big or too small. It was just sufficient for the image of an incorruptible man you could trust and had the courage to articulate what you were thinking. A home like this, among lots of similar detached houses with their regular-sized gardens, showed that Isaksson was no better, or no worse, than the average Swede. He fitted in. He was one of us. Except Chief Inspector Erik Moberg knew that he would take an instant dislike to the man, though he had never actually met him in the flesh. Moberg tended to take instant dislikes to people – it saved time. It was well known that Isaksson was quick to criticise the police. They were an easy target, and it was a simple way to garner cheap popularity among an increasingly sceptical public. Ironically, if Moberg hadn't been a cop, he might have voted for Isaksson's right-leaning brand of politics. Isaksson never went as far as the Sweden Democrats when it came to the hot topic of immigration, but disapproval was often implied. His line was: where had the all old Swedish virtues gone? Hence his championing of family values. To some, it struck a chord. To others, it seemed hopelessly out of tune with modern life and living in a country with a divorce rate that had reached a forty-year high the previous year with over 25,000 couples separating. As Moberg himself had done his bit to inflate the figures, he felt even more antipathy towards the man he was about to meet. Yet this model family man with strong Christian beliefs appeared to be paying a prostitute for sex that he presumably wasn't getting at home. Moberg could smell a hypocrite a mile off.

The sun was warm again as Moberg eased his substantial frame out of the driving seat of his car. He prayed that the weather would break soon as he slipped on his jacket. It covered his already sweat-stained shirt. His approach would be very informal, which was why no one else was with him. He needed to rein back; not mention anything inflammatory like the nun's habit. He knew he was taking a risk. Commissioner Dahlbeck would haul him over the coals if this interview went wrong and someone as high profile as Isaksson complained of police harassment. Moberg waddled up the garden path.

It was Isaksson's wife who answered the door. She showed him through the house and into the back garden, where Axel Isaksson, cup of coffee in hand, was sitting at a wooden garden table covered in paperwork.

'And this is meant to be a paperless society,' said Isaksson as he rose from his chair.

'It's much the same with the police.' Moberg was on his best behaviour. He even managed a kind of lopsided smile.

Isaksson wasn't as tall as he looked on the television. He had short, greying, ginger hair that was receding at the temples. The nose was long – a feature relished by cartoonists to give their subject a distinctive look – and was accentuated by the thin-rimmed spectacles. The eyes behind the glasses were hard and uncompromising. The intense stare was even unnerving for someone like Moberg, who had met the gazes of murderers, rapists, arsonists and abusers. Despite the pleasant greeting, this man wouldn't pass up a chance to promote himself at someone else's expense. Moberg would have to tread carefully, as he realised that he had taken the inevitable aversion to the politician. It was as Isaksson offered his hand to shake that Moberg tried to gauge whether this man could have run up behind Julia Akerman and knifed her in the back. He wasn't overweight, and the handshake was firm. Yes he could, concluded Moberg as he tried to balance on the flimsy garden chair where Isaksson indicated he should sit.

'Chief Inspector Moberg. I know your name, but from where...' Isaksson made great play of thinking about where he had come across it before.

'The death of Inspector Karl Westermark.'

'Ah, yes!' Moberg knew that Isaksson had the answer all along. 'The detective who shot himself in front of a fellow officer while you listened in from another room.'

'The same.'

'I recall it was Inspector Anita Sundström who was the one who witnessed it all. I hope she has been able to return to duty after such an experience.'

'She's serving again.' Moberg was trying hard not to rise to the taunt. Isaksson had described the whole incident as a "shambles". How could they let a murdering policeman get away with suicide instead of bringing him to justice? The implication was that they had given him a way out.

'Anyhow, how can I help you today, Chief Inspector?' said Isaksson as he picked up a packet of cigarettes from the table. 'I haven't got long. There's a council meeting in an hour.' He took out a cigarette and popped it into his mouth. He flicked a plastic lighter with his right hand, the implication of which was not lost on Moberg. 'Not a nice habit. My only vice. My wife won't let me smoke inside. Good for her.'

'I expect you've read about the murder in Pildammsparken of a woman in her thirties?'

Isaksson blew out a plume of smoke. 'Of course.'

'The woman in question was called Julia Akerman. Does that name mean anything to you?'

'Should it?' This was accompanied by another exhalation of smoke.

'Julia Akerman had a Swedish passport, but she lived in Switzerland.'

'I can tell you now, Moberg, that I have never been to Switzerland.'

'I'm sure you haven't. Akerman was a frequent visitor to Malmö. In fact, she rented an apartment on Kronborgsvägen.' None of this information seemed to be having any effect on Isaksson, who sat impassively smoking opposite him. 'We believe that her real name was Ebba. But it was her profession that is of particular interest.'

'And?' Isaksson was beginning to lose patience.

'She was a prostitute.'

'The newspapers didn't indicate that.'

'We haven't released that information... yet.'

'Look, I know you have a difficult case on your hands, but I have a meeting to go to soon. Can you come to the point? Why are you here?'

'It's delicate. I didn't want to approach you anywhere official.' This was the bit that Moberg was going to enjoy. 'We've been to Switzerland, and we've discovered Akerman's client list. There are two Swedes with Malmö connections on it. Do you know a Markus Asplund?'

'Should I?'

'He runs Malasp Travel. Appears on telly adverts.'

'Now you mention it, I have heard of the company.'

'And the man himself? Have you come across him?'

Isaksson shook his head and took another drag on his cigarette.

Moberg paused, savouring the moment. 'The other name on the list... it's yours.'

For a moment, Isaksson just stared at him.

'Is this what the police have been reduced to?' he barked angrily, throwing his cigarette on the ground. 'Because I hold you publicly accountable, you have to stoop this low to get back at me. Try and besmirch my name, make me look—'

'I'm not making you look anything,' Moberg interrupted angrily. 'I'm just saying your name's on a high-class call girl's client list, and we have to carry out our duty and ask you why. It's my job.'

'This is absolute rubbish. I've never heard of this woman. And I find the suggestion that I would consort with such a person totally offensive.'

'You're religious, aren't you?' Moberg knew he was losing it, but couldn't stop himself.

Isaksson was momentarily taken off guard. 'Of course.'

'Do you like women dressing up as nuns?' The moment it came out, he knew he'd gone too far.

Isaksson exploded. 'You've made a huge mistake crossing me, Moberg. You won't know what's hit you when I've finished with you.'

Isaksson turned his back on him.

'I'll see myself out then. But I'll be back.'

Moberg sat in his car and hit the steering wheel in frustration. Yet again, he had let someone get under his skin. He had blurted out the one piece of information he was intending to keep quiet about – the nun's habit. It was something he could have used against Isaksson at a later date. Now he had blown the advantage and given the politician time to cover his tracks and throw up official obstacles. But at least he hadn't left empty-handed. He fished out the unfinished cigarette that Isaksson had tossed away, and carefully wrapped it in his handkerchief. It wouldn't be admissible in court, but at least they could check if the DNA from the butt matched that from the semen stain. He was hoping that it would.

Hakim had been on the phone all morning. The picture emerging of Markus Asplund fitted in with what they already knew. He was certainly affluent. The travel business *was* lucrative, especially if there was a sizeable number of corporate clients. Several of Sweden's top firms used Malasp Travel. Asplund had travelled to America three times this year alone, and he had been to Geneva once. His background wasn't remarkable. Born in Ystad, his father worked on the ferries and his mother was a medical receptionist. He hadn't gone to university but had worked in the building trade for a few years. When he was twenty-one, he had taken himself off round the world doing odd building jobs to pay his way. That must have kindled his love of globe-trotting because on his return, he joined a travel firm in Malmö. Within five years, he had set up his own office. By this time, he was married and had his first child. Hakim had found a connection of sorts.

He popped his head round Wallen's door. 'Do you know where the chief inspector is?'

'Called in to say he was dropping something off in Lund. Would be back after lunch. Have you got anything?'

'Well, not between Akerman and Asplund as such. But Asplund set up his first travel business from his home. It wasn't Malasp Travel then because he wasn't in Malmö. It was called Adventure Travel. It was aimed at young people who wanted to hitchhike round the world. When that took off, he set up an office in Lund to be near students. Then he graduated to Malmö, and more sophisticated clients and holidays.'

'What's the relevance?'

'Asplund's wife, Ella, comes from Sjöbo. That's where they lived for a couple of years when they were first married, and that's where he set up his first office.'

'And Isaksson's from Sjöbo.'

'Exactly. Both clients of a woman who happens to have one number in her mobile phone – a nursing home just outside Sjöbo. Is Sjöbo the connection we're looking for?'

CHAPTER 26

They stood inside *meditationplatsen*. In the distance, beyond the undulating grassy slope and the scattered clumps of trees, the sea looked serene. Anita had suggested this trip to the summer home of Dag Hammarskjöld because she thought Kevin would be interested. In reality, it was to give her somewhere to sort out the unsettling thoughts which had been running away with her over the last twenty-four hours. The Meditation Place was what Anita needed right now.

It was composed of a low ring of stones with a large boulder in the middle inscribed with the word *PAX*. It was a relatively recent addition to Dag Hammarskjöld's thirty-hectare estate at Backåkra, round the coast from Ystad. She had explained to an interested Kevin that he had been the second Secretary-General of the United Nations in the 1950s. He had bought the farm as a summer residence in 1957. The half-timbered farmhouse up the hill had been turned into a museum after his death, but there was no sign of life in it when they had peered through the windows. Anita took a photo of Kevin standing next to a large bronze of the great man's head and giving a cheeky peace sign with his fingers.

'People come to this ring for weddings and baptisms. And in a week's time, at Midsummer, thousands will gather here. Pity you're going to miss that. It's the biggest day of our year.'

'So what happened to Dag thingy?'

'Hammarskjöld's plane crashed over Africa. Everybody on board was killed. He was flying from Leopoldville to a place in Northern Rhodesia... I can't remember the name. He was trying to negotiate a ceasefire between various rival factions in the Congo. Many believe he was the best Secretary-General ever. John F. Kennedy called him "the greatest statesman of our century".'

Kevin took off his sunglasses and looked quizzically at Anita. 'How come you know so much about him?'

'I did a project on him at school,' she admitted bashfully.

'Now you mention it, it does ring a few bells. How did the plane crash?'

They moved out of the circle as the peace was shattered by a group of talkative middle-aged women brandishing walking poles.

'Surrounded in mystery. Many believe it was deliberately shot down. The first investigation put the crash down to pilot error, but since then, there's been talk of a second plane sighted nearby. Some say that some of the crash victims had bullets in them. There appeared to be lots of inconsistencies.'

'And reasons for shooting his plane down?'

'Complicated. Possibly something to do with commercial interests in a mineral-rich part of the Congo. Katanga, I think it was called. America worried about it falling into Soviet hands. The Belgians and the British were also involved, as well as the UN. There are lots of conspiracy theories.'

'Yeah, I must read up about all this. Sounds just my sort of thing.'

'Something to keep you busy on long winter nights in Penrith.'

They stopped on the brow of the hill, the farmhouse behind them. 'If you're not there to keep me warm, I'll have to do something.' He leant over and gave her a soft kiss on her lips. Any further endearments were interrupted by Anita's mobile phone. Kevin's exaggerated sigh didn't distract her from seeing who the call was from. Eva Thulin.

'I've got to take this.'

Anita seemed pensive when she had finished her call. Kevin knew that Eva Thulin had something to do with forensics and that Anita had phoned her before they set out on their trip to Hammarskjöld's retreat.

'Any luck?' he asked.

'You love a conspiracy theory?'

'Yes.'

'Well, what about this? I've just spoken to Eva, and she said that neither Rylander's nor Klas's bodies were brought to Lund. They should have gone there. They would need autopsies because of the ways they both died.' The strong light glinted off her sunglasses. 'She's double-checked, but they definitely didn't come in.'

'But the bodies will have to appear at some stage for their respective funerals.'

'I'm sure they will, but it would be good to make sure that they were properly examined beforehand.' Anita threw her arms up in the air. 'But the whole thing doesn't make sense. What if Klas was right about being suspicious of Rylander's death? Moa the nurse wasn't convinced either. Then Klas suddenly gets killed. What if that wasn't an accident? What if, as the tyre tracks indicate, he was deliberately driven off the road?'

'Come on, that's difficult to buy. This isn't the Cold War.'

Anita stared at him. 'But it might have something to do with it. Rylander was at the heart of things at the time.' Even to Anita, it was starting to sound outlandish, but she pressed on. 'Klas said that Rylander indicated that it all started and finished in Berlin.'

'I think he said Wilhelmstrasse.'

'But that's in Berlin!' Kevin was being annoyingly pedantic. 'So what happened in Berlin?'

'Well, two things must have happened if it started and finished there.'

'Are you always like this?'

'What do you mean?'

'Quibbling.'

'It's one of my best qualities,' he tried to joke.

'It's not a quality I like.'

'All right, I'm sorry,' Kevin said hurriedly. He needed to placate her before it blew up into their first row. 'Look, I'll tell you what. We've got all Klas's notes back at the house. Maybe we'll find some answers in there.'

Moberg didn't give the team a blow-by-blow account of his unsuccessful meeting with Axel Isaksson. And he didn't inform them about the cigarette butt, which he had handed over to Eva Thulin, who would pass it on for DNA testing. Naturally, he hadn't told her how he had come by it, as he knew she wouldn't have allowed herself to be involved in such a deception. He knew he couldn't do anything with the evidence, but if he could connect Isaksson to Akerman, then he had some ammunition. What he wasn't looking forward to was the expected call from Commissioner Dahlbeck wanting to know why he had visited the politician – he expected Isaksson to use the word "harassment" – and why he had disobeyed specific instructions to leave well alone until there was some firm evidence. He knew he had possibly buggered up any chance of nailing Isaksson. Which is why he was in a foul mood when the team assembled, and he opened the meeting with: 'Give me something fucking positive!' And they did on the Asplund front. The Sjöbo connection sounded encouraging.

'Do we know whether Asplund and Isaksson knew each other?' Moberg asked. 'They'd both be young men then.'

'Asplund was only there for a couple of years, but they might well have come across each other,' chirped up Wallen. Hakim was impressed how assertive she was being on this case; maybe she was emerging from Anita's shadow. 'The population is only around six thousand for the whole municipality. But we haven't anything positive yet.' She took a deep breath. 'But one tack I thought worth taking was to follow up the well-publicised fact that Isaksson is a devout churchgoer.'

'Mmm.' Moberg was about to blast off on an anti-church invective but reined himself in.

'He's an upright member of *Svenska Kyrkan*. So, I thought I'd check out the local Church of Sweden in Sjöbo. He wasn't a member of that congregation, but it turns out that he was attached to a lot called the Church of God's Mission on Earth.'

'Who the fuck are they?'

'It was more of a sect than a church. It was run by a charismatic pastor who'd broken away from the official church because he didn't believe that they were engaging enough with young people and too many were slipping away from the path of righteousness as a result. His church appealed particularly to young families.'

'And is this Mission on Earth outfit still going?'

'No. A number of followers left Sjöbo, and it closed down after a few years because the congregation had dwindled to virtually nothing.'

'And Isaksson was one the church members? Is that any use to us?'

Wallen's face lit up. 'I was thinking back to Julia Akerman's cross and the Bible that Hakim saw by her bedside in Switzerland. She was connected with a church over there. So, as she may well have a link with Sjöbo – the number in her phone points to that – I thought a visit to the pastor might throw up something. He's still alive and living in the town.'

Moberg went over to the crime scene photos of the dead woman. Next to them were photos of the wooden cross and the inscribed page of Akerman's Bible, that Hakim had taken with his mobile phone while in her apartment.

'You think she may have been one of the Mission on Earth worshippers? Did they have an Ebba in their congregation?'

'We should ask the question.'

Before Moberg could speak again, there was a knock on the door and a young secretary slipped into the room.

'What?' Moberg shouted angrily, annoyed that his train of thought had been disturbed. The secretary winced.

'I'm sorry, Chief Inspector. Commissioner Dahlbeck would like to see you.' Her voice was muted.

'Can't you see I'm busy?'

Despite her trepidation, she stood her ground. 'He wants to see you *now*.'

CHAPTER 27

Anita was uncharacteristically nervous. She stood outside the Simrishamn police station, unsure whether to go in. Initially, she had had no intention of doing so, but that was before her visit to the letting agent of the holiday home next to Albin Rylander's. She had gone in to get the name and address of Fanny and Benno. The girl on the desk had been reluctant to give out the information until Anita had flashed her warrant card. That had done the trick, and she had the name – Källström. After further prompting, the girl had produced a Stockholm address and phone number. Anita had gone out into the sunshine on a busy Storgatan and phoned. The elderly lady at the end of the line said that she was called Källström, but she had no idea who Fanny and Benno were. Anita checked the address with her. That was correct; so was the phone number the letting agent had given her. Further questions about whether Fanny and Benno might be a nephew or niece or grandchild were indignantly rebuffed, and when the old woman threatened to call the police about nuisance calls, Anita gave up. As she put her phone away, she was faced with the obvious question – who were the young couple?

To double-check, she went back to the letting agent. Yes, they had paid in advance. It was a fairly late booking, but they had been in the holiday home for three weeks. The woman who picked up the keys matched Kevin's description. And the keys were returned to the office. They had been shoved through the letterbox before any staff had arrived on the Friday morning.

'We were a bit surprised,' the girl remarked.

'Why?'

'Well, the Källströms had booked the house for six weeks. It doesn't worry us because it's all paid for. Maybe they had to go back to Stockholm for some emergency. It just seems a waste of a nice holiday let.'

Anita's mind was now working overtime. 'Can I borrow the keys? Just until tomorrow.' The girl immediately looked worried. 'It's police business,' Anita said firmly. 'You'll have them back before the office closes tomorrow. I'll sign for them.'

'I suppose that's all right,' she said uncertainly.

Alice Zetterberg feigned surprise at seeing Anita enter her office. They surveyed each other like a mongoose and a cobra. The mutual mistrust and loathing was taken as read. Zetterberg didn't offer Anita a seat.

'Are you so bored with your holiday that you have to come and pester us? I assume this isn't a social visit.'

'It's about Albin Rylander's suicide and Klas Lennartsson's death.' There was no point in any preamble.

'Neither of which have anything to do with you.'

'Are you in charge of those cases?'

'I would hardly call them cases. But, yes, I'm overseeing them.'

Anita suddenly felt uncomfortable under Zetterberg's unflinching stare. Why the hell had she come to see this ghastly woman?

'I have some information that might be useful.'

'And what could you possibly have that would be useful to me?'

'Both Lennartsson, and Rylander's nurse, Moa Hellquist, felt there was something not right about the suicide. Rylander's positive state of mind at the time made them sure that he wasn't contemplating killing himself.'

Zetterberg gave a mirthless laugh. 'And that's it? You've been listening to the wrong people. Lennartsson seemed to have his head up his arse most of the time; and the nurse is busy covering herself for neglecting her patient. She should have made sure he wasn't storing away his pills.'

'So why were the bodies not taken to Lund for the autopsies?' Anita snapped back.

Zetterberg scrutinised her old foe. 'You have been a busy little bee. The reason they didn't go to Lund is that they had too big a workload, so they were sent up to Stockholm instead. And *they* found nothing suspicious.'

'You've seen the reports?'

'Yes.'

'What about the tyre marks at Lennartsson's crash scene? The angle of the swerve?'

'I saw nothing wrong with the scene. The man either tried to avoid an animal or just nodded off for a moment and lost control. He'd just come back from Germany, I'm led to believe.'

Anita was about to mention that Klas was returning from Berlin with some important information concerning Rylander; then she thought better of it. Pointless mentioning the Källströms, too.

'Who was the other cop who turned up at Rylander's on the morning his body was found?'

Zetterberg's eyes blazed with fury, but she kept her voice calm. 'Why are you coming to me with this shit? Trying to get your name in the papers again?' she added nastily. 'Either a colleague feels he needs to blow his brains out in front of you, or you're shooting the wrong person. If I were you – and thank God I'm not – I would avoid publicity in the future. Go back to your little holiday with your skinny British boyfriend, and leave the professionals to do their jobs.'

*

Moberg picked up his office phone and dialled an internal number.

'Wallen. I want you and Mirza to go and see Asplund now. Do a DNA swab. If he objects, threaten him with something. Obstruction. Anything. We need to make things happen.'

He slammed the phone down. His meeting with the commissioner hadn't improved his mood one jot. Not only did Dahlbeck want action on this case, but he was tying his hands behind his back because Isaksson was off limits. The politician had made a formal complaint.

'You've got no evidence. And what on earth were you doing going to the bloody man's house? Are you completely stupid?'

'But he's a genuine suspect,' Moberg had protested; he had had difficulty keeping his temper in check.

'He's not now because you barged in there after I expressly told you not to.'

The dressing-down continued for another ten minutes. Moberg left with the commissioner's orders ringing in his ears: 'Asplund sounds like our man. Put pressure on him and get a result.'

Moberg was sure that the politician had a lot to hide. In his opinion, all politicians did. They would have to crack Asplund first, but he would get Axel Isaksson in the end.

Anita was still spitting feathers by the time she reached the cabin and found Kevin at the living room table, surrounded by notes. He had a beer in his hand. By the thunderous look on her face, he didn't think it worth bothering to ask how she had got on.

'That fucking woman!'

'What woman?'

'Alice Zetterberg!'

Kevin put down his bottle and shook his head. 'What on earth did you go and see her for?'

'What do you think?'

Kevin stood up. 'Come and sit down. And calm down. I'll fetch a bottle.'

'Make it a big one.'

He went into the kitchen and picked up a bottle of Shiraz. He made sure that the wine glass was full before handing it over. Anita nodded gratefully and took a huge gulp. She was more composed by the time she had related the tale of her discovery about the non-existent Källströms and then her fruitless approach to Zetterberg.

'What did you think that would achieve?' Kevin asked after she had finished.

'Oh, I don't know. Maybe I thought it would awaken her curiosity if nothing else. But she's too brainless.' By now, she was on her second glass, and Kevin had opened another bottle of Honeybee beer from the local Bohman & Brante Brewery, which he was growing fond of.

'But you didn't give her much to go on.'

Anita's eyes blazed. 'She wouldn't have listened, whatever I said. As far as she's concerned, there isn't anything suspicious in the deaths.'

'You have to find out more before you can go back. You need something concrete. Something like evidence!'

Anita's fierce expression melted. 'Oh, fuck off!' she grinned. 'I'm sorry.' She leant across the table and squeezed his hand.

'I'm afraid you'll have to go through this lot,' Kevin said nodding in the direction of Lennartsson's notes. 'They're all in Swedish. And there are some CDs, too.'

'Forget it. I'll have a look through later.' Her hand was still on Kevin's. 'Thank you.'

'For what?'

'Just being here.'

'I wouldn't want to be anywhere else.'

She gave his hand another squeeze. 'Wouldn't you rather be

in the bedroom?'

'But it's still the afternoon.'

'Does that matter?'

Hakim and Wallen tracked Markus Asplund down just as he was leaving his office in Västra Hamnen. He glanced at his watch in an agitated manner.

'We need another word,' opened Wallen.

'Look, I've got a train to catch.'

'Where to?'

'Gothenburg. I've got a trade event this weekend. I need to get up there tonight to make sure that the stand is ready.'

'Well, you might have to miss it.' Wallen was being firm. Again, Hakim was impressed.

'Can you be quick then?' Asplund said, anxiously glancing around. The wide avenue was nearly empty.

'You lived in Sjöbo some years ago.'

'So? My wife comes from there.'

'You said you didn't know Axel Isaksson other than by reputation. He comes from Sjöbo. Isn't it possible that you came across him?'

'No. It's not a very big place, but I was busy trying to establish a business and raise a family. Besides, we weren't there for that long.' Again, his eyes strayed to his watch. 'Anything else?'

'We need a DNA swab.'

Asplund looked momentarily stunned.

'What if I don't want to cooperate?'

'We can do this down at the polishus. But you'll miss your train.'

'We can give you a lift to the station in our car,' Hakim put in helpfully.

'Why do you want it?'

'To compare it with a DNA sample in Julia Akerman's

apartment,' answered Wallen, who felt there was nothing to be gained by hiding any details. The more he knew what the police knew, the more he was likely to panic and give himself away.

For a second, Hakim thought he saw a flicker of relief in Asplund's eyes.

'OK, but can we please be quick?'

Hakim exchanged a surprised glance with Wallen as they turned towards their car, which was parked just along the pavement. On the way over, they had speculated about how accommodating Asplund would be. They knew that if he refused outright, there would be very little they could do, despite what Moberg had ordered.

By the time they got to the station, Hakim had swabbed Asplund's mouth in the back of the car.

'Can I go now?'

Wallen turned from the driver's seat and smiled. 'Thank you for your cooperation. When will you be back in Malmö?'

'Late Monday. I'll be going home on Sunday first. If that's OK with you,' he added sarcastically.

Asplund climbed out of the back of the car. He looked thankful to be able to get away.

'Oh, by the way,' Hakim suddenly said. 'When you lived in Sjöbo, did you hear anything about the Church of God's Mission on Earth?'

'No,' he said in exasperation. 'I'm not religious. Not my thing.'

They watched him as he hurried off through the doors of the expensively refurbished station.

'We'd better get his DNA off to Eva Thulin to keep the chief inspector happy,' Wallen said as she manoeuvred the car into the traffic. 'Do you think it'll match what we found at Akerman's?'

Through the glass wall he could see Asplund disappear down the escalator. 'I wouldn't bet on it.'

CHAPTER 28

Kevin woke to find that Anita wasn't in bed beside him. After their afternoon lovemaking, he had gone down to the beach for a swim, followed by a leisurely supper of fried chicken pieces with salad. Kevin was amused at Anita's supposed indifference to Klas Lennartsson's research material, which she had cleared away for the meal. He knew she was itching to have a look at it. So, he wasn't surprised when he found her in the kitchen poring over Lennartsson's notebooks at two in the morning.

'You were snoring, so I thought I'd get up.'

'Cheeky bugger! I don't snore.'

Anita gave him a tired grin. 'That shows how long it's been since you shared your bed with someone.'

Kevin slumped down in a chair opposite her.

'Well, we're both awake now. Cuppa?'

'Coffee for me.'

'Blimey, you'll never get to sleep. It'll have to be instant.'

He filled the kettle up and flicked it on. With a big yawn, he turned and watched Anita, in a blue T-shirt and black knickers, intently sifting through the paperwork that covered one man's extraordinary life. Yet the most extraordinary piece was missing. Would they ever find it?

She didn't acknowledge him when he placed the mug of black coffee next to her. She was so absorbed that he took his cup of tea outside with him. He'd slipped on a jersey and shorts. He shivered as he stood on the porch. Despite the heat of the day, it was nippy at that unearthly hour of the morning. He sipped the warm liquid greedily. The lack of urban illumination meant that the myriad stars had free rein in the night sky. It was as though they had scooped up all the light from the earth and scattered it randomly about the universe. In the stillness, he could hear the sea lapping the shoreline below. He might be falling in love with Anita, but he was definitely falling in love with Sweden. Was it always like this? At that very moment, he felt he could chuck it all in back in Britain and come and live here. Then again, this was only a holiday, despite Anita trying to turn it into an investigation. And it was notoriously easy to be seduced into thinking of moving abroad after a great experience. Grass always greener. He remembered that he and Leanne had thought of buying a small place in Spain after a surprisingly argument-free fortnight in the sun. But he knew deep down that he could never be too far from his girls – and Anita might not be too happy to have him hanging around on her doorstep. Any remotely profound thoughts always left him gasping for a cigarette. Best not. He didn't want to go back to bed with Anita, smelling of smoke. Not very romantic. Not that he was sure that she would be going back to bed anyway. He finished his tea and went inside.

To his surprise, Anita was dressed. She had a bunch of keys in her hand.

'Where are you going?'

'To the Källströms' house.'

'At this time of night! Can't we do it in the morning?'

'They're mixed up in this. I don't know how or why, but they were here for a reason, and I suspect it wasn't to soak up the sun.'

She went into the kitchen and rummaged around for a torch.

'Is this really necessary?'

'Do you want to come or not?'

Kevin sighed. No chance of getting her back into bed while she was in this resolute mood. It was a side of her that he hadn't come across before. He rather liked it.

'Just let me get some trousers on. It's cold out there.'

Ten minutes later, they were making their way across the damp grass in front of Rylander's house, and beyond to the third property. Like their cabin, it was all on one floor. From this side of the buildings, the only noise was the soft pad of their footsteps; the sound of the sea being blocked out.

'I feel like a burglar.' Kevin found himself whispering.

Anita ignored him as she carefully slotted one of the keys into the Yale lock by the light of her torch. They stepped inside. They found themselves in a small hallway with a row of hooks for coats and an empty rack for shoes. Anita found a switch. The hallway opened out into a corridor. Further switches were flicked on to reveal a kitchen at one end and a large wet room at the other. Across the corridor from the hallway was an open door, through which a large space loomed. Once she had turned on the light, Anita's immediate impression was of a very well-appointed living room. The furniture was stylish in a deliberately rustic way. At the far end, large picture windows overlooked the sea. Off the living room were two bedrooms. By now, the house was ablaze with light.

'Nice place. But what are we looking for?' Kevin asked.

Good question. Anita wasn't entirely sure why she had rushed over here. Her famously unreliable female intuition? More on an impulse really. She had suddenly remembered the keys she had borrowed from the letting agent in the middle of reading Klas's notes, a lot of which were transcriptions of the CDs that Klas had used for his interviews. She could see that Rylander had had a fascinating career with spells around the world, particularly in London, Washington and East Berlin. He had some scurrilous things to say about certain ex-colleagues and leading political figures whom he'd come across in the course of his long diplomatic career. As he would be dead by the time the book was supposed to come out, no one would be able to sue him, and many of the people he referred to were also dead anyway. But the references in themselves would certainly get the press excited. She had also found Rylander's father's incredible story about saving Lenin's life. Was it really true? Rylander was convinced. Had that turned the son, like his horrified father, against Communism for the rest of his life? But none of that explained why she was standing in the middle of the Källströms' living room with her new lover at three in the morning. The sun would be coming up soon.

'I have no idea.'

'That's a good start.'

'You're a policeman. You should be used to having no idea what you're looking for. I don't know. Could they have left something to give us a clue as to why they were here?'

Kevin wandered over to a small bookcase, which only housed about a dozen paperbacks.

'Won't they have had a cleaner in by now? They went a week ago.'

'Not necessarily. They'd booked six weeks. The cleaners might not come until the next occupants are due to arrive.'

Kevin ran a finger along the top of the bookcase. 'Looks pretty clean to me.' He shrugged. 'Well, we've nothing to lose.'

Anita left Kevin to scrutinise the living room while she went into the bedrooms. One had a double bed, while the other had two singles. All the beds were neatly made. The fitted wardrobes yielded nothing except empty hangers. Nothing in the drawers. Maybe the cleaners had been in. Before leaving, she pulled back the duvet on the double bed. The bottom sheet was neatly tucked in, but she could tell by the small creases that it had been slept in. So, no cleaners after all. This made her go back and re-examine the room with the twin beds. She did the same with the duvet on the first bed. This definitely hadn't been slept in. It made sense that a couple would use the double bed. But when she idly whisked back the duvet covering the second single, someone had definitely been in there.

'Kevin!' she called. He came into the bedroom.

'Did you say that the woman, Fanny, indicated they were a married couple?'

'She referred to him as her husband. Something like: "my husband works in IT".' Anita pointed to the sheet. 'Well, it doesn't look as though they shared a bed. This and the double bed have both been slept in.'

'Maybe he snores!'

'Mmm.'

They both went back into the living room. Kevin flopped down on the sofa.

'This is more comfortable than yours.'

'You can move in here if you want. It's been paid for.'

Kevin yawned widely.

Anita strolled over to the window. The first streaks of morning light were appearing in the distance. The spell of good weather appeared to be continuing.

'If Fanny and Benno weren't wife and husband, and had separate rooms, what were they doing here? And why did they suddenly cut their supposed holiday short? Right on the morning after Rylander killed himself – or not, as the case may be?'

'She said that they had to get back to work. Perhaps that was just an excuse. Maybe they had a falling out. Couples do. Leanne was forever shutting me out of her bedroom. Or shutting herself in other men's bedrooms,' he added bitterly.

'I know what you're saying. But don't you think the timing's odd? They obviously aren't who they say they are. They gave someone else's address when they booked this house.'

'Maybe they're married to other people. This was an illicit hideaway.'

Anita gave him another of those withering looks he was starting to get used to. 'You're not helping.' She came over and sat next to him. 'That figure you saw outside watching Rylander's. Could you describe him?'

'No. Too dark.'

'But was the figure small, medium or large? Fat or thin?'

'I'm not sure. Well, I suppose he was large. Otherwise, I might not have noticed him. But it was all shadows.'

'Large,' Anita muttered to herself. 'Large.' She suddenly put a hand on his knee. 'Was he bald? Totally bald?'

He thought for a moment. 'Could have been. Actually, come to think of it, the moonlight caught him for a moment on the second occasion. Yes.' Now even Kevin sounded excited.

'Moa the nurse said that the policeman with Zetterberg was large and bald. The one who didn't say anything. And Zetterberg didn't answer my question when I asked her about him. Who's the mysterious herr Large?'

'I thought you said he had no hair.'

'Very funny. Mr Large, then.'

Kevin sat up. 'What if Mr Large wasn't watching Rylander's place, but this one? Where I saw the figure in the trees, he could easily have seen over here. Especially with these picture windows. Maybe that's what drove the Källströms away. He might have been a private investigator.'

'Trust you to complicate matters!'

Kevin sniggered. 'It's only a theory. Now I've got one too!'

Anita raised her hand quickly and slapped him playfully on his knee. 'It's not a competition.'

Kevin pretended to be hurt, but he couldn't keep it up and dissolved into laughter.

'Can we go to bed now?'

'Wait!'

'What?'

'Was that a car coming along the track?'

They both sat listening. It definitely was. The crunch of tyres on rough gravel. A car door opened and shut.

'Lights,' Kevin whispered.

'Bit late for that.'

They both stood up. Through the open door to the corridor and hallway, they could hear footsteps outside. Then someone tried the front door. It opened.

CHAPTER 29

Two uniformed police officers entered the house. Anita didn't recognise them. The shorter one had the flap undone on his gun holster in readiness for use. He was the one who spoke.

'What are you doing here?' The question was dripping in aggression.

Anita had to take charge of the situation, as Kevin had no idea what the policeman had said, though he got the gist.

'I'm Anita Sundström. I'm holidaying in the house at the end of this row.'

'That doesn't answer my question. This house is meant to be unoccupied.'

Were they a passing highway patrol?

'My friend here,' Anita said, indicating Kevin, 'thought he heard someone trying to break in, so we came to investigate.'

'What did you hear?' the officer said, turning to Kevin, who stared blankly back.

'Kevin's from England. He doesn't speak Swedish.' She stared straight at Kevin and said in English. 'These boys want to know what you heard.' Kevin frowned. 'The sounds you heard from *over here*. That's why you woke me and we came to investigate.' Fortunately, she could see that he was cottoning on.

'Yes... yes, that's right. I thought it might have been glass breaking. So I woke Anita up, and she said we'd better take a shufti.'

Torquil MacLeod

'What is a shoofty?' the policeman said in English with some puzzlement.

'Sorry. Have a look. But, as you see, nothing.'

'And how did you hear these sounds when there is another house in the way?'

'Ah, I was outside having a smoke.'

'Did you see anyone?'

'Afraid not.'

The bigger policeman muttered something to his colleague.

'How did you have a key?' asked the shorter one. This was in Swedish and aimed at Anita.

'When I knew that this was empty, I went to the letting agent in Simrishamn. I wanted to have a look around.' She gave a little laugh. 'It's nicer than mine. Thought I might swap. You can ask them.'

This seemed to placate the officers.

'OK. We'll have a look round and make sure there hasn't been a break in. You can go.'

Anita raised her eyebrows to Kevin and nodded towards the door. He didn't know what had been said.

'Oh, Inspector, I might as well take the keys back to the agents.' The accompanying smile wasn't warm. 'It'll save you a trip.'

Dawn was breaking as they made their way back towards their house. Ribbons of golden light were replacing the stars.

'That was interesting,' ventured Kevin.

'Wait till we get back,' Anita said quietly.

When they got home, Anita made her way into the kitchen and filled up the kettle. Kevin disappeared into the bathroom. She could hear him peeing loudly. Why did he never shut the bathroom door? Or put the toilet seat down? He'd been living on his own too long.

By the time he returned, she had made them both a cup of

tea. They sat at the kitchen table.

'You covered up well,' she said with a thin smile.

'There wasn't much else I could do. And we couldn't exactly have told them the real reason we were in there. They'd think we were barmy.'

Anita raised her cup and sipped her tea thoughtfully.

'Didn't it strike you as odd?'

Kevin shrugged. 'Not really. We'd do the same back in Britain if something looked suspicious.'

'But how did they know someone was in the house?'

'All the lights were on.'

'What's to stop somebody putting all the lights on when they're at home? It's no one else's business.'

'It was three in the morning. Not many people are likely to do that.'

'But burglars aren't likely to light up a house like a Christmas tree, that they're trying to rob.'

She took a further sip and then put the cup down firmly on the plastic table top.

'At first, I thought they must have been a passing patrol. But because of the apple orchard, you can't see that house from the main road.'

'Someone else reported it,' Kevin suggested.

'Who? No one else lives round here. We're the only ones.' Then she wagged her finger back and forth. 'They also knew the house was meant to be empty. How? Holiday lets that finish early aren't exactly the sort of thing the local police are informed about; they've got enough on their plate. Besides, the letting agent wasn't fussed, as they'd already been paid.'

'All right, I admit that it's a bit strange.'

'So, how did they know we were there?'

All Kevin could offer was a shrug.

'More to the point, how did they know who I was?'

'What do you mean?'

Now Anita was looking out of the kitchen door as though she was concentrating on some object in the living room.

'When he asked me for the keys to take back to Simrishamn, he called me "Inspector".'

CHAPTER 30

The drive to Sjöbo took forty-five minutes. Wallen had reluctantly agreed to let Brodd drive. He had insisted, as he said he knew the small town reasonably well. She had only been there on a couple of occasions as far as she could recollect. She didn't mind giving up her Saturday to work on the case, but why did she have to share it with Pontus Brodd? She had summoned up the courage to question Moberg's decision. Instead of shouting at her, he had explained that sending a Muslim detective to interview a Christian pastor in a town known for its anti-immigrant stance might not be a good idea. Anita would probably have said bollocks to that and taken Hakim with her, but Klara could see where the chief inspector was coming from. So, it was Brodd she was stuck with, but she had made it clear that she would do the talking and he could take notes.

Sjöbo sits in the middle of Skåne, virtually halfway between Malmö and Simrishamn. It grew in size after it became a halt on the train line between the two. Though the train has long gone, it is now the meeting point of roads that cross the region from east to west and south to north. Wallen remembered it was a dull town with few interesting buildings except round the central square. Sjöbo's most incongruous feature was a large, old, Dutch-style windmill that now sits in the middle of a housing estate. From what she could remember, it was derelict.

They entered on the road from the west. Instead of heading

straight into the centre of the town, Brodd turned the car off to the left and they found themselves on a wide, straight road fringed by anonymous houses. Further along Planteringsgatan he took another left. He came to a stop in front of a modest single-storey house with a neat garden. The home of Pastor Elias Kroon was as unremarkable as those they had already passed.

The pastor didn't seem to want to let them in until Wallen explained that they were the police. He may have been a charismatic preacher in his day, but this was a remote and suspicious man. Probably in his mid to late sixties, he was nearly bald with, to Wallen's mind, off-putting staring eyes. His nose was angular, his lips thick; and his stubbly chin indicated that he hadn't shaved for a couple of days. Medium height, he was still a fit man, as evidenced by the bicycle she could see through the window, propped up in the back yard. He had reluctantly shown them into a very sparse living room, totally devoid of anything on the walls except for a wooden cross above a crammed bookcase. Wallen immediately noticed there wasn't a television. There was a wireless; it certainly wasn't modern enough to qualify as being described as a radio. A Bible was open on a table near the hearth. She couldn't remember the last time she had seen a fireplace that looked as though it was actually used. There was a musty whiff about the house as though, even in the warm summer they were having, light and air never really penetrated the rooms. And to be honest, she wasn't entirely sure whether the pastor had washed recently. Personal hygiene didn't seem to be a priority.

They all stood around awkwardly, as Kroon didn't offer them a seat. Wallen heard Brodd mutter 'Not very Christian.' behind her.

'We're here because we're investigating the murder of a woman in Malmö early last week.'

Kroon didn't speak. Wallen found his intense gaze disconcerting. She ploughed on.

'This woman was called Julia Akerman. Does that name mean anything to you, Pastor?'

'No.' The voice was deep and rumbling.

'We think she may have a connection with Sjöbo. We know that there is some link with Axel Isaksson, the politician. I believe he was a member of your church.'

'He was. An important member. He was a believer.'

'Do you mind if we sit down?' said Brodd, who was finding it difficult to write his notes while standing up.

Kroon nodded. Both Brodd and Wallen sat down on an old, worn, uncomfortable sofa. Wallen was wondering if they had done the right thing – the sofa, too, had an unpleasant smell – and she shifted uneasily before putting her next question to Kroon, who remained standing.

'If he was such an important member, why did he leave your church?' To Wallen's annoyance, this had come from Brodd.

'His political career took him to Malmö.'

'So why isn't your church operating now?'

The pastor's piercing eyes twitched as though Brodd had stumbled across a topic that pained him.

'We live in an ungodly world. Fewer people want to hear the Lord's word and live by his teachings. This is particularly so of the young, whom I did my best to help. But the foreigners that have invaded our land have brought evil beliefs with them and are undermining our society.' Wallen thought she could be listening to one of Isaksson's speeches. 'Our numbers dwindled and it was no longer financially viable to keep the church running. I still hold prayer meetings here for those who wish to attend.'

Looking around, Wallen thought few would want to venture into this uninviting room.

'When did the church close?' Again this was Brodd.

'I believe in millennialism.'

Brodd stifled a laugh. 'What's that? The end of the world?'

Kroon gave him a pitying look. 'No, not Armageddon; a

new beginning. We are now in the penultimate age… the age when the final battle with Satan is being fought out.' His eyes began to blaze, his voice became animated; his features bursting into life in front of them. He seemed to grow in stature. This was the tub-thumping preacher of the past, the passionate persuader. 'Look at the Middle East today. Iraq and Syria. Look at the ghettos of Stockholm and Malmö full of immigrants. That's where we must root out Satan from our midst. Defeating the devil is God's mission on earth. When we win, we will see a New Earth in God's kingdom.' Then he produced an unexpected smile. 'So you see, my "church" will never close. But the building closed its doors in 2001.'

Wallen was glad that Hakim wasn't present to hear Kroon's invective. And they didn't seem to be getting anywhere, so she jumped in before Brodd came up with yet another irrelevant question or remark.

'We think Julia Akerman may well have some connection with Sjöbo. In fact, we think her real name was Ebba. We don't know the surname. Did you have an Ebba amongst your congregation?'

'We had two.'

'Yes?'

'Ebba Persson and Ebba Pozorski.'

This was promising. Even Brodd was paying attention.

'Our Ebba was in her mid-thirties. Born, we think, in 1979.'

'Ah, that wouldn't be Ebba Persson; she's in her seventies. It could be Ebba Pozorski.' At last, he sat down on a high-backed wooden chair, no longer wary of their presence.

'How do you spell that?' asked Brodd. 'Doesn't sound Swedish.'

Kroon slowly spelt the name out for him. 'She had a Polish father. Boleslaw.'

'I've heard or seen that name somewhere,' pondered Brodd out loud.

'Can you tell us about Ebba Pozorski? Her family? What happened to her?'

Kroon's eyes seemed to be drawn to the cross on the wall when he eventually spoke. 'Ebba's mother was Swedish, or to be exact, first generation Swedish of Polish extraction. Elzbieta, as she was called, returned to Poland from time to time to visit her relations. I'm not sure where.' He paused. 'Actually, it was somewhere that used to be in Germany but became Polish after the war...'

'Wroclaw? It used be Breslau.' Wallen found herself being amazed that Brodd would know such a thing.

'Yes, it was Wroclaw. It was on such a visit that Elzbieta met Boleslaw. He was older than her, but they became attached to one another. They married over there, and Ebba was born in Wroclaw. She must only have been an infant when they came to Sjöbo to live. They thought that Sweden would offer them a better way of life than in communist Poland.' Kroon's face darkened. 'It was sad. Ebba was such a pretty girl. Very devout.'

'She was wearing a cross when we found her,' Wallen said.

'Is that right?'

'Yes.'

He nodded his head slowly. 'I am pleased. She must have retained some of her faith.'

'Why do you say that?'

Kroon leant over and picked up the Bible, and cradled it as he talked.

'The Pozorski family joined my church in the early days. It wasn't easy for Boleslaw in a town like this, but we embraced him and his family.'

'If you don't mind me saying so, it sounds as though you don't care too much for immigrants,' Brodd said unhelpfully.

Kroon held the Bible up. 'Those who follow the true path will always be welcome.'

'Fine. Can we hear about the Pozorskis, please?' said Wallen impatiently. This was a real breakthrough, and she wanted to make sure they got as much information out of Kroon as possible.

'They were fully involved in the church and our activities. Little Ebba had let God into her heart, and the Lord's beauty shone out of her. But then, when the child must have been about twelve or thirteen, Elzbieta died. Boleslaw found it difficult to cope. He turned to drink. He lost his job. And he lost control of Ebba. She became what you might call wild. She came under a malign influence within my own church. I will never forgive myself for being blind to the perverted designs of one of my own flock until it was too late. Ebba had turned to the path of sin and depravity.'

'She became a prostitute,' said Brodd as he looked up from his note scribbling.

'It is awful to say, but I'm not surprised. She succumbed to the evils of the flesh. I fear damnation awaits her.'

'Sorry, can I get this straight?' Wallen said. 'Are you saying there was a particular individual who corrupted her?'

'Oh, yes. He was sent packing. But by then, it was too late to save Ebba. She left Sjöbo and, so I was told later, went to Malmö. I never saw her again. Poor Boleslaw. His mind started to go. He has Alzheimer's now.'

'That's it!' exclaimed Brodd. 'I knew I'd seen the name. He's on the list of the nursing home. Boleslaw Pozorski.' He said the name with such vehemence you would have thought he'd solved the case.

'Pastor, who was the malign influence? Was it Axel Isaksson?'

Kroon looked appalled. 'Of course not. It was a man called Markus Asplund.'

CHAPTER 31

Jazmin wandered through the malls of Mobilia, which had now become an excellent shopping centre. It had most of the stores you'd find in the centre of Malmö. She had spent some time in Indiska. She loved the clothes there, but she couldn't afford any at the moment. Next door, she browsed in Akademibokhandeln. She couldn't believe how many cookbooks there were. Sweden must have the highest percentage of published chefs per head of population in the whole of Europe. She spent most of her time glancing through the shelves of feminist literature; she was hoping that the Feminist Initiative under Gudrun Schyman would at last gain a few seats in the upcoming September general election. She smiled to herself as she thought of how supportive Lasse was trying to be; more out of trying to please her than any conviction on his part. His politics were far from radical, but she was working on him. Sweden must change and adapt, and she wanted to be part of that process.

After buying a book which she knew was an indulgence, as she and Lasse had little money, she compounded her guilt by having a fika at Espresso House. She took out the mobile Lasse had bought her and sent him a text to say that she would be home by lunchtime. Despite the café area being full of Saturday morning shoppers – she even had to move over to let a woman into the seat next to her – she was soon engrossed in her new book. She lost track of time, and suddenly realised she had been there longer than she had planned. In a panic, she quickly gathered up her bag and shoved the book inside. But something was wrong. She stared at the Formica-topped table. Where was her mobile? She bent down and looked on the floor. It wasn't there. She then scrabbled inside her bag and emptied the contents out onto the table, knocking her cup and saucer onto the floor in the process. The cup broke.

'Oh, shit!'

She was now totally fazed. As she attempted to clear up the pieces of crockery, all she could think about was how cross Lasse would be.

Why had she let Brodd persuade her to have lunch at the Gästgifvaregård? He wasn't her idea of a dining companion. The ornate, baroque building was in Sjöbo's central square. Brodd had said that the food was really good and inexpensive. She had to admit that she was now hungry, as she had skipped breakfast. The surroundings were faded plush. The high wooden doors, long windows, wainscots, plinths and urns gave it a somewhat over-the-top old-world feel. Wallen didn't much like it; she favoured modern eating places. They wandered through a number of dining rooms until Brodd found one with an empty table that satisfied him. On Brodd's recommendation, they both ordered *bruna bönor med stekt flask*. She preferred more imaginative dishes than this basic fare, but it would fill a gap. When the pork and beans arrived, she found herself tucking in. She had to admit it was really tasty.

'What did you make of Pastor Kroon?' Wallen asked when there was an interval in Brodd's munching.

'Something weird about him. Funny sod.'

'A useful one, though.' Brodd nodded at her as he shoved another forkful of meat into his mouth. 'At least we now know who Ebba really is. And we've got some good background. No wonder we couldn't find any trace of her birth if she was born in Wroclaw. But we should be able to find out more about her past now. I'll give Hakim a call before we leave so he can get some digging done. One thing's clear, the passport's definitely false.'

'Not necessarily,' Brodd said in between some complex chewing. 'Someone might have fixed up a real one for her with the false name. Asplund could possibly have done that. He has travel contacts.'

'She'd probably need more than tourist contacts to organise something as complex as that.' Wallen put down her fork. She couldn't believe she had cleared her plate so quickly. Brodd was still eating, but he'd put a mountain of the free salad on first. 'Fancy Asplund's name coming up like that! That's the link to Isaksson we wanted. Interesting that both Asplund and Isaksson denied knowing each other.'

'Isaksson probably doesn't want to be associated with Asplund if he's such a degenerate. Anyway, if you ask me,' said Brodd, wiping his mouth, 'we've got our man.'

'Certainly everything points to Asplund. He must now be our prime suspect. Carries on with the young Ebba. Corrupts her, according to Kroon. They both end up in Malmö. Then we know they're connected through her "business". He probably met her the day she was killed. Now we have his DNA, we can match it up with that from the semen in her body.'

'Do you mind! I'm still eating.'

'Wouldn't have thought that would put *you* off your food.' She pushed her plate into the middle of the table. 'The only thing we don't know is why Asplund would actually want to kill her. What's the motive?'

'Maybe he was jealous of someone? Didn't like what she did?'

'Possibly.' Is that where Isaksson comes in? Wallen wondered. She could see that Brodd was losing interest. He suddenly smiled at her.

'Talking of jealousy, I think the chief inspector is jealous of me.'

'Pardon?'

'I haven't been able to go drinking with him lately.' He followed this statement up with a confidential wink. 'And I've got another date tonight.'

Wallen suppressed a smirk. 'A date?'

'Yes. Second one. She's a bit of all right.'

'Is she myopic?'

He looked quizzical, then: 'Oh, very funny.' He pulled out a toothpick and began to de-meat his teeth. When he'd finished, he brandished the toothpick. 'I'm a bit of a catch, actually.' Wallen began to conjure up an image of some very plain woman with bad skin and thick glasses. 'She's blonde.'

'A lot of Swedes are!' Wallen was always piqued that she wasn't fair- haired like so many of her contemporaries. It was the blonde Anitas of this world who seemed to attract the men.

'Nora. That's her name. Do you know, I think she's into policemen. Some people think being a cop is sexy.'

'Really,' Wallen murmured sceptically.

'Oh, yes. She's very interested in what I do.'

'Lucky you.' Her various partners had never shown the slightest interest in her career. 'Anyhow, I think we've been here long enough. While we're in Sjöbo, I want to go and visit the nursing home where Boleslaw Pozorski is.'

Brodd pulled a long face. 'I've already been there. Besides, we'll get nothing out of the dad if he's got Alzheimer's.'

'But now we know his daughter's name, we can find out when she last saw her father. She might have been there during her final visit to Sweden.'

Brodd put away his toothpick. 'Can I have a pudding first?'

'No!'

Moberg was coming out of China Box laden with a variety of oriental fare. This would keep him going until his supper. He had started off towards the polishus when his mobile phone went off. It took some ingenuity to retrieve it from his pocket without dropping his food.

'Yes!' he bellowed into the phone.

'Eva Thulin here.'

Moberg's tone changed immediately. 'Hi there. Have you anything for me?'

'Nothing back from Asplund's DNA sample yet. Should get that on Monday. But news on Isaksson.' Moberg could feel a surge of excitement. 'He made love to your victim while she was in Malmö. I'm surprised we found anything as I assumed she'd have protected sex.'

'Not necessarily. She knew all about her clients, remember. Not any riff-raff off the streets. Probably explains her extortionate charges, too.'

'One other thing: it's Isaksson's semen on the nun's habit.' When she didn't get a reply, 'Did you hear me, Chief Inspector?'

'Oh, I heard you all right, Eva. Many thanks. Enjoy the rest of what's left of the weekend.'

'That's if I ever get finished here,' he heard her start to moan, but by then, he was switching off the call. He stood in the middle of the pavement, and a huge grin slowly spread across his face.

CHAPTER 32

Kevin had gone out for a long walk along the coast and left Anita to carry on going through Klas Lennartsson's research material. She had already started making her own notes as though she were working on an actual case. The events of the early hours of the morning were playing on her mind. Too many things weren't right. But there wasn't any evidence – real evidence that she had access to – that there had been any foul play in either Rylander's suicide or Klas Lennartsson's crash. Yet there were too many things that she couldn't explain. The call to a harassed Eva Thulin hadn't helped. She was in the middle of chasing up DNA results for an investigation that the team were working on. But she did confirm that Lund should have been able to handle the Rylander and Lennartsson autopsies if they had come in. Zetterberg had lied about that. So why had the bodies been taken to Stockholm?

She returned to Rylander's career. Germany seemed to be the key, according to Klas. He had worked at the Swedish embassy on Otto-Grotewohl-Strasse in the Berlin of the German Democratic Republic. Rylander was in Berlin for two years between 1974 and 1976, shortly after the GDR had at last been recognised by many Western states, including America. Immediately before that, Rylander had been in Bonn, so he must have been a bit of a German expert. He would have been in his mid-forties by the time he pitched up in East Berlin. Ten years before that, he had been in London, as well as having spells in Algiers, Amman and Buenos Aires. Back to London after Berlin, and eventually the big one – Washington. A very successful man. So, if he had been murdered, as Klas clearly thought, where along the line did he upset someone enough that they wanted him dead? The motive must have been the imminent appearance of his posthumous memoires. Who would they affect? Who would want them suppressed? There had been a few indiscretions along the way, but surely none bad enough for someone to set up the elaborate death of an already dying man. The trouble was that no one that she knew would be able to provide the answer that Klas had discovered in Berlin. Who was it he'd gone to see? This led to further scrutiny of Klas's notes to discover a name. She couldn't find anything. Klas didn't appear to have written down the information.

Anita left a note for Kevin to say that she was popping into Simrishamn. She decided to listen to the CD of Klas's last interview, dated a couple of days before Rylander's death, in the car. She packed away the notes along with all the CDs into the box file and threw it onto the passenger seat. She had already listened to sections of the conversations between Klas and Rylander. The old man was a good raconteur and had a fund of interesting stories and wise observations on world events of the 1970s and 1980s. But she could tell that near the end of each session Rylander's voice began to break up; his flow distorted as tiredness got the better of him. Again, doubts crept back; maybe he really had got fed up with life and just wanted a swift conclusion. She put the CD into the player as she drove, and heard Rylander talking about his life after retirement and the many conferences he was asked to attend, committees he had sat on and TV interviews he had given.

Anita drove to the far side of Simrishamn and called into the house of Klas's cousin, Ida Svensson. After a sympathetic chat, she managed to get the keys to Klas's house. Anita knew that most Swedes don't entrust their keys to neighbours, but to family members, however far away they may live.

Ten minutes later, she had parked on Stenbocksgatan and opened Klas's front door. It was always a strange feeling going into the home of someone who had recently died, but it had been part of her job for over twenty years. There was always an element of sadness, especially if the death had been tragic or unexpected. The ghosts of the past, both good and bad, still lingered. This, of course, was particularly poignant, as Klas had been a person she had known and liked.

Her first port of call was his study. It was a temple to Scanian history: shelves of books and box files, and old newspapers stacked in piles on the floor. Photographs of local landmarks haphazardly covered the walls. The room was an organised mess, much like Klas himself. The mahogany, rectangular desk with a green leather inset was as neat as Klas was ever going to get; everything in its dusty and disordered place. As she sat down in the hard wooden chair behind it, she had a strange feeling that someone had been there before her. It was the round-based lamp on the desktop that caught her eye. It had been moved – the telltale crescent of dust-free surface gave it away. She opened the desk drawers. They were crammed with what, to Anita's untutored eye, looked like junk. In one, she found an old school year book. She flicked through it, and there was Klas beaming awkwardly out of the page alongside headshots of his classmates. It must have been his final year. A few pages on she found her own photo. She would be coming up for sixteen. Heavens, she had forgotten how long her hair had been then. The face staring out was of a bright-eyed innocent with the happy expression of one who was looking forward to whatever life had in store. Had that young girl really turned into the distrustful old bitch she often felt like these days? Wasn't that the reason why she was sitting here right now? Had what she'd experienced in her police career – and a less than successful domestic life – really made her so cynical and unable to think the best of people? What would she tell her sixteen-year-old self? Don't go near a police station, for starters. And secondly, if you see any handsome academics, run a mile!

She replaced the year book. She got up and inspected the rest of the study. She could now see that some of the book shelves had been disturbed – the scuffed dust marks again looking suspicious. A night-time intruder wouldn't have noticed. Then she went round the rest of the rooms. It had been a lovely house until Klas had taken it over and neglected it. He hadn't the money or the time. He was not a man who had the practical skills to mend or repair his home. Anita suspected that changing a light bulb would have been a major challenge. Klas was a man who had lived in the past and not in the present. And was it Albin Rylander's past that had resulted in his death? By the time Anita had returned to the study, she was convinced that someone had been in the house. Not burglars who were taking advantage of an empty building, but somebody searching for something who didn't want anyone to know they had been there; trying to cover their tracks. Were they searching for Klas's Rylander research material? It was a disquieting thought.

Half an hour after her arrival, she was ready to leave. She had already phoned Stefan at the police station from Klas's study. Luckily, he was on duty. She asked about whether there had been any official written report on the patrolmen's visit to the holiday home in the early hours of the morning. He couldn't find anything. In fact, he was surprised any patrol was in the vicinity and at that time. 'They didn't come out from here. Maybe they were from Ystad.'

It was a thoughtful Anita who locked up the house. Already a plan was forming in her head.

'I hope you've got a good explanation for being in a dead man's home?'

Anita swung round guiltily and saw the menacing figure of Alice Zetterberg hovering on the edge of the pavement.

Holding up the keys, Anita said: 'I got these from Ida Svensson, Klas's cousin.'

'Doesn't answer my question,' Zetterberg snapped back.

'That's all you're going to get. You can't arrest me for breaking and entering because I've had Ida's permission.'

The glare in Zetterberg's eyes was almost manic. For a moment she didn't respond. Then, at last, she spoke very slowly.

'I don't know what you're playing at, but I'm warning you to keep your nose out of business that's not yours.'

Anita smiled sweetly. 'I wouldn't do anything to upset an old friend like you, Alice.'

Zetterberg flushed with fury, and she angrily wagged her finger in Anita's face.

'You're heading for a big fall, Sundström.' Without another word, she stalked back up the road towards the police station.

Anita returned the house key and drove back to the cabin. On the way she continued to listen to Rylander. She could hear the sea in the background, so he and Klas must have been sitting outside. He was describing life in East Berlin and how few people would talk to him, as they were afraid that the Stasi would be listening in – or that anything they said to a westerner would be reported back to the authorities by an army of informers. But he said he was amazed at what the GDR was doing in terms of reconstruction.

'*You must go to Berlin, Klas.*'

'*I would love to.*'

'*Quite a place. Quite a history. I remember the first time I walked down Karl-Marx-Allee. I was staggered. This wasn't the East Germany of western imagination, or that portrayed by the western press. It is an extraordinary boulevard, about ninety metres wide, over two kilometres long, stretching from Frankfurter Tor right up to Alexanderplatz. Had it been built in the 1920s, the architectural snoberati – I'm sure there's no such word, but you know what I mean – would have raved about it. In retrospect, it's now viewed favourably by the postmodernists. It was built on one of the routes the Russians used to fight their way into Berlin in 1945. Originally, it was called Stalinallee, until de-Stalinisation. It was used for May Day parades.'*

There was a long pause. Anita parked the car on the grass next to the house and was about to eject the CD from the player.

'Ah, yes. I sometimes get forgetful. There was a specific reason I mentioned Karl-Marx-Allee. When my story's fully told, you must have verification.'

Anita took her finger away and listened intently.

'No one will believe me, you included possibly, unless you know what I reveal can be corroborated. You must make that first trip to Berlin and head for 64 Karl-Marx-Allee. There you'll find a man – not quite as old as myself – called Hans-Dieter Albrecht. Once I tell you the final part of my tale, you'll realise his importance.'

Anita ejected the CD and sat quietly with it in her hand. Had Klas deliberately not written down the name and address when he began to suspect that Rylander's suicide wasn't a suicide at all, and that he was being watched? He had been right to hide his research with them. Somebody had been in his house after his death. Right, she had things to sort out. Kevin would either have to fit in with her plans or just lump it.

Kevin was still wet when he came back.

'I was so hot after the walk, I couldn't resist a swim. I've had a lovely time.'

Anita passed him a cold bottled beer, which he gratefully accepted.

'Anyway, how's your day been? Get anywhere with that lot?' he asked with a nod in the direction of Klas's notes.

'Yes,' she said thoughtfully. 'Let's sit out in the sun.'

They made their way onto the grass where a couple of garden chairs and a picnic table had been placed by Anita before Kevin's return. She wanted him to be sitting down and relaxed before she told him what she (or possibly they) was going to do.

'It's a beautiful coastline along here. Magical.'

'I'm going to tear you away from it.'

'Oh,' said Kevin, the bottle halfway to his mouth. 'Where are you taking me?' Then he took another swig of his beer.

'Berlin.'

His snort sent beer spurting through the air. Anita waited for the spluttering to stop and for him to compose himself as he wiped the alcohol off his T-shirt. When he had finished, he simply smiled and said, 'Great.'

'Is that all you can say? Don't you want to know why?'

'I don't have to. I've never been to Berlin. Always been a place I thought would be interesting. And whatever we British may think of the Germans, we're partial to their beer.'

He was being annoyingly reasonable.

'This is *not* a holiday, Kevin,' she said sternly, as though she were reprimanding an eight-year-old Lasse. 'Well, it is, but the Berlin bit isn't.'

'Why can't we do both? I assume you've tracked down Klas's contact.'

'Yes. I heard it on the last CD of the interviews he did with Rylander. Said this man, Hans-Dieter Albrecht, would verify his story. Lives in a street called Karl-Marx-Allee. But this Albrecht must have told the story to Klas, so he can tell it again to us.'

Kevin stood up. 'I'm going to get another beer. Want one?'

She watched him go inside. She couldn't believe how easy it had been. She had expected some resistance, and that he would try and persuade her not to go, and say she was barking mad to meddle in something that had nothing to do with them. The truth was that she would have gone even if he had stayed behind, but she realised that she really wanted him to be with her. Give her support. Believe in her, however hare-brained the scheme was. That's why she had carefully prepared an argument in her head as to why they should go, and then present him with the evidence to back up her reasons for pursuing their own investigation. And he had just agreed without the slightest quibble. Bloody men! She couldn't fathom some of them. He came back with another bottle of beer, and hers poured into a glass; he knew she wasn't a natural bottle-swiller.

'So, when do we go?'

'Tomorrow. Late morning. The flight's only an hour.'

Kevin lazed back in his chair. 'For how long?'

'Two nights.'

'Well, when you've finished this, you'd better go and book the flight and hotel.'

Anita started to laugh. 'I have already.'

He joined in. 'Bugger me! You don't waste time, do you? How did you know I'd agree?'

'I didn't. But then I thought you were the sort of man who'd follow me to the ends of the earth,' she teased.

He leant over, took her hand and gave it a mock kiss. 'Maybe not to the ends of the earth, but I'll go as far as the Brandenburg Gate.'

Later on, over an outside supper at the picnic table of cold sill in mustard and hot potatoes, they got down to the business of the trip. Kevin had insisted that they go Dutch on the expenses for the flights and hotel. She had tried to dissuade him, as she knew this was only happening because of her insistence, but he wouldn't budge.

Anita told him of her conversation with Eva Thulin about the autopsies, and her visit to Klas's home and the strong feeling that it had been searched. 'Professional job,' was her assessment. She went on to graphically describe her brief encounter with Alice Zetterberg. 'I don't know whether it was a coincidence that she was there, or if she was having the house watched and had a tip-off. Put it this way, she wasn't pleased.'

'So, you reckon this Hans-Dieter fellow will give us the answers?'

Anita reached over to the wine bottle and topped up their glasses.

'That's what I'm hoping.'

'Do you speak German?'

'I can get by in French, but not German. How about you?'

'Look, Anita, you've heard my Essex accent. Most of my current colleagues don't even think I speak English.'

Anita chuckled. 'If I hadn't worked in London, I wouldn't understand you. Anyway, don't worry. I doubt if Klas spoke German either, so I suspect he communicated with Hans-Dieter Albrecht in English.'

Kevin pulled out a cigarette. 'You know, he might be suspicious of us just turning up out of the blue. It's not as though we've been sent by Rylander in the way that Klas was. I suspect that Rylander had already warned this bloke that Klas would turn up at some stage. Should we give him a call to find out, before jetting off?'

Anita shook her head slowly. 'I can't find a number for an Albrecht living there.'

'Ah, so we may get there and he's not around or he won't see us. Even worse, we might not be able to communicate with him.'

'Come on, Kevin, don't you like a challenge?'

'Bloody hell!' he said, waving his unlit cigarette at her and almost knocking over his glass of wine in the process. 'Just going on holiday with you is a challenge. You entice me over here with the promise of sea, sand and sex, and I get murder, mystery and... and... I can't think of another thing beginning with bloody "m", all thrown in.'

'What are you complaining about?' She fluttered her

eyelashes at him and playfully blew him a kiss. 'I've lived up to the first three promises.'

'I'll let you off then.' Then his expression turned serious. 'You know; if you're correct about all these things – and I have to agree something's not right here – this isn't going to be some jolly Agatha Christie jaunt. If Rylander *was* murdered and Klas *was* killed deliberately because he was getting too close to the truth of Rylander's big secret, there is one very dangerous person out there. Probably more than one.' He pursed his lips. 'You've already ruffled a few feathers. If whoever it is has already killed, and gone to huge lengths to do so – and we're going to follow the exact same path as Klas – I think we're going to have to be bloody careful from now on.'

CHAPTER 33

Nine o'clock on a Sunday morning wasn't the easiest time to get one's brain in gear, but Moberg had called them in to go over all the evidence that had been gathered the day before. The fact that they had made some headway ensured that Moberg was in a positive frame of mind, even though Wallen had been desperate for a lie-in, Brodd was still hung over after his date, and Hakim had had to postpone a promised visit to see Jazmin and Lasse's apartment. Since returning to Malmö full time, he hadn't had the time to go round and see them. He hated himself for feeling a slight sense of relief; he knew he'd probably end up arguing with his sister. He still couldn't get his head around the fact that Lasse had taken her on. In fact, it was Lasse he'd had to phone to apologise to because he couldn't reach Jazmin's mobile.

The meeting-room table was strewn with pieces of paper, photographs, cups of coffee, and the detritus of the various versions of breakfast the team had brought in with them. Hakim had a laptop with him. Moberg pointed at Wallen to begin.

'Yesterday, Pontus and I visited Pastor Elias Kroon of the Church of God's Mission on Earth.'

'Excuse me, Klara. Pontus, are you with us?'

Brodd sat up guiltily.

'Sorry, Boss. Night with the lady.'

Wallen's face twisted in disgust, Hakim glanced at the ceiling and Moberg frowned.

'I hope it was worth it.'

'You could say that.' Whatever he was trying to imply, everybody else in the room knew that Brodd's chances of getting laid were pretty remote. And there was no way he could admit to them that she had left the bar without him at around eleven.

'Just keep your mind on the fucking job. Klara, carry on.'

'Initially, the pastor wasn't keen to have us there, but he did open up eventually. Our victim was a member of his church. Her real name was Ebba Pozorski. She was born in Wroclaw in Poland, which is why we couldn't find her birth anywhere here. Moved to Sjöbo when she was little with her Polish father, Boleslaw, and her Swedish mother of Polish extraction, Elzbieta. The family joined Kroon's church. What has now emerged is that both Axel Isaksson and Markus Asplund were also members, so now we've got an historic connection between our two main suspects. It seems that it was Asplund who was mainly connected with the young Ebba.'

Moberg held up a meat plate of a hand.

'We'll come to that. I think we need to know everything about our victim first before we go through the suspects – much as I'm looking forward to that.' Brodd summoned up a laugh as he knew he needed to get back into the chief inspector's good books. 'From now on, to avoid confusion, I want Julia Akerman referred to by her real name, Ebba Pozorski.' The team nodded agreement. 'Anything further from your end, Klara?'

With a wry glance in Brodd's direction, she went on: 'As we were in Sjöbo, we decided that it might be an idea to go to the nursing home where Boleslaw Pozorski is a resident. He suffers from Alzheimer's, so wasn't any help.'

'He called you "Elzbieta",' contributed Brodd.

Wallen ignored his comment. 'Though we got nothing out of him, we were able to confirm through the staff that Julia... sorry, Ebba, visited him nearly every month. In fact, her visits tally with her known trips to Sweden.'

'And her last visit?' asked Moberg.

'The day before she died. The staff were helpful and said that Ebba was very affectionate towards him, even though most of the time he didn't know who she was. She was also very generous with funding for the home. Though it's state run, Ebba's donations have helped them buy extra equipment and improve the facilities.'

'Presumably, they don't know how she made the money for her donations?'

'Not yet. It'll come as a shock when all this comes out. But the picture that is emerging is of a woman who didn't spend extravagantly or live the high life, despite her well-paid profession.'

'Her home wasn't as you would expect,' added Hakim. 'Smart but basic. And she didn't fly first class or anything like that.'

'Basically, a good Christian girl who was corrupted.'

'I'd agree with you, Klara.' Moberg shifted in his seat. The room was warm even at that time in the morning. The scorcher was continuing. 'OK, have we got anything else on Ebba Pozorski?'

'I have,' piped up Hakim. 'After Klara discovered her real name, I was able to search the usual sources – criminal record database, tax office records, vehicle licensing, old electoral registers et cetera. She was certainly living in Malmö in 1996; she was working in a convenience store down in Möllevången. That didn't last long though, and she seems to have drifted from one job to another. In 1998, she was caught soliciting; that was before the law changed. She was let off with a warning. Then she disappeared from official sight until February 2003, when she found taxed employment.'

'Where?'

'Lund. Do you want to guess the name of the company she worked for?'

Moberg clapped his hands together. 'Malasp Travel!'

'Yeah.'

'Fantastic! How long was she there?'

'Five years. She was classed as a travel representative, whatever that means. Then she suddenly drops off the radar.'

Moberg rubbed his chin thoughtfully. 'Right, so she disappears in 2008 and turns up in Switzerland...'

'A year later; but with a new name.'

'And a new profession – or returning to an old one,' Moberg mused. 'So how come she goes from travel representative to high-class call girl in a year?'

'Well, I think Markus Asplund must be behind all this,' weighed in Wallen, who was horrified at the role this man must have had in the poor girl's life.

'That neatly brings us on to our first suspect.'

Wallen went up to the board, wrote Pastor Kroon's name, and then linked it with red arrows to the photos of Asplund and Isaksson. 'According to Pastor Kroon, it was Asplund who turned Ebba from sweet Christian girl into call girl. That's why he was expelled from the church. Despite the fact that Asplund was a man with a young family, he took an unhealthy interest in Ebba, and led her down the path of depravity, if Kroon is to be believed.'

'And is he?'

'I didn't like him,' Wallen confessed, 'but there's no reason for him to lie. He seemed to have liked the Pozorskis.' She sat down.

'Is that your impression, Pontus?'

Brodd looked momentarily startled. 'Yeah. Bit creepy if you ask me. In a religious sort of way, of course.'

Moberg stood up, went to the board, and looked hard at Markus Asplund's smiling face.

'We've got a lot against him now. We know that he knew Ebba from an early age. If the pastor is correct, he knew her too intimately. We don't know what relationship they had between him leaving Sjöbo and her becoming one of his employees in 2003. She leaves five years later. By 2009, she's living in Switzerland under a false name, servicing clients all over Europe. We know they're still in contact because he's on her client spreadsheet. Fast forward to twelve days ago, and she's murdered in the park. Asplund, we think, probably had sex with her the day she died. We should have that confirmed tomorrow, according to Thulin. He's got an apartment in town not far from hers. Where did they meet to shag? His apartment? He has no proper alibi for the time of the murder, and we know he's fit – runs and works out – and is right-handed; so that tallies with the attacker. And, as a frequent visitor to America, he could easily have got hold of the murder weapon. So, he has means and opportunity.'

'I don't know if it's relevant, but he lied about knowing Isaksson,' said Wallen.

'No, that's interesting. Why? Is Isaksson involved in the murder too?'

'We still haven't got a motive.' This was still a detail that was nagging Hakim.

'She must have had a lot of dirt on him,' Brodd suggested as he emerged from the fog of his hangover.

'He did have sex with a prostitute but, of course, we can't arrest him for it,' reasoned Hakim; 'he never seems to have paid for it. Anything else she might have said would simply be her word against his, and his professional reputation would carry more weight than hers.' Brodd sniggered. 'I'll tell you what's been troubling me from the moment I found out what she did for a living, and even more so now we've found out a bit about her background: how did she find these wealthy clients all over Europe?'

There was silence as they all pondered the question.

'It's quite a leap from travel representative to trollop,' agreed Moberg.

'Maybe that's it.' Hakim said suddenly. 'Travel is the key. All the clients were in cities that had an Easyjet flight to and from Geneva. That's probably not a coincidence. The flights are well priced, so she could save money, much of which she passed on to her father's nursing home. Budget travel's also low profile; she wouldn't stand out in the crowd. She'd know all about that sort of thing from working for Malasp. And she might have met her future clients on business trips while working for the agency. We need to check how often she worked out of the office during her time there – and how often she went abroad. And go through the names on the spreadsheet to see if the men listed have travel connections.'

'It's still not the easiest thing to do,' Moberg pointed out doubtfully. 'You can't just walk up to someone and say "oh, by the way, I'm going to be a freelance whore soon; do you want to sign up here?"'

'It might have been difficult for *her*,' rising excitement was creeping into Wallen's voice, 'but it's something that Asplund could do. In his business, he must have made masses of contacts all over the place.'

'Fuck me, Klara. That's a helluva thought. Asplund is Ebba's pimp!'

'That would make sense of all those free shags he was getting.' Even Brodd had perked up now.

'He really would have everything to lose if that came out,' Moberg said with a certain amount of glee. 'Maybe she was fed up with their arrangement, whatever it was, and wanted out. That might explain all the religious stuff. She wanted to repent.'

'Or maybe she was becoming a liability,' Wallen had a further thought. 'There might have been an argument when they met that day, and she said something that forced him to act quickly and get rid of her that night while she was still in the country.'

'That might answer another question that's been bugging me,' ventured Hakim. 'He would probably know that she jogged in the park when she was in Malmö. As she wasn't a frequent visitor to the city, and if we accept that the murder was premeditated, then the killer would have had to be familiar with her routine. He'd probably be the only person who'd know her movements.'

'Someone else might.' They all turned to the chief inspector.

'Who?' Hakim asked.

'Axel Isaksson. I haven't told you this because, unfortunately, it's not official. But it's been confirmed by Thulin that one of the DNA samples found in Ebba belonged to the esteemed politician. What's more, it's his semen on the nun's habit. Isaksson definitely had sex with her during the two days she was here. Probably on the Monday.'

'Could you see him running after Ebba with a knife?' Wallen enquired.

'Oh, I think he's fit enough. Though he is a smoker; that's how I got his DNA. So, you see, our problem is that it can't be used in evidence against him. And anyway, I've been warned off by the commissioner. However, I think another little visit is called for to put the wind up him. After all, he paid for sex from a known prostitute, which is illegal. He also lied about knowing Ebba, who, as a member of this daft church, he'd probably known off and on for thirty-odd years. And what intrigues me is that both Isaksson and Asplund deny knowing each other. Why? They're both on the spreadsheet. I can't believe they haven't been in contact recently. The question remains, are they in this together?'

'So what action should we be taking, Boss?' It was as though Brodd had made a major contribution to the meeting and was now helping to tie it all up.

'As soon as we hear from Thulin tomorrow about the other DNA sample, I want Asplund brought in for questioning.

When's he back?'

'Tomorrow sometime,' Wallen confirmed.

'He's bound to want a lawyer in, but I want him to feel the pressure. I want him to know we're after him. And make sure you get his phone. I want that checked for any link with Ebba Pozorski, or Isaksson.'

'What about Isaksson?' Hakim asked.

'An unofficial visit. I'm going to twist the knife tomorrow.'

'What about the commissioner?'

'Sod him. I've got two good reasons to talk to Axel Isaksson. One, he's a serious suspect. Secondly, I can't stand him.'

CHAPTER 34

Jazmin plonked the Willy's supermarket bag on the small kitchen table. The apartment had looked very clean when she had come in through the front door. Lasse had been hard at work getting their home ready for Hakim's visit, and had managed to hoover up nearly all Messi's cat hairs. As she was about to unpack, Lasse came in from the living room.

'He's not coming.'

'What!' Jazmin exploded.

'Sorry. He's been called into work,' Lasse said, giving her arm a consoling rub.

'You've nothing to be sorry about! It's typical of him. Any excuse. We make an effort and he can't be bothered.' She angrily banged a packet of rice on the table top.

'He really did sound apologetic. But he's working on that case of the jogger murdered in Pildammsparken.'

'Look, Lasse, don't make excuses for my brother. If he doesn't want to come, then I wish he was honest enough to tell me.' Further items of shopping were aggressively disgorged.

'He did want to explain to you, but he couldn't get an answer on your phone.'

This gave Jazmin a jolt. She hadn't had the courage to tell Lasse that she had lost her new mobile. This was a good moment to come clean, but she found herself making a feeble excuse instead. 'Must have forgotten to switch it on. Just being dozy.' It had the effect of deflating her indignation.

Lasse put a consoling arm round her shoulder. 'Don't be so hard on him. With Mamma being a cop, I know how many extra hours they have to put in on a big case. And I also know how difficult Chief Inspector Moberg can be to work for.'

'I suppose you're right.' She gave him a rueful grin. 'I just wanted to show him the apartment. Show him that I can stand on my own two feet.' He pretended to look hurt. 'With your help, of course. Now make some coffee!'

'It should be the other way round. Have you seen all the cleaning I've done? Messi's flaming hairs were everywhere. Sometimes you feminists don't appreciate all the housework men do.' This was answered with a good-natured slap.

As Lasse started to brew some coffee, she reflected on the real reason she was disappointed that Hakim hadn't turned up. That *person* had been there again last night. She'd recognised the green hoodie. She had gone out to the garbage bins with the kitchen rubbish about midnight, just before heading for bed. There had been movement on the far side of the hut. She thought it must be a kid playing – they were often out long after they should be. But as she re-emerged, she saw the figure in the light of a streetlamp, disappearing round the far end of the apartment block. That in itself had troubled her. When she had mentioned it to Lasse, he had dismissed it again; it was some kid causing trouble. But it wasn't an adolescent. And before she went to bed, she had peered out of the living room window – and the figure was back. She had rushed through to the bedroom, where Lasse was already asleep. By the time she had dragged him to the window, there was no one to be seen. Lasse had got annoyed and said that she must stop this paranoid behaviour. Then they had argued, and he had ended up sleeping on the sofa. At three in the morning, she had gone through and told him to come back to bed. The make-up sex had patched up the quarrel, if not exactly putting her mind at rest about the person who seemed to be stalking her.

*

The plane landed bumpily on the runway at Schönefeld, which had formerly been East Berlin's airport and was now home to busy budget airlines. It had none of the seductive trappings of most international airports. It was simply a place for moving people from one destination to another with the minimum of fuss. Kevin was glad to be back with Anita, as they had sat miles apart on the plane because of the last-minute booking. Once they found themselves out in the sunshine, there was a long covered walkway to the train station. They were greeted at the ticket machines by queues of Berliners returning from weekends away. When they reached the end of their queue, the machine wouldn't take notes or Visa cards, and, as they had no coins at this early stage of their visit, they had to return to the airport terminal and buy tickets at the tourist information counter. Kevin saw the funny side of it – Anita didn't.

The journey into the city took nearly an hour. Through windows besmirched with graffiti, they saw nondescript suburbs, which gradually developed a more interesting character as they got nearer to the centre. This was East Berlin awakening from its years of communist rule and now becoming a fully-fledged part of the new Germany. Many of the boring old GDR-era blocks were interspersed with eccentrically innovative modern design. At Frankfurter Allee, they had to change to the underground, and they stepped onto a yellow train with stencilled images of the Brandenburg Gate on the windows. The plastic seats were sticky to sit on in the heat. It made Kevin feel nostalgic for the London tube.

They emerged at Alexanderplatz under the shadow of East Berlin's most prominent structure, the 368-metre-high television tower – a soaring concrete spike supporting a huge gold and silver bauble, from the top of which protruded an antenna. The ball and the antenna, to Kevin's mind, resembled one of those fancy decorations which you see on top of Christmas trees. The whole thing was impressive, he had to admit. This showpiece of the GDR must have been a gigantic v-sign to the West. Seen from every viewpoint and a useful marker for tourists, it loomed large over Anita and Kevin as they trundled their cabin bags over the bustling Karl-Liebknecht-Strasse and found their way to their hotel on the corner of Dircksenstrasse and Rosa-Luxemburg-Strasse. The hotel was clean and modern, as exemplified by the Arne Jacobsen turquoise egg-chairs in the lobby. The bedroom was the usual neat box with a large flat-screen TV. Kevin immediately switched on the television, while Anita inspected the bathroom. After freshening up, she returned to see Kevin stretched out on the bed glued to some drama.

'What are you watching that for? You don't understand German.'

'No, it's funny. This is *Midsomer Murders*. There's Inspector Barnaby talking German. It's nothing like his real voice.'

'Of course it isn't. You're like a child.'

Kevin smirked as he turned off the TV and put the remote on the table. He wandered over to the window. 'You realise that the elevated railway is just over the road? We're not going to get much sleep.' Just then, a train screeched its way towards the Alexanderplatz station.

'We're not here to sleep.'

'That sounds promising,' he said suggestively.

'And we're not here for that either. I think we should go and try to find Hans-Dieter Albrecht's apartment now.'

'You're joking! Can't we do it tomorrow? I'm starving. Let's find a nice restaurant, have a few beers, and then come back here and discuss a plan of action, preferably in that bed.'

Ten minutes later, they were back on the street with Anita consulting a map she had bought at Kastrup Airport.

'It's not too far from here.'

They crossed Alexanderplatz – a big, anonymous thoroughfare surrounded by concrete GDR tower blocks.

'Alexanderplatz was named in honour of Russian Tsar

Alexander I in 1805.' Kevin had used the last twenty-four hours to mug up on Berlin's history via Anita's computer. The flight time hadn't been wasted either, as he'd bought a pocket guide to the city before they set off. 'Do you know the Peaceful Revolution started here in 1989 with the largest demonstration in the history of East Germany?'

Anita let Kevin chunter on as they made their way, under a canopy of lime trees, along the pavement. On their left they passed the Kino International cinema with a huge painting on the front wall of some actress she didn't recognise. She was thinking about what might await them. Was this a fool's errand? Why had she got involved in all this in the first place? The events that had taken place were unfortunate. She could have ignored them and still be enjoying a relaxing holiday with Kevin, who was proving to be good company, despite drivelling on about history she wasn't particularly interested in. She was growing fond of him. Whether she could ever love him was another matter, but she was pleased that he had happily gone along with her impulsive notions. And what if they did find out Rylander's secret? What then? Would it be of the magnitude that made someone willing to go to extraordinary lengths to make sure it never came out? Or would it prove to be just another interesting tale, like his father saving Lenin's life, that would fascinate people for five minutes before they moved on to something more attention grabbing? And even if it were the former, what could she actually do to bring someone to justice? There would never be anything official – Zetterberg would see to that; her mind was stubbornly closed to any shady possibilities surrounding the deaths. The point was, without an official investigation being opened, there was no chance of finding evidence – particularly forensic – and proving guilt. She had no proof. All her evidence was circumstantial. And as for finding someone responsible; where to start? The holiday couple? Suspicious, yes. But they had left on the Friday and weren't around when Klas came back from Germany. All these negative thoughts were beginning to sow the seed of self-doubt: maybe Rylander wasn't murdered, and Klas's death had been a genuine accident, after all.

'Blimey, Rylander was dead right what he said on that CD.' Anita's jumbled thoughts were abruptly interrupted. They had reached the Strausberger-Platz roundabout with its fountains jetting high above their circular splash pools. In front of them, Karl-Marx-Allee really opened out with dramatic eight-storey blocks of apartments on either side of a road which seemed to stretch into infinity. They were built in the wedding-cake Stalinist style. Covered in architectural ceramics, they still retained the harsh beauty that made them a worthy flagship project for the fledgling German Democratic Republic. The boulevard was wide enough to accommodate three lanes of traffic on each side of the road and a grass-covered area in the middle.

'Constructed between 1952 and 1960,' she heard her unasked-for guide explain. 'And it's here on the building sites that the first workers' uprising took place in 1953. Led to a hundred and twenty-five deaths.'

'Thank you. Now, can you use your vast local knowledge to find number 64?'

'Well, I reckon it's this side of the street,' he said as the green light beckoned them across the road.

'And how do you work that out?'

When they reached the other side, there was a bust of Karl Marx staring at them.

'The numbers on the other side of the street are odd. So, I'd hazard a guess that this side will be even.'

'Very good. You should be a detective.'

They walked along the road, looking for number 64. The ground floors of the complexes were made up of shops, offices and eating places. Across the road was a sports bar and a tanning centre. Anita assumed that neither would have been around even in a workers' paradise. They found the portico of number 64 just beyond the entrance to the Strausberger-Platz underground station, which emerged from underneath the block itself. They found around thirty names listed next to their respective buzzers. On the fifth floor, they saw the name "Albrecht". There didn't seem to be any first names.

'That must be him,' Kevin observed. 'I thought you couldn't find a phone number under that name.'

'I couldn't.'

He saw Anita hesitate. 'Aren't you going to buzz him?'

She still didn't move. 'Are we doing the right thing?'

Kevin looked aghast. 'Bloody hell, girl! You've dragged me all the way to Germany to meet this bloke. You can't back out now.' Before she could say anything, he reached across her and pressed the buzzer. 'Too late now!'

A young woman's voice answered in German.

Anita leant up to the intercom and said slowly in English. 'Is that the home of Hans-Dieter Albrecht?'

There was silence at the other end, and then the voice responded in German-accented English. 'No, he does not live here.'

Anita's face dropped. All this way. What a waste of time!

'We were given Hans-Dieter Albrecht's name – and this address – by a Swedish man called Klas Lennartsson. Did he come here at the beginning of last week?'

Another lengthy pause. 'Who are you?'

'I am Anita Sundström. I am a friend of Klas Lennartsson's. And we both knew a Swedish gentleman called Albin Rylander, who was a friend of Hans-Dieter Albrecht's.'

After what seemed like an eternity, the voice spoke again. 'You'd better come up.' This was followed by a buzzing sound, and they were able to push the door open. They went through a further glass door, and the hallway opened out. The tiled floor was cool after the warmth outside. There was a staircase rising to their right. 'Fuck that for a lark,' muttered Kevin. Then he spotted a lift tucked away in an alcove on the left. They came out onto a small landing, and a door at the end was open. A young woman stood waiting. She was in her mid-twenties, and had long, black hair flopping over half her face, while the other side of her head was shaved. The ear in view featured an arc of glittering rings, and her sleeveless white top highlighted an arm that was completely tattooed from shoulder to knuckles.

'I did not expect two of you,' she said suspiciously.

'Hello. I am Anita, and this is my friend Kevin, from England. He is also a friend of Klas Lennartsson's.'

The young woman reluctantly let them over the threshold. The apartment had a spacious hallway with one wall covered in a half-finished mural, the message of which wasn't yet apparent in the flurry of paint. They got no further. Anita could smell something tempting coming through the half-open kitchen door.

'I am sorry to interrupt you. You must be about to eat.'

'Why do you want to see Hans-Dieter Albrecht?' the young woman asked; her gaze intense. The cooking might be giving off pleasant aromas, but Anita still caught a whiff of the spliff that she must have just smoked.

'Our friend, Klas Lennartsson, came to see Hans-Dieter last week. I believe they met.' There was no response from the woman. 'Unfortunately, Klas is now dead. An accident.' Suddenly, her eyes widened in alarm. 'Your reaction confirms to me that they did meet.'

'Come,' the young woman said, indicating the living room. This was chaotically arranged with a couple of aging sofas in the middle of the floor and a television in front of them. In one corner were two easels on which were unfinished canvasses portraying something Anita didn't recognise. Hakim would possibly appreciate them, she thought. Paints and clothes were strewn around, as well as papers, books and magazines. The table by the window was laid out for a meal for one. Anita recognised both the table and standard lamp next to it as being from IKEA. Peering beyond the disorganisation, she could see that, once upon a time, this had been an elegant apartment, even if it had been built for the comrades. She and Kevin gingerly found places to sit, while the young woman disappeared into the kitchen. When she came back in: 'I turn off the cooker,' she explained.

'I'm afraid we thought this must be Hans-Dieter's apartment. It had the name Albrecht by the door downstairs.'

'That is me.' Again a wave of disappointment hit Anita. Kevin just raised his eyebrows. 'I am Manja Albrecht. Hans-Dieter is my grandfather.' Relief flooded onto Anita's face. 'This used to be his home.'

'I did try to find your phone number before we came. To fix up an appointment.'

'I only have mobile.'

'That explains it. We were wondering if it was possible to meet your grandfather.'

'And why?'

'Klas Lennartsson was writing the life story of a man called Albin Rylander, a well-known diplomat in Sweden. Sadly, Rylander died before the book was completed, but he had given Klas Herr Albrecht's name. Your grandfather had some important information about Rylander's life, and Klas came to Berlin last Monday to meet him. Tragically, that information has been lost because Klas died in a motorbike accident before he could tell anyone.'

Manja sat on the floor and curled up like a cat.

'I still do not understand why you two are here.'

Kevin was interested to know how much information Anita was willing to give away. He certainly wasn't expecting what came next.

'The publisher is still keen for the book to be finished. I am a writer, and they have brought me in to complete it.' Kevin had to turn his head away to avoid being seen to smile.

'And the Englishman?'

Without batting an eyelid, Anita continued: 'Kevin here is working for the publisher of the English language rights. They have already paid out money, so they are trying to protect their investment.'

'That's correct,' Kevin confirmed. 'I work for... Rooney and Bale.'

Now it was Anita's turn to stifle a grin as Kevin produced the names of Britain's two most famous footballers. She reflected that in their job, which required them to be able to spot lies, it helped to be an accomplished liar oneself.

Manja eyed them both up before speaking: 'Your Swedish friend came here Tuesday and met my grandfather. They had long talk. I do not know what about.'

'Do you think he will talk to us?'

Manja shrugged. 'I do not know.'

'Can you get in touch with him? It is important.'

She nodded in reply. 'I will ask, but I cannot promise he will come. He is not happy with strangers. He does not trust people.'

'That's fine.' It wasn't, but Anita wasn't going to press the young woman too hard.

'How long are you in Berlin?' Manja asked.

'Two nights. If we could see him tomorrow, it would be fantastic.'

'I will speak to my grandfather. Then it is up to him. I cannot do more. Give me your number, and I will ring you.'

Once they were out in the street, Kevin burst out laughing.

'What's with all the publisher stuff?'

'What about Rooney and Bale?' she countered, beaming at him.

'To back up your daft story.'

'Well, I wasn't going to frighten her off with stories of people being murdered and that we were cops investigating their deaths. We'd have got nothing out of her, and then we wouldn't have had a hope in hell of talking to Albrecht.'

Even at eight on a Sunday evening, the traffic flow along Karl-Marx-Allee was steady.

'I need a drink,' said Kevin, who had spotted the sports bar on the other side of the road.'

'So do I, but I could do with some food with it.'

They crossed the road, but on closer scrutiny of the sports bar, there was no chance of anything substantial to eat there. A small café on the corner was closed. They wandered down a side street and found a Vietnamese restaurant-cum-carry-out. The smiling lady who served them couldn't speak English, but they could point to the photos of the dishes available on the wall. They ordered two Berliner Kindl beers, which they thirstily drank at a table on the street. Anita was having second thoughts about the food, but was surprised to find that they were given huge portions, and it tasted delicious. And it was incredibly cheap.

'I can't believe this,' said Kevin, gazing at his plate of lemon chicken. 'It's just over four quid if my maths is correct. And the beer was bugger all. Why haven't I come to Germany before?'

There was a steady stream of customers coming to order or collect their meals. There were only a couple of other tables occupied by diners.

'Enjoy it; cheap prices might be the only thing we'll get out of this trip,' Anita observed pessimistically.

'Manja said she would ring tomorrow. There's no reason why he won't see us.' Kevin tried to sound encouraging, though he knew they might well leave Berlin disappointed.

'I hope so. Otherwise, we'll have discovered nothing.'

Kevin finished chewing a particularly succulent piece of chicken.

'Not so. We've found out something really interesting.'

Anita appeared baffled. 'What?'

'Those flats.'

'What about them?'

'I know you weren't listening to me jabbering on while we walked down Karl-Marx-Allee.'

'I had other things on my mind.'

'I could see,' he said, waving his fork at her. 'But its history tells us something. After the East-West split, this bombed-out street became Stalinallee, and the buildings were created as a showpiece for the new Republic. They're not the sort of buildings we associate with Eastern Europe under the communists.'

'I don't see the significance,' said Anita as she scooped up a forkful of rice and pork.

'If you listen to Kevin, you will be enlightened.' He swigged the last of his beer. 'Fancy another one?'

'Just bloody tell me!'

'OK. Those posh flats were built for the leading party members. And Manja's flat used to belong to Hans-Dieter Albrecht, presumably at the height of the GDR.'

'And?'

'That makes our Hans-Dieter an important party member.' The implication began to dawn on Anita. 'So, why did the right-wing Albin Rylander want a leading communist to verify his mysterious story? I think we may have got Rylander all wrong. Far from having the same views as his father – who felt guilty for saving Lenin's life – and devoting his career to standing up to the evils of the East; what if his political affiliations were the other way round?'

'You mean sympathetic to the Soviets?'

'Or the Stasi.'

'No, that can't be right.' The thought was too preposterous. She herself had heard Rylander being very derogatory about the Russians.

'We might find out tomorrow.'

CHAPTER 35

Moberg had got up early that morning. It promised to be another warm day, and the forecast didn't seem to offer any respite in the near future. The drive through town had been easy, and he parked opposite Axel Isaksson's house at a quarter past seven. He had no idea when the politician would leave for work, but he wasn't going to go up to the house and knock on the door. That really would be harassment. Isaksson could still make that claim when he was accosted in the street by the chief inspector, but what the hell! As he sat behind the wheel of his car and idly flicked through the pages of *Sydsvenskan,* he was shrewd enough to realise that he was flirting with a potentially dangerous enemy. His career could be seriously damaged by this man, yet he had a strong gut instinct about him. It wasn't one of Sundström's daft, girlie-intuition-type feelings – this was years of policing and dealing with liars, manipulators, killers and conmen. Something about Isaksson wasn't right. It wasn't the man's politics he objected to – just the fact that he was a politician. What's more, a politician that happily used the police as a political punch bag.

Though Asplund must be their number-one suspect, Moberg wasn't totally convinced that he was the killer, despite the evidence stacking up against him. Having come face to face with Isaksson, he was now certain that he was heavily involved. He knew that he was connected with Ebba Pozorski through her client spreadsheet. Now, he had the DNA to connect him to her directly. He had made love to her the day she died – or the day before if Ebba's diary entry was correct. Then there was the stain on the habit. That was his. He was a man of supposedly deep religious convictions, but those convictions didn't seem to preclude him getting a prostitute to dress up as a nun. More significantly, he must have known Ebba when she was a young member of Pastor Kroon's bizarre church. Then there were his denials about not knowing Markus Asplund. Had they been in contact in the last few days since the murder – or before then? There was no chance of getting the go-ahead to chase up Isaksson's phone records. But once they'd had a look at Asplund's mobile; that could be telling. Above all, what put Isaksson ahead of Asplund in Moberg's mind was the motive. Asplund's business and marriage might be damaged by the Ebba revelations, but he would survive. Isaksson, on the other hand, had far more to lose. His whole image as trustworthy Christian politician promoting family values would have been shredded forever. There would be no way back.

At ten to eight, Axel Isaksson appeared at his front door, turned to kiss his wife goodbye, and headed down the road towards the bus stop. Moberg got out of his car and lumbered after him.

'Excuse me, herr Isaksson,' he called out.

Isaksson swung round. His eyes opened wide in disbelief.

'I thought I'd seen the last of you. That's what Commissioner Dahlbeck promised.'

'Lovely morning,' Moberg said as he switched on what he assumed was his best smile.

'I've a bus to catch.'

'I won't keep you long.' By now, the chief inspector had reached his quarry.

'I've got nothing to say to you.' And he was about to continue to the distant bus stop when Moberg spoke again.

'It's only one question.' This time Moberg even managed to summon up a pleading expression. Isaksson hesitated. 'Why was your DNA found inside Ebba Pozorski's body?'

Isaksson was momentarily paralysed. It gave Moberg another few seconds to continue his unsubtle attack. 'And your semen on a nun's habit she wore?'

Isaksson recovered. 'This is fucking outrageous.' Not an expression that Moberg had expected from such a religious man, but one that assured him that he had hit home.

'And you didn't tell me about knowing her from your church in Sjöbo. You've got history with this girl.'

The politician advanced menacingly towards Moberg, his finger raised. 'It's you that's going to be history after this. I'm going to bury your career.'

'Is that a "yes" then?'

Isaksson seemed to be about to explode, but found enough self-restraint to turn away and stride past the chief inspector back towards his house. A minute later, the front door was slammed shut so loudly that the sound reverberated down the quiet street.

Moberg waddled back to his car and eased himself into the driving seat. He wondered how long it would be before Commissioner Dahlbeck called to haul him over the coals. He switched on the ignition, and the engine sprang into life. When he had started out this morning, he wasn't sure what he would be able to achieve, or even what he was trying to accomplish. He hadn't quite anticipated Isaksson's dramatic exit. He gunned the engine, and a wry grin enveloped his massive face. He had rattled the bastard.

They emerged from the underground station at Stadtmitte. As they made their way out, they passed an old man playing the *Blue Danube* on an accordion. Anita had allowed Kevin to set the day's agenda while they waited for Manja Albrecht's call.

She had dragged him to Berlin, so he might as well make the most of it. Checkpoint Charlie was first on his itinerary.

Over breakfast earlier, Kevin had outlined the things he thought they should try and see.

'I think we should visit places that are relevant to your investigation.'

'Our investigation.'

'Sorry, our investigation. Firstly, we know that Rylander was in East Berlin in the 1970s. It was the height of the Cold War. He must have got to know Albrecht then, whom we can be fairly certain was a significant member of the communist party. So, I thought we should get a feel of what it was like at the time. There's a museum next to Checkpoint Charlie which should give us a good idea.'

'OK,' said Anita as she drank the dregs of her coffee. She wasn't sure if she wanted to spend the day trailing round museums, but it was his holiday.

'When we're there, we'll be near Wilhelmstrasse.'

'Klas mentioned that.'

'Yep. According to Klas, Rylander said it all began and finished there. I can see why it started there because of his father's story about Lenin. Wilhelmstrasse was like Whitehall in London. A lot of the big government departments were located on the street, so it's from the Foreign Office there that Lenin's train was financed and organised.'

'That's the start, but how does it finish there?'

'I knew you'd be awkward. I don't know.'

'From what I read in Klas's notes, Rylander worked at the Swedish embassy on Otto-Grotewohl-Strasse. I can't find it on the map.'

'Mmm. Never mind. We'll still visit Wilhelmstrasse, and then head off to the Brandenburg Gate. That's not relevant; I just want to see it.'

Once back in their room after breakfast, Kevin suddenly

emerged from the bathroom, toothbrush in hand and mouth covered in white toothpaste as though he were frothing.

'Do you know what we've overlooked?' He didn't wait for Anita to answer. 'Klas came to Berlin and talked to Hans-Dieter Albrecht and, being a good historian, he would have gathered other information significant to the story, just as we're trying to do.'

'And your point?'

'Where is it all?'

Anita slapped her forehead in annoyance. 'God, how stupid! I'm an idiot! He would either have had it on him when he was coming out to see us—'

'Or it was in his house,' said Kevin, completing her thought.

'But then, Klas can't have had it with him when he crashed because the police would have it now.'

'Doesn't follow. The murderer or murderers could have taken his stuff away from the crash site before the police arrived.'

'Or maybe that was what they were looking for at his house?'

'I suspect,' Kevin said, wagging his toothbrush at Anita, 'that they got his Berlin material from the crash site but were still looking for all the stuff he deposited with us. Whoever's behind this seems to want to obliterate anything to do with Rylander's secret past.'

'If they've got Klas's Berlin notes, which presumably covered his chat with Hans-Dieter Albrecht, then they know what he found out.'

'Makes sense.'

'But where does that leave us?'

'Haven't a clue,' said Kevin as he retreated to the bathroom and finished his brushing.

They walked down the road from what would have been the GDR side of the famous crossing point in the Berlin Wall and saw a sign: YOU ARE ENTERING THE AMERICAN SECTOR. The replica sentry post was manned by two mock American guards, whose roles were to be photographed by the thousands of tourists who flocked to the scene of the one of the Cold War's great stand-offs, when Soviet and American tanks faced each other across the physical and ideological divide in October 1961.

The museum proved more satisfying, and they were both fascinated by the ingenious ways in which desperate East Berliners had planned escapes to what they hoped would be a better life in the West. A life that Albin Rylander symbolised, yet Anita was now having doubts about where his loyalties had lain. The museum held surprising interest for her as a Swede because there was a section devoted to Raoul Wallenberg, the Swedish diplomat who saved the lives of thousands of Hungarian Jews during the war before disappearing into Soviet captivity, never to be seen again. Would Rylander's final chapter remain as tantalisingly elusive as Wallenberg's?

As they left Checkpoint Charlie and made their way through the crowds onto Wilhelmstrasse, Anita's mobile went off. She took it out of her pocket and glanced at Kevin expectantly.

'Hello, Anita Sundström.'

'This is Manja.'

Anita mouthed 'it's her' to Kevin. 'Will your grandfather see us?'

'Yes. But I am not sure he is so happy about it.'

'What time?'

'Eight o'clock. And please use the back entrance of the building.'

'OK. Thank you, Manja.' Anita was about to end the call... 'Sorry Manja, just a quick question. I'm trying to find a street called Otto-Grotewohl-Strasse?' She listened intently to Manja's reply before finishing with a 'Danke.' She clicked her phone off and gave Kevin a triumphant look.

'He's seeing us tonight at eight.'

'And Otto-Grotewohl-Strasse?'

'It doesn't exist now; it's changed its name again. But it was the name that the East Germans gave to what was... Wilhelmstrasse.'

Moberg was sitting in the car park of the polishus, wondering if he had just wrecked his career, when his mobile phone started to go off in the pocket of his jacket, which had been flung carelessly over the passenger seat. At first, he was unsure whether to answer it. Had Isaksson been that quick? It made sense that as soon as he had stormed back into his house, he'd been straight on to the commissioner. Moberg reluctantly took out his phone, and was relieved to see that the incoming call was from Eva Thulin. He grunted his name in greeting.

'I hope you're having a nice day, too.' Thulin could be equally as sarcastic as Sundström.

'Shit start to the day. What have you got for me?'

'Markus Asplund's DNA. It matches the anal sample from your victim. You see, even forensics can get to the bottom of things.'

Moberg ignored the joke. He never understood how the forensic technicians could find humour, particularly of the childish variety, in their work. He didn't even offer a 'Thanks' before he quickly cut the call off and dialled Wallen's office.

'Wallen, I want you and Mirza to bring Markus Asplund in and grill the bugger. We've now got the DNA confirmed. He did screw Ebba Pozorski the day she died. I want him really pressured. Above all, I want you to try and establish a connection with Isaksson. So, go through his mobile phone. If he's wiped his calls, then check out everything with his provider.'

'Yes, we will.'

'And I've just had a thought. Once you've confirmed that he knows Ebba – and he can't deny it now – find out what he knows about that old stab wound that Thulin found on her body. It might be his handiwork.'

Wallen paused at the other end of the line. 'Don't you want to lead the interview?'

'No. You'll do a good job.' He could almost hear her purr.

'And if the commissioner rings down for me, say I'm out.'

'Shall I say what you're doing?'

'Just say I'm out!' he shouted down the phone. He threw his mobile onto his jacket and started up the car. He was going to Sjöbo to see if he could dig up any dirt on Axel Isaksson.

It was an incongruous setting for a friendly fika. But here she was with Kevin having a coffee and cake in the middle of what had been the Gestapo headquarters, the site of some of the most barbaric and evil goings-on that the world has ever witnessed.

They had walked round the gravelled area that surrounded the Topography of Terror museum, before entering it. All the different buildings were described. The SS Headquarters next door; the Reich Main Security Office; and even the editorial office of *Der Angriff*, the main organ of Nazi propaganda set up by Joseph Goebbels. Along the northern perimeter of the site was one of the last vestiges of the Berlin Wall. Beyond, stood Hermann Goering's vast Ministry of Aviation – a perfect example of Nazi architecture at its most intimidating, which, ironically, survived the aerial Allied bombing that destroyed everything else around it. The largest office block in Europe at the time, it later served the GDR Council of Ministers before becoming the German Ministry of Finance after unification. All this information was lapped up by Kevin.

'I can't believe where we are,' he said with obvious excitement, which Anita found difficult to share. 'Do you know, it's been very strange since we arrived yesterday, but whenever I see people over... say... eighty, I can't help thinking that they might have been in the Hitler Youth or Nazi sympathisers, brainwashed into adoring the Fuhrer. A bit weird. It's probably a British thing.'

'I noticed the obsession when I lived in England as a youngster.'

'Exactly. We were brought up with war films and documentaries. My dad remembered the sound of the bombers coming over and the night ablaze with the lights of the anti-aircraft guns and the red flames from buildings in London. His family lived near Brentford in those days. Brentford itself was hit a lot at the time of the Blitz. We weren't occupied, but it left an indelible mark on the British psyche. We still hate the Germans when we play them at football.'

'Isn't that because they keep beating you?'

'Not in 1966!'

Anita scooped up the crumbs from her cupcake with her finger. It had been delicious; nice and light, which was a surprise because the café was more like a works canteen.

'Isn't it time the British moved on?'

'That's easy for you to say. Your lot weren't in the war.'

Anita could feel an argument brewing. She had had this a couple of times during her year seconded to the Met, when colleagues had taken the mickey out of the Swedes for their lack of involvement. She knew her country's reasons, but they seemed less valid now after what she had just seen and read.

'The Germans appear to have come to terms with their past. They seem upfront about everything if this is anything to go by.'

Kevin's mouth was still half-full of cake when he pronounced: 'I'll reserve judgement until I've seen a bit more of Berlin.'

'I just hope your daughters' generation is more forgiving.'

He suddenly laughed. 'My daughters have no clue about the war. They probably think Hitler's first name was "Heil".'

'Surely not,' said Anita in all seriousness.

'Maybe not,' he conceded. 'Might be being a bit harsh there. They're lovely girls, but Abigail and Hazel live in a different world to mine or yours. Like Lasse, I suppose.'

'I'm sorry, Kevin. I've been so absorbed with this Rylander business, I haven't even asked you about your girls.'

Kevin drained the last of his coffee. 'They're good. Abigail's twenty-first is coming up next month. My ex is generously allowing me to pay for the night out.'

'But you're going?'

'I'll put in an appearance. Abigail wants to have a few drinks at her mum's place and then go off with her mates clubbing in Newcastle. I'll have to meet Leanne's new bloke. Works in advertising, apparently, so he's probably a dick. And Abigail's boyfriend will be there too. Darren isn't going to become a member of Mensa any day soon, but he's all right. They met at work in the council offices In South Shields. That's the other side of the Tyne from—'

'North Shields.'

Kevin grinned. 'Of course, that's where we first... you know.'

'I think that was one to forget.'

He toyed with his coffee cup, still with an amused look on his face. 'Anyway, they live in a flat down there. She gave up a hairdressing course when she realised she would never earn enough to go out all the time. As for Hazel, she's getting on for eighteen now. Doing 'A' levels at Newcastle College. Might even be the first one in our family to go to university. Still lives at home, but she's got a sensible head on her shoulders. She comes over to see me from time to time for the weekend. Likes the countryside and getting out. Her big sister is too like Leanne for comfort. Abigail took one look at Penrith and decided it was the most boring place on earth because it didn't have the nightlife you get in Newcastle; and she hasn't been back since.'

'It must be hard not seeing them that much.'

'They could be at the other end of the country. Or abroad.'

'I'm lucky to have Lasse in the same city, even though I don't see that much of him since he moved in with Jazmin.'

'Feisty girl. I wouldn't like to get the wrong side of her.' Anita nodded in cheerful agreement. 'Anyway, I hope you'll meet the girls sometime. I'm sure they'll like you, if Leanne doesn't poison their minds first. It's all right for her to have lots of men but, strangely, she's not keen on me moving on.'

'And I think we should be moving on,' Anita said decisively. She stood up before Kevin launched into a tirade about his ex-wife. 'You're the tour guide. Where next?'

'We'd like you to accompany us to headquarters,' said Wallen firmly, Hakim standing rigidly at her side.

Markus Asplund stood wavering at the end of the platform. He could see that the two officers weren't going to budge. His eyes suddenly lost the usual brightness that shone out of the glossy photos of him in the Malasp Travel advertisements. The haunted expression showed Wallen and Hakim that their number-one suspect had been expecting this.

CHAPTER 36

'Here it is.'

Kevin and Anita stood on the pavement, gazing at a long block of apartments with shops and offices underneath, made up of prefabricated concrete panels, only broken up visually by some low trees and straggling bushes. Even by GDR standards, the blocks were dreary, yet, according to the various information boards dotted all along Wilhelmstrasse, this was where some of Germany's most historically important buildings once stood: a street of palaces that had gradually morphed into offices of state. The one they were looking at now was the site of the Foreign Ministry. To the left had been the Reich Chancellery and to the right, the Presidential Palace; behind them was the office of Hitler's Deputy, Rudolph Hess, and the Reich Ministry of Public Enlightenment and Propaganda run by Joseph Goebbels.

'To think, nearly a hundred years ago, the people in there,' said Kevin pointing towards the apartments, 'were planning to surreptitiously whisk Lenin across Europe and let him loose on Russia and change the world forever. Yet without Oscar Rylander's intervention, he might never have made it. Think of what might have happened... no Bolshevik takeover. There might not have been the spread of communism. Hitler might never have happened, but if he had, there wouldn't have been an implacable communist enemy like Stalin to help swing the war, and we might all be part of the thousand-year Reich right now.'

They moved off slowly along the street in the direction of Unter den Linden.

'More to the point,' said Anita with some exasperation, 'what effect did Oscar's story have on his young son? We know that, in retrospect, Oscar was ashamed of what he did. In the light of that story, it's given credence to what everybody in Sweden saw as Albin's anti-communist stance.'

'But maybe that was all a front. I once saw a TV programme about Kim Philby and Guy Burgess. They were famous communist spies who joined an organisation called the Anglo-German Fellowship. It was a pro-Hitler group in Britain before the war, made up of aristocracy, politicians and businessmen. This was a way that the future traitors used to publicly show that they were right-wing and disguise their communist affiliations. It certainly worked for them. What if Rylander was doing the same? He doth protest too much... and all that. He had the opportunity when he worked here between 1972 and 1974.'

They turned off Wilhelmstrasse before they reached the new British Embassy at the top of the street. Outside the embassy the road was cordoned off to traffic to stop bombers driving up and attacking the building. They were now in Behrenstrasse, which housed the American Embassy.

'But if he *was* working for the Soviets, I don't understand how that can be so important now.' Kevin shrugged. 'It's all just history.'

'Well, that's something I do know about, being Swedish,' Anita responded. 'During the Cold War, we were neutral.' She added, 'Of course,' before Kevin had time to say it. 'It was a delicate situation because we were physically close to the Soviet Union. That's why we didn't fight in the Second World War: because of the fear of communism and Russian invasion. After the war, Moscow had to believe that Sweden was credibly neutral. And to the Americans, we had to keep alive the notion that we were a neutral country, but on their side. That's why we've never joined NATO. It was a constant balancing act. In many ways, things still haven't changed. We're still pulled between Obama's America and Putin's Russia.'

Kevin nodded. 'So, if a very senior Swedish diplomat was spying for the Soviets in the heart of Washington, that would be incredibly embarrassing for the Swedish government even now. Treasonous, of course, but is it reason enough to kill him in order to keep him quiet? Were his revelations going to expose someone who is still alive?'

They had had to wait an hour for Markus Asplund's lawyer to turn up. On his arrival, they moved into the interrogation room. While Asplund appeared calm, even relaxed, Wallen was nervous, as she hadn't conducted such an important interview before, though she had sat in on a few. Usually, these had been carried out by the late Henrik Nordlund or Westermark or Anita Sundström. Part of her tenseness was down to the fact that Hakim was sitting in with her. She knew how close he was to Anita. Would he be judging her against his friend? Would he report back to Anita about how she was doing? Would they end up laughing at her behind her back? But Hakim gave her an encouraging nod, and she started: Asplund gave his name and address for the benefit of the recording.

'First of all, could you confirm your movements on the evening of Tuesday, the third of June? That was the night that Julia Akerman was murdered in Pildammsparken.'

'As I've already told you, I was in my apartment at Östra Rönneholmsvägen.'

'And you skyped your wife and son for twenty-three minutes that night?'

'As I've mentioned. I have fully cooperated,' he said with a nod to his solicitor.

'Which still leaves you without an alibi. But we'll leave that for the time being. Now, when we visited you last Thursday, we asked you if you knew the victim, Julia Akerman. You denied all knowledge.' Wallen was warming to the task.

'That's correct,' he answered confidently.

'What about Ebba Pozorski?'

For a second, Markus Asplund's composure was ruffled, and he didn't answer. The moment soon passed.

'I believe we had someone of that name briefly working for the company some years ago. I've had quite a staff turnover as the business has expanded.'

Wallen turned to Hakim, who spoke next: 'According to her tax records, Ebba Pozorski was with you for five years. Between 2003 and 2008. She was a sales representative. Do you remember her?'

'I've had lots of them working for me over the years. The name rings a bell, but I don't keep track of those that leave.'

'Not even the attractive ones?' This was Wallen.

'I think that's a totally inappropriate comment to make,' put in Asplund's solicitor.

'I only mention it because we have matched your client's DNA with that of a sample of semen found in the body of the victim. He appears to have had anal sex with Ebba Pozorski shortly before she was stabbed to death. How would your client like to explain that?'

They moved along Behrenstrasse as far as the Memorial to the Murdered Jews of Europe. To Anita, this was an extraordinarily sombre site, even in the sunshine, as she viewed row after row of concrete blocks laid out linearly over undulating ground.

'It's like a faceless cemetery,' Anita said thoughtfully.

'Maybe that's what it's meant to be. I'm going to have a wander in. Coming?'

Anita shook her head. She had no idea why she didn't want to enter the labyrinth of concrete, but something held her back. She watched Kevin disappear between the rows of blocks, among which crowds of visitors, particularly parties of school children, were walking and contemplating and playing and shouting.

For a weird moment, it felt as though the memorial was being desecrated by all this activity, yet she reflected that maybe that was the point. Possibly the best way of remembering the millions who had died was to fill it with the living: those with futures in a better world than the one experienced by those who had been murdered. Suddenly, she was aware that Kevin, standing a few blocks in, was waving to her to join him. When she showed reluctance, his hand gesture became more frantic. What was the matter? It was probably him just being silly, and there'd be some joke at the end of it. She entered into the grid and found that he wasn't where she thought he'd been standing. She called out his name and moved further through the memorial, stepping down a gradient. A noisy group of kids appeared to her left, and she let them through.

'Anita!' It came in a loud whisper.

This was pathetic. She wasn't in the mood for games. Then she noticed him up a slope to the right.

'What the f—'

He shushed her, finger to his lips. He did a double shake of his head to motion her to join him.

She was about to get cross with him when she registered his expression. This wasn't a game.

'You were being watched.'

'What?'

'I could see from in here that you were being observed.'

'An admirer?'

'If it had been, I would have come out and smashed his face in. It's more serious than that.'

'You recognised someone?'

'Yes. It was Benno Källström.'

She looked at him in disbelief. 'Surely not! Mind you, I wouldn't have recognised him. Didn't even see him at the beach house.'

'I did. So what's he doing in Berlin?'

227

CHAPTER 37

'I would appreciate it if I could have a few words with my client alone.' Wallen and Hakim glanced at each other and left the room in silence.

Out in the corridor, they saw Brodd coming towards them with Asplund's mobile phone in his hand.

'Well?' asked Wallen.

'He's made fifteen calls to Axel Isaksson since the sixth; three days after the murder. And received ten.'

'What about before?' asked Hakim.

'Nothing. No contact; then suddenly, mad activity.'

'Good,' said Wallen holding out her hand to take the phone off Brodd. 'That'll help us in there. Sounds as though Moberg might be right and that they're in this together. Go and tell the chief inspector what you've found out.'

Brodd slouched off.

'He'll make the most of it,' Hakim commented wryly as Wallen handed him the mobile.

Asplund was ill at ease when Wallen and Hakim returned.

'My client wishes to cooperate as much as possible in your investigation,' explained the solicitor.

'That's very good of him,' Wallen replied with mock civility. She stared straight at Asplund. 'Did you have sex with Ebba Pozorski on Tuesday, the third of June?'

Asplund nodded.

'Sorry, can you speak up for the recording?'

'Yes.'

'At what time did you meet?'

'That afternoon.'

'Where?'

'My apartment.'

'Is that where you met each visit she made to Sweden?'

'No. I used an apartment of a friend of mine. I didn't want to leave... traces of her that my wife might discover.'

'So why not there this last time?'

'We were scheduled to meet at my friend's place. But she just turned up at my apartment before I was due to leave. I wasn't happy for her to be there, but she was acting oddly. Upset.'

'Upset?'

'Something had spooked her. I don't know what. She wanted comforting.'

'So, anal sex was your way of comforting her.' Wallen couldn't keep the bitterness out of her voice.

'She calmed down first. Then we...'

'And afterwards?'

'We agreed to meet in a month's time at my friend's flat, and she left.'

Wallen consulted some notes she had laid out on the table.

'Did you pay for the sex?'

'No.'

'But you knew she was a prostitute?'

Asplund glanced at his solicitor and then back at Wallen. 'Yes.'

Wallen pushed a copy of the Julia Akerman spreadsheet across the table.

'We've shown you this spreadsheet before. Why are you on it if you're not a paying client like all the others?'

Asplund pursed his lips. 'Maybe for old time's sake. As you

reminded me, she had been an employee.'

'Come on, you don't expect us to believe that. My colleague here, Inspector Mirza, has a theory about that. Haven't you, Inspector?'

'We think that Ebba Pozorski probably met her clients while working for your travel business. Either that, or you made the initial contact.' It was Hakim's turn to consult some notes. 'We've done a bit of digging over the last twenty-four hours, and the names we've been able to check on turn out to be members of the travel industry in their various countries. It can't be a coincidence.'

Asplund sat mutely.

'Were you – I can't think of another suitable word – Ebba Pozorski's pimp?'

'This is outrageous!' cut in the solicitor. 'You can't accuse my client of such a thing.'

'And why not?' Hakim asked innocently. 'Ebba Pozorski's a high-class call girl with clients all over Europe, many of whom are in the same business as herr Asplund. Your client has admitted that he regularly had sex with this woman, who was one of his ex-employees. She had to find the clients somehow, and we've no evidence from her computer to suggest that she advertised her services over the internet. I think it's a perfectly legitimate question.'

Asplund stared hard at Hakim. 'No comment.'

'OK, let's go back,' continued Wallen. 'As you were having sex with her, we can safely assume that you remember her as an employee. Were you sleeping with her then?'

'Is this relevant?' The solicitor was starting to annoy Wallen.

'We are establishing the relationship between your client and the murdered girl. We want to know how far this relationship went back.' Turning her gaze back to Asplund: 'Were you sleeping with Ebba Pozorski when she was working at Malasp Travel?'

'Occasionally,' Asplund admitted.

'Is that why you employed her?'

The solicitor was about to jump in again, but Asplund answered.

'No. She was good at her job. She was a hard worker. Honest.'

'What experience did she bring to the role of sales representative?' This was Hakim's turn to probe.

'I can't remember exactly. But she must have had a good CV.'

'That's odd,' said Hakim shaking his head as he bent over a typed sheet of paper. 'The jobs that she seems to have done don't seem to tally with being a qualified sales rep – unless working in a convenience store counts. Or the fact that she was caught soliciting in 1998.'

'Look, she was down on her luck. I gave her a break. And she didn't let me down.'

'That's very good of you,' Wallen weighed in. 'Giving her a break. Did you know that she had been soliciting for sex?'

'No. Of course not.'

'Are you sure that your kindness to a girl who had hit the skids was entirely altruistic?'

'If you mean I just employed her to have sex with her, you're dead wrong!' he said angrily.

'I don't mean that,' she carried on calmly. 'I think you knew her before she came to work for you.'

'I don't know what you're on about,' he blustered.

'You knew her when she was a teenager in Sjöbo.'

'Of course I didn't!'

'Along with her parents, she was a member of the Church of God's Mission on Earth. You've already denied being a member of that church. Do you still deny it?'

'Yes.' But there was a hint of uncertainty in his voice.

'That's strange, because Pastor Elias Kroon, the founder of

the church, reckoned you were a member for a time. Well, that's what he told me. So, I ask the question again.'

'I was, briefly,' he said dismissively.

'Why only briefly?'

'I got fed up with all that millennialism nonsense. And I didn't like Kroon.'

'The feeling seems to have been mutual. And during your "brief" time as a member of the church, you must have come across the Pozorski family.'

'Yes, I remember them. They were nice.'

'And Ebba Pozorski?'

Asplund licked his dry lips. 'OK. I did know her. Can I have some water?'

Hakim got up and left the room.

'Inspector Mirza has left the room to fetch some water,' Wallen said for the benefit of the recording. Until he returned, they sat in silence. Wallen was feeling good, as she could see that they had got to Asplund. Not a trace of his trademark smile had appeared, and he was flustered. She suspected the water was a ploy to gain time to marshal his thoughts. Hakim returned with a bottle and a plastic cup, and passed them over the table. Asplund slowly unscrewed the bottle top and carefully poured himself a cup full of water. After he had drunk the whole lot, Wallen proceeded.

'Now we've established that you knew Ebba at least twenty years ago, can we come back to your long-term relationship?'

'There was no long-term relationship,' Asplund protested.

'Then explain why you took her on at Malasp Travel.'

Asplund fixed his eyes on the bottle of water, which he was now twisting back and forth in his hands.

'As I said, Ebba was down on her luck. Things hadn't gone well for her since leaving Sjöbo. I took pity on her.'

'Then took advantage of her?'

'It wasn't like that!' The flash of temper was there again. In an instant, it was gone. He gripped the bottle tightly and spoke evenly. 'I'd heard that she'd been on the game, and I thought this would help get her off it. By then, her mother was dead and she was estranged from her father. That upset her because she loved him more than anyone. That's why she used to visit him at the nursing home whenever she was in Malmö.'

'We hear she gave a lot of money to the home.'

'She was that sort of girl. And, believe it or not, she was very religious.'

'So, why did she leave Malasp?'

'I don't know.'

'More to the point, why would someone want to kill her?'

'I've no idea. It's tragic.' Asplund looked across to Wallen directly, the hint of tears in the corners of his eyes. 'She didn't do anyone any harm. But her life was blighted.'

Wallen returned the stare. She wasn't going to fall for the emotional act. 'That brings me neatly back to Pastor Kroon. You use the word "blighted". According to Kroon, it was you who blighted her life.'

'What?' He was incredulous.

She referred to her notes again. '"She came under a malign influence within my own church. I will never forgive myself for being blind to the perverted designs of one of my own flock until it was too late. Ebba had turned to the path of sin and depravity."' She finished reading and looked up. 'According to him, that was you.'

'That's totally wrong. It's rubbish.'

'That's why he threw you out of the church.'

'That's *not* true. I wouldn't have touched a teenager. I can't believe he's saying such a thing.'

Wallen let him wallow in the implications of what she'd just accused him of and then nodded to Hakim, who took up the attack.

'Can we talk about Axel Isaksson? You denied knowing

233

him.' Asplund remained mute. 'Not only was he a member of the church, so you must have known him there, but also you've been in regular contact with him since Ebba's murder.' Hakim held up Asplund's phone. 'Fifteen calls. And ten from him. Why?'

Asplund didn't bother with the cup and took a swig of water straight from the bottle. He put it down on the table very deliberately. 'Ebba,' he said quietly. 'It was about Ebba.'

'What about her?'

'Well, her death, of course. We both knew her. I phoned him as soon as I saw her picture in the paper, but I didn't know he was sleeping with her until I saw his name on that spreadsheet,' he said, nodding towards the table. 'I asked him if he could find out what was happening. He can find things out... you know, in his position.'

'And in "his position", could he clear up your mess?' Hakim pressed. 'An old connection from the church.'

'No! Absolutely not.'

'Do you possess a butterfly knife?'

'A what?'

'A butterfly knife. They're sold in the US, which you visit regularly. It was the murder weapon.'

'I have no idea what you're talking about.' He sounded very agitated.

'She was stabbed with it. But it wasn't the first time. Someone had previously stabbed her in the shoulder. With your preferred type of lovemaking,' Hakim said pointedly, 'you must have spotted the scar.'

'She never talked about it.'

'It doesn't look good for you. We know you had sex with her the day she died. Maybe an argument took place. Did she threaten you?' Asplund just kept shaking his head. 'She could have ruined your marriage and damaged your business if your relationship came out. You could have had access to the murder weapon; and you have admitted that you run and train regularly, so you could easily have jogged up behind her and killed her. After all, you knew where she lived, which isn't far from your own apartment. Most tellingly, you were probably the only person in Malmö who would have had any idea about her routine. Motive, means and opportunity.'

'It's not true! I didn't kill her; I loved her.' And, virtually in a whisper, 'I protected her.'

'Protected her?' Hakim queried.

Asplund's head sank onto his chest, and he muttered: 'Ask Axel Isaksson.'

CHAPTER 38

Chief Inspector Moberg scooped up his last dollop of pie and ice cream. Even he was struggling, but he had had two main courses. Brodd had recommended the Gästgifvaregård in Sjöbo, and, as he had had no luck finding anything about Axel Isaksson that would be useful to the investigation, he might as well take advantage of the local facilities while he was here. He had talked to some people in the town hall, and they had spoken highly of the politician. A couple of the shops had been the same. He'd even gone round to Pastor Kroon's house, but the cleric hadn't been in. There must be someone round here who didn't like the pompous prick. Even the middle-aged waitress had said he was a decent enough fellow – so she wasn't going to get a tip.

He had turned his phone off, as he was sure that Commissioner Dahlbeck would be trying to get hold of him. And, yes, when he had checked it before sitting down to his meal, there had been three missed calls from his secretary. There was also one from Brodd. He ignored that, too, as he assumed that he wanted to arrange a drink after work. He didn't mind boozing with Pontus as long as he didn't drone on about this supposed new girlfriend of his. She sounded too good to be true. Let's face it, Brodd was no catch. Moberg, being naturally suspicious, was beginning to suspect that he had invented this woman to give him some much-needed credibility among his colleagues. He checked his phone again as he drank his coffee, and saw that he'd missed a recent call from Wallen. He would ring her back as soon as he was finished. She might have news of

the Asplund interrogation. Everything seemed to be pointing in
the travel agent's direction, but Moberg still wasn't sure about
the motive. In his mind he was convinced that Isaksson had
most to lose. But that didn't mean Asplund wasn't involved.
They were connected, but what was the specific link other than
the bizarre religious cult created by Elias Kroon? His appetite
sated, Moberg hurriedly paid his bill, and left. Outside the
ornate portal of Gästgifvaregård, next to a pole on which the
national flag dangled wistfully, he dialled Wallen.

He was pleased with what Wallen had to report, even
though Asplund had flatly denied murdering Ebba Pozorski.
They had established the Sjöbo link when Ebba was a teenager,
the fact that he'd employed her to give her a break when she had
fallen on hard times, and that he knew she was a prostitute both
before and after working at Malasp Travel. Asplund wouldn't
be drawn on whether he had fixed up her clients, but they had a
good case against him except for a clear-cut motive.

'What about Isaksson?' Moberg asked.

'Didn't Brodd get in touch?'

'Must have missed his call,' he answered vaguely.

'Asplund's mobile showed he'd phoned Isaksson fifteen
times since Ebba's killing. And Isaksson had rung him ten.'

'I bloody knew it!' he said, smacking the flagpole with his
free hand. The jolt left the metal pole vibrating.

He heard a little chuckle at the end of the line. 'You're going
to like this. When Hakim presented the case against Asplund,
he reacted by saying that he didn't kill her, that he loved her,
and that he protected her. Then, when Hakim pressed him on
what he meant by protecting her, all he would say was "ask
Axel Isaksson".'

Moberg felt a surge of excitement. It was the feeling he got
when his gut instinct had been confirmed.

'Is Asplund still there?'

'Yes. We're waiting for Prosecutor Blom to decide whether

we've enough evidence to keep him.'

'OK, I'm coming straight back.'

'By the way, the commissioner wants to see you.'

'After what you've told me, Klara, I want to see him!'

Anita emerged from the shower. She began to rub herself down with a towel. Kevin sat on the bed and watched, admiring her body. He was still pinching himself that this woman was sleeping with him. He had had attractive – and not so attractive – women in his life before. Leanne was regarded as a "looker", which was why so many of his colleagues had tried their luck with her. Some had succeeded. But Anita was different. Smarter for a start. There was something sexy about intelligent women; that irresistible combination of brains and beauty. She was fun, too; when not chasing after invisible killers. What she saw in him, he had no idea. His dad had always said that you should never question luck. Now he knew what his old man had meant.

Anita slipped on a pair of black knickers and stood thoughtfully in front of him.

'Are you really sure it's him?'

'Positive. That was the guy we know as Benno Källström, and I could see him plainly from inside the memorial. And he was definitely watching you. I've done enough surveillance in my time to spot the signs.'

Anita frowned. Even with the first wrinkles of middle age, her face seemed beautiful. 'Do you think he's followed us back here?'

'I was pretty sure I saw him again when we got off the train at Alexanderplatz, so he probably has.'

He was trying to stop himself becoming obsessional, but a few days with Anita had created that worrying mindset. All the time they had been wandering round the sights of Berlin – the Brandenburg Gate, the Reichstag, the Tiergarten – he had been keeping an eye out for Benno. He hadn't seen him and was starting to doubt himself until he caught a glimpse of him at the busy station.

'Do you think the woman is here too?' Anita asked as she slipped on a T-shirt.

'I didn't see her. Doesn't mean she's not here.'

Anita started to rub her hair again with the towel.

'If they're not who they say they are, who are they? What were they doing in the holiday home next to Rylander's? Besides being very suspicious, it's bloody unnerving. To be followed all the way here. What do you think we should do?'

That had been uppermost in Kevin's mind since the Jewish Memorial.

'Whoever these people are, they're serious. We don't know when Benno got to Berlin, so we can only hope that he didn't follow us to Karl-Marx-Allee last night. If what Klas found out from Albrecht on his visit here led to his death, we have to make sure that the source of that information isn't put in danger.'

'But if Benno's following us, he, or someone he's working for, already knows what Albrecht told Klas – that's if they got hold of his Berlin notes somehow.'

'Not necessarily. If they *had* found the notes, Albrecht would probably have been disposed of by now. I'm sure they want to silence him, too, but they don't know who he is, or where to find him. Basically, we mustn't lead them to the granddaughter's flat.' Kevin got up from the bed, went to the window and glanced out as though he was expecting to see Benno standing there across the street. He turned back to Anita. 'I think you should go alone tonight. I'll leave the hotel first and see if he starts following me. If he does, I'll ring you, and you can head off to Karl-Marx-Allee.'

She stopped rubbing her hair. 'And if not?'

'If not, you'll have to make sure you lose him if he tries to follow you.'

'You'd better give me a good description of him then.' She threw the towel down on the floor in exasperation. 'This is like one of those stupid spy movies Björn used to love.'

Kevin flashed a wan smile. 'Except in this one real people seem to be dying.'

He could see that Commissioner Dahlbeck was furious. He also looked weary. Years of arse-licking must take its toll, Moberg thought uncharitably.

'You've gone too far this time, Moberg. I gave you strict instructions not to harass Axel Isaksson, and instead, you've gone out of your way to do just that without the slightest justification.' Moberg wondered if the commissioner was about to burst a blood vessel. 'I'm going to have to take you off the case. I'm going to give it to Larsson's team.'

Moberg calmly let him finish. Normally, he would have lost his temper by now, but he realised this wasn't the right time and place.

'Before you do that, Commissioner, have you thought *why* Isaksson is so keen to stop us asking him questions?'

'A man of his standing is entitled to protection against baseless accusations,' Dahlbeck said defensively. He hadn't expected to have to justify his decision.

'So it's all right to hassle the scum of our streets, but not the politicians whose policies create most of the problems we have to clear up.'

'I'm not going to argue with you, Moberg.'

'Well, you might want to tell Larsson that your family-values politician has not only been paying for sex with a prostitute, but has been in regular touch with our chief suspect ever since the murder. They knew each other in Sjöbo, where they attended the same church. The victim, Ebba Pozorski, was also a member, so they both knew her from a young age. And now our chief suspect's only defence is that we should talk to Isaksson. Apparently, he has all the answers. But that depends on whether you're willing to let Larsson ask the questions.'

That was Moberg's parting shot as he headed for the door. His hand was on the handle when the commissioner spoke:

'Maybe I'm being hasty.' Moberg managed to smother a smile as he swung back round. 'I don't like the man any more than you do, but he's been beating us with a stick for some time now. We have to use the softly, softly approach.'

'He's broken the law for a start. Having sex with a prostitute.'

'I'll have a word with Blom first. See where she thinks we stand.'

'I don't want to arrest him... yet. But we need to talk to him as soon as possible.' Commissioner Dahlbeck's face creased into a worried frown. 'The longer you wait, the more time he has to cover his tracks.'

The call from Sonia Blom came more quickly than even Moberg had anticipated. He was given the go-ahead to talk to Axel Isaksson, but she warned him that he must tread carefully. 'An informal chat at this stage. We don't want to give him any more opportunities to denigrate the Skåne County Police. And he has powerful friends.'

'He might lose some of them by the time I've finished,' Moberg answered gleefully before putting the phone down. He had the satisfaction of knowing that his last comment would get her fancy knickers in a twist. Since her much-heralded arrival from Stockholm, Blom's cautious, image-conscious approach to her prosecuting duties had stymied many of his investigations over the years. He prayed for the day when she would return to the bright lights of the capital, and they'd get someone in who was more effective.

To Moberg's surprise, a call to Isaksson's office had elicited an immediate response from the politician himself. He was suddenly being cooperative, in a cagey way. The commissioner must have warned him that there was nothing he could do to prevent the inevitable questioning. Isaksson would help if he could, but he'd rather not have the interview at his office, or at his home. Of course he bloody wouldn't, thought Moberg. They agreed to meet in Kungsparken; near the casino at four o'clock.

Moberg took Wallen along with him because she was fully up to date with the Asplund situation. Isaksson was already there when they arrived. He looked cool in a short-sleeved shirt; his jacket discarded back at the office because of the warmth of the afternoon. He was smoking. Was this to calm his nerves? It did nothing to dim the hostility in his stare. And he appeared surprised at seeing Wallen accompanying Moberg. 'I have to cover my back too,' is how the chief inspector justified her presence. When Isaksson had finished his cigarette, they all sat down on a bench, with Wallen squeezed on the end next to Moberg.

'When I spoke to you before,' started Moberg, 'you denied any knowledge of Markus Asplund and Ebba Pozorski. But the fact that you're talking to us now indicates you were lying about that.'

'Lying's a strong word.'

'Mistaken, then. You forgot.' Moberg was hoping that this would wind the politician up. Get him angry and he might be less guarded. 'We now know that you knew them both from your Sjöbo days in the Church of God's... something or other. And we also know you've been in constant contact with Asplund ever since Ebba's death.' Isaksson's eyes screwed up behind his glasses in puzzlement. 'We've seen his mobile. He's called you fifteen times, and you've been on to him ten.'

'I can't deny it then.'

'What were the conversations about?'

Isaksson's gaze wandered towards a group of young mothers with pushchairs and waddling toddlers in tow.

'About Ebba. They were always about Ebba.'

'This is a prostitute that you both slept with. One that seems to have dressed up in a nun's habit for your gratification. This we can prove.' Moberg quickly moved on before Isaksson asked the obvious question as to how they could be sure of that without him giving them a DNA sample. 'Put it this way, if you are going to stand in September's general election, your chances will be well scuppered if this comes out.'

Isaksson looked sharply at the chief inspector as though the realisation of what he had done had suddenly hit home. He didn't crumple as Moberg thought he might, but, being a politician, he seized on his words. 'You said, "*if* it comes out".'

'That depends.'

'On what?' Moberg could see Isaksson's mind whirring; weighing up the possibility of negotiation and compromise.

'How cooperative you are.' He decided to put the squeeze on him. 'With your status and future ambitions, your relationship with Ebba Pozorski could have jeopardised your whole career. Not to say your marriage and reputation as an upright Christian. That gives you one helluva motive.'

Isaksson gave a bitter laugh. 'You've no idea. Ebba would never have betrayed me. She wasn't that sort of girl.'

'You mean client confidentiality,' Moberg commented derisively.

'Despite her profession, she was a good Christian girl.' Moberg couldn't get his head round this, though it echoed Asplund's thoughts about Ebba on the interview recording he had listened to before they had come out to the park.

'Her killing was a premeditated act. If she was such a saint, why would anybody want her dead?'

Isaksson spread his hands hopelessly. 'I have no idea. Neither has Asplund.' To Moberg, this was tantamount to confessing to collusion between them. But which one actually did it? 'Look, if I tell you all I know, can you put a lid on everything that's happened concerning me?'

'We might be able to if you're really helpful.' Moberg knew he was lying, but if it made the job easier, sod it. 'OK, let's go back to the beginning. When did you first come across Ebba Pozorski?'

Isaksson fumbled for the packet of cigarettes stuffed in the breast pocket of his shirt, and took one out. He lit it. This was trying Moberg's patience, but it would be worth the wait if he got his man.

'She must have been about nine or ten when she joined the church with her parents. I wasn't too keen when Boleslaw Pozorski was accepted into the congregation.'

'Because he was Polish?' Wallen asked as she scribbled down what Isaksson was saying.

'Too many immigrants were coming in. Nothing like the appalling situation we have now, of course. I thought that by making them welcome, it was just encouraging them. But Elzbieta was a good person, and I accepted him for her sake. And Ebba was such a sweet thing.' He puffed hard on his cigarette and let out a cloud of smoke.

'What about Markus Asplund?'

'Oh, he joined the church later.'

'Your old pastor, Elias Kroon, described Asplund as... what was it Klara?'

'He said that Asplund had perverted designs on Ebba, and that due to him, she turned to a life of sin and depravity.'

'Not exactly a ringing endorsement of your fellow worshipper. Was that how you saw it?'

Isaksson idly flicked the ash from his cigarette and reproduced the harsh guffaw of before.

'Of course not. Whatever the circumstances may seem to be, Asplund is an honourable man.' This wasn't the opinion that either Moberg or Wallen had formed of the travel agent.

'According to Pastor Kroon, he expelled Asplund from the congregation.'

'Asplund left the church because he could see what the rest of us were blind to. When the church began, we were so full of hope, and Kroon seemed to tap into and articulate our beliefs and expectations. We were entering the Golden Age before the final judgement. He promised us a New Earth in God's

Kingdom. We were the chosen ones. But as the church grew, he began to change, to become more manipulative, more secretive.' He threw away his cigarette with a heavy sigh. 'Kroon took a shine to Ebba, who was now a very impressionable teenager. Her parents were old-fashioned in their attitudes and outlook, and she was incredibly naïve for her age. That innocence is wonderful in many ways when you see what today's youth is like, but easy to mould in the wrong hands.'

Moberg looked at Isaksson in astonishment. 'Are you saying that it was Pastor Kroon who had the perverted designs on Ebba?'

Isaksson slowly nodded his head. 'Asplund saw that Kroon was exploiting her unwavering faith in order to groom her; to use that sickening modern phrase. He raised concerns. We thought he was mad. We knew he'd already become disillusioned with Kroon's teachings, but we thought his accusations were wild; that he had some agenda of his own. We still believed that Kroon was a great man; a visionary. So, Asplund left the church.'

'What about you, then?'

'A couple of years later. I was moving to Malmö anyway. I realised that Kroon was making a mockery of the God that I worshipped. By then, I knew that he was... you know... with Ebba.'

'And you did nothing?' Wallen shouted in disbelief.

A middle-aged couple further along the path turned round in surprise, before continuing their constitutional.

Isaksson took off his glasses and scratched behind his left ear, then replaced his spectacles. 'I'm ashamed,' he gulped. 'I've had to live with that knowledge... and now her awful death.'

Moberg couldn't weigh up this man. From the haughty politician with such strident views, here was a vulnerable human being. A man admitting failure. Was it an act?

'So what happened then?'

'Nothing for a few years. Then, when I was checking out the Skåne County Police in my capacity as a council member...' he ignored Moberg's scowl '... I came across an old police report that mentioned that Ebba had been found soliciting. I'd heard from Sjöbo contacts that she'd run away from home and that her father wasn't speaking to her. I don't think he ever realised what was going on under his nose.'

'And you found her?'

'Yes. She was living in a hovel in Rosengård. Still a beautiful girl; but in a mess. I wanted to get her off the game. So, I approached Markus Asplund. His company was successful, and I asked if he could give her a job. He was happy to help and, gradually, she seemed to turn her life around. I think that's when he fell in love with her.'

'You mean started shagging her,' Moberg said brutally.

'He wouldn't have seen it that way.'

'What went wrong?'

Isaksson reached for his packet of cigarettes and then changed his mind. 'Despite everything, she slipped back into her old habits. I know Asplund tried hard to keep her on the straight and narrow, but she was too damaged by then.'

'But it's quite a jump from trawling the streets of Malmö to a nice house in Switzerland and some well-heeled clients.'

'Do you mind if we walk? I'm getting stiff.'

Moberg nodded reluctantly. He was comfortable, and he avoided exercise as much as possible. They all stood up and began to wander slowly through the park.

'Asplund was at the end of his tether when he came to me. He knew that she would never change her ways. It was a case of if you can't beat them...' He was lost in thought for a moment, and then he was back. 'He came up with this idea that if she was going to be a "professional", then she must do it as safely as possible. With more respectable people. No, that's not the right word. Discreet people. Men who wouldn't beat her up and abuse her; treat her badly. Ebba had been on occasional business trips with Asplund, and she was always being chatted up by his contacts. It wasn't a huge step to charging them.'

'So, are you saying that Asplund found the clients?'

Isaksson came to a halt and nodded.

'They were *his* business contacts?'

'I believe so. He wanted Ebba to earn enough so she didn't have to have too many men. Just a select few. Maybe it was easier for him to come to terms with that. It would enable her to fund a better lifestyle, and, to be honest, I think he thought it would enable him to wean her off the game altogether. Deluded. It was too late by then.'

'But where did you come in? I assume you came in?'

Isaksson began to walk off slowly with Moberg and Wallen in tow.

'Asplund wanted Ebba to have a fresh start in a new country. He went to Switzerland a lot, and she would be able to keep a low profile there. It's a place where people don't ask questions. But he wanted her to make the break complete by giving her a new identity. I managed to arrange a passport for her as Julia Akerman.' He stopped again, and Moberg nearly bumped into him. 'I failed her once, but at least this gave me a chance to help her.'

'And sleep with her.' Isaksson wasn't going to get any sympathy from Moberg.

'I'm not proud of it. But my wife...' His voice trailed off.

'Ebba played out your religious fantasies? The nun thing?'

'It was her way of repaying me.' Moberg could feel Wallen bridling next to him.

'If that's the case, why did she charge you?'

Isaksson adjusted his glasses as he eyed the chief inspector.

'She didn't. But it was my way of giving her something. Gifts of money, not payment for services. I'm not a rich man. I don't know what her real "clients" paid... a lot I suppose.' He sighed. 'Maybe it was to salve my conscience.'

'It's semantics. It's your way of trying to get round Swedish law. Trouble is that she put it all down on a spreadsheet, so whatever you say, it looks like you paid for sex.' Moberg enjoyed keeping him wriggling on the hook.

'Look, I've been totally honest with you,' Isaksson said earnestly. 'Doesn't that count for anything?'

Moberg grinned at him. 'Afraid not.'

'Where were you on the night of Tuesday, June the third between nine and midnight?' Wallen asked formally.

Isaksson's eyes showed relief. 'I was at a council meeting until nearly ten. Then I had a private meeting with another councillor, Emeli Nilsson, until nearly eleven. Then I went home. You can check it all out.'

Moberg had to admit this was a blow, but if the politician had been telling them the truth, then – sadly – he wasn't in the frame. That didn't mean that he still couldn't land him in the shit.

Isaksson looked at his watch. 'I've got a meeting in fifteen minutes. You'll have to excuse me.'

'I'm sure we'll be seeing more of you, herr Isaksson.'

The politician hurried away.

'Hang on!' Moberg called after him. Isaksson hesitated, not wanting to return. But he waited for Moberg to rumble up to him.

'Ebba had a scar on her shoulder. I'm sure you noticed. Know where it came from?'

'She got it in Sjöbo. I only found out long after it happened. After I'd left the town.'

'How did it happen?'

'Pastor Kroon attacked her.'

CHAPTER 39

By the time they reached Moberg's car, he was sweating profusely and he leant against the vehicle.

'I hate the heat.' Wallen could tell he wasn't happy. He'd just seen his favoured suspect slipping through his fingers. 'You'd better look into his alibi. If it checks, he's not our man. But it doesn't mean I'm not going to shaft the sanctimonious bastard.'

Wallen had to agree. She was appalled, if not totally surprised, that a man who supposedly cherished Christian values could, once he eventually became aware of it, stand by and let the young Ebba Pozorski be abused to such an extent that her whole life was wrecked. And then to compound it by taking sexual advantage of her after he had tried to make it up to her. She would quite happily see his career crash and burn.

'Do you think that they could still be in it together?' she suggested, resurrecting an earlier idea of the chief inspector's. 'They both had possible reasons to get rid of her. The murder still could have been carried out by Asplund.'

'They're not exactly casting stones at each other.' Moberg kicked at a pebble on the pavement and it went scuttling into the grass verge. 'I want you to have another go at Asplund and see if he corroborates the whole setting-Ebba-up-abroad scenario.'

'What about Pastor Kroon?'

'That was a turn up for the books – if Isaksson's right. Of course, Kroon might be the scapegoat the two of them need.

What did you make of him?'

'Like Brodd, I thought he was weird. Not likeable.'

'Could he have done such things to Ebba?'

Wallen reflected on the question for a few moments.

'Possibly.'

'More to the point, could he have physically committed the murder? He must be getting on in years.'

'He has a bicycle, so he's fit enough to ride that around. Whether he could have jogged up behind Ebba, I don't know. Of course, he might have been hiding in the trees waiting for her, so he wouldn't have had to run far.'

Moberg unlocked the car and opened the door. 'We'll wait for it to cool down a bit. It'll be bloody hot in there.'

'There's one thing that Asplund said that I didn't think about at the time. Ebba turned up at his apartment, which annoyed him. Off limits because of his wife. But he said that she was upset. Something had spooked her, he said. She didn't say what it was. But what if she had seen Kroon, here in Malmö?'

'Well, that's another thing we need to check out. His movements on the day. We also need to speak to former members of his wacky church and see if they back up Isaksson and Asplund. Because if this whole thing isn't an elaborate story concocted by those two, we're looking at a new suspect – Pastor Kroon.'

Anita and Kevin emerged from the front of the hotel. They stopped to talk.

'Any sign of him?' asked Anita as Kevin went through the routine of lighting up a cigarette and scanning the street in both directions.

'Not that I can see.'

'OK, off you go. Hopefully, he'll follow you.'

As they had planned, she turned to go back into the hotel. Kevin was going to try and act as a decoy.

'Well, aren't you going to give me a goodbye kiss? Make it

look authentic?'

She stepped back towards him and gave him a full-blooded kiss on the lips.

'Does that look authentic enough?' she said teasingly after prizing herself away.

'That'll do.' And he set off towards Alexanderplatz.

Anita went back to their room. Even if Kevin managed to waylay Benno Källström, his female companion, Fanny, might be waiting for her to make a move. Before Kevin left, they had agreed that Anita would take the underground to a couple of stations beyond the one beneath Manja Albrecht's apartment block, and then switch back. Fortunately, Anita had glimpsed Fanny on a couple of occasions and knew what she looked like. She would take care when approaching the apartment, and the fact that she had been asked to go in the back way indicated that Hans-Dieter Albrecht didn't want anybody attracting attention.

She paced the room, her nervous tension growing. What would she unearth tonight? Would she find out anything? She couldn't assume that Albrecht would tell a perfect stranger all he knew about the secret life of Albin Rylander. She was also worried about Kevin. In her crazy attempts to discover what she thought was the truth behind the deaths of Rylander and Klas Lennartsson, she had possibly put Kevin in danger. If something happened to her, it was entirely her own fault. But Kevin had come because she knew that he was probably falling in love with her and would do anything she asked of him. But this? It was madness. She would ring him and tell him to return to the hotel. She wouldn't go and see Albrecht. They would go back to Sweden tomorrow as planned and forget all about it. And then he could enjoy the last few days of his holiday. She was on the verge of picking up her mobile when it sprang into life. She grabbed it. It was Kevin.

'I've no fucking idea where I am, but Benno was on the train.'

'Where is he now?'

'Outside this building.'

'What building?'

He laughed. 'Once I knew he was on the train, I got off at the next station. And then I walked confidently into this apartment block. Followed someone in; made it look like I knew where I was going.' Anita could tell from his voice that he was having fun, like a big kid. 'I'll hang around here for half an hour and hope I'm not reported for loitering!' She was about to call it all off when he said, 'You'd better head off now.' He paused. 'Be careful.'

Moberg had Wallen, Hakim and Brodd in his office for an early-evening briefing.

'OK, tomorrow we hit Sjöbo. We've got a list of some of the church members from Asplund.'

'We've started checking where they live,' said Hakim. 'Most still seem to be in and around the town.'

'If we need to draft in extra officers, so be it. The commissioner is so relieved that our murderer might not be Isaksson that he'll grant us anything. I want confirmation of what Isaksson and Asplund have told us before we move in on the pastor. Any luck with the bus CCTV, Pontus?'

'Not yet, Boss.' Brodd had been given the task of finding out if Pastor Kroon had taken a bus into Malmö on the day of the murder, as they had discovered that he had no registered car.

Hakim and Wallen's second interview with Asplund a couple of hours before had verified Isaksson's version of events. He had made complaints about Kroon's behaviour toward Ebba, which had fallen on deaf ears amongst the congregation. But not even Asplund had known the extent of the sexual abuse that she had been subjected to until years later, when he had got to know her at Malasp Travel.

'Why didn't you bring it to the attention of the authorities when she was working for you?' Hakim had asked.

'I wanted to, but Ebba begged me not to. She didn't want to be reminded of what had happened, or relive it in a very public court case.'

Asplund also confirmed that Isaksson had approached him about offering Ebba a job and how, when she drifted back into prostitution, he had helped set her up in Switzerland; and that Isaksson had supplied the passport. He was still non-committal about whether he had actually procured her clients – 'I assume she met them through the job' was all he would say. The team knew it would be difficult to prove otherwise, as all her former clients resided outside the jurisdiction of Swedish law, with many living in countries where prostitution wasn't illegal.

The fact that the two stories tallied had meant that Blom was unwilling to keep Markus Asplund in custody: they didn't have enough real proof to hold him, and she couldn't see them finding enough to officially charge him within the mandatory three-day period. That pissed off Moberg, who couldn't help feeling that it was far too convenient that each suspect was backing up the other with exactly the same story.

'Now that Asplund has left us, we have to concentrate all our efforts on Pastor Kroon. The quicker we can do it, the faster we can either find he's the killer or rule him out. If it's the latter, then it's straight back to the dynamic duo. But from what I hear of the cleric, I'd like to pin something on him. There must be a whole host of sexual-abuse-related charges. Anything will do.'

'It might be difficult, as the chief witness is conveniently dead,' Brodd pointed out.

'Well, make sure he's the fucking killer then!'

Anita hopped off the underground train at Frankfurter Allee. So did a number of her fellow travellers, who were making for the overground station with its numerous connections to other parts of Berlin. Anita crossed over to the other platform and couldn't see anyone doing the same, though there were quite a few people, including a large group of garrulous students, already waiting for the Alexanderplatz-bound train. Within three minutes, she was on board and heading back into the centre. Only three passengers got off at Strausberger-Platz. She had decided that once off the train, she would walk along the other side of the road from Manja Albrecht's apartment block because there the pavement was wide, and it would be difficult for someone to follow her without her spotting them. She walked down to the Strausberger-Platz roundabout, where she noticed an Italian restaurant. That might be a good place to meet Kevin afterwards for a debriefing session – if there was any debriefing to do.

Halfway down Karl-Marx-Allee, on Manja Albrecht's side of the road, Anita came to the entrance to the underground. She darted down to the station. She walked the length of the platform, came up the other end and turned right. Steps brought her back into the bright light of another cloudless evening on Andreasstrasse and the eastern end of the apartment block. A couple of minutes later, she was round the back of number 64 and standing at the door. Before pushing the intercom button, she took one further glance round, scoping the road behind the building. Opposite were trees, through which she could see a children's play area. Further along were more modern apartments, pristine white with neat metal railings hemming in the narrow balconies. A woman passed her on the pavement; middle-aged – too old for Fanny Källström. She was as sure as she could be that she hadn't been followed. She turned and pressed the buzzer, and Manja's voice answered.

The door clicked open, and Anita stepped into the unknown.

CHAPTER 40

Hans-Dieter Albrecht was younger-looking than Anita had expected. She knew he must be at least eighty, but the man who stood up when she entered Manja's living room was tall and held himself upright. His hair was silver, and though thinning, still covered most of his head. A grey moustache adorned his upper lip. The face was lined, yet had a healthy, flushed pallor. This was a man who had looked after himself. But it was the dark eyes that Anita's gaze was drawn to. They were guarded, and she knew that he was sizing her up. The hand that he offered to her was deeply wrinkled and veined, but the fingers pressed firmly as they enveloped hers in a handshake.

Manja brought in coffee, and then departed after a brief conversation in German with Albrecht, which Anita couldn't understand.

'I leave you with my grandfather,' Manja explained to Anita, who was now sitting. 'He does not like me to listen to the stories of the old days.' Whether this was a warning, Anita wasn't sure.

After Manja had left, there was silence as Albrecht continued to stare at Anita. Then he suddenly waved his hand in the direction of the easels.

'Decadent art,' he said in English with an amused smile. 'The Nazis would have hated it. And also in my time, Manja would have attracted the interest of the authorities.' Anita was impressed by his excellent, if accented, English. 'But she is young, and the world in which I lived has gone. But why exist in such a mess?'

This loving indictment of his granddaughter was delivered despite the fact that Anita could see that Manja had actually made some sort of effort to tidy up.

'I've a son of a similar age. They think differently. They expect more.'

Albrecht took a sip of coffee. He put the cup down slowly.

'So, why do you want to see me?'

'I explained to Manja that I've been brought in by the publishing company that is producing the biography of Albin Rylander. Due to Klas Lennartsson's sad and untimely death, I've been assigned to complete the book.' She produced a pocket voice recorder. Kevin had gone out and bought it in the shopping mall at Alexanderplatz after she'd invented the replacement-writer story for Manja. 'At least you can make an attempt to look like a real writer,' he'd said as he explained how to work the little machine.

'Manja said there were two of you.'

'Yes. But Kevin can't make it tonight. He had another meeting.'

He smiled at her, but there was no warmth in the expression.

'Bullshit! You may be a pretty lady, but you are no writer. I can smell police at fifty kilometres. Why are you really here, Anita? That is if "Anita" is your real name.'

Anita held her hands up as though someone was pointing a gun at her.

'I didn't want to deceive you, but I thought you might not see me if you knew the real reason I have come to Berlin. And I am Anita, by the way. And a cop.'

His face hardened. 'I think your visit is over.' He stood up.

Anita jumped to her feet. 'No, wait! I'm here unofficially. The Swedish police know nothing of this. When you met

Klas Lennartsson last week, I don't know if he told you that he thought Albin Rylander had been murdered.' There was no reaction from Albrecht, so Anita carried on. 'Then Klas died. He was a friend of mine. I think he may also have been killed because of what you told him about Rylander. I'm trying to discover the truth. Only by finding out Rylander's story can I uncover a reason for these two deaths. And you're the only person who has the answer.'

'And if you get the answer you want, what will you do then?'

'That depends on what it is. I don't know what I would do, but at least I might know what I'm up against.'

Albrecht rubbed an eye and then let his hand drop to his side.

'If your friend died because of what I told him, are you not putting yourself in danger?' This uncomfortable thought had been growing in her mind since their arrival in Berlin, and had waxed dramatically from the moment Kevin had spotted Benno Källström. But she couldn't let it go now.

'I know I could be.'

He gazed at Anita intently as though he was weighing up whether to cooperate or not. Then he slowly lowered himself back down onto the sofa and indicated that she should do the same.

'Put that away,' he said firmly, pointing to the recorder. As Anita compliantly slipped it back into her bag, he could see the mixture of fear and resolve in her eyes.

'I've seen the same determination in the eyes of many who passed through Lichtenberg. After we had finished with them, they no longer had that defiance. Dazed, broken, haunted; mere shells.'

'Stasi?'

'And proud. But I am sensible enough not to proclaim it from the rooftops. *Schild und Schwert der Partei.* We were the

Shield and the Sword of the Party. We did our job well, and there were rewards.' He waved at the walls. 'This. This was my reward. Karl-Marx-Allee. The best. But when the Wall came down and our Lichtenberg headquarters were occupied, life was difficult for a former member of *Staatssicherheit*. That it is why I do not live here. I learnt to keep a low profile and blend into the background. I am just an old Berliner who is seen wandering off to the local shops to buy his newspaper, his loaf of bread. I am invisible – and I intend to stay that way.' He pointed at the window. 'There are people out there who would happily harm me if they knew exactly who I was and what I did. I have no regrets. It was for a cause that I believed in. I still do. My father had been a communist, but the Nazis shipped him off to the death camps with so many other political prisoners. I remember the day they came to take him away. My mother crying, my sister screaming. None of the comrades returned. But our time came...' He drifted off in thought, and Anita waited. She had time. She knew he'd tell her all.

'Klas Lennartsson told me that Rylander said it all began and ended in Wilhelmstrasse.'

'Did he?'

'I think Rylander meant that Lenin's journey to Russia was masterminded from the German Foreign Office in Wilhelmstrasse. It was in Malmö that his father Oscar saved Lenin's life, and we think – that's Kevin and I – that the event coloured the whole of Rylander's life. But how did it end in Wilhelmstrasse? Was it because the Swedish embassy was there in the Cold War days?'

Albrecht crossed his legs and sat back in the sofa. She could see him relax, and his eyes brightened.

'You are right about Lenin. But Albin Rylander did not grow up being a political animal. Far from it. He enjoyed life. I think he was what you call in the West a *bon viveur*. That man could hold his drink. But he found Sweden dull. After the war, he wanted to see the world and get the Swedish government to pay for it, so he joined the diplomatic service. He knew nothing of the Lenin connection until his father told him before he died. He gave him a red handkerchief that Lenin had given him.'

She clicked her fingers. 'Yes! He used to wear it in the top pocket of his jacket. And he was clutching it in his hand when they found his body.'

'I am pleased. He showed it to me once. He had not thought about it much at the time of his father's passing, but he realised the story explained why his father was so vehement about the evils of communism. It was guilt, especially at the time shortly before the war broke out, because of Sweden's fear of being swallowed up by the Russian Bear. It was only when Rylander junior had been in a number of diplomatic postings that his admiration for Moscow and what the Soviet Union stood for was kindled. But until then, he made the most of his life. He was tall, handsome, and had many homosexual encounters, especially in places like Algiers, London and Buenos Aires. In the days before mass communication, you could get away with almost anything... in the West that is. I did not approve of his sexual behaviour, but it proved useful to us. And so did he when he was based at the Swedish embassy in Otto-Grotewohl-Strasse—'

'Wilhelmstrasse?'

'Correct. That is when I first came into contact with him. But this goes back further. It really begins with a man called Bruno Krell...' Anita sat on the edge of her seat and concentrated hard, as she knew Albrecht wouldn't allow her to take notes. She wanted to get the story exactly right for when she repeated it to Kevin.

Bruno Krell was born near Lübeck in 1923. His real name was Gunter Ringel. As with many young, impressionable teenagers of his day in Germany, he was in awe of Hitler and the ideals of the National Socialists. He was in the Hitler Youth, and when the war broke out, he was absorbed into the army. He was brave and resourceful and very, very ruthless. These qualities were highly prized by the Nazis, and attracted the attention of a senior member of the Gestapo. Though young, Ringel was an enthusiastic participant in many Gestapo operations on the Eastern Front, where they followed the assault troops and barbarically "cleansed" the population.

In 1943, he was brought back to Germany and, because of his youth, was used to infiltrate the student unrest that was highlighted by the White Rose movement led by Sophie and Hans Scholl at the University of Munich. As the war was nearing its close and the Russians advanced steadily through the east of Germany, Ringel found himself working out of the Gestapo headquarters here in Berlin. He had been involved in rounding up the increasing number of dissidents, deserters and defeatists emerging from the woodwork when the war was obviously lost; there were still plenty of their own people for the Gestapo to kill even in the last days of the war. However, Gunter Ringel was astute enough to know that his time was up, and he managed to flee Berlin. He made for Lübeck, but realised that he would never get as far as the Baltic coast. Like many Nazis, he recognised that his Gestapo background would count against him if he was taken by the Allies. He found a fellow German soldier of a similar age, got him drunk, killed him, and stole his identity. Bruno Krell emerged and blended into the background; an ordinary trooper who had been separated from his unit. Who would have believed that a man of twenty-two could have packed so much death into his short life? Unfortunately for him, he was captured by the Russians and not by the Americans or British.

By 1950, Bruno Krell, the vehement communist, was living in East Berlin, and had started working in a lowly position for the recently formed Staatssicherheit. His old Gestapo skills came into their own. Surveillance, infiltration, interrogation and persuasion. There were a number of ex-Nazis who wormed their way into positions in the new GDR. You could not run a country on old communists alone. Not that anyone knew of Krell's past at that time.

In the late fifties, he came under the influence of Markus Wolf, the head of Hauptverwaltung Aufklärung – the HVA – the foreign intelligence section of the Stasi. Again, he had the qualities and qualifications to be a good spy. He was attached to various embassies abroad – those that would accept a GDR embassy. And he spent time in Moscow, where he impressed the KGB. And it was the Russians who sent him to London in 1964 because the GDR did not have a diplomatic presence there at the time. He spoke good English, Russian and, of course, German. He was soon gathering intelligence. Both the KGB and the Stasi appreciated how valuable he was becoming. But he had one weakness that he had hidden during his Gestapo days. He was homosexual. It was illegal in Britain then, as it still is in Russia. Yet it was also a strength, in that he made a number of useful contacts in what would now be called the gay scene. He knew the pubs and clubs where they gathered – civil servants, scientists, MPs, lawyers, aristocrats, diplomats and the like, who could then be blackmailed if necessary.

And then one day, he was recognised in the street by a woman who had been arrested by the Gestapo near the end of the war. Krell, or to be more exact, Gunter Ringel, had interrogated her. She had survived and married an army captain who was part of the occupying force in the British Sector of Berlin. She was now living in London. She reported the sighting to her husband, and he passed the information on to MI5, the domestic counter-intelligence and security service. They did some digging and pieced together Krell's past. Because of his youth in the war, he was not exactly in the first rank of war criminals. And besides, the diplomatic immunity of the Russian embassy would make *arrest impossible. Expulsion from the country seemed to be the only option. However, MI5 felt there might be another choice. They put him under surveillance and soon realised what he was doing and the connections he was making. They had a spy in their midst but, because of his background, not a spy who was ideologically committed. He was a man of transferable loyalties – a man who could be turned.*

That is where Albin Rylander came in.

Rylander was working at the Swedish embassy in London at that time. He came on the radar of the MI5 watchers who were keeping an eye on Krell because of his visits to similar haunts. Then, MI6, the agency for gathering foreign intelligence, got involved, and they made the decision that they would try and recruit Krell through a staged homosexual contact. But they didn't want to compromise him or themselves by using a British or American man for the seduction. That was something the KGB could have sniffed out. So, what better than a neutral, who would seem to have no partial views? A Swede. MI6 contacted Sektionen för särskild inhämtning – the SSI – the Section for Special Collection; a very secret part of the Swedish Armed Forces, whose role was to liaise with foreign intelligence agencies. After carefully monitoring Rylander's promiscuous activities, MI6 suggested Rylander would be suitable, and the SSI went about recruiting him on behalf of the British. He did not take much persuading. Money was probably an inducement to a socialite on a junior Swedish diplomat's pay in the expensive London of the decadent sixties. But what really appealed to Rylander was that it was a dangerous adventure.

It was not difficult for Rylander to run into Krell and befriend him. They became lovers, and, gradually, Krell was turned. In fact, he was easily bought. His only loyalty was to himself. And once he started to provide information, the fear of being caught by the KGB or the Stasi was further inducement. And if it all went wrong and he tried to defect to the West, his

Nazi past would be dragged up. That was made quite clear by MI6. He was trapped. In effect, he became a double agent and MI6 provided him with seemingly useful but ultimately useless information to feed back to Moscow and East Berlin. MI6 thought that by sharing Krell's secrets with the CIA, they could win back the Americans' trust after the exposure of Kim Philby and the other Cambridge spies.

The trouble began when Rylander began to change his view of the world and the West. The more he thought about his father's Lenin story, the more he saw it as fate that he should be attracted to communism. That was cemented when he came to work in East Berlin. That's when he contacted the Stasi. He knew that Krell was away in America, where Markus Wolf thought he would be of most use. Albrecht was the Stasi contact that met up with Albin Rylander. At that stage, they were aware of his sexual connection with Krell, but it never occurred to them that he was working for MI6. He told Albrecht about the saving of Lenin's life and said that he was interested in working for the communist cause, but insisted that Krell was not to know about him contacting the Stasi because of the personal nature of their link. The truth was that though he was in love with Krell, he didn't trust him. That's why he had come directly to the Stasi's domestic section and not Wolf's foreign operation. Initially, they did not know what to do with him. He was not exactly in a position to be of much use, but he might be one for the future if he got higher up the ladder; if he could aim for an important London posting – or even better, Washington – then he might prove useful. Until that time he was, in diplomatic corridors, to outwardly distance himself from any connection to communism. To become an anti-communist hawk was how Albrecht described it. And that is what he became until his death.

Rylander reached Washington in the early 1980s. Ronald Reagan had become president and was ramping up the Cold

War. It was a dangerous time. Krell was now back in Berlin and in a very senior position. That was when Albrecht came across him. A very dislikeable, cold and arrogant man – and not one to cross. The trouble was that he now had access to vital information that he was passing back to the British, which was then shared with the CIA in Langley. Sometimes he used Rylander, who managed to take out some of the most sensitive material before it reached the desks of MI6. Rylander was becoming alarmed at the quality of the information that Krell was now sending. He realised he had to do something. They met one last time – somewhere in Sweden when Rylander was home on leave. It was a sad parting for Rylander because he knew he was about to betray the love of his life. And that is exactly what he did, through Albrecht. At first, no one could believe it, but the Stasi's interrogation methods were infallible. Krell was hard to break; he knew what it was like to be on the other side, both with the Gestapo and the Stasi, and he knew how to handle even the most difficult of questions and the physical force that accompanied them. But when he heard who had betrayed him, all the fight seemed to go out of him. He was finished. He had been in love with Rylander. Of course, they made sure that Rylander was in no way connected to Krell's sudden fall from power and subsequent execution. He needed protecting.

Albrecht remained Rylander's contact until the Wall fell. That was a bad time to be a Stasi agent. He could tell the way the wind was blowing. Unlike many of his colleagues, he could see that his days were numbered. He may have been a communist, but he was also a pragmatist. He got rid of all the files connecting him to the Stasi, which, of course, included everything to do with Albin Rylander. He did it before the panic, when everybody was desperately trying to get rid of everything. When the Stasi headquarters were occupied by protestors, apparently they found 16,000 sacks of shredded documents, much of which they have painstakingly pieced together since.

But there is no mention of Albrecht in there – or Rylander, or Krell. He disappeared from sight and remained anonymous until his granddaughter was contacted by Rylander a couple of months ago. He agreed to meet Klas Lennartsson after Rylander's death. Rylander told Albrecht that he was going to tell all in a book, though Albrecht's name wouldn't be revealed.

Rylander's legacy? Above all, he gave Krell to the Stasi. It was a huge blow to the British and Americans when one of their top sources throughout the Cold War was silenced. After Krell's death, he continued to provide Moscow and East Berlin with sensitive information; his time in America was particularly fruitful. Incredibly, Albrecht firmly believed that Rylander went on serving the communist cause even after his retirement; even after glasnost. Albrecht wasn't totally sure, as he had been out of the game for a long time, but his guess was that during Putin's first presidency, Rylander was still supplying the Russians with intelligence. The Russians have snooped around the Stockholm archipelago and Sweden's east coast for years. Could Rylander have played a part in that? Albrecht could only speculate. None of this, of course, was known to the West. Rylander was so respected that he served on various important committees – diplomatic and military – both in Sweden and internationally. And the diplomat's death? Albrecht was pretty sure he knew who had killed him – and why.

CHAPTER 41

The evening had started to cool, and Anita was quite happy to have her meal inside the Vesuvio trattoria off the Strausberger-Platz roundabout and not at a pavement table. After leaving Manja's apartment, she had phoned Kevin, who had holed up in a bar near Alexanderplatz waiting for her to contact him. She had taken a table, and Kevin joined her fifteen minutes later when she was on her second glass of the house red. He wasn't sure if Benno Källström had followed him, but it didn't matter now. As long as he didn't know where Anita had been.

Over their antipasti, she filled him in on Albrecht's story. Kevin was fascinated with all aspects of the tale, and annoyed Anita by constantly interrupting her to clarify certain points. By the time their main courses arrived – a *Tortellini alla Panna* for him and a *Petti di Pollo al Pepe Verde* for her – they were entering the area of speculation.

'Did he produce a suggestion as to why Rylander might have been killed?' Kevin asked in between mouthfuls.

'Yes,' she answered as she waved to the waiter to bring them a second bottle of wine. 'And very disturbing it was too.'

'Disturbing?' His fork stopped short of his mouth.

'He thinks that it could be our own people behind it.'

'What do you mean, "own people"?'

She lowered her voice. 'The Swedish government. Or more likely, some Swedish agency within the government.'

'Wow! I know we've been talking conspiracy theories, but I didn't think there was any real possibility of that.'

'It's all to do with what I mentioned to you about Sweden's balancing act during the Cold War. There have been a couple of Swedish spies unmasked, like Stig Wennerström, who worked for the Soviets in the 1960s. Like Rylander, he was based in Washington at one stage. But he was an individual acting on his own. The difference is that Rylander was recruited by the Section for Special Collection. Even today, most Swedes know nothing about this organisation. Basically, they were getting into bed with the British at a time when they were meant to be neutral.'

'I remember reading about all the Edward Snowden stuff, and it was revealed that Sweden had signed a top secret agreement with the Yanks, us, Canada and Australia, I think, to share intelligence.'

'Well, Rylander in his memoirs would have revealed the SSI connection. This would further damage the supposed neutral stance that Sweden still has today, and give Putin even more ammunition. The problem is that I suspect the SSI at the time didn't bother to inform the Swedish government. They acted alone in their recruitment of Rylander. But to make it worse, having been involved in creating one of the West's most useful spies, Rylander then changes sides and hands Krell over to the Stasi. That fact coming out would have damaged the relationship Sweden's secret service and MI6 had with the CIA. And then, of course, he was spying for the Soviets and East Germans in Washington, and may well have carried on supplying the post-communist Russian government with vital secrets. Depending on what those secrets were – which presumably would have come out in the book – that would have further destroyed trust with the Americans. It would have also led to a witch hunt among the government secret service agencies in Sweden. God only knows what kind of power struggles go on there.

Whatever the situation, the revelations in the book would have been explosive, and the repercussions and recriminations would have had major international implications. I don't think the British, Americans, Russians or the Swedes come out of it well, so there are a lot of people who might have gone to great lengths to make sure nothing ever came out.'

Kevin filled Anita's glass up from the fresh bottle. 'It's certainly all been kept very quiet. I've never heard of Bruno Krell. And the media have named and shamed most of the Cold War spies over the years. Bloody hell!' He topped up his own glass. 'Who does Albrecht think is behind it – specifically, I mean?'

'He reckons it could be the modern equivalent of the SSI. It's now *Kontoret för särskild inhämtning* – KSI – The Office for Special Collection.'

'That's only one letter different.'

'And the same, very secret organisation.'

Kevin pulled a strained face. 'If that's all true, then they're not going to be very happy about us.' He leant over the table and held Anita's hand. 'Are we getting in too deep? I don't want anything horrid happening to you. Not to me, either.'

She gazed at his hand on hers. 'I don't know what to do. Pretend it never happened? In some ways I no longer care about Rylander. He was a traitor, though I'm sure he could justify it to himself. In fact, the whole book thing was him just being mischievous on a giant scale, knowing he wouldn't be around to take all the flack. But Klas? That's different. He was an innocent in all this. Just doing the most exciting job to ever come along in his ordinary life.'

Kevin squeezed her hand. 'Pudding?'

Anita slowly removed her hand. 'I think they call it dessert.'

'If you want to be posh. I can't finish without ice cream. Isn't that what Italian restaurants are all about?'

*

They walked back to the hotel. They had eaten and drunk too much and realised they needed the exercise to settle their stomachs. Even at that late hour, the traffic was still swishing past on its way out of the city centre. Lights were gradually disappearing from the apartment blocks they wandered past. Anita slipped her hand into Kevin's. They knew their unspoken thoughts were about what they should do. The moral dilemma of cops who suddenly realise that whatever action they take, they can't bring to justice an organisation that has the power to brush everything under the carpet. What made it seem even more hopeless, more impossible was that there was no way they would be believed because they didn't have access to the facts that would support their case. Kevin broke the silence.

'There was something that Klas said about Rylander not being ashamed of what he'd done, but he felt guilty about the person it most affected.'

'I remember.'

'Whatever we think of Rylander now, the most difficult thing in his life must have been to betray his great love. I can't imagine doing that.' He gripped her hand tightly.

'Krell sounds like a self-serving monster.'

'But even monsters can love. It sounds as if discovering it was Rylander who had grassed him up was what broke his resistance. And Rylander still had regrets at the end.'

Anita turned to him. 'Have you any regrets?'

'A few. But none that I'll worry about on my deathbed; unless you're not there holding my hand.'

Anita smirked. 'I don't know about that.' She let go of his hand. He was getting into uncomfortably intimate territory. This wasn't the time.

They walked on in silence. What on earth were they going to do about Rylander and Lennartsson? All the options seemed to spell danger.

CHAPTER 42

Moberg was also weighing up his options. Sandwiches, a pizza, or a Chinese carry-out? Waiting for the team to report back from Sjöbo had made him hungry. He had gone over all the material, interviews and evidence surrounding the case. Notwithstanding his natural loathing of Axel Isaksson, he was beginning to think that the politician, though guilty of various crimes – supplying a passport in a false name, paying a prostitute for sex, withholding information from the police – wasn't the murderer. The aggravating thing was that Isaksson's alibi checked out, despite Moberg's attempts to circumvent the timeframe of his movements and the murder. It still added up to the fact that he couldn't have been in two places at once. And Moberg was coming to a similar conclusion regarding Markus Asplund's possible guilt. He had carefully listened to the interviews again. Though Asplund was clearly avoiding admitting to setting up Ebba with her clients, he did sound like a man who was telling the truth most of the time. Moberg had been in and around interview rooms long enough to know when someone was lying through their teeth. It might be frustrating in terms of progressing with the case, but, with that in mind, he'd had a brief meeting with Prosecutor Blom about what they already knew about Pastor Kroon and what the team were busily trying to dig up.

What Brodd had found out was that Kroon had been in Malmö that Tuesday. CCTV had shown him getting off the direct SkåneExpressen 8 bus at Södervärn bus station at 9.38 am. It had arrived three minutes late. He hadn't been able to find Kroon making a return journey from there. But that was enough to give the cautious Blom the nerve to say that if the team found witnesses willing to substantiate Isaksson's assertion of Kroon's behaviour towards Ebba, then they could bring him in for questioning.

Moberg was still undecided about his early lunch when his office phone rang. He grabbed the receiver. It was Hakim.

'We've found four people who have reluctantly admitted that they were uncomfortable with the pastor's unsavoury relationship with Ebba. One elderly ex-member, according to one of the constables I spoke to, said that she was expelled from the church for raising the subject. She didn't report it, as she thought the police wouldn't believe her because Kroon was well respected in the town. But they've all kept quiet. I think they were frightened of Kroon. Still are. And they justified their silence by the fact that Ebba suddenly went away. Out of sight, out of mind, I suppose.'

'That's good work. Right, I want you and Wallen to go round to Kroon's place now. Pick him up and bring him in.'

Another decision. A Chinese carry-out. Things were looking up.

The Stasi Museum at Lichtenberg was a five-minute walk from the Magdalenenstrasse underground station. It was the sheer size of the old Stasi headquarters' twenty-two-hectare complex that blew Kevin's mind. As they didn't have to be at the airport until one o'clock, he had convinced Anita that they could spend the morning going round the museum and find out what sort of organisation Hans-Dieter Albrecht had worked for – and Albin Rylander had spied for. And it was sort of on their way.

The museum was in the building which had housed the Stasi hierarchy. It was much like any other unimaginative early

1960s office block you'd find anywhere in the world – except the business of "house 1" was more ominous. Its role was to police, spy upon and terrorise a whole nation; to seep into and control every aspect of its citizens' lives.

The centrepiece of the museum was the office suite of the Minister for State Security; the fiefdom of Erich Mielke, who held this position for thirty years. It was just the same as it was when the frenzied citizens of East Germany forcibly occupied the administrative buildings before all the documents could be destroyed; and they were able discover the files on themselves, their families, friends and colleagues. What they found was an organisation that had compiled 111 kilometres of paper files, 1.7 million photos and 28,000 recordings. Kevin was much taken with Mielke's conference room and private quarters. They were vivid snapshots of 1960s design with wood-panelled walls, parquet flooring and clunky furniture. Not too ostentatious, of course, but solid, practical, comfortable; reeking power. Mielke's vast, plain, highly polished desk still had the telephones of the time in place. Kevin mentally speculated about what dreadful instructions and fateful decisions must have been conducted over those lines.

In various rooms the story of the Stasi was told through their imaginative, yet often clumsy, listening and photographic devices in what was a surveillance seventh heaven. Many aped the technology of the early James Bond films – the watch with a recording device, the clothing that contained miniature cameras, and innocent handbags that picked up idle but subversive snippets of conversation; even the Rosa Klebb shoe with the metal spike at its tip. What tickled Kevin most was the watering can with a concealed camera – even gardeners weren't safe.

As he moved through the rooms, he realised that Anita was not with him. He made his way back and found her staring at a case containing domestic listening devices.

'There's some fascinating stuff through there, Anita.'

She didn't acknowledge him but continued to be transfixed by the objects in front of her.

'We'd better not be too long; we've got to get to the airport.'

'That's what all this has been about.'

'What?'

Anita swivelled round to face him. 'Surveillance. Listening in. That's what they've been doing.'

Kevin was still unsure what she was alluding to.

'Rylander. They were listening in.' The penny dropped. 'That's what the Källströms were doing next door. They had Rylander under surveillance. There must be bugs planted in his house. They were listening to his conversations with Klas. When they realised that he was going to reveal everything, they killed him. Maybe not they themselves, but other members of their team or organisation. That's why they left when they did before their holiday rental was up.'

'Maybe it was our Mr Large I saw in the trees observing the house.'

'He's obviously the same man Moa Hellquist saw with Alice Zetterberg when she reported Rylander's death.'

A young couple came wandering into the room, and Anita and Kevin slipped out into the corridor.

'They must have bugged Klas, too. They would have suspected that he would find out at least some of Rylander's life story that he hadn't yet told.' Anita suddenly smacked the wall with her hand in exasperation. 'The text! The text he sent me. They would have intercepted that. Oh, the poor fellow!'

Kevin took Anita by the arm. 'Let's get out of here.'

'That text was Klas signing his own death warrant.'

They had gone through the airport security and made their way past the shopping area. Normally, Anita would have automatically stopped at the duty free to pick up a bottle of spirits, but she

273

couldn't concentrate on anything other than their present predicament, which she was solely responsible for landing them in. They hadn't seen Benno Källström on either of the two trains they took to reach the airport, but both of them had been aware that he was probably somewhere close by. Kevin may have fooled him once – but not twice if he was a real professional. They found seats in the corridor leading to the departure gates.

'They must also have bugged your holiday home.' Kevin was simply articulating what she had already worked out.

'I know. They must have been listening in to all our conversations – and were probably watching us once they knew our suspicions had been aroused, and I had started asking questions. That would explain the police patrol materialising at the Källströms' that night.'

'And Zetterberg turning up when you went to Klas's home.'

'You're right. How the hell does she fit into all this?'

'Of course, she may have been unwittingly involved. Just doing her job. Given a tip off that someone was in Klas's house. That sort of thing.' The scowling glance she threw in his direction immediately had him retracting the theory: 'Then again, maybe not.'

'I'm not inclined to give her the benefit of the doubt. But you may be right,' she conceded. Anita opened her bag, rummaged around and then gave a heavy sigh. There was no comforting snus to help calm her.

'What surprises me,' started Kevin. He stopped for a moment, then continued: 'What surprises me is that as they obviously knew we were coming to Berlin, why didn't they contrive to stop you meeting Hans-Dieter Albrecht? They must have known that we couldn't discover a motive for the murders without his background story. Actually, now I think of it, why didn't they stop Klas from coming? They must have heard Rylander telling him. You got the address from a recording.'

'I did, didn't I?' mused Anita. Then she suddenly sat bolt

upright. 'No, no, they didn't know. I remember now, that recording had the sound of the sea in the background. They must have been sitting outside. It wouldn't have been picked up by the microphones in the house. So, they might not have even known that Klas was going to Berlin until they realised he'd already been from the text message to me.'

'He told *us* though. If—'

'But they probably hadn't started listening into us at that point; we only started fishing after Klas's death. At that stage, they'd assume that Klas hadn't got enough to finish the book. Other than the Lenin story, it wasn't exactly best-seller material. And nothing to shed light on their activities. Then, to their horror, they realise he's been in Berlin and probably knows the whole truth, or at least some of it. The fact that he texted me alerted them to us – perhaps they bugged the house after that.'

'Yeah; I can't work out when they could have done that.'

Anita went quiet. 'I reckon they only had one opportunity to do it; you were out on a walk and I was in Simrishamn.'

'I wonder why they didn't find Klas's file. I reckon they would have searched the house while they were bugging it; they obviously gave his place the once over.'

'They wouldn't have found it,' she said with some glee. 'I took it with me!'

'Clever shite! So, what about when we talked about Albrecht? They would have heard us then.'

'We were outside, remember? Having a beer. That's when I told you we were coming here. Now it all makes sense! Once we were being monitored, they would have found out about our Berlin flight bookings. That's why Benno Källström followed us here.'

'This is doing my head in. I need a drink. Fancy one?'

They got up and walked back along the corridor and found a bar. Kevin ordered himself a beer and Anita a glass of red wine. They took sanctuary at a corner table.

'I don't know what the hell we're going to do. I'm so sorry for getting you involved in this.' She took his hand and pressed it between hers.

With his other hand, he gently pushed back a couple of stray hairs that had flopped over her glasses.

'I'm just glad I'm here for you. I lo...' He checked himself. 'I'm really fond of you, Anita.'

She beamed back at him gratefully. Then they both returned to their drinks in silence.

After a long draught of his beer, Kevin spoke.

'Look, Anita, can you go to your boss in Malmö with this?'

She shook her head. 'Hardly. We've got no evidence. We've got a nurse's suspicions about Rylander's suicide; we've got the theories of a local historian who's now dead; plus some other weird stuff like the Källströms finishing their holiday early – and that they're certainly not called Källström at all. We've got a cow of a police detective acting oddly but, on the face of it, not operating outside the law. We think we've been followed to Berlin but can't prove it. We're basing our theories on the word of a shifty ex-Stasi operative who won't come out of hiding to back up our story. We can't prove a damn thing. We've got no autopsy or accident-scene reports. Nothing concrete. And Moberg certainly wouldn't contemplate sniffing around someone else's enquiry, because it's officially Zetterberg's remit. He'd think I was on drugs. I'd do the same in his position. So would you.'

'I suppose you're right.' He gave a little groan. 'I've got to go back on Thursday, but I can't just sit in Penrith waiting and wondering what's happening to you, and then get some message that you've been in a fatal accident – or whatever these spooks dream up to keep you quiet.'

She could see the worry etched across his features. She realised at that moment how much he cared for her.

'I can look after myself. I'll be fine.' Not that she felt remotely fine.

'Anita, that's not enough,' he said forcefully. 'These people – whatever the fuck they're called – have killed twice. You now know too much. They know you know. Do you think they'll let you just carry on merrily as though nothing's happened? They can't be sure you'll not let the cat out of the bag at some stage, even if you don't pursue it now.'

'Kevin, why would they harm me? They know I can't prove that Rylander and Klas were killed. End of story.'

'But that's not the story, Anita. Rylander's *past* is the story. What he did, with their connivance, is what they're worried about. They know you can't touch them for the murders, but it's all the other stuff they'll be afraid might come out. That's what's putting you in peril.'

Anita was quite shaken by what Kevin had just said. She hadn't thought it through properly; hadn't grasped the real significance of what she had done. Suddenly, she realised with alarming clarity that she was totally out of her depth.

He drained the last of his beer decisively and slammed down his glass. 'Right, the first thing we both do is turn off our mobile phones so they can't be traced.'

'My last text was to Lasse, just to tell him we'd be away for a couple of days.'

'That doesn't matter because they followed us here. But we don't want to make life easy for them from now on.'

They both took out their mobiles and switched them off.

'What if Lasse—'

'No "what ifs",' he said firmly, putting away his phone. 'Now, you lot carry guns, don't you?'

'Yes. But I'm not allowed to carry a weapon around with me when I'm not on duty.'

'Is it back at the holiday home or your flat?'

'Of course not. Locked up in headquarters, where it should be,' she said primly.

'Right, as soon as we reach Malmö, I want you to go and get it.'

She placed her hand on his. 'This is daft. I'll be OK,' – though she knew she wouldn't be. And she was now dreading his return to England; she would be lost without him.

'Just do as I say,' he said resolutely. 'I've got a plan. It's probably a shit plan, but it's all we've got.'

CHAPTER 43

Moberg just had to look into the demonic eyes to know that they were dealing with a seriously strange man. A man who had wielded extraordinary power over his congregation. He must have assuaged a need in these people. Not that Moberg was remotely sympathetic to their spiritual wants, whatever they were. It was their own damn fault that they'd been sucked in by his manipulatory rhetoric. If they had chosen that route to heaven, they had mistakenly stumbled across the devil. This might be the first time he had clapped eyes on Elias Kroon, but he could easily imagine the creepy pastor quite capable of unspeakable behaviour towards the young Ebba Pozorski. Now they were going to have to prove that and place him at the scene of the crime. That might be difficult. Having taken Kroon's fingerprints on his arrival at the polishus, Moberg had got straight onto forensics to recheck their findings from Akerman/ Pozorski's apartment to establish whether he had been there. There was no match.

The one ace Moberg had up his sleeve was conducting the interview with Hakim. The young Muslim's presence in the room made a disquieting impression on the pastor, who wouldn't look at him directly. This was the effect Moberg had wanted.

'You have no right to hold me here. I should be doing God's work; I'm late for an appointment already.' He made a show of looking at his watch, which, Moberg noted, was on his left wrist.

'We have every right. Surely even your God would approve of you, one of his disciples, helping us try to find the murderer of an innocent young woman.'

'She was a whore. Ungodly. She got what she deserved.'

Moberg restrained an impulse to reach across the table and grab the pastor by the throat.

'OK, let's find out why she became a prostitute. I want to take you back to when you were running the Church of God's Mission on Earth. The Pozorski family join the congregation. They bring along their pretty daughter, who becomes obsessed with religion. When she was killed, she was wearing this cross.' Moberg pushed the object into the middle of the table.

'She shouldn't have been wearing that.'

'Despite everything that had happened to her, she still believed. Despite everything you'd done to her.' The chief inspector nodded to Hakim. Hakim produced a sheaf of papers.

'These are statements by ex-members of the Church of God's Mission on Earth that claim that, at the very least, you sexually abused Ebba Pozorski. They include one from Axel Isaksson. Do you deny the allegations?'

Kroon stared at the pieces of paper before returning his gaze to Moberg.

'There is only one being I'm answerable to. I won't be judged by the likes of you.' He stabbed a finger in the direction of the statements. 'Or them.'

'Are you saying you played no part in corrupting Ebba Pozorski?' Moberg pressed angrily.

Kroon remained collected. 'All I will say is that if anyone was doing the corrupting, it was that girl. She was evil disguised as innocence.'

'So, you're trying to tell us that it was Ebba who led *you* astray?' He ramped up the astonishment in his voice for the benefit of the digital recording.

'I will let you draw your own conclusions. She died a harlot.'

Hakim could sense that Moberg was about to lose it.

'Is that why you attacked her with a knife?' Moberg roared.

Kroon was not intimidated. 'I was defending myself.'

'She was stabbed in the shoulder. How could you have been defending yourself if she had her back to you?'

'I have nothing further to say about that incident.'

Hakim could see they would never get him to admit culpability. In his own warped way, Kroon had probably justified his actions by transferring the guilt to Ebba. Before Moberg lost control, Hakim quickly changed tack.

'Why did you come into Malmö on Tuesday, the third of June?'

'Did I? I can't remember.'

Hakim pushed across the table a CCTV image of the pastor getting off the bus.

'This is the bus station at Södervärn. It's SkåneExpressen 8 from Sjöbo. You can see the time and date there,' said Hakim, pointing. Kroon still avoided looking at the young detective.

'I must have then,' he said absently.

'What was the purpose of your visit?'

'I am not sure whether it was that date, but I came into Malmö to return some books to the city library.'

'And doesn't Sjöbo have a library?' said Moberg taking over the interview again, his temper now under control.

Kroon gave the chief inspector a contemptuous look. 'Not with the kind of religious or philosophical works that I find mind-improving.'

Moberg was beginning to dislike Kroon even more than Isaksson.

'And how long were you at the library?'

'I spent much of the day there.'

'And then?'

He sucked in his thick lips. 'I visited a member of my flock.'

'Former flock,' Moberg corrected.

'The believers – the *true* believers – will always be loyal.'

'And how long did the visit take?'

He wafted a hand in the air. 'As long as I was needed.'

'We can't find you getting the bus back that day,' put in Hakim.

'That's because I didn't get the bus back. I stayed the night.'

Both Moberg and Hakim tensed.

'Can we have the name and address of this person?' Moberg snapped.

'He is not well.'

'Name and address?'

Reluctantly, the cleric gave them the name of man called Jaspar Lindroth living in Dammfri.

'That's not far from Pildammsparken. Hakim, get Wallen to check that out immediately.' Hakim hurried from the room.

'I don't want you to distress Lindroth. The man has cancer, for goodness' sake.'

'I'm sure Inspector Klara Wallen will be gentle with him. Now, did you go anywhere near Pildammsparken that night?'

'No.'

'Are you sure?'

'As God is my witness.'

'We'll let him sweat,' Moberg said to Hakim as he helped himself to coffee from the vending machine. He took a sip and pulled a face. 'Why do I buy this crap? It never gets any better.'

'What do you think?' Hakim asked.

'Is he our man? I bloody hope so, but I suspect we'll have a job proving it. Well, finding enough evidence to satisfy Blom anyway.'

'He was in Malmö on the night of the murder. He'd attacked Ebba before with a knife.'

Moberg gave a heavy sigh. 'Again, we can't prove it. There's a medical record showing she was treated for the wound in Ystad, but no formal complaint was made by her or her father.

So that won't stand up in court. It's hearsay.'

They began to wander along the corridor towards Moberg's office.

'He's got a motive. She could still have brought charges against him at any time.'

'But why now?'

Hakim had to agree that the timing was odd. He could have tracked her down when she was living in Malmö before she moved to Switzerland.

'Unless he ran into her on that Tuesday. Probably accidently. Maybe something was said, and he realised that she was still a danger to him. She could have threatened to expose him.'

'And the butterfly knife?'

'I don't know. There might be a number of ways he could have got hold of one. Maybe a member of his congregation had been to the States at some time. Or maybe he had. There are a lot of weird religious sects over there.'

'It's a problem when there's no sign of the murder weapon. Look, while we're waiting for Wallen to speak to Lindroth, get Brodd to go down to the city library and see if the pastor *was* there and for how long. And I know it's a long shot, but see if Ebba Pozorski went in there that day, too.'

The call that came in from Wallen was encouraging. Lindroth had confirmed that Pastor Kroon had visited him on the afternoon of Tuesday, 3rd June at about four o'clock. They had talked and prayed together and, as it was getting late, Kroon asked if he could stay the night. 'Are you sure it was Kroon who suggested he stay the night?' Moberg had asked. Wallen confirmed that it had been Kroon's suggestion. Lindroth had become very tired after their discussions, so he had gone to bed shortly after eight. He left Kroon to fend for himself, but he was adamant that he heard the front door open and close before he dropped off. He wasn't sure of the time but says it must have been before nine.

He has no idea when Kroon came back because he was asleep by then.

Moberg and Hakim were back in the interview room soon after the call from Wallen ended. The chief inspector came straight to the point: 'The night you stayed with Lindroth; where did you go out to?'

'It was hot in Jaspar's apartment. I went out for some fresh air.'

'And where did you go?'

'Along the streets. I'm not sure where. I don't know the district well.'

'You didn't happen to go to Pildammsparken?'

'Do you not listen? I have already told you that I did not go to the park.'

Moberg had already recognised that Kroon was going to be a tough nut to crack, but at least they knew he had motive – and now, opportunity. He could feel that they were getting closer.

Kevin was on his second cup of tea when Anita returned from the polishus. He had taken up a seat in one of the café areas in the newly laid out Central Station. It reminded him of Kastrup Airport, which they had just come through a couple of hours before. He had been tempted to wander round Malmö for a while to get to know the city a little, but decided that he didn't want to go sauntering off with the possibility of secret service operatives in the vicinity. From the station, he had allowed himself a peek at the Savoy Hotel. In its art nouveau magnificence, it purported to be every bit as chic and expensive as its London counterpart. It was there that the mess they had got themselves into had begun in 1917. It was extraordinary to think that Lenin had walked through the very arch he was standing under, had crossed that bridge over the canal to eat at that hotel, and there have his life saved by a Swedish waiter – an action which impacted on millions. And caught up in the dying ripples of that one brave deed were the deaths of the saviour's son and an innocent historian nearly a century after the event.

Over his cups of breakfast tea, he had played over again in his mind the mad plan he had concocted. There was no way that they could take on a secret government organisation like the KSI, or whoever it was behind the killings. It would be impossible for Anita to bring anybody to justice for the murders. The system would make sure that never happened. So, instead of waiting nervously for their adversaries to make a move on Anita once he had gone back to England, he'd reckoned that it was best to go to them and try to put them on the back foot. His idea was to flush them out – with himself as bait.

Anita arrived looking pale. She tapped her bag, and he understood that she had collected her police pistol.

'Any questions?'

'No. I didn't bump into anybody. They must all be busy.'

She glanced at her watch.

'Train's in five minutes. We'd better go.'

With a sense of foreboding, Kevin gulped down the last of his tea and followed Anita towards the platforms.

CHAPTER 44

Jazmin had slept heavily last night. The two paracetamols had helped. When she turned over and stretched out, she saw that Lasse was not lying next to her. The first hint of panic was when she realised there was no indentation in his pillow. She had changed the bedding yesterday afternoon. He worked at the Kungsgatan café until late on a Tuesday but would normally be back around midnight. Usually, he crept into bed and they'd snuggle up. Last night, she had gone out like a light. Maybe he hadn't wanted to disturb her and had slept on the uncomfortable sofa they'd bought second-hand at Myrona. He'd probably started playing his stupid football computer game and just dropped off. She opened the door to the little living room and was greeted by Messi, who nuzzled around her ankles before darting off into the kitchen for her to feed him. There was no Lasse. After his late shifts, he never left early the next morning because he didn't have lectures until eleven. It was now 8.03 am.

She looked around the apartment, which was so small that the task took under a minute. Why? She didn't know, because it was obvious he wasn't there. A reflex reaction? Her mouth was still dry from the night's sleep. Now she could hardly breathe. She tried to gulp in lungfuls of air and had to grab the edge of the draining board for support. As she gradually calmed down, she chided herself for her loss of control. There must be a simple explanation. Maybe he'd stayed the night with one of his fellow workers. He was friendly with a guy called Leo. That would be it. He'd probably left a message on her mobile. And then it hit her again that she hadn't had a mobile since it had been stolen at Mobilia. She still hadn't had the courage to mention that to Lasse. She would definitely tell him later today and face up to his anger and annoyance. He'd probably go straight to lectures instead of coming out to Rosengård, but he should be back by four. She'd cook him his favourite meal. After all, she had been a bit cranky lately. All this business about being watched had made her tetchy, and it hadn't helped that he hadn't believed her. Maybe she *had* dreamt the whole thing up.

Jazmin felt better now as she scooped out the last of the cheap tin of cat food into Messi's bowl. She watched him devour the fishy-smelling mash. As she boiled up the kettle, she resolved to go out and get a cheap pay-as-you-go mobile phone to tide her over. They couldn't afford a landline telephone, so she felt that she had to have some point of contact. And to ring Lasse, just to make sure he was all right.

'It's not a good idea. I don't want you anywhere near.'

'You can't go alone.'

'It'll be fine. Anyway, they'll be keeping an eye on you. Not me. You're the one who's stirred things up. I'm the outsider.'

'But he's my contact.'

'I'm sure I can give him all the details. And once it's in the public domain, then we'll be OK. They can't move against you then. You do trust him, don't you?'

'He's good; one of the best investigative journalists in the business. A conspiracy like this is right up his street. And with his contacts, he'll help blow it wide open and give it massive coverage. It's a helluva story.'

'I'm meeting him at nine. It should be quiet then.'

'You must be careful,' she said with obvious concern. 'Remember what happened to Klas.'

'Don't worry; they won't be stupid enough to kill a British police officer – there'd be too many awkward questions. And I won't be stupid enough to let them.' He turned away from her. 'I could do with a swim. Are you coming down to the beach?'

'Give me a minute.'

Five minutes later, Anita and Kevin were heading down the path to the beach.

'Do you think we sounded convincing?' Anita asked as she walked in front of Kevin down the steep incline.

'I hope so.'

They had rehearsed the conversation a number of times. They'd decided to keep it simple and not give away too much information. The bugging devices would have picked up the whole thing. The listeners would have to piece together some of the details themselves so it didn't sound too contrived. Enough to whet their appetite. Who was Kevin going to meet? Without an actual name, they would have to speculate. Whoever it was would be a threat to them if he was an investigative journalist; how much had they told this guy? And though they'd been given the time for the fictitious meeting, they didn't know the location. They would have to follow Kevin. He and Anita had selected Stenshuvud. Anita would have plenty of cover among the trees. Kevin would drive her car the long way round to the site, coming in from the Kivik side. In the meantime, using her friend Sandra's car, Anita would get to Stenshuvud before Kevin and his shadows. They knew they were taking a huge risk. Klas had been going to tell what he knew, and now he was dead. But anything was better than living in fear.

On the beach Kevin stripped down to his bathing trunks while Anita spread out a blanket, which she sat on with a book at her side.

'I hope to God they're still listening.'

'You can be bloody sure they are.' Kevin paused and then: 'I've just had a nasty thought.'

Anita looked up abruptly. Was there a defect in their plan? She was worried about it as it was. Everything could go horribly wrong, and it was all her fault for being so bloody inquisitive. The very characteristic that had served her well in her career had now put her and her friend in serious danger.

'What about?' she mouthed anxiously.

'Those bastards have probably been listening in on our lovemaking.'

Anita found herself laughing, a welcome break in the tension she was feeling. 'I hope we were good then.'

'All that screaming!'

'And that was just you.'

Pastor Elias Kroon's photograph had been placed in prime position on the whiteboard next to a large map of the centre of Malmö. He was their main suspect now. Not that Brodd was paying much attention as they gathered for the review meeting that Moberg had called them to.

'She didn't turn up!' moaned Brodd to a disinterested Wallen. 'Nora, that is. Booked a flaming restaurant as well. Expensive, too. I looked a right berk just sitting there on my own.'

'That's hard to believe.'

Her sarcasm went straight over his head as he wittered on. 'No call. Nothing. What did she think she was playing at? I mean—'

Fortunately, Moberg's entrance stopped him in mid-flow, and they all took their seats round the table.

'Right, let's find out where we are with him,' Moberg said, jerking a thumb over his shoulder in the direction of Pastor Kroon's photograph. 'Have we anything new? Pontus?'

Brodd was caught off guard, as he was still bewildered by the fact he had been stood up.

'Em... yes...' he mumbled as he flicked through his notebook.

'The city library. Kroon did go there and he was caught on the CCTV.' He scrutinised his scrawly writing. 'Arrived 11.27 and left 15.32. As he said, he was returning some books. He also took out three new ones. Do you want the titles?'

'No, I fucking don't,' Moberg said petulantly. Anything that didn't further the case against Kroon was an aggravation best avoided. 'Did Ebba Pozorski turn up at the library that day?'

Brodd shook his head. It produced a heavy sigh from the chief inspector.

'Any luck with his movements at the time of the murder?'

Wallen and Hakim had been beating the streets around Lindroth's address, searching out possible sightings by people living in the area and possible CCTV coverage.

'Kroon did go out that night.' This was brighter news from Hakim. 'He passed a school building on Ribevägen and they have CCTV. He appears walking past the entrance at 21.31.'

'Did he go back that way?'

'No. Not that we can find. But the thing is, if you look at the map there, Ribevägen literally leads straight into Pildammsparken.'

Moberg thumped the table and made the coffee mugs jump. 'Yes!'

There were smiles around the table. They knew that they were on the right track, and that all the pieces were falling into place.

'OK. Kroon comes into Malmö to take his books back.' Moberg got up and stood next to the map. 'He gets off the bus at 9.38 down here at Södervärn. He makes his way through town. He doesn't reach the city library until 11.27. That's nearly two hours. What was he doing in between times? My guess is he bumps into Ebba Pozorski during that period. They argue. She threatens him. Something of the sort.'

'Or it's the other way round,' suggested Hakim. 'She was

upset when she turned up at Asplund's apartment later on.'

'Fair point. He spends the rest of the day at the library. What next?'

'He's planning what to do,' Wallen advanced.

'But how does he know where to find Ebba?' asked Hakim, to which Moberg's reply was a scowl. 'Unless someone told him,' Hakim said quickly to make amends. 'Isaksson?'

'That's an interesting one,' observed a placated Moberg. 'Despite what Isaksson says now, they must have been close once. Isaksson and Asplund knew where she lived. Asplund wouldn't have told him, but a slimeball like Isaksson might. I expect Kroon has dirt on him which he could use to get that information out of him. If he knew in advance she would be there, that would explain why he had the knife on him. Anyway, we can fill in those gaps later.'

He turned his attention back to the map. 'After the library, he goes to visit his friend in Dammfri over here. After nine, he slips out of the apartment when Lindroth's in bed. He passes along Ribevägen at around half nine. So we now know that he was in the vicinity of Pildammsparken; something he vehemently denied. And the timing's right for him to get into position to kill Ebba when she came out for her jog.'

'What next?' Wallen asked. The growing excitement was infectious.

'We've virtually got him on all counts. But I want a team down at Pildammsparken tonight with Kroon's photo,' indicating the one on the whiteboard. 'He's got such a creepy face that someone must have noticed him. Once we place him in the park, we'll have nailed the bastard.'

Jazmin was getting desperate. She had gone and bought a pay-as-you-go phone in Mobilia. Immediately, she had rung Lasse's mobile. All she got was his answer message. She had tried twice more without success. She had convinced herself that he must have turned his phone off while he was waiting on tables and had forgotten to turn it on again. But it wasn't like him to do that. She had become increasingly restless around the apartment and had even shouted at Messi for tipping over his water in the kitchen. It was then that she had phoned the café in Kungsgatan. Lasse hadn't turned up for work last night. They assumed that he must be ill. Would he be all right for his Thursday-evening shift?

This was startling news. Where the hell was he? There was probably some rational explanation, which he would have innocently left on her stolen phone. Oh, why hadn't she said something about the phone before? Maybe Anita would know where he was. She had phoned her, but her mobile was switched off. She had cursed. Too busy having a good time with her English boyfriend! Yet Lasse would probably walk through that door any moment now. She would give him a piece of her mind when he did; out of relief more than anger. At half past five, she tried Lasse's and Anita's phones again. Nothing. She was feeling sick. Something just wasn't right. Who could she turn to? Reluctantly, she picked up her new mobile and rang her brother.

CHAPTER 45

'Missing? Are you sure?'

Hakim had never heard Jazmin so upset before. Her story was garbled and difficult to follow, but he got the gist.

'I'm sure there's nothing wrong. He'll turn up soon.' His attempts to calm his sister weren't working.

'Something's not right, Hakim.' He could hear the frenzy in her voice. 'He didn't turn up for work at the café. And with all this being-watched stuff.'

'What are you talking about?'

'I mentioned it to Lasse's mamma. I told Lasse but he wouldn't listen, and now he's gone missing. And my phone, too. I don't know what to do.' It all came out in a rush.

'Wow! Wait on, Jazmin. What's this "being watched" business?'

'Someone has been watching the apartment.'

'Since when?'

'I don't know. A week or so ago and then the last few days. I'm frightened.'

This really wasn't like his sister at all. She had a strong personality, which is why so many arguments had broken out within the family.

'Look, you stay put. I'm sure Lasse will come back. I'm working at the moment in Pildammsparken.' He could see Wallen with a couple of uniformed officers intercepting walkers and joggers further along the path. 'I'll be here for a few hours. But if you've heard nothing by then, I'll come round. I'm sure it's nothing.' He attempted to sound reassuring. 'Don't worry.'

Anita drove along the main coast road. She wasn't going fast, but her mind was racing. What had she let Kevin in for? At the last minute, before he was about to head off, she had changed her mind. She had begged him not to go. But he had been obdurate. This was the only way. She had considered calling Moberg, but that would have been futile. Kevin was risking his life. These people, whichever secret service department they worked for, were ruthless. They had thought nothing of getting rid of Klas. Her only hope was that it would be harder to explain the death or disappearance of a foreign policeman. She no longer cared what happened to her, but realised that she didn't want any harm to come to Kevin. It was dawning on her what a great support he was; more than the friend she had been happy to have fun with while emotionally keeping at arm's length. The one thing she could do for him now was to not let him down; to be there when this appalling situation reached its climax.

She turned off to the right, and put her foot down as she hit the side road that led to Stenshuvud. It was vital that she got to the car park before Kevin did. She glanced in the mirror to see if there was any vehicle following her. The long, straight road behind her was totally clear. At least that was good.

There were two other vehicles in the dusty car park when she reached it ten minutes later. She hoped the occupants would have gone down to the sea and not up the hill, as that was where they had prepared their trap. It was a clear, warm evening with just a light breeze – and it wouldn't get dark for a while. She locked the car and carefully scanned the area as though the tree-lined car park would be bulging with armed secret service personnel. She felt for her Sig Sauer pistol. She had checked it and rechecked it before leaving the house. Satisfied at last, she quickly made her way towards, then past, the information centre and up the path into the trees. She had instructed Kevin to go up the main path that would take him to the South Head first and then onto the North Head. He was to wait there in the open. She would stealthily make her way by an alternative route that encircled the side of the hill and came out at a different point on the North Head. From there she would have an open view so that anyone following Kevin would be in clear sight.

When Anita reached the fork which was signposted to the North Head, she stopped. She decided that she would change her plan. Instead of going and waiting close to the rocky outcrop, it made more sense to find out as soon as possible if Kevin *was* being followed – and how many people she was going to have to deal with. She glanced round for a good piece of cover so she could linger out of sight. The trees were thick here, and there was a convenient rock to hide behind. It gave her a perfect view of the path leading up from the bottom of the hill. She took out her pistol and checked it yet again. Now the time was 20.47. Kevin should be here within minutes. She couldn't remember being more nervous, and she could feel a trickle of sweat running down her spine. Her mouth was dry, and she tried to moisten her lips with her tongue. So much could go wrong. Running round a hillside brandishing a pistol was idiotic. It went against her every instinct. She wasn't a maverick. It was breaking all the rules by which she worked. For the hundredth time, she cursed her own stupidity and single-mindedness that had landed them in this increasingly terrifying situation. And where was Kevin? Had he got lost driving here? Then an even worse thought struck her – had they already intercepted him?

Moberg had emerged from one of his few positive meetings with Prosecutor Blom. He hadn't had to battle with her to keep Pastor Kroon under lock and key for the next three days. Maybe it was the late hour that had helped and she wanted to get home to whatever poor sap was waiting for her there. She had pointed out it was Midsummer on Friday, and that the whole of Sweden would be partying by then. He assured her that he was confident that they would have the final piece of the jigsaw – Kroon's presence in Pildammsparken on the night of the murder – in place in time for the national holiday in two days' time. Blom thought that his team had built a good enough case, and she was confident that, with more time, they would be able to gather further, conclusive evidence, such as how the pastor had got hold of the murder weapon and where it was now. Moberg was convinced that he'd be able to sweat it out of the repugnant reverend. He was also sure that he could get Isaksson to dish the dirt as a way of saving his own skin.

As he sat down in his office and began deciding where he was going to eat on the way home, he was congratulating himself on a job well done. They had wandered up a couple of blind alleys but, luckily, they had led them to the killer. And when the murderer was as despicable a character as Pastor Kroon, then it made it all the more satisfying. And all achieved without Anita Sundström throwing her usual spanner in the works.

He still hadn't heard from Wallen about how they had got on with any Kroon sightings in the park, which was an irritation. They might have to spend another day on that, but the truth would emerge in the end. There was a note on his desk asking him to ring Eva Thulin as soon as he got the message. He looked at it in some surprise. She must be working late. Maybe she had found some evidence of Kroon being in Ebba Pozorski's apartment after all. That would tighten up the case even further. So, he was more than happy to punch in Thulin's number and wait for her to answer.

'Moberg here. Returning your call. Got something for me?'

'Yes,' came a guarded reply.

The tone of her voice immediately troubled him. 'Well?'

'I didn't want to leave you a message. Thought it best if I talked to you direct.'

'Just cut to the chase.' Moberg hated wafflers.

'It was a bit of a long shot, but we've managed to get some DNA from Ebba Pozorski's running vest.'

'What do you mean?' he asked warily.

'She was jogging when she was attacked. She was stabbed twice. Whoever stabbed her was sweating because they were running as well. Basically, there was sweat on the hand that inflicted the blows and, because the knife was quite short, when it was shoved into Pozorski's back, the killer physically touched the material of her running vest at the point of the second, deeper incision. There was a stain. A minute one, barely noticeable, and we didn't think we'd be able to get anything from it at first.'

Moberg found he was getting excited and concerned at the same time. 'And that stain has given you a DNA match?'

'Yes, it has.'

'It better be Pastor Kroon because we've got the fucker locked up downstairs.'

'I'm afraid not.'

'Well, tell me for Christ's sake!' he demanded fiercely.

Thulin paused at the other end of the phone. Then she spoke: 'You're not going to believe this.'

CHAPTER 46

It was the twig crunching that Anita heard first. Then voices. Surely Kevin couldn't be in contact with them already? Her body went taut with anticipation, pistol gripped tightly in her hand, when she realised that the sounds were coming from the wrong direction. She couldn't see anyone, but she could make out the voices of a man and a woman. They were descending the hill. As they passed by her hiding place, they were laughing. A young couple out for a flirtatious evening walk judging by the bandied remarks. At least that accounted for one of the vehicles down in the car park. Then she heard Kevin's voice saying 'Good evening,' in English. Typically polite; and the Swedish couple returned the greeting. She could pick up their surprise; it wasn't what they were used to. But she was hugely relieved that Kevin was all right.

Within a minute, she could see him striding up the path within spitting distance of her vantage point. She couldn't tell if his heavy breathing was nerves, or if he was finding the climb hard. She so dearly wanted to call out to tell him she was there, ready to back him up, but he might be under surveillance and it would give the game away. And then he was gone. The only sound left now was the low rustle of the leaves around her in the light wind.

Just when she was starting to think that nobody was coming and their bait hadn't attracted the fish, she was aware of movement in the trees beyond. Then she caught a glimpse of a blond head. The man was not coming up the path, but keeping among the trees and shrubs that bordered the track to the hilltop. He was moving stealthily. Now she could make him out as he flitted between the foliage. He was tall and well-built, and wore a lightweight, beige jacket that was half-zipped. She could see the unmistakable bulge of a gun framed by the material. She had never seen Benno Källström, but the figure furtively moving less than five metres away matched Kevin's description. She weighed up the situation quickly. His body language didn't seem to be of someone working in tandem with a partner. Once he had gone on, she would wait a short time to see if anyone else emerged. The two minutes she remained pressed against the rock seemed like hours, but it would be reckless to overlook any possibility that he wasn't alone.

She managed another agonising minute before slipping away along the very narrow path that took her round the side of the hill. She tried not to rush, though her instinct was to run and protect Kevin before Benno caught up with him. It took her five minutes to reach the edge of the rocky outcrop. There was Kevin. He was gazing out to sea, rhythmically rocking from one foot to the other. He glanced at his watch, creating the effect that he was waiting for someone. She didn't expect Benno to make his move until Kevin's "journalist" appeared. What he had planned to do then, Anita could only speculate. Surely he wouldn't try and kill them both? A lot of people would be needed to cover that up, unless it turned into an unexplained shooting by some maniac who is never found and brought to justice. It might be that simple. In which case, she reckoned she couldn't hang around. She needed to find him fast. He wouldn't be on the path leading from the South Head, but in a position to watch it and still keep an eye on Kevin.

Slowly, she worked her way round the edge of the outcrop, using the trees and bushes as cover. Every step she took, she made sure that her foot came down quietly. After a few paces, she stopped and listened. There was nothing to give away Benno's position. As she edged forward again, she was frightened that her uneven breathing would betray her; it sounded so loud. She pressed herself against a thick tree trunk and then crept away from its protective overhanging branches. She almost stumbled upon Benno, who was just in front of her facing the opposite way. He swivelled round instantly, his hand automatically reaching into his jacket. But he never had time to get his gun out, as Anita was pointing her own pistol at his head.

For a moment, she just stood there wondering what she should do next. From this point forward, there had been no decisive plan. Kevin had had a vague idea that if she was able to arrest Benno – possession of a weapon would be a good enough excuse – then the police would have to take official action, and that would give them some sort of protection. By bringing it into the public domain, they might be able to keep the shadowy spooks at bay. She told him to put his hands on his head.

'Move!' she ordered. He stepped down onto the path and walked towards the North Head. At that moment, Kevin appeared. She could see the relief on his face.

'He's got a gun. Can you get it?'

Kevin swiftly strode up to Benno and yanked the gun out of his jacket.

'Is he alone?' Kevin asked as he inspected Benno's gun.

'Are you?' demanded Anita in Swedish.

He didn't answer. Anita pushed her pistol into the small of his back so that he would step forward. She made him sit on one of the protruding rocks. All was quiet around them. The sky was hazy blue and the deep azure sea virtually unrippled. It was a picturesque scene, yet here they were, brandishing weapons and about to interrogate a double murderer. The irony wasn't lost on her.

'Who do you work for?' She was still speaking in Swedish.

'Are you going to kill me?' he answered without a hint of fear.

'No, I'm going to arrest you.'

He even smiled. 'I wouldn't bother. I wouldn't be in custody for very long.' There was a hint of a laugh when he asked: 'What are you going to charge me with?'

'Carrying a firearm.' It was as lame as it sounded. 'Why were you following us in Berlin? Why were you spying on Albin Rylander? Did you kill Klas Lennartsson?' The questions flew out randomly and Anita cursed herself for her unprofessionalism.

'You have no idea who you're messing with, have you?' Benno Källström was perfectly unruffled.

'We've a pretty good notion,' said Anita. 'You killed Albin Rylander to protect your agency before he had time to tell Klas Lennartsson his full story. Is it the Office for Special Collection?' For the first time, Benno showed a hint of concern. 'Then, when you realised that Klas Lennartsson was still carrying on with the book and had found out Rylander's secret, you contrived his accident.'

'Prove it.'

'What's he saying?' asked an exasperated Kevin, who hadn't understood any of the exchanges.

'He's not telling us anything.'

'Can I kick the shit out of him then?' She grimaced in horror.

'You can tell you're not from Sweden,' Benno commented wryly in English. He turned to squint up at Anita; the evening sun was still shining brightly. 'You'd better arrest me then. But I warn you: when I get out, I'll be coming after you.' He let the threat linger in the air.

'Get up,' Anita ordered. She glanced across at Kevin. He looked as helpless as she felt. Any thoughts of reasoning with this man were flying out of the window. He couldn't be intimidated. They had nothing to bargain with.

Benno Källström stood up. He grinned at Anita. Then, suddenly, his expression changed, and he crashed to the ground at her feet. Anita gawped at Källström, then at Kevin, who was obviously as dumbfounded as she was. Then she noticed the blood pooling over the rocks. She hadn't taken in the thud of the shot, as it had been so neatly carried out. She swung round and saw a burly, bald man standing a few metres away with a gun, elongated by a silencer. Kevin had swivelled round and was on bended knee, Benno's weapon pointing at the intruder – Mr Large.

'Put your pistol away, Inspector Sundström,' he ordered in Swedish. His voice was deep and confident. 'You're not in danger.' Turning to Kevin, he said in immaculate English. 'And I'll take that gun, if you don't mind, Detective Sergeant Ash. It's government property.' Kevin appeared uncertain until Anita nodded to him. Kevin stood up and held the gun out for the man, who casually walked over and took it from him.

Anita was still stunned. She gazed at the blood, already congealing, and she knew that Benno was dead. When she looked up again, she was given another start. Behind the large man, who had now put his own gun and Benno's weapon away, was Alice Zetterberg. What the hell was she doing here?

'This is all very unfortunate,' the man said, still speaking English.

'You're bloody right!' exploded Kevin. It was a release of tension. 'He's the bloke I saw watching Rylander's house before he died.'

'And was at the scene afterwards with *her*,' Anita said accusingly.

'I suspect that you've pieced together much of what has happened and why. I do not intend to enlighten you much more, other than to say that there was never any intention to do Klas Lennartsson any harm. We had ways of ensuring that the story would never enter the public domain. If you know as much as

I think you do, then you'll appreciate that it isn't in Sweden's interests that Rylander's activities should emerge.'

'But you still killed Klas.' Anita's anger was beginning to bubble up.

He ignored her remark. 'Lennartsson's trip panicked our operative here,' he said with a nod in the direction of the dead body. 'He took it upon himself to solve the situation without official sanction, which would not have been given.' Looking at Kevin: 'I think he became what you English would describe as a "rogue agent". We realised he had become a serious liability when we discovered he had followed you to Berlin. He had you two in his sights from the moment it became obvious that you were determined to follow up Rylander's and Lennartsson's deaths.' He waved in Zetterberg's direction. 'We tried our best to discourage you. Your colleague here tried to block your every move, but you wouldn't desist.'

'She's always poked her nose in where it wasn't wanted,' Zetterberg said snidely in Swedish.

Anita just scowled. So Zetterberg had been colluding with the secret services to conceal the crimes! At that moment, she couldn't think of anybody she loathed more.

'How are you going to explain Källström's death? Or whatever his real name is.' Anita's fury blinded her to the fact that there was no guarantee that she and Kevin wouldn't end up the same way.

He shrugged. 'This never happened.'

Another cover-up. And with the willing Zetterberg helping out. How could she? Anita wondered furiously.

'What about Anita?' Kevin's voice broke through her troubled thoughts. 'What about the both of us? Are we going to be two more incidents that never happened?'

'Of course not. We don't go round killing British policemen. Or our own, either. You are free to go.'

Kevin looked at the large man incredulously.

'What if I report all this?' said Anita aiming her comment at Zetterberg. 'Three murders have been committed. We're witnesses to this one.'

'Besides the fact that you'll never be able to prove it, I think you'll be sensible.' The big man was in total control of the situation. 'After all, you wouldn't want anything nasty to happen to Lasse and Jazmin at their crappy little apartment in Rosengård.' Anita's jaw dropped. 'Or you, Inspector Ash, with those lovely daughters of yours. Abigail's the oldest, I believe. And young Hazel,' he carried on pleasantly. 'She'll be going to university next year. Bright girl, apparently.'

'How the fuck do you know?' Kevin demanded.

'We have friends in Britain.'

'It'll be MI5 or something. You bastards are all the same.'

'You can't threaten us,' Anita protested.

'What a stupid thing to say, Inspector. That's exactly what I am doing. And remember, it's not only your families you should think about.' An edge came into his tone. 'You would be destroying your careers and your reputations. We would see to that.' He paused to make sure that they had got the message. 'We do not want either of you being loose ends that we have to tie up.'

Anita looked down at the body of the dead agent, then at Kevin. He held out his hand to her. She moved across to him and he took her by the arm.

'Before you leave,' the big man said, 'you don't happen to know where Lennartsson's Berlin notes are, do you?'

Anita shook her head in reply. As they left the hilltop, the image that would remain with her for ever was Zetterberg's self-satisfied sneer. They were aware of shadowy figures appearing from the trees. The clearing-up operation had begun. Another cover-up – and there wasn't a damn thing she could do about it.

CHAPTER 47

Jazmin was startled by the apartment buzzer. Could it be Lasse? He might have forgotten his key. But it was Hakim.

When he entered the apartment, she immediately told him that she had heard nothing from Lasse, and she still couldn't get hold of Anita. She was now so worried that she didn't know where to turn or what to do. Hakim tried to calm her down, but he could feel that something was wrong, if not necessarily suspicious. It was very unlike Lasse just to go off. He also knew that he hadn't been missing long enough for the police to take any action – Jazmin had last seen him yesterday morning when she went off to her lectures. At his sister's insistence, Hakim had tried Anita's home phone and her mobile but had got no response, though he had done it reluctantly because he didn't want to alarm her. He then tried the hospital to see if Lasse had been taken in after an accident. Again, there was no joy.

He stayed with Jazmin for over an hour. He tried to persuade her to spend the night with their parents, but she wanted to stay put in case Lasse suddenly came walking back into the apartment. She needed to be there for him. Then he excused himself. He had to be at work at half past six tomorrow morning. That in itself had been strange. They had been in Pildammsparken when Wallen had got a call from Moberg telling her that they were to pack up immediately. No reasons were given. The only instruction was that he wanted to see the team assembled at half six. It must be important because it wasn't a time you'd usually find the chief inspector at his desk.

The bottle of red wine was empty. Anita went into the kitchen and opened another one, even though it was past midnight. When they were leaving the Stenshuvud car park in their respective cars, two unmarked blue vans and a police car were the only other vehicles in the area. Anita had burst into tears on the drive back. She felt bitter, saddened and belittled by her experience on the North Head. Everything she believed in and stood for in her years of policing seemed to have lost any coherent meaning. Three people had been killed to protect an inconvenient truth – one of them totally innocent of the machinations of governments and their secret services. A friend whom she hadn't believed until it was too late. She was beginning to wonder if she could carry on working to uphold the law that was treated in such a cavalier, contemptuous fashion by those who wielded real power. How high did these decisions go? Or were the present-day politicians unaware of the exploits of those who were acting in their name? The only answer was to give Kevin a long and strong hug when they got back to the holiday cabin. And more tears.

Neither of them felt like eating, and it was the wine that got them speaking again, albeit spasmodically. Though it was the elephant in the room, the subject of the specific threat to their families and careers was not mentioned. It seemed too frighteningly surreal for them to articulate. Maybe this was the beginning of the silence that the large man was demanding of them. One practical point that Anita did mention in passing was that the person who had spooked Jazmin was probably one of the secret service team doing background checks on the family. However appalling that was, she was relieved that it was nothing else.

'Thanks for everything.'

Kevin raised his glass as though about to propose a toast. 'I'm just glad I was here. Not exactly to help, but to support.'

'Oh, you helped all right. I'm just sorry for involving you

in all this. It's been so awful for you. This was meant to be a holiday.'

'Put it this way: when I go home tomorrow, I won't be writing this up on TripAdvisor.'

She gave him a good-natured kick for lightening the mood. 'I was being serious.'

'So was I. I'm not exactly going to recommend a holiday like this one. Come to sunny Skåne: stay next to a suicidal Scandinavian spy with a secret; follow a blonde bombshell as she tracks down a multiple murderer, before being threatened by Swedish security services. That'll have 'em rushing over here.'

They didn't finish the second bottle. They headed for bed and made love. Not the passionate, animal, selfish love of before, but a thoughtful, we've-been-through-a-lot-together, glad-to-be-alive love. They moved not as two individuals seeking pleasure from the other, but as one.

The only person in the meeting room who wasn't bleary-eyed at six-thirty in the morning was Chief Inspector Moberg. That was the first surprise. The second was that there was no sign of the photograph of Pastor Elias Kroon or the images of Markus Asplund and Axel Isaksson on the board. But the news that greeted them was even more astonishing.

'Right. We're starting again. Pastor Kroon has been released. I hope we may be able to bring some charges against him, but murder isn't one of them.' As he saw Wallen about to question him, he held out a huge hand to stop her before she had time to speak. 'Eva Thulin rang me last night. They've been able to extract DNA from a sweat stain on Ebba Pozorski's running top. She found a match to our old associate, Karl Westermark.'

The three other officers in the room looked stunned.

'But he's dead,' Hakim pointed out. Moberg, Wallen and Hakim had all heard the shot as Westermark had blown his own brains out in front of Anita Sundström in his apartment on Ön – and seen the bloody aftermath as a shocked Anita was led away. Not that any of them had had any sympathy for the detective who had murdered their much-respected colleague, Henrik Nordlund, as well as raping and killing a young teacher.

'I said forensics had found a match. It's a familial match. Someone in his family.' To Hakim this also sounded far-fetched. How could there possibly be a tie-up with the murdered woman? 'And the only living close relative Westermark seems to have had is his sister, Sigyn. I've had a couple of the night-duty boys trawling for details. She lives in America. What we've found out so far is that she was following her brother into the police and spent a year at the Academy in Stockholm, but she dropped out when she hooked up with an American called Brad Guzman. They went to live in Boston, where she trained as a teacher in physical education, which is what she's been doing for the last few years. She married Guzman, but they're now divorced. No kids. But she left her job earlier this year, and no one seems to know what she's been up to since.'

'But what could Westermark's sister possibly have to do with Ebba Pozorski?' Wallen's question echoed the thoughts of everybody else.

'Good question. Why should an expat gym teacher want to kill a Swiss-based prostitute in a Malmö park? I have no fucking idea! I can't find a connection. The Westermark family have nothing to do with Sjöbo as far as we can see.'

'What about when Ebba was picked up for soliciting? Was Westermark the arresting officer?' Hakim suggested.

'Looked into that, and it wasn't him. Doesn't mean Westermark wasn't shagging her when she was working the streets before Asplund and Isaksson came to her rescue. God knows what he got up to before he killed Greta Jansson.'

'At least the American connection would explain the butterfly knife,' observed Wallen.

'Yes. We've got means. But opportunity? We know she must

have been in Malmö that night. Her DNA shows that. But we've got to prove beyond doubt that she was here. So, I want flights from Boston to Copenhagen checked from February up until now. You'll need to look out for Westermark and Guzman, as she could be going under either name. Has she been in Malmö since she left her teaching job? If she has, what's she been doing? Where's she been living? We need to build up a picture of this woman. That's the only way we can find a connection with Ebba. Maybe they met when Ebba was working at the travel agents, and she fixed her up with a flight to America. Maybe her husband was screwing prostitutes, and they've become hate figures. There must be something. We've got to find that link. More to the point, we've got to find her. If she's back in America, we'll need lots of evidence to get her extradited.'

Moberg took a photograph from his hastily compiled file and placed it on the whiteboard where Kroon's had been the day before. Sigyn Westermark had short-cropped, blonde hair; and sturdy but pretty facial features with a wide mouth and a hint of her brother's jaw. And for anybody who was familiar with Westermark, she had the same cold, piercing blue eyes. It was only Hakim who noticed that Pontus Brodd had turned white at the sight of the photograph.

Hakim caught up with Brodd in the toilets. Brodd was dousing his face in water. It did little to make him look any less wretched than he had been minutes before when Moberg had produced Sigyn Westermark's picture.

'Are you OK?'

Brodd wiped his face on a paper towel.

'You know that woman, don't you?'

Brodd nodded dolefully before tossing the paper towel in the bin. He leant back against the basin and held on to the sides behind him as though they would stop him from collapsing. Hakim waited for him to speak.

'It's Nora.'

'Nora?'

'Yes. She's the woman I've been seeing lately.'

'Are you sure?'

'Oh, yes. You don't forget a face like that. She's even more gorgeous in the flesh.' She was too like the hated Westermark for Hakim to see any beauty there.

'You've got to tell the chief inspector. This is important. It means she's still in Malmö.'

Brodd shook his head. 'She might not be. She didn't turn up for our last date.'

'When was the last time you saw her?'

'Saturday. Then we were meant to meet up at The Pickwick on Tuesday evening. She didn't show.'

Hakim's mind was whirring. 'Where did you meet her? The first time, I mean.'

'It was there, actually. Not my usual sort of place, but I'd heard Anita talking about it, and I thought I'd give it a try.'

'What did she tell you about herself?'

Brodd gave him a puzzled look. 'I don't know really. Said she'd come from somewhere up north and didn't know anybody in Malmö. She was a good listener, though. Really seemed interested in me.'

I bet she was, thought Hakim. Brodd wasn't the obvious choice for a woman to pick up at a bar.

'And what so interested her about you?'

He gave a pained grimace. 'Well, this actually.' He waved his hand at himself. 'She liked the idea that I was a cop. She said she'd always wanted to join the police, but things hadn't worked out.'

'Did she ask anything specific about the job?' Hakim was starting to worry.

'I may have let slip that I was working on the Ebba Pozorski murder.'

'Please, no.' Hakim was becoming incensed. He knew that Brodd would have exaggerated his importance. He'd probably indicated he was running the case. 'Did you give her details of how it was progressing?'

'I might have,' he mumbled. 'She just seemed fascinated.'

'So, our killer knows exactly how the investigation's been run?' Brodd gazed back at him helplessly. 'You've got to speak to Moberg right now.'

'Oh, Christ!' Brodd stood rooted to the spot, unable to tear himself away from the basin. 'I can't believe this is happening to me.'

'At least she'll not know that she's under suspicion. That's one thing. Have you got her number?'

Brodd shifted uneasily. 'No. She rang me.'

'What did you do with this woman?' Hakim asked incredulously.

'Nothing, actually,' he confessed shamefacedly. 'We talked a lot. But she did kiss me goodnight on the second date,' he added as an afterthought. Hakim couldn't believe that a man could be so full of bullshit. His pathetic attempts at self-aggrandisement had put the whole case in jeopardy. At least they would be able to trace Sigyn's calls to Brodd, which might give away her whereabouts.

'Just go.'

Hakim thought Brodd was going to be sick on the spot. He was pale and drawn. He could see the fear in his eyes. Eventually, he tore himself away from the comfort of the basin and walked out of the toilets. Hakim reckoned that Moberg's explosive reaction would reverberate round the whole of the polishus once Brodd told him the news. But it still wouldn't get them any closer to a connection between Sigyn Westermark and Ebba Pozorski.

CHAPTER 48

Hakim put the phone down. He was deep in thought. The impossible was entering his head. He had kept this particular notion at bay for a while, but it kept resurfacing. Sigyn Westermark (not Guzman) had arrived in Copenhagen on an SAS flight from Newark on March 25th – and had taken the same route back on Wednesday, June 4th, which was the day after Ebba Pozorski's murder. Then she had returned on a Norwegian Air Shuttle flight from New York-JFK three days later. Why? It was a question to which he was beginning to form an answer. And it wasn't one he liked.

And where was she now? He flicked onto Google and brought up a map of the streets around Pildammsparken. His eyes followed the route from Ebba Pozorski's apartment on Kronborgsvägen through to where she was murdered in the park – the point where Sigyn Westermark struck the fatal blow. Now he could see it all clearly. How had they got everything so wrong from the word go? He suddenly had a second thought which was even more disturbing. He was out of his seat in a trice, and rushing down the corridor into Moberg's office. A shell-shocked and grey-faced Brodd was sitting slumped in a chair opposite the chief inspector who was finishing off the bollocking of a lifetime.

'What the fuck—' Moberg started.

'We've got to find her! And find her fast!'

*

The weather was showing signs of turning, with puffs of grey cloud languidly building up in the blue sky. It was still a lovely day to be driving over the expanse of the Öresund Bridge, and Kevin drank in the uninterrupted view. Ahead was Copenhagen. He arched round to gaze at Malmö and the white finger of the Turning Torso as it spiralled above the city. It was a bittersweet moment. He was leaving Sweden. This was the country of Anita, and her presence here would always make it a place to return to; a place to dream about when he was back in England. But it held bad memories too. He could never dismiss or forget the events of the last fortnight. That was partly why they had left the holiday home at about ten, after one last swim down in the bay. What had occurred had soured the location for both of them. Anita was cutting short her stay and was going to spend the rest of her summer vacation back in Malmö. He had a late night flight from Kastrup, so they decided they would spend their last day together in Copenhagen. He could do some shopping to find presents for his girls. They also planned to do a bit of sightseeing, and then spend a leisurely evening at a nice restaurant before Anita dropped him off at the airport on her way back to Malmö. He didn't want that moment to come. But he knew he would have to bid her goodbye. Would he have the courage to say that he loved her? How would she react?

At the other side of the bridge, the road was swallowed up by a tunnel which funnelled traffic through to the Danish side of the Sound. He took out his mobile phone and switched it on. It was the first time he'd done so since Schönefeld Airport in Berlin. After everything that had happened yesterday, he'd forgotten all about their phones. Now they were in the tunnel, there was no signal. Anita glanced across at him.

'Just want to see if there's a message from Abigail. As the flight gets in at an unearthly hour, I'm getting a taxi to her flat to crash out till the morning.' He sat fiddling with the phone.

'Don't forget to turn yours on.'

Anita shook her head. 'Forget it. We've been through too much the last few days for me to want to get in touch with the world, or the world with me. It can wait a day.'

'She killed the wrong person?' Moberg's disbelief was obvious.

'Yes. I think she was trying to murder Anita.'

'Anita Sundström?'

'Exactly.' Hakim could see that the chief inspector needed some persuading. 'Firstly, I need to ask Brodd a question.' Moberg's wave in the direction of the distraught Brodd was the granting of permission. 'At any stage in your evenings with Nora did she mention Anita?'

Brodd shifted uneasily in his seat and then gave an apologetic cough. 'Yeah. Well, I did. When she was asking me about members of the team, I must have dropped in Anita's name. But I told her that she was away on holiday.'

'And that was it?'

'Erm... she did ask if she had gone anywhere nice. You know how people talk whenever holidays are mentioned. It was just that sort of thing. Perfectly innocent...' his voice trailed off.

'And did you tell her?'

'No. Because I didn't know where she'd gone. I wasn't that interested.'

'What's this all about?' demanded Moberg.

'Sigyn Westermark – that's what she still calls herself – chucked in her job in Boston in February. She flew over here in March. The day after the murder, she took a flight back to America. Three days later, she was back here again. I believe that's because she found out that the person she had killed was the wrong one. It's Anita she's after.'

'Because of her brother?' Moberg was beginning to see where Hakim was coming from.

'I think so. The timing of her quitting her job and leaving

America fits in with the release of the official report on Karl Westermark's death. She probably got it into her head that it was Anita's fault that he killed himself – or that she put him in such a position that he had no other option. A grieving, vengeful sister.'

'You think she was planning it for some time?'

Hakim was busy ordering his thoughts so that they would come out coherently. 'I imagine she was watching Anita and her routine, which often included late night jogs. What Sigyn couldn't have known was that Anita was going on holiday. But Ebba Pozorski, blonde with a baseball cap similar to Anita's; roughly the same size and shape, appeared in the dusk coming from the direction of Anita's apartment. The path from Kronborgsvägen to the road across from the park goes down the side of Anita's building. Sigyn assumed it was her intended victim. Afterwards, she flies back to Boston, only to discover she's killed the wrong person. So, she comes back to finish off what she failed to do. But she can't find Anita, so she hangs around the pub that Anita frequents – The Pickwick – to try and find out where she's gone. She strikes lucky because she finds Brodd there, who is not only a cop, but working on the case.' Brodd winced. 'Now she knows how the investigation is going and she realises that she's in the clear for the moment – we're chasing other suspects. The only problem is that Brodd doesn't know where Anita's gone. And this is why we have to act quickly. As you may know, my sister is living with Anita's son, Lasse. Jazmin reckoned that their apartment was being watched. It must have been Sigyn. Then Jazmin had her mobile phone stolen; the only thing she remembers is being aware of a blonde woman sitting next to her before the phone disappeared. Sigyn again.'

'But why?'

'Lasse has disappeared. I think Sigyn lured him using Jazmin's phone. However it was done, my guess is that she's got Lasse holed up somewhere.' His eyebrows knitted into a worried frown. 'Or has even killed him already.'

'An eye for an eye?'

'Absolutely. Either that, or it's Sigyn's way of guaranteeing that Anita returns to Malmö so she can complete the job.'

Moberg wiped his forehead. 'Shit! Shit, shit, shit!' He quickly weighed up the options. He couldn't afford not to act decisively, even if he wasn't totally convinced by Mirza's theory. But it did make chilling sense, and if there was a young man out there facing a death sentence, they had to move heaven and earth to find him – and Sigyn Westermark.

'Right! It's even more urgent that we find out where she's been over the last few months – house, work, et cetera. That might give us a clue as to where she is now. What's your sister called again, Mirza?'

'Jazmin.'

'You say she had her mobile nicked. If Sigyn used it to get at Lasse, we should be able to trace where she made the call from – or any subsequent calls. Might give us a location to work on.'

'Should we circulate her photo?' Brodd suggested tentatively.

'No!' barked Moberg. 'That'll alert her that we're on to her, and she might just kill Lasse and get the hell out of here. The one thing we've got – *thanks* to you – is that she doesn't think she's a suspect.'

'And Anita?' This was another major concern for Hakim.

'Yes, Anita. I don't want her alarmed. If she thinks her son's in danger, she'll go off the deep end and try and do everything herself and get in the fucking way.'

'But I reckon she's the real target. She's got to be warned.' It came out as an impassioned plea.

'I'm well aware that one of my officers is in peril. Leave her to me.' The implications of what was happening began to dawn on Moberg and simultaneously raised his blood pressure. 'Get Wallen to get as many people as we need on this – on my authority. Everybody meet again in two hours. Now fucking go!' he bawled.

Moberg lumbered into Hakim's office. He wore the expression of an extremely frustrated man.

'Anita. I can't get hold of her. She's not answering her mobile or home phone. Do you know where she was spending her holiday?'

'Up the coast from Simrishamn.'

'Where exactly?'

'Not really sure. But Jazmin went over there last week with Lasse. She'll know.'

'Right, get the address out of her, and then I'll get someone from the Simrishamn station to go and pick Anita up. We can't afford to have her wandering around if Sigyn Westermark's on the loose. I want her here, or at home under protection.'

The meeting room was buzzing, but the underlying tension was inescapable, as they knew that one of their own was being targeted. Besides Wallen, Hakim and Brodd, there were seven other officers who had been hastily co-opted onto the investigation. Moberg came storming in.

'Right,' started the chief inspector before he had even taken his place at the head of the table. 'Anita Sundström. She's still out of mobile phone contact. I've been onto the police in Simrishamn and they're sending a couple of officers round to where she's staying. I just hope she's there. OK, background on Sigyn Westermark, please.'

A petite detective called Ylva Forsgren chirped up. 'She was brought up in Trelleborg with her brother Karl. Parents both dead; and the only living relative we've managed to contact is an aunt who's still living there. Said she hadn't seen Sigyn since Karl's funeral. Hardly anyone turned up to that. I got the impression that the family had been badly affected by

Westermark's cop-killing antics and his sticky end, and they didn't want to be associated with his memory. That's why the aunt wasn't even aware that Sigyn had returned from America in March. She did say that Sigyn was deeply troubled by her brother's death. As far as she's aware, no one she knew had seen Sigyn recently.'

'What about America?'

'Per here,' she said pointing to a prematurely balding man in his thirties, 'has spoken to the husband, Brad Guzman.'

Per Mattinsson took over. 'They were married for four years. He says that Sigyn worshipped her big brother. He admitted he never really took to Karl, though he made an effort for her sake. The marriage seemed happy enough, but everything changed after Karl's death. She became moody and distracted. Started taking all sorts of medication. The job she loved at the local high school no longer interested her. Brad puts their split directly down to Sigyn's inability to cope with her brother's death. He's had no contact with her since the divorce. He'd heard that she'd left her job and assumed she had probably gone home to Sweden.'

Moberg puffed out his cheeks. 'So, we're dealing with a seriously disturbed lady who seems to be putting the blame for her brother's death at Anita's door. Klara, where are we up to with Sigyn's movements?'

'We found out that she's been living in an apartment near the Torso. Three-month rental: paid up to the end of June. We've had a squad car out there but there's no sign of her. Doesn't appear that she's gone back there on her return from the US. So we're now doing the rounds of hotels, hostels, and bed and breakfast places. Nothing yet.'

'Hakim?'

'Through the tax people, we've discovered that she was working most of that time as an attendant at the Kallbadhus down on the beach. As soon as this is finished, I'll head down there.'

'Good,' snapped Moberg. 'Where are we at with your sister's phone?'

'Brodd was dealing with that.'

All eyes turned on Brodd. News of his "girlfriend" had quickly spread through the corridors of the polishus.

He answered nervously. 'There's no signal at the moment. The last time it was used was last night at 22.03. Nothing since. We've managed to trace the location where the phone was last used. It was somewhere in the vicinity of Roskildevägen.'

'Where Anita lives?'

'Yeah.'

'And the last call made was to Sundström's mobile.'

'Fuck! So has Sigyn already made contact with Anita?' Moberg fell silent. Everybody watched him as he swiftly evaluated the situation and decided what action to take.

'Maybe once she'd got hold of Lasse, she assumed that my sister would get straight onto Anita, and she'd come rushing back to Malmö. Eventually she'd go home, and Sigyn would be waiting for her. But she didn't appear, so she tried to ring her.' This was Hakim.

'That makes sense. But if Anita's phone is still off, Sigyn might still be hanging around hoping that she'll turn up. Klara, take Brodd and as many officers as you need, and comb the area. Now, what about Lasse? This is a question we've got to ask – is he alive or dead?'

Wallen gave Hakim a pitying glance. 'I'm sorry to say that there must be a good chance he's not alive. If Sigyn was in the vicinity of Anita's apartment last night, what's she done with Lasse? There can't be many places she could keep him captive. It's simpler stashing away a dead body than a living one.'

Hakim was clearly upset by the thought. 'But on the other hand, would she get rid of Lasse before she knew that Anita was back in the city? Unless killing Lasse is an end in itself,' he admitted reluctantly.

'OK, until a body turns up, we've got to work under the assumption that he's still alive. We need to find him fast. Where's your sister, by the way, Mirza?'

'She's still at her flat.'

'Right. I'll send round an officer to keep an eye on her, just in case. We've got a bitter and twisted woman running around our patch and she might get it into her head...' He didn't have to complete the sentence; they all understood the scale of the task they faced.

CHAPTER 49

Hakim walked along the white pier that jutted out from the beach, towards the Kallbadhus. Built in 1898, the low, wooden cold bathhouse, painted a restful willow green, stood on stilts in the water, veering off at two symmetrical right angles at the end of the pier; the whole forming the shape of a T. Visiting it for a sauna and sea dip, whatever time of year, was a Malmö institution. Not that Hakim was a regular visitor. He had only been twice, and that had been in the company of Lasse, who was grateful that Hakim was paying. Saunas of increasing heat alternated with jumping into the sea to cool off. It hadn't been his idea of fun, but he had to admit he had felt better afterwards.

There was a café at the entrance, and it was a pleasant place to while away a few hours in the shadow of the Turning Torso, which loomed over the surrounding sea. The Kallbadhus was on the first pier of five dotted along the length of the beach at Ribersborgs, stretching out like a bony hand into the Sound. This was the only one with a large building at the end. Pier number three was also T-shaped, while the other three were just straight. The beach itself was filling up, as this was now the school vacation, and with the Midsummer holiday long weekend beginning tomorrow, it would get even busier.

At the small reception, Hakim flashed his warrant card at a gangly young man with short, brown hair and the beginnings of a moustache. 'I need to speak to someone about Sigyn Westermark.'

The young man pulled a face. 'Well, I know her. As much as anyone. We worked shifts together.'

'Can we have a word? Outside, preferably.'

The young man looked round and called over to a girl who was cleaning one of the café tables. 'Saga, can you take over reception for a minute?'

She nodded. 'No problem, Magnus.'

He followed Hakim out onto the pier decking. Hakim got straight to the point.

'When did you last see Sigyn?'

'Is she in trouble?'

'Just answer the question.'

Magnus thought carefully. 'It was a Sunday. I remember that. Beginning of the month.'

'That would be June the first – that fits in. Did she resign?'

'No. She just didn't turn up on the Tuesday. Monday was her day off. Never heard anything from her. Mind you, she was a bit weird.'

'In what way?'

He raised his eyebrows. 'You know, just strange. Not very friendly. Kept herself to herself. Didn't join in much – unless someone or something was useful to her. The old, wrinkly guys loved her, though. She's attractive. Good body,' he said admiringly.

'Did she ever talk about living in America?'

His surprise was obvious. 'I didn't know—'

'Did she ever mention having a brother?'

He shook his head. A steady stream of clients wandered in and out of the building. A middle-aged couple came walking up and hovered near where Hakim and Magnus were standing. They were more interested in the design of the building than Hakim's conversation. Nonetheless, Hakim moved away a few steps. Magnus followed.

'Did she ever talk about the police?'

'Don't think so.' Then he clicked his fingers. 'There was an incident on the beach. Some lads getting obstreperous. Too much drink. The police were called. I remember her being really rude about them. The police, that is. "Murdering bastards." That's what she said. I was quite taken aback. They were only breaking up a fight.'

Hakim was beginning to wonder if Sigyn had come across Lasse in one of his visits to the bathhouse; he knew he came as often as his wallet would allow. Maybe that's when her plan B had been formed. Plan A had worked a treat, except she'd got the wrong person.

'You say she didn't mix much. Was she friendly with anyone?'

'Not really. Didn't make an effort. Not even during lunch breaks and things. She would just wonder off down the beach. Sometimes, I'd see her at the end of one of the other piers over there, usually having a smoke.' He chuckled. 'Not something she'd do in front of our clients, who are all trying to stay fit or live as long as they can.'

'One last thing. Can you ever remember her mentioning an Anita Sundström or a Lasse Sundström?'

'No. Definitely not; though Lasse Sundström sounds familiar.'

'He sometimes comes here.'

'Ah, that's probably it.'

Hakim took out his notebook, wrote a number on it, ripped off the page and passed it over to the man. 'That's my number. It's a long shot, but if Sigyn turns up here, ring me immediately, though make sure you don't tell her that the police are asking after her.'

'She must be in trouble.'

The clouds were now starting to gather. The hot spell was drawing to a close. It was typical that the weather was about to break in time for Sweden's biggest annual holiday. But it wouldn't dampen the celebrations. Every Swede would embrace this high point of the summer, even if the sun they worshipped failed to appear. As he didn't drink, Hakim was never a great participant in the pagan festivities, though he was happy to see people let go of their inhibitions for a change. That in itself showed how Swedish he was, despite his heritage.

He wandered down the beach, as Sigyn Westermark must have done on numerous occasions to escape her colleagues and customers. What bitter thoughts must she have harboured to go as far as killing someone whom she blamed for her brother's death? Karl Westermark's last selfish act had destroyed his sister's life as well. As he walked along the path towards the second pier, more and more groups of young people were heading for the beach itself. There was excitement in the air. The summer stretched in front of them. He'd better report in; he rang Moberg. His boss didn't sound in a good frame of mind at all. Before he could report his conversation at the Kallbadhus, Moberg immediately launched in: 'We can't find her. Bloody Sundström. Simrishamn have reported that she's not at her holiday home, and her car's not there. Where the fuck is she?'

Hakim knew that Moberg and Anita had a long history of conflict, but he could tell that the chief inspector was worried about her.

'Anita can look after herself.' He tried to sound reassuring.

'But she might not know she's in danger. I just hope this mad bitch hasn't got to her already,' Moberg spluttered angrily. 'OK, have you got anything for me?'

'Not really. Sigyn was a bit of a loner. Didn't turn up for work the day of the murder. I think she may have come across Lasse at the bathhouse. But it doesn't get us any nearer to finding her, or him.'

There was silence at the other end of the phone. Hakim thought that the chief inspector might even have rung off.

His gaze wandered to the next pier; the other T-shaped one. Nestled in the corner where the pier changed direction, was a small wooden cabin with a metal roof and short black chimney stack. There were a couple of swimmers climbing out of the water nearby.

'Look, if Sigyn's got Lasse somewhere, we have to think of the sort of place she might have access to or know about.' Hakim's attention returned to his phone. 'She didn't know Malmö that well until she came to live here in March, so where would she choose?'

'I gather she didn't socialise,' said Hakim thoughtfully, 'so she'd be most familiar with everything between here, where she worked, and over near the Torso, where she was staying. Other than hanging around Anita's and Pildammsparken – and following Jazmin, of course.'

'Maybe it's somewhere she passed every day on her way to work. OK, what I want you to do is go from the Kallbadhus, trace her route back to her apartment and see if anything jumps out at you as a hiding place on the way. I'll send more men to help.'

'I'll do that. Anything from Klara?'

'Zilch.'

Anita drew the car up at the drop-off point for Terminal 2. They hadn't spoken much during the drive from the underground car park in the centre of Copenhagen to the airport. They had had a congenial day of shopping and sightseeing, and an expensive farewell meal at a waterside restaurant in Nyhavn. Kevin hadn't been his normal jokey self. Maybe the events of last night had knocked the stuffing out of him as much as they had her. And now that they were briefly parked outside the blazingly lit terminal building, she suddenly wanted to say so much. To thank him for the umpteenth time for his unquestioning support, to say how close she now felt to him; yet she was afraid that he would blurt out that he loved her. She suspected it to be the case, but she still didn't feel she could truthfully reciprocate those feelings. Huge affection, strong friendship and physical desire were all part of how she saw her relationship with him – but not love. Not yet, anyway.

Kevin got his luggage out of the car. He turned to her.

'You'll come over to see me before Christmas?'

'I'll try.'

He took her in his arms and kissed her full on the mouth. It was fleeting.

'I...' The words failed him at the last minute. 'I'll text you when I get back.'

'Good. I'll want to know you've arrived safely.'

He picked up his case.

'Next holiday, can we make it less complicated and dangerous? I hear Syria's very nice.'

She watched him go through the swing doors. He gave her one last wave through the glass wall, and he was gone. She suddenly felt empty. Alone. She would send him a text, just to thank him again. He'd get it before he boarded. Maybe she liked him more than she would admit to herself. She got back in the car. She reached into her bag, pulled out her mobile and switched it on. She glanced at the car clock – 23.27. It was too late to call Lasse. She'd do it in the morning, after a night back at her apartment. She'd planned to have a quiet Midsummer in Simrishamn with her friend Sandra but couldn't face that now. But she would have to go back to the holiday home sometime and collect her gear before her rental ran out. She couldn't bring herself to spend another night there.

She noticed that she had a number of missed calls from Hakim, Moberg, Jazmin – and five from a number she didn't recognise. She had four voice messages.

The first message – from the unfamiliar number – turned out to be from a very agitated Jazmin:

'Please call back. Lasse's gone missing. I don't know where he is. Please, Anita. Come and help me find him.'

The second was from a now distraught-sounding Jazmin:

'He's still not turned up. Please, please call!'

Fear struck her like an icy blast. She decided to head straight for Lasse's apartment immediately. What on earth was going on? She switched on the ignition as the next message played, this time from Jazmin's number. She didn't recognise the woman's voice:

'Anita Sundström, your worst nightmare is happening. I have your son. Now listen very carefully. If you want to see Lasse alive again, I want to see you at the end of pier three on Ribersborgsstranden at midnight tomorrow. Come alone. If I think anyone else is around – and that includes your incompetent colleagues – I will slit your son's throat. That's no empty promise. And then you'll know the agony of losing someone you love. Midnight tomorrow.'

Anita sat in dazed confusion. Then the fourth message came on and the familiar voice of Chief Inspector Moberg:

'Anita, Moberg here. Look, as soon as you get this, call me immediately. I've got to speak to you.'

While the car was idling, Anita quickly replayed the messages as though she'd been unable to really believe them the first time round. The menace in the unknown woman's voice seemed even more vehement the second time. Her thoughts whirled. My God, my little Lasse! What's happened? After the initial panic, which left her shaking, she managed to concentrate her mind, to psych herself into police mode. Her breathing became more controlled. Jazmin's message about Lasse going missing fitted in with this appalling threat from the unknown woman. But why? She obviously knew her because the threat was very direct, but who was she? And was Moberg aware of this? Was that why he was trying to contact her? She had to think this through. She methodically beat the steering wheel with her clenched fist as she tried to map out a plan of action. She'd get onto Jazmin first, but the threatening woman's message had come from Jazmin's phone. Maybe best to get onto Moberg initially. She suddenly stopped herself in the middle of returning Moberg's call – the threat had been very specific. This woman didn't want her colleagues involved. And she knew Moberg of old. He might just charge in there; and Lasse's life was at stake. But the woman had given her twenty-four hours – midnight tomorrow. Maybe she could catch Kevin before he went through the security check. Then a dreadful thought barged in and pushed all the others out of the way. She played the awful message again. This time she listened to the time of the call – 22.03 on the 18th of June. Oh, my God! That was last night! The back-lit digital clock on the car's dashboard appeared to shout at her – 23.33. She had twenty-seven minutes to reach the beach – and she was even in the wrong country. She'd never make it in time.

'Still here?' Moberg popped his head round the door of Hakim's office. 'Go home and get some sleep.'

'I can't.'

There were still groups of officers out searching. Others had been told to stand down for the night and resume at first light. All leave had been cancelled, and there were going to be a lot of disappointed police families who would have to celebrate Midsummer on their own. But the whole of the polishus was on high alert. The teams involved were trying to walk the fine line between searching for the kidnap victim and not alerting the kidnapper. If Sigyn Westermark knew what was going on, that would be the surest way of ending up with a dead body. They knew that she meant business.

Hakim's own hunt had been unproductive. There were a couple of places he had searched, but they had been outside chances. Most of the area between the beach and the Turning

Torso was new. There were building sites with sheds and portakabins. But there were plenty of construction workers around using them, so it would have been impossible to store a body, let alone a living person, without it being spotted.

'Still nothing from Anita.' Moberg was now hovering as he engulfed the doorway. Hakim suspected that he felt as impotent as he did.

'Well, I'm going outside for a smoke. It might help. Fancy joining me?'

Hakim was taken aback. Moberg had never been this sociable before. He was about to refuse, then changed his mind. He could sense that Moberg needed to talk to someone. He stood up and followed the chief inspector down the corridor. They made their way out into the car park. The usual Malmö wind was picking up, and it was drizzling lightly; the first rain they'd had since the night Ebba Pozorski was murdered. The forecast for the weekend wasn't good; not that it mattered to them. Moberg offered Hakim a cigarette, which he politely refused. The chief inspector lit up and blew a cloud of smoke into the air. Hakim watched the smoke – and it was at that moment that it suddenly hit him.

'Smoking! That's it!'

Moberg stared at him uncomprehendingly.

'The guy at the Kallbadhus said that Sigyn used to wander down to the other piers during her lunch breaks to have a smoke. That's the part of Malmö she knows best.'

'But it's just beach and piers.'

'Pier three has a cabin at the end. It's been shut up for years. She had months to work out how to get in. What better place to hide someone? Not the sort of place you'd think to search because it's so public – swimmers and the like. But no one goes in; and there's no one around at night, which is when she must have lured Lasse there using Jazmin's phone.' Hakim's voice was trembling with excitement.

Moberg threw away his cigarette with one hand and reached for his car keys with the other.

Anita was mesmerised by the car clock as its bright figures ticked over inexorably towards midnight. She had raced onto the motorway junction at Kastrup and had swiftly reached the bridge. She was way over the speed limit and hoped that she wouldn't be stopped. Rain was now falling from the scudding clouds, and spotting the windscreen. Her inadequate wipers only smudged the drops, and headlights coming in the opposite direction made her blink. It helped that there was very little traffic on the roads now. There was the infuriating stop at the toll booths on the Swedish side of the bridge, which seemed to take minutes but, in fact, she got through in forty seconds. She almost wept when the motorway shot over Kalkbrottsgatan, which would have taken her directly through Limhamn and straight onto the beach road, but there was no junction there. She'd have to go all the way round by Hyllie. And that meant roundabouts that would slow her down.

The car was juddering as she came off the motorway and onto the slip road. Her second-hand Peugeot wasn't built for such handling. She managed to negotiate three roundabouts at speed, narrowly avoiding a truck on the second one. She ignored the irate hooting. Now she was on Annetorpsvägen and heading for Limhamn. 23.51. She was definitely not going to get there for midnight. All she could think about was Lasse and not being able to help him. And she still couldn't figure out who the woman was. Was it someone she had been responsible for imprisoning in the past and was now out? Her thoughts were too cluttered to single out a possible candidate. Now she was on Kalkbrottsgatan. As she rushed through built-up Limhamn, she jumped the red light by the Shell garage at the Hyllie Kyrkoväg intersection, almost knocking over an unsuspecting pedestrian trying to cross the road.

There was a minute to go when she reached Limhamnsvägen, which would take her straight up the coast road adjacent to the city's long beach. Now she was terrified; her hands were glued to the steering wheel through sweat and fear. She was so intent on reaching the pier on time that she hadn't decided what to do once she was there. Would Lasse still be alive? Why hadn't she turned on her mobile earlier? She found herself yelling out loud. What came out of her mouth, she didn't recognise; some sort of primal scream of a mother unable to protect her child. The clock moved to 00.00. She howled as tears of desperation streamed down her face. She was too late.

By the time she screeched to a halt at the beach end of pier number three, it was five past midnight. She jumped out of the car, leaving the driver's door wide open; rushed down the short path; bounded up the five wooden steps; and burst along the wet decking. There didn't seem to be anyone else around. She ran as fast as she could, and halfway down she nearly lost her balance in the dark and had to grab the wooden railing to stop herself falling. She reached the cabin and turned the corner. She peered into the gloom. Only the dim outline of the pier was visible in the faint glow of the sodium lights of the city. Nothing else. No one was there. Was this woman playing games with her?

'You're late.'

Anita swung round. There were two shadowy shapes standing at the far end of the other arm of the T. Here, instead of railings was solid fencing for protection against the wind, and a gap to allow swimmers access to the steps down to the sea. Anita brushed the rain from her face and stepped forward. At that moment, the moon broke through the eddying clouds. Now she could see a light-haired woman. She was standing next to a tall figure. With a jolt, Anita realised it was Lasse. He had his hands tied behind his back, had thick tape over his mouth, and was unsteady on his feet as if he'd been drugged. Anita felt

angry and sick at the same time. But at least he was still alive.
The moon disappeared again.

'Lasse! Are you all right?'

As her eyes grew accustomed to the dark, she could see that
the woman was holding something up to Lasse's throat. Could
it be a knife?

'You've been hiding from me.'

'I don't know what you're talking about. I don't know who
you are, or why you've kidnapped my son.'

She laughed. 'Thanks to you, I've killed an innocent
woman. How does that make you feel? Yet another death at
your door. But you won't have long to think about it because
you're next – and then your darling Lasse.'

Anita held up her hand. 'No, don't! Can't we talk this
through? Just tell me what I've done wrong. It can't be anything
to do with Lasse. Let him go. It's obviously me you want.'

'My name is Sigyn Westermark. Ring any bells?'

Anita gave a sharp intake of breath. 'Is this about Karl?'

'You were responsible for his death.'

'But he killed himself!'

'You forced him.'

'I didn't. He took his own life. It was his decision.'

The moon made another appearance and its pale light
glinted off the knife. 'No! He had no choice. You destroyed
him.'

'Karl killed and raped a young teacher. He murdered one
of his own colleagues. No one forced him to do those things.'

Sigyn took a pace towards Anita and brandished the knife
in front of her. Lasse sank to his knees.

'He loved you. He told me. He was besotted. And you
rejected him.'

'You mean I wouldn't sleep with him. That's all he was
interested in.' The more enraged Sigyn became, the further she
moved away from Lasse and the closer she got to Anita. Anita

could now make out the resemblance to her brother. 'The only person Karl ever loved was himself.'

'He loved me!' she shrieked. 'You took him away from me. That's why I'm going to kill you!'

Anita strained her eyes. The light was dim, but the frenzy of the deranged woman in front of her was palpable. Somehow, she had to get Sigyn off her guard. Disarm her. She played for time. 'You'll not get away with this. Even if you kill us, you'll be caught.'

Another bitter laugh: 'You're a cop through and through. Don't you understand; I no longer care? They can do what they like with me after you're dead. I'll have paid my debt to Karl. My beautiful Karl.'

It was then that Anita realised that someone had appeared at the beach end of the pier. Her glance alerted Sigyn. In that moment, Anita leapt at the woman and caught her off balance. The impact took them both to the edge of the sea steps, and they plunged through the gap and into the water. They went under. Anita clung to Sigyn as she struck out with the knife, which caught Anita on the shoulder, ripping through her thin jacket and piercing her skin. Their bodies were enmeshed in an aggressive rhythm as they surfaced and gasped for air. Anita had lost her glasses. Sigyn grabbed at her again, pushed her back under the water and, the knife still in her hand, raised her arm. Anita twisted furiously as the blade missed her by a hair's breadth. Now she had the advantage. She caught Sigyn round the waist and pulled her under the waves. It was a bitter battle of avenging sister and protective mother, both emotions driving their fury in a whirligig of flailing limbs. Once more, they broke the surface, panting for air. Again, Sigyn lunged at Anita who, in a last surge of strength, parried the blow, grabbed the hand wielding the knife, and deflected it towards her attacker. Sigyn gave a sudden, loud, rasping gasp. Anita let go, and Sigyn went limp. The moon lit her face: wide-eyed; unbelieving. She tried to speak. Then, with a gurgle, she slowly slipped out of sight.

Exhausted, Anita swam on the spot for a few moments, trying to get her breath. Then she slowly paddled back to the pier. Her left shoulder was throbbing. She tried to haul herself up the steps. She could feel the blood oozing down her back. She felt faint and nearly plummeted back into the sea, but a strong arm grabbed her hand and hoisted her up. She was in the firm grip of Chief Inspector Moberg. What was he doing here? Behind him, she could see Hakim freeing Lasse from his bonds. Moberg pulled her onto the top step.

'Happy Midsummer, Sundström!'

EPILOGUE

BERLINER MORGENPOST – Friday, 20th June
STOP PRESS
TRAIN DEATH CAUSES DELAYS
A man fell to his death in front of an underground train approaching the platform of Pankow station on the U2 line. The incident occurred at 17.03 yesterday evening during the height of the rush hour. Services were disrupted for two hours. Late last night, the police named the man as 80-year-old Hans-Dieter Albrecht.

Other titles by the author

Meet me in Malmö is the first in the series of the best-selling crime mysteries featuring Inspector Anita Sundström. *Murder in Malmö* and *Missing in Malmö* are the second and third titles.

A British journalist is invited to Malmö to interview an old university friend who is now one of Sweden s leading film directors. When he discovers the directors glamorous film star wife dead in her apartment, the Skåne County Police are called in to solve the high-profile case. Among the investigating team is Inspector Anita Sundström, who soon finds the list of suspects growing. As Anita battles to discover the answers amid the antagonism of some of her colleagues, she even begins to think that the person she is becoming attracted to could be the murderer. This is the first in a series of the best-selling crime mysteries featuring Inspector Anita Sundström.

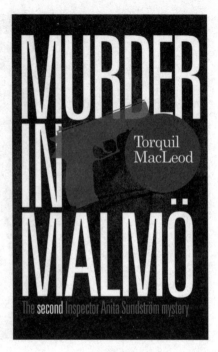

Torquil MacLeod

The **second** Inspector Anita Sundström mystery

Murder in Malmö is the second in the series of the best-selling crime mysteries featuring Inspector Anita Sundström.

A gunman is loose in Malmö and he's targeting immigrants. The charismatic head of an advertising agency is found dead in his shower. Inspector Anita Sundström wants to be involved in the murder investigations, but she is being sidelined by her antagonistic boss. She is assigned to find a stolen painting by a once-fashionable artist, as well as being lumbered with a new trainee assistant. She also has to do to restore her professional reputation after a deadly mix-up in a previous high-profile case. Then another prominent Malmö businessman is found murdered and Sundström finds herself back in the action and facing new dangers in the second Anita Sundström Malmö mystery.

Missing in Malmö is the third in the series of the best-selling crime mysteries featuring Inspector Anita Sundström.

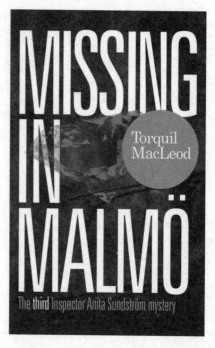

When a British heir hunter fails to return home after a trip to Malmö, Inspector Anita Sundström doesn't want to get entangled in a simple missing person's case. She shows a similar reluctance when her ex-husband begs her to find his girlfriend, who seems to have disappeared. But when the mysteries take a sinister turn, Sundström finds herself inextricably involved in both baffling affairs, one of which seems to be connected to a robbery that took place twenty years earlier. As the cases begin to unravel, tragedy awaits the investigating team in the third Anita Sundström Malmö mystery.